Paraic O'Donnell read English and French at University College Dublin and Linguistics at Trinity College Dublin. He has worked for many years in the translation industry, and travels extensively in Europe, Asia and the United States. He lives in Wicklow with his wife and two children, and can usually be found in the garden. *The Maker of Swans* is his first novel, for which he was shortlisted for the *Sunday Independent* Newcomer of the Year at the Bord Gáis Energy Irish Book Awards 2016.

@paraicodonnell
paraicodonnell.com

Praise for *The Maker of Swans*

'Compulsive reading . . . rich, strange, beautiful'
Helen Macdonald, author of *H is for Hawk*

'A strange, new and captivating look at a magical realm . . . Lavishly entertaining'
Sam Kitchener, *Independent*

'The prose in O'Donnell's first novel is glorious, combining an ear for deep cadences of language with a phenomenal acuity of vision'
Tim Clare, *Guardian*

'I devoured this book and it kept me guessing right to the very end. Line by line, Paraic's writing contains some of the most beautifully turned phrasing I've read in a long while'
Laura Barnett, author of *The Versions of Us*

'There are novels that are effortlessly filmic while retaining all their integrity as works of literature . . . Beguilingly fantastical and written with great visual acuity, it is almost impossible to read it without trying to cast its central characters in your mind . . . Kinetic and pacy, it is a page-turner in the very best sense of the term, with a central scene of extraordinary heart-in-mouth excitement . . . It would not be surprising if the reading public clamours for a second instalment of this vividly imagined and deeply pleasurable gothic fantasy'
Melissa Harrison, *Financial Times*

'Wonderfully dark, magical'
Elle

'O'Donnell creates an atmospheric and gothic world that wavers between fantasy and reality . . . Ambitious and original'
Sarah Gilmartin, *Irish Times*

'A fabulously assured, elegant gothic-flavoured tale'
Fanny Blake, *Woman and Home*

'Rarely does a writer stop you so fully in your tracks . . . a bold new talent'
Sunday Independent

'A tale about magic and art, power and responsibility . . . There's sufficient invention and engaging strangeness to keep the reader enfolded, though it is O'Donnell's arresting descriptions of the natural world that are likely to live longest in the mind'

Stephanie Cross, *Daily Mail*

'A powerful thriller set among the fading grandeur of an English manor house'   *Vogue*

'Exquisite'   Liz Nugent, author of *Unravelling Oliver*

'Poetic and strange, this gothic novel is a dark, elegant celebration of the power and beauty of words and the spells they weave'

Eithne Farry, *Sunday Express S Magazine*

'Eerily mesmerising . . . O'Donnell generates genuinely page-turning excitement in a series of murders, chases and kidnaps . . . We have here the emergence of a new and highly original literary voice'

James Moran, *Tablet*

'Dazzlingly inventive'   Jane Casey, author of *After the Fire*

'Extraordinarily readable . . . almost cinematic'   *Irish Independent*

'O'Donnell's eloquent descriptions and old-world characters make it a charming, lyrical read even when tension is high. I admired the depth of O'Donnell's imagination, which allowed him to conjure up this enthralling tale . . . A literary feast'   Gemma Crisp, *Stylist*

'An oddly beautiful tale of magic and art, this reminded me of Alain-Fournier's *Le Grand Meaulnes*'   Cathy Rentzenbrink, *Bookseller*

'A mesmerising book whose prose absolutely soars'

Sandra Newman, author of *The Country of Ice Cream Star*

'Sonorous, beautifully made . . . disquieting and unfathomable'

The Spectator

'Cleverly combines literary references and Dickensian intrigue'

Sydney Morning Herald

The
Maker of Swans

PARAIC O'DONNELL

WEIDENFELD & NICOLSON

A W&N PAPERBACK

First published in Great Britain in 2016
by Weidenfeld & Nicolson
This paperback edition first published in 2017
by Weidenfeld & Nicolson
an imprint of the Orion Publishing Group Ltd
Carmelite House, 50 Victoria Embankment
London EC4Y 0DZ

An Hachette UK Company

ISBN (Mass Market Paperback) 978 1 474 60103 0
ISBN (eBook) 978 1 474 60038 5

A CIP catalogue record for this book is
available from the British Library.

Typeset by Input Data Services Ltd, Bridgwater, Somerset

Printed and bound in Great Britain by Clays Ltd, St Ives plc

MIX
Paper from
responsible sources
FSC® C104740

www.orionbooks.co.uk

I

A Lamentation

One

I*n the dream*, there was nothing. Nothing, and then fire.

It came upon the house with the fury of a sudden storm, a gale of flame that swept the cedars from the lawns and obliterated every window. It flung open the doors and thronged the staircases, possessing rooms with effortless violence. It surged among the hallways, avid and primrose bright, inundating the ballroom, rising in moments even to the chandeliers.

Eustace saw it all, and he did nothing. He stood in the fire's midst, unmoving and somehow unscathed as he waited to be consumed in his turn. He could not see her, the child, could not have hoped to find her in time. He could not see her, and knew she could not call to him.

It was that despair that ruptured his sleep, that flooding grief. When he heard the shots, he had lain awake for some moments already with the bedclothes thrown back, his hand spread on his chest to quieten his heart. He started slightly at the sounds – there were two, in quick succession – but almost welcomed the distraction. Eustace was accustomed enough to gunshots. They were not quite usual, perhaps, but they caused him no particular alarm. But the dream – the dream had been another matter. He could not remember when he had last felt such dread.

He clawed at the nightstand for the chain of his watch and found, when he had wrung the dimness from his eyes, that it was a shade after one. It might have been worse. His duties were often irregular, and it was not rare for him to be called from his bed at unpardonable hours. Still, he did not welcome such disturbances. The years of his service had done nothing to soften them.

Wearily, but with the smooth economy of long habit, he rose and drew a dressing gown about him. The house, even in these last days of October, was wretchedly cold. The great drapes, as he parted them, were heavy with damp. They would, even at noon, betray almost nothing of their original colour. There was little here that did.

He saw the Jaguar first. He had left the lamps lit on the avenue, and the car was a little way beyond the fountain, whose pair of stone dragons reared above it, mossy and hugely opposed. It had been brought to a halt, Eustace judged, from a considerable speed, and with no great excess of deliberation, veering from the driveway before returning to it, and gouging an almost elegant scroll of turf from the lawn. The driver's door was open, the interior spilling a yolky light.

Mr Crowe – for of course it was him – had taken a position astride the car's bonnet. His legs were planted staunchly apart, his cloak swelling and snapping in the breeze. From this vantage, he commanded the avenue northwards to the gates, in which direction he appeared to be bellowing. When a second set of headlights appeared, in the darkened parkland beyond the fountain, he gave emphasis to his address with a volley from a pair of pistols. Eustace knew those guns. Mr Crowe had collected them at the card table from a brigadier general who had been left insensible by a stroke.

They had first seen service against the Boers, sixty-odd years before, and were capable now of little more than a healthy racket.

The other car flared fully into view, pulling up with some violence only a little way short of the Jaguar, so that Mr Crowe was forced to raise an arm against the glare of its headlights. Its sole occupant was a bearded and wary figure whose leather coat had been cut for a bigger man. He emerged with a considerable show of animation, only to retreat behind his car door when Mr Crowe opened fire.

Eustace yawned and scratched one cheek. As his attention returned to the Jaguar, he noticed for the first time that it held a passenger, a young woman. His gaze had been drawn by her movements – she was winding down the passenger-side window – and by the colour of her dress, which announced itself even at this distance.

It was a remarkable red, almost exultant. In a house like this, living always amid an ancient and untouchable drabness, you seized upon colours. Your eye was snared by them. The only other such colours that Eustace saw were those of the fruit that Mr Crowe would want on those occasions – they were infrequent now – when he would set his mind upon some lavish entertainment, when he would assemble a houseful of showgirls and disreputable peers, insisting that no extravagance be spared.

On such evenings, there was always fruit in plenty. It would go all but untouched, but it was never stinted upon. Grapes lay on salvers in bloated and dusty heaps, liver-dark or the green of new oak leaves. Plump figs, tawny and oozing, were piled splendidly in crystal bowls. And the nectarines – Eustace was always taken by them – these would be massed in wide dishes of pewter, tumbling in lush avalanches onto the surrounding linen. They seemed, on some part of their voluptuous surfaces, to exemplify every imaginable red: here coral or fox blood, there cinnabar or claret, chrysanthemum or rust.

Having lowered her window, the woman in the red dress hoisted herself, with the sluggish ceremony of those drunk on wine, to a seated position on its frame. Thus established, she lit a cigarette and rested her cheek on the dark lustre of the Jaguar's roof. The back of her dress was cut in a deep delta, baring a tongue of tenderly shadowed skin.

Mr Crowe crouched for a moment. With the extremity of one pistol, he traced the knotted sequence of her spine. He plucked the cigarette from her fingers, wolfing and releasing a lungful of smoke before returning it. Finally, he placed a kiss on his fingertips, delivering it to her cheek before rising regretfully to his feet.

The bearded man, during this interlude, had crossed most of the distance between the two cars. Eustace had marked him already, coming by way of the grass so as not to give the warning of his footfalls. Mr Crowe, when he saw him, set about reloading his pistols, hurling at his adversary some expressions of derision that Eustace could not hear.

The other man paid little attention. He seemed intent only on the woman, directing at her some harsh words of his own. When she ignored him, or answered only with a toss of her head, he began to taunt her, snatching at her hair with a clawed hand. She turned to him, finally, and blew a contemptuous plume of smoke over his face. Then she spat, precisely and copiously, at his feet.

Eustace took a quick breath. This would not end well.

The bearded man stared at the ground as if he doubted the physical truth of the insult. When he raised his eyes, the reason was gone from them. His chest rose and shuddered, as if some inner binding had been ruptured.

He slapped her face. It was a mean and unsparing blow, given with the heel of his hand. She fell forward, stunned, and slumped from the car door. Lowering herself out onto her hands, she crouched against the Jaguar. Mr Crowe leapt from where he stood, his cloak spreading behind him. The other man could no longer be seen.

Eustace swore softly and let the curtain fall.

He let his pace slacken as he clattered down the front steps. He was too late, of course. That much had been evident the moment he hauled open the great oak doors, though he had hardly expected it to be otherwise. His living quarters were on the second floor, chosen for their remoteness from the grand rooms below. Even twenty or thirty years earlier, he would not have closed the distance in time.

In other respects, Mr Crowe was a man of easeful habits, and never more so than in these last years. He would be unhesitating, though, in response to a provocation like the one Eustace had witnessed. His ferocity would be ungovernable. Whatever had happened, it had happened swiftly. It had been over, in all likelihood, by the time Eustace had reached the head of the stairs.

As he crossed the gravel towards the drive, he slowed further, allowing some evenness to return to his breathing. He took in what he could of the scene, on the avenue before him and in the surrounding shadows. The contours of what had taken place were already plain, but there were things he must discover quickly, particulars without which he could make no reckoning of its consequences. He could not yet tell what this might bring to their door.

The cars, the Jaguar and its meek counterpart by the fountain, sat idling, their doors splayed. The woman in the red dress crouched below the window, her head lowered to her knees. Mr Crowe had dropped to his haunches. He held her to himself with one arm, his head canted sorrowfully towards hers. He was singing to her, Eustace realised as he drew nearer, his tone tender and indistinct. He could not be sure of the aria.

The bearded man lay where he had fallen. Mr Crowe's cloak had been cast over him with no particular ceremony. One foot protruded, and a trouser leg was hoisted above a white haft of shin.

Mr Crowe had heard him approaching. When Eustace was twenty paces away, he raised his right arm in a gesture that was half an acknowledgement, half a warning. In that hand, he held one of the pistols still, but loosely; the trigger guard rested on two upturned fingers. The gun was not part of the gesture. Eustace took its meaning from elsewhere; from the stark tension of the upraised arm, the way it was held opposite to the woman. He was encircling her, it said, in his protection, sequestering what had occurred here. Mr Crowe was turning him away.

Eustace knew all the forms of deference. He observed them, for the most part, with an almost unseen grace. He knew much else also, too much to be so easily deflected. He disregarded Mr Crowe's raised arm, coming to a halt with a brisk snap of his heels. His impatience, as he surveyed the scene, was thinly glazed with calm.

'The cars must be attended to first,' he said. 'The lights, at least. May I take it that the field day has concluded?'

Mr Crowe gestured again with that right hand. A brief, dismissive flicker.

'Who called you out, Eustace? I did not. I am in conversation.'

'You are in the middle of the avenue, sir. As is the lady, who must forgive my disadvantage in having no means to address her. Shots have been fired – quite a number. The cars, the lights – these things must be attended to.'

Mr Crowe loosened the muscles of his neck and massaged the bridge of his nose with an unoccupied finger. 'This is Arabella, Eustace, who performs at *L'Étoile*, though her gifts are squandered in that place.'

The woman did not look up. She hunched her shoulders slightly, as if suppressing a shiver.

'I am delighted to make Miss Arabella's acquaintance. I would be glad to see that she is made comfortable in the drawing room.'

When Mr Crowe responded by resuming his singing, Eustace persisted. 'The fire has been banked down,' he said, 'but it will draw out the worst of the chill. The lady has suffered a shock.'

Mr Crowe broke off. For a moment, he looked away in silence, his jaw stiff. 'You never loved music, Eustace, or the fires that give rise to it.'

'I have not, I hope, ever much burdened Mr Crowe with the matter of what I love or do not.'

Since this elicited no answer, Eustace paused to summon what delicacy he could.

'The young man, sir. Perhaps there is something that may be done for him.'

Mr Crowe looked up, at last. His locks, never excessively tended, were in wild disorder. His face, with its strong juts and faint skew, was smirched – with oil and gunpowder, at least, and likely with much else. He seemed, as he spoke, to labour against some agitation in himself.

'Eustace, will you not be told with gentleness? I did not call you. Let me tend to these private matters.'

'These private matters, if we do not prevent it, will not remain so for long. We know well enough the difficulties that may follow such disturbances. The young man, Mr Crowe. What is to be done for the young man?'

Mr Crowe stood. It cost him some effort and discomfort, but he was roused and managed it quickly. He brought Arabella to her feet too, supporting her beneath her elbows. His courtliness had been eroded a little by his impatience. Towards Eustace, certainly, his manner was unvarnished.

'Nothing is to be done for him, do you hear me? There is nothing to be done.'

He started towards the house. He would have marched there in fury, Eustace knew, if he did not have the girl to tend to. Fury or no, however, this could not lie until the morning. What must be done, whatever little advantage was to be saved from this, it fell to him.

'The young man, sir.' Eustace made no move to follow them. When he spoke, he gave a careful weight to his words. 'What is done cannot be undone, but we must make certain arrangements, if we are not to invite further unpleasantness.'

When this brought no response, Eustace spoke more plainly.

'Am I to leave him where he lies, then? Sir, as a matter of decency—'

Mr Crowe turned fiercely. He had hardened his features, though they were crossed by an unruly spill of hair. The woman, momentarily overlooked, seemed slight as she steadied herself by his side. He could make himself imposing still, when he was moved to it.

'*Decency*, Eustace? *Decency*?' He swung his free arm towards the form beneath the cloak. 'What did that son of a whore know of *decency*, who accosted me on my own lands like a brigand, who raised his hand against such a creature as this? I have dispatched him in the manner he deserved. Do you expect me to deliver a eulogy?'

Eustace said nothing.

'And you, Eustace – you were not always so punctilious in attending to the dead. Do not presume to lecture me.'

He was about to speak, but clamped his jaw to prevent himself. He looked away, shaking his head.

'Well, Eustace? You wish to interrogate me no further, then? We are free to go?'

He said nothing, keeping his eyes averted. Mr Crowe turned away with a grunt, and began lurching again towards the house, still somewhat encumbered by his companion. Negligently, he discarded the pistol that he still held, tossing it out across the dark lawn. Eustace marked the place.

'Our aria, my love.' Mr Crowe gave his attention again to his companion. 'It is an act of insufferable philistinism not to finish an aria that one has begun. Do you not agree? Come, we will conduct you to safety. And not merely safety, eh? For we have not abandoned all sport. We are not barbarians, after all.'

They trudged towards the house and its almost unlit majesty. Mr Crowe growled through what remained of the aria.

'*Ah, cielo! Si può! Si, può morir!*'

Eustace crossed towards the gun. He would retrieve it before he lost its position.

'*Di più non chiedo, non chiedo.*'

Underfoot, the grass had begun to thicken with frost. The pistol would already be touched by it.

'*Si può morir! Si può morir d'amor.*'

The cars too, when he stilled their motors. Over everything, there would be a gauze, a skin of cold.

Two

It is *Clara* who wakes first.

The house is entirely silent as she slips from her bed and begins her preparations. Outside, it is not yet light. Though it is not rare for her to stir before dawn, she has done so in recent days with unusual purpose. She dresses, in clothes she laid out last night, without ceremony or hesitation. She is quick-limbed and precise, her bare feet crossing and recrossing the floorboards as she busies herself. They are shipwreck-cold, but she will not pull on her calfskin boots just yet. She is quieter without them.

Clara is a child of gentle but inexorable habits. There are things she attends to in the mornings, rituals she observes in careful and deliberate order. Although she is anxious to be on her way, there are some customs she will not forgo. When she has washed and dressed, as always, she takes her seat at her writing table. In the hour after she wakes, the world through which Clara moves is at its most thickly inhabited. She is surrounded still by the creatures of her sleep, and she must clutch at their wraiths before they have vanished beyond recall.

She must write it down, all of it, just as she must set down the stories that sometimes crowd her thoughts, or her observations of the patterns of swifts in flight. It is a need she feels; a need, she supposes, that is not common. She fills countless notebooks in this way, hoarding them as other children do seashells or brightly coloured stones. Every scrap of paper is carefully indexed, and she will allow no one to disturb the arrangement of her desk or the meticulous ordering of her shelves.

Still, it is not that she is secretive exactly, or that she shares nothing at all of what she writes. To Eustace, especially, she shows a great many things, and she knows that he takes particular pleasure in her more fanciful inventions. She describes to him the impossible fauna of her imaginings: the birds with feathers of silver leaf or spun sugar; the insects sculpted from polar ice, whose wings are hardly more than flakes of finely worked cold. A single breath, and they would vanish.

She tells him of the intricate and devious machines that assemble themselves in the darkest chambers of smugglers' caves, snatching secrets from the fug of rum and the loose talk of sailors. She describes the automata that emerge in the lightless upper recesses of cathedrals, summoned into being by certain passages of music. During performances of Bach's great masses, for instance, dozens of these machines may appear, elaborating themselves from nothing more than dust and shadow, and from the tiny golden filaments of melody and counterpoint that drift upwards on the heat. Once fully formed, they proceed to teach themselves Latin, or to pelt the heads of cardinals with mouse droppings.

These phenomena Clara explains in jottings that Eustace might find anywhere in the house or grounds, at any hour of the day or night. She might scrawl five or six lines on a napkin and leave it behind her at the table. It is not uncommon for him to discover, while dusting off a bottle of Montrachet in the cellar, a stack of Mr Crowe's calling cards, neatly bundled and bound with ribbon. On the backs of these, in her dense and fastidious cursive,

Clara will have set forth some branch of her personal cosmology.

Today, because she will pass his rooms on her way downstairs, she decides to leave her pages by his bed. He is a fitful sleeper, but her comings and goings rarely disturb him. She is slight, and has the practised stealth of the solitary child who lives among old and undisturbed things.

At his bedside, even in her quiet haste, she is stilled by something unfamiliar. On the nightstand, loosely wrapped in a soiled handkerchief, lies a pair of ornate pistols. Clara lowers her face to the bundle, drawn by a thread of scent. There is oil in it, and heated metal, a sweet but faded charring. With a throb of disquiet, she studies the stains on the handkerchief, their peculiar complexion of darkness. In this house, the appearance of such things might have a thousand explanations, but she would be less surprised to encounter them among Mr Crowe's possessions. Eustace dislikes untidiness; it is rare, in his quarters, to find anything out of place.

Clara glances uneasily at him as she arranges her pages. She has chosen rather formal stationery today, the notepaper bearing the letterhead of a hotel in Biarritz where they spent the last summer but one. The nights there, she remembers, were clouded with hydrangea blossom, and with some scandal that Mr Crowe had either instigated or put right. She thinks of it distractedly as she looks over the title page.

Natural History of the Nebula Snail, Vol. XI, no. iv

While it cannot be observed directly from Earth, the nebula snail (*Helix nebulosa*) is endemic to certain regions of interstellar space, where it grazes on helium and hydrogen and leaves in its wake a diffuse and garishly coloured smear (see fig. (a) below) that is not only extremely unsightly but also very difficult to remove from the fabric of the universe (some authorities suggest that vinegar in solution may be effective).

[Eustace, can we try snails like the French do? Next time there is company, we could impress them with our sophisticated continental habits. Also, when can I have wine with dinner? I think you'll find that I am rather more grown up than certain other members of the household. – Ed.]

Over millions of years, a large enough colony of such snails can leave trails covering such an immense ~~area~~ volume of space that they are visible from Earth, forming what we know as nebulae.

The monograph continues in this vein for a further four pages, and includes several detailed illustrations. She pictures him waking to find them, knowing just how he will appear as he reads them: his chin raised slightly as if in wariness, his eyes seamed and intent. His expression will soften, though, as he comes upon some oddity that amuses him. He may shake his head gently, tapping a line or passage that gives him particular enjoyment or cause for incredulity.

Eustace stirs as Clara is leaving. The sheets are roped about his chest, and he grips one of his pillows as if it were a dog intent on mauling him. She hesitates at the door. It is the pistols that are troubling his sleep, and whatever business brought them here. She ought to stow them in her knapsack and take them with her. It would be easy, where she is going, to put them where they could do no more harm. But Eustace would notice at once, and would be alarmed. He might even come looking for her.

No, it is ridiculous even to think of it. And it is getting late. She cannot deliberate any longer.

She descends by the back stairs. The stone under her bare soles is mortifyingly cold, but on these steps she can be entirely noiseless.

Nor is she likely, taking this way, to encounter Mr Crowe, who keeps no particular hours and often bids her goodnight as she goes down to breakfast. He would not question her business abroad, of course. He would be far more likely to lead her in a foxtrot across the vestibule, or to introduce her to a film actress. Mr Crowe is kindly towards her, even protective in his rather abstract way, but he certainly does not concern himself with her whereabouts when she is not in his presence. If her care were left entirely to him, she reflects, she could make camp in the beech woods and live on sardines and tinned peaches. He himself might well die of hunger, without someone to bring him chops and burgundy.

The truth is that Clara's comings and goings are subject to very little scrutiny by anyone in the household. Eustace generally requires that she present herself for meals with some regularity and fit herself out in such a way as to avoid pneumonia, but he does not otherwise hinder her projects and excursions. Even so, on this particular morning she would just as soon meet no one.

In the pantry, she begins filling her knapsack with provisions. First, she bundles up an entire loaf of bread, not worrying that Alice will notice. After all, Alice herself seems to mislay a considerable quantity of Madeira. And in any case, the bread is the most important thing. The books she consulted in the library were all in agreement on that. In the wild, of course, they can scarcely depend on bread, but they are happy to accept it when they must.

Next, Clara takes whatever greens are to be found. Some tender lettuce leaves would be best, but it is too late in the year for those. She makes do instead with half a head of cabbage, chopping it as finely as she can, and unbraids and shreds the necks of some onions that have been hung for winter. None of it is quite right, she thinks, but it will have to do.

Finally, she takes a small blue tin from a high shelf. On its lid, a sturgeon is curled so that its back forms a menacing ring of serrations, encircled in turn by gold lettering in elaborate Cyrillic script. She has been eyeing it for days, faltering always at the last moment. It will be missed, of course, and there will be a fuss. It will have cost a great deal – not that Mr Crowe ever seems concerned about such things – and Alice will have written its price in her book of accounts, even if it is a price she arrived at unaided. It cannot be helped, any of it. It is not the time to skimp on these things.

She glances up at the narrow, mullioned window. Outside, the darkness has the faintest leavening of lilac. It will not be long until daybreak, when a whole day will have passed since she last fed them. It is time to go. Now, at last, she sits on a low bench and tugs on her boots, then fastens her knapsack and slings it over her shoulder. She is ready.

Leaving by the kitchen door, she takes her first breath of the cold, feels the quick, knifing surge of it. Under the cold, there is a faint richness, the muted savour of damp leaves and turned earth. She quickens her step, the anticipation rising in her. She feels light and heavy at once, both alert and serene. She cannot explain it.

In the west lane, she breaks into a gentle run. In the mist and the scarce light, the hedgerows are a parade of shapes that at first she can barely decipher, but then it is only a tall nettle, slackening and discoloured, or the stark coronets of cow parsley gone to seed. A scrawny fox appears in her path, darting quickly aside as it catches sight of her, its teeth clamped over some furred and feebly twitching thing.

Above the orchard, as she passes, colours are seeping into the hem of the sky. She hurries on, past the neglected herb beds, until she comes to the narrow ironwork gate, partly obscured by ivy, that leads from the walled garden to the wilder grounds beyond. From here the way is downhill, and in the beech woods she begins to run again, scuttling through the thick drifts of leaves until she realises that she is scaring up all manner of birds. Their alarm calls might easily spread through the woods and beyond, and that could ruin everything. She keeps instead to the middle of the track, skipping over the dry leaves and brittle twigs, finding the soft and mossy places to tread.

When she stumbles from the quiet shade of the woods, she is surprised, as always, by the sudden and limitless air, by the scale and openness of the country before her. She pauses for a moment, looking out over the broad valley of grassland. Though it is not yet fully light, she can see all the way to the mountains, a swell and fall of bluish shadow some eight or nine miles to the west. From there, a peaty stream threads its way to the mere, the wide and dark-watered lake that lies at the heart of the Estate, its shape so irregular that it seems somehow mutable, its edges half hidden always among the reeds.

If it seems unreal, this place, its boundaries shifting and indistinct, it is perhaps because she has dreamed of it so often, or of things that happen here. She has come here sometimes, even in daylight, and has wondered whether she *is* dreaming. In the same way, she has been deeply asleep but believed herself to be out walking in the last hour before nightfall, watching the swans that gather here. This is the more disconcerting experience, especially when it is something forcefully unreal that makes her realise her mistake. She remembers a scarecrow that she saw once. It was starkly upright in the dark water of the lake, and the wind tugged at its tatters of cheesecloth until it pivoted on its post. Beneath its flannel coat gaped a hull of grey and vacant ribs.

It was this scarecrow, in fact, that gave her the name by which she knows this place. It is a name she uses freely, though she has otherwise kept that particular dream to herself, and even Eustace has come to adopt it.

'The Windbones,' he said once, appraising her choice. 'It is apt for that place, for the way the wind chases a whiteness through the grasses. It will chase through you also, if you do not wrap up. You had your woollens on, I trust?'

She smiles at the recollection, but only briefly. She is nearing the place and must be slow and cautious. She found them in the lee of a young willow, huddled in the ruined heap of the nest. Though it is only yards from the water's edge, it lies deep enough in the reeds that for now, at least, they have gone unseen from the lake. It is not unheard of for orphans to be nurtured by other adults, but it is rare. Their fate, if they are discovered, is likely to be much less kind.

She picks her way through the reeds, parting them as gently as she can. Though the woods were already stirring, the lake shore is almost silent. They have come to accept her, she thinks, but they are fearful still. She must be careful, above all, not to startle them from their hiding place. She has learned to tread with laborious slowness as she approaches them, moving her limbs in such tiny increments that she wonders, at certain moments, if she has become entirely still.

She finds them sleeping, the cygnets. Pushing at last through the fringe of reeds that surrounds the nest, her breathing eases. They are safe, if only for another day. Moving with the utmost care still, Clara lowers herself to her knees. They have woken now, each untucking its head from the downy pouch of its body and staring at her, but they do not take fright. They seem always to know her when she is this close, though whether it is by sight or scent she cannot tell. Tenderly, she strokes the plumage of the one closest to her. It gazes at her for a moment, meekly quizzical, its eyes no more than gleaming pips in the soft tuft of its head. It flexes its tiny neck towards her offered knuckles, as if to accept her touch, and the softness she encounters is barely palpable, like the weightless glancing of dandelion seeds.

Clara relaxes her posture, sinking lower on her knees. She spreads a cloth over her lap and begins unpacking her provisions. Taking a bowl from the knapsack, she scoops water from the channel that partially encloses the nest. To the water she adds the shredded greens, refilling the bowl each time they empty it. She tears the bread into dainty morsels, moistening these too, and letting the chicks snatch them from her palm.

On the evening she first found them, she swaddled them in an old eiderdown, covering it with tarpaulin so that it would not become sodden. Their parents were hunted from the mere, she thinks, by another pair of swans nesting nearby. They may even have been killed. She has seen such things before.

She sees how frail they are still, as the food draws them from beneath the quilt, how matted and patchy their down. Taking out the tin of caviar, she works it open and spoons it out in small, glistening heaps. The cygnets hesitate for an instant, peering down their bills at the dark clusters of roe, then lunge towards them. They eat greedily, snapping at each other's bills and scouring the tin after she has emptied it. When she offers them more bread, they turn their heads disdainfully away.

Clara smiles, caressing one of the chicks along its underside, but she feels the meagre heat beneath its ruffled softness. She gets to her feet, aware suddenly of the chill. It will be November soon. The days will grow raw and comfortless, in the woods and on the shore. The nights will widen, welcoming everything that hunts. She has tried not to think of it, but they are only weeks old, and far from fledged. There will be only so much she can do, as winter patiently encircles them.

She notices something then that has caught on her sleeve. It is the tiniest of feathers, hardly more than a wisp of down. She detaches it carefully, meaning to inspect it more closely, but it is so slight that she cannot keep hold of it. She sees it only for an instant before the wind takes it, a thread of brightness that shivers from her fingertips and is gone.

Three

When *he woke* again, Eustace thought first of running. The impulse was fleeting – he had silenced it by the time he sat on the edge of his bed to straighten his cuffs – yet it was curious, after all this time, how easily it had come to him. But perhaps it was not so strange that he should feel the old urge, that the memory of running should persist. He had seen enough of it in his time.

He had been no more than a boy the first time. He had been left with little choice, after what had happened – after what he had done. If he had not run, they would have come for him. What awaited him had never been in doubt.

After that, it was something he became accustomed to. They had fled to Paris first, he and Mr Crowe, when that city was in the last of its true glory. There he had been admitted to another world, to a world of carriage rides and opera houses, of scandals whispered behind silk-gloved fingers; a world of sonatas and cigar smoke, of toothless princesses and jasmine-scented whores.

It was a world where he knew nothing, but he learned quickly. He was shown without introduction into the lower rooms of half the fine houses in the *septième*. While he waited for his master to emerge from the salon or the boudoir above, he listened to the talk of the servants, even when there was hardly a word of it that he understood. He kept his eyes on his untouched absinthe, and he tried to pick the sense from the noise. He learned.

He stood with the valets in the passageways, or among the grooms in the stables, and his education came without order or sequence. He learned the word for horseshit and the word for iron; the words for lice and sores, for maidenhood and stillbirth. But he listened, and he learned.

He learned the ways in – *on se tutoie, hein?* – and the ciphers that were meant to warn him off. He learned to look for what might be of use, for the few true secrets that fell unintended among the scraps. He learned that this, as much as anything, was his purpose in those places, that he must be the first to read the signs. He learned to see things coming.

And he learned when to run.

For that was the nature of running. You knew, almost without exception, that it was coming. The rabbit kit, still half-blind, learns of the hawk's intention when it finds itself upside down in the harsh wind, trailing a bright tether of its guts. A man – even a boy, unless he is a halfwit – will have some means, however slender, of warning himself. A woman, in Eustace's experience, possesses a sharper faculty still. The fine threads of which our safety is woven – these are like a hand that she reads without effort. Not even the slightest twitch that might begin their unravelling is invisible to her.

It took many forms, Eustace learned, the sign that puts paid to the last of your doubts. The hand that is slipped, at a late hour and before some disreputable doorway, into a coat that hangs too heavily on one side. The blunt smack of the gavel, echoing above the tumult. Or perhaps only the back of a fine gown, turned gracefully against you in a glittering ballroom. Such events, however unlike each other, were equal in their effects.

Whatever its nature, the thing that you cannot mistake is only the last in a disquieting procession. For days or weeks before, all ease has been wrung from the life you had. Your sleep is thin and easily torn. You eat only what you must to keep you from weakening. In the sump of your chest, a sour dread is pooling. It will be loosed in your blood, all of it in one rush, when the time comes.

That much he had learned the first time he had taken to the road, with no provisions but those he could bundle together in ten or fifteen fevered minutes. That was long ago, before he had taken his present name. Since then, there was little about running that Eustace had not come to know. Nothing in its cramped rituals, however calamitous or exotic the circumstances that gave rise to them, was ever fresh or new. The first time, nonetheless, had been set apart in at least one respect. In one detail, it was not repeated.

Though he had done so many times since then, Eustace did not flee that first night in the company of Mr Crowe. He set out alone, and it was Mr Crowe that he pursued.

It was a morning he might otherwise have taken pleasure in. The air had a rasp of cold in it, and the sky had the clean, mineral blueness that is seen only in the declining months. He spared it little more than a glance. There would be other such days.

He began by pacing out the avenue. In the dark, there was only so much he had been able to do. There had been the body, of course, which he had consigned for now to the luggage compartment of the young man's own car. He had walked the half-mile or so to the main gates, where the avenue joined the public road that bounded the Estate to the north. It carried little passing traffic, even by day, and the country round about held only a scattering of households.

If anything had been heard, he knew the lights to look for. He had cleared away the guns, and had seen to the cars. The young man's was in the old stable yard for now, as any visitor's would be. He had done what he could with the disfigured lawn.

It would have been useless, he knew, to have attempted more before daylight, yet he had gone to bed uneasy. He had not done a tenth of what was needed. There would be much he had missed. Now he could bring some thoroughness to the task.

In the low October sun, the grounds were harshly lit. Every blade of grass was finely etched, every leaf underscored with shadow. If anything had been dropped or flung from the cars, he would pick it out. He did not look his age, he was told, but he was slower on his feet than twenty years before; he would emerge sorrier from a brawl, if he were to enter it at all.

Of all his faculties, his sight had aged least. Even at twenty or thirty feet, he could tell a mistle thrush apart from its more common cousin. He did not hunt now, since Mr Crowe had lost his taste for it, but he could still take down a buck from a quarter of a mile, if he were pressed to it. His scouring of the lawns, then, yielded items that even a diligent sergeant might have overlooked. He was further rewarded when he inspected the great lime trees that lined the avenue.

Gathering the spent cartridges gave him rather less satisfaction. Of all the chores that would fall to him from the antics of the night before, he was least enamoured of this one. His post had its vexations; he was long enough accustomed to them, and it was not his habit to hold himself aloof from his work. It gave him no pleasure, however, to find himself bagging and counting buckled casings like the lackey of a common murderer. If he accommodated himself to such things, it was not that he did so always without discomfort; it was not that he never grew weary.

Tiresome as it was, accounting for the cartridges gave him an occupation that blunted his unease. When it was done, there was little else for his attention to fasten upon. The woman had left two white cigarette ends, each mint-scented and lightly fretted with carmine gloss. Mr Crowe had let fall a scarf, a fine thing in black and dove-grey silk. It had been ground under a heel, most likely his own, and was no longer serviceable. In agitation, Eustace tapped at his palate with his tongue.

What else? What else was there?

He could see or think of nothing. It gnawed at him, making him doubt his own subtlety. For lack of any less obvious occupation, he turned his attention again to the car and its contents. He had moved it to the stable yard only until it could be put beyond recovery. He would see to that later. What he wanted, for now, was what it might reveal to him. Who and what was he, this man? Where had he come from? How soon would he be missed, and by whom?

The woman, Arabella; she might have answers to give them. Mr Crowe might have gleaned something from her himself as they became acquainted, but he could not now be depended upon to approach the matter with rigour. He had never been diligent, except in a handful of cherished pursuits, and he had begun to neglect even those. In any case, there was no telling what cause she might have to keep things from them.

Even if she were to reveal nothing, Eustace was inclined already towards certain inferences. She was an entertainer, that much he knew, and Mr Crowe had encountered her at one of the dives he now frequented. But what had he been to her, this young man? A lover? A husband? He had been ardent in his feelings, but what of hers? The unfaithful, he had observed, were apt to renew their old attachments when they were finally freed of them.

He set about rummaging through the car's cramped and dismal interior. It was upholstered in a cheap, grey fabric and had been indifferently cared for. The bearded man had often been content, it appeared, to take his meals in the vehicle, even to pass the occasional night there. On the back seat, there were remnants of sliced bread and a half-eaten jar of fish paste. Under a bundle of thin and stale-smelling blankets, Eustace found an empty bottle – some inferior gin – and a magazine of lurid photographs.

On the front passenger seat were five or six gramophone records with pictures of performers on their sleeves. In music, their visitor had favoured the work of those whose beards and leather coats most closely resembled his own. His literary tastes, on the evidence of the three flimsy paperbacks in the glove compartment, tended towards poetry. There was something in this that Eustace found both unsurprising and indistinctly loathsome.

Aside from these items, there was little else that revealed much. If he had possessed a driving licence, he had not been punctilious enough to keep it in the pocket of the windscreen visor, or in any other obvious place. There were receipts and other such ephemeral things, but nothing that put a name to the face Eustace had seen. He might have been a vagrant, but he might just as easily have been the wayward middle child of a cabinet minister.

Eustace reclined in the driver's seat and let out a slow breath. Idly, he picked up one of the volumes of poetry and began to leaf through it. Mr Crowe, of course, was steeped in verse, as he was in all forms of writing. Clara, he had long since realised, was made in the same way. Words, in their minds, were not fixed to things as a tendon is to a muscle. Every particle of creation, to them, was submerged in a flux of words. Everything was contiguous with everything else, the touching of one word or object setting up currents and mutations that seemed never to stop. They described the world by ceaselessly unsettling it, never letting anything rest. He saw the enticements of all this, or he did sometimes, but it exhausted him too. And he distrusted it.

He made a desultory survey of the poems, scanning titles and first lines. His eye snagged here and there on a form of words that had been twisted, like a fishing lure, into an arresting brightness. The rest was merely wearying. He turned the book over, glancing idly over the back cover. Here, the poet's handful of achievements was made much of. He had put out a few others like this one. He had won this or that prize.

Eustace tossed the book back onto the seat. His breath had formed a mist on the windscreen, obscuring the familiar bulk of the house, and he found that he could no longer tolerate the sour air of the car's interior. He would wash again, when he went back inside; he would put on a fresh suit and shirt. But it would stay with him for hours, he knew. He would find its taint at the edges of his breath, clinging with faint insistence to his skin.

He found them in the orangery. They had contrived to sleep there somehow, gathering up what soft furnishings there were and piling them beneath the piano. From the depths of some closet, Mr Crowe had procured a fur coat and this now covered the woman. Even with this improvised bedding, they could hardly have passed a restful night. Though it retained some of its grandeur, the domed chamber of glass was frigid and comfortless after sunset. He surveyed the bottles and decanters that had been abandoned on various surfaces about the room. They had put themselves, he supposed, beyond the need for comfort.

He set the breakfast tray on a wicker table and stood for a moment, listening to the magniloquent blare of Mr Crowe's snoring. Eustace rarely woke him under any circumstances, and rousing him in this condition was particularly unappealing. Still, there was some urgency in today's business. There was much to discuss.

He circled the piano, glancing at the sheets of Chopin that had spilled from the music stand. Mr Crowe had taken a run at a nocturne, it seemed, before thinking better of it. The lid had been closed over the keyboard, and on it rested a heavy crystal ashtray containing several cigar ends and a scrap of cloth. An intimate garment, Eustace realised as he cleared the items away.

Though he opened the piano lid with no particular object in mind, he found himself measuring out the familiar intervals. He had no particular aptitude for music, but had been fascinated enough by this unsettling clutch of notes to observe how the chord was played, to practise it at odd moments of leisure. With his left hand, he stroked the white keys. With two fingers of his right, he clawed the pair of sharps. It was satisfying, somehow, simply to form the shape. The gesture felt appropriately large, even before a note sounded. He raised his splayed fingers and held them, allowing himself a moment or two of relish. He brought them down like a landslide.

The chord clanged immensely, resounding in the chilly vault of marble and glass, and its effect was immediate. An incredulous whimper rose from beneath the piano, followed by the scuffing of agitated movement and a sequence of resonant thuds, each attended by an anguished moan. The noises culminated in a colossal roar.

'*What in the name of the living and writhing Christ?*'

'I believe it is known as the Tristan chord,' Eustace said, barely raising his own voice. 'I may be wrong, of course. I am not a lover of music, as you know.'

Still supine, Mr Crowe worked his head and shoulders clear of the piano. He was in considerable disarray. To the grease and smut of the night before, he had added wine stains and a small quantity of some kind of sauce. His hair, entirely flattened on one side, was arranged on the other in a violent outward spray. He did not have command over his right eye.

'Eustace, you intolerable scourge! What are you thinking of, hammering at the piano like that? You have ruptured something in my heart, I think. I almost vomited with fright.'

'That does sound alarming. Stand up, sir, and let me examine you.'

'I will let you examine the toe of my boot, Eustace. Can a man and his guest not couch themselves in comfort without suffering a deranged musical assault? Look at this poor girl. She is trembling.'

'I apologise, of course. Had I realised that you were servicing the instrument—'

'Oh, you are a rare wit, Eustace. The instrument requires no servicing, I assure you. It is in fine temper. Is it not, Arabella? We banged out a tune or two before Morpheus claimed us. Hup, hup! Bestir yourself, girl. Breakfast is served.'

Arabella emerged, pulling the fur coat about herself and regarding Eustace with blurred hostility. When Mr Crowe had availed himself of a kipper, they arranged themselves with some labour on a sofa.

'What time is it?' Arabella asked him. Her manner suggested that the onset of morning had been brought about by some unnatural means.

'A little after eight,' he said. 'You do not care for breakfast?'

'Isn't it considered uncivilised to be waited on at breakfast?'

'It is generally considered uncivilised,' Mr Crowe put in, 'to pass out in the orangery. Our disgrace, I fear, is already complete.'

Arabella glanced at the tray and shuddered. 'Just coffee.'

She lit a cigarette as Eustace set out her cup, watching him through her hair with unabated resentment. He returned her gaze, studying her for as long as decorum allowed, looking for signs of what lay beneath her composure.

'I was still eating,' said Mr Crowe.

Arabella gave him a level and unrepentant look. 'I was still sleeping.'

Mr Crowe's indignation dissolved then into a look of fond indulgence. Arabella, spooning partially melted sugar from her coffee cup to her lips, answered this with a pantomime of contrition. Even with his long habituation to such things, Eustace could take only half a minute or so of this exchange before interrupting.

'If you will forgive me, sir.'

Mr Crowe looked up.

'It is inopportune, I realise, but you will recall that there were matters arising from last night's proceedings.'

'For the love of God, Eustace. You are like a senile terrier. I am at breakfast with a noted soprano.'

Arabella snorted. 'You noted that first, did you?'

Eustace gathered and dispersed his fingertips in a gesture of regret. 'It grieves me, Mr Crowe. If it were within my power, I would attend to these matters without troubling you.'

'How is it not within your power, Eustace?'

'The young man—'

'Christ, Eustace. You will not be told.'

'It is distressing for you, sir. And, of course, for Miss Arabella.' She doused her cigarette in her coffee. Her distress, if she suffered any, was for the moment held in check. 'However, it is no longer simply a matter of the gentleman's unfortunate—'

'There was nothing unfortunate about it,' Mr Crowe said. 'This, now—' he gestured towards Eustace. 'This is unfortunate.'

'Perhaps,' said Eustace. 'Nonetheless, it cannot be avoided. The matter is now more pressing than we first apprehended. There is something we must discuss, when you are at leisure.'

Mr Crowe reclined and belched. 'I am always at leisure, Eustace. Particularly so this morning. And surely you would not have me forsake Arabella when she is at her most desolate?' She slid towards him, the fur coat slipping lower about her shoulders.

'Very well,' Eustace said. 'But if we are to pursue this here, I am afraid we must be frank. I can no longer be delicate, even for the lady's sake.'

Mr Crowe pushed out the chair on which he had been resting a boot. 'Sit down, Eustace, for the love of Jesus. Sit down and have at it. I did not spring Arabella from a convent. She is well enough inured, I think, to what passes between men of the world.'

Eustace took his seat. He loosened his cuffs and set aside the starched cloth that had been draped over his forearm. The view from the orangery was over the formal gardens to the south. His gaze wandered over the neglected hedges, seeking out what remained of their order and symmetry.

'I am sure,' he said at last, 'that we all feel great regret at what has occurred. And Miss Arabella, of course, must be assured that she has our utmost sympathy.'

She looked at him warily, pulling the fur more closely about her shoulders.

'I will not pry, of course, into a quarrel whose nature may have been intimate. The grievance, real or imagined, that brought the young man here; that is not my concern. These afflictions are common enough in the world. As for what passes between you and Mr Crowe, well – for all that it is an exalted thing, I'm sure, it did not drag me from my bed.'

Mr Crowe sucked at his teeth. 'I trust, Eustace, that there is some object to this disquisition.'

'The deceased, sir. The young man—'

'His name was David,' Arabella said. 'David Landor.'

'Indeed?' Eustace paused. He bowed his head fractionally. 'I had discovered Mr Landor's name, then, without realising that I had.

You will understand that I was obliged, under the circumstances, to examine his personal effects and – forgive me, miss – his person. I was obliged to discover what little I could about him, and about last night's unfortunate events.'

'Suffering Christ, Eustace,' said Mr Crowe. 'It is like being trapped in a tea room with a lady detective. Tell us what this investigation of yours has revealed. What did this Landor do with himself when he wasn't battering young girls and getting in the way of bullets.'

Mr Crowe had dispensed, it seemed, with all tenderness and circumspection. Eustace studied Arabella for her response, but she seemed troubled only by the chill.

'As to his occupation, I had discovered only that he was perhaps somewhat irregular in his habits, and that he had a liking for poetry. But it was more than a liking, it now seems: one of the volumes I found was by a man of that name.'

Arabella looked away, as if in distaste. 'The poems – yes, of course. He used to read them to me sometimes. It was all terribly solemn, as if he were the prime minister announcing that we were at war. They were about seagulls, and feeling sad on buses, that sort of thing. He didn't do much of anything else, apart from spending my money. I don't suppose you found any of that?'

'What may be of more concern,' Eustace continued, 'is the deceased himself; the state of his person.'

'What about it?' Mr Crowe said. 'I trust it has not changed? He did not get up in the night and ask if he might ring for a cab?'

Eustace plucked at his sleeve. 'I mean only that it bore no signs of grave injury. Some bruising, nothing more.'

Mr Crowe said nothing. He massaged his scalp, retrieving some items of detritus from the roots of his hair and depositing them upon his saucer. From the floor behind the sofa he retrieved a decanter of Armagnac, half-filling his cup before adding a splash of coffee.

'That's ridiculous,' Arabella said. 'I saw it all myself. I heard the shots, and he – he went down. I heard the shots. There must have been half a dozen.'

Eustace drew the bundled handkerchief from his pocket, unwrapping it carefully to reveal the bullets. Some were blunted and misshapen, others merely discoloured. 'I dug two from the bark of a lime tree,' he said. 'And you intended, no doubt, to clip one of the stone dragons. It will survive, I daresay, as will the lawn. I believe I have accounted for all of them. Mr Landor's death, it seems, had some other cause.'

Mr Crowe remained silent. When he had drained his coffee and liqueur, he lit a cigar and moved to an armchair facing the gardens. He stared, as Eustace had, at the elaborate enclosures of box, disfigured by weeds and unchecked growth.

Eustace addressed him directly now. 'You asked me what I had concluded, and I will admit that I was far from certain of any conclusion. You know, however, what it is that I suspect, and it seems you will say nothing to persuade me otherwise.'

'I don't understand.' Arabella looked from Eustace to Mr Crowe, who gave no sign that he was listening. 'What does he suspect? What happened to David? What did you do?'

'It is something I myself do not pretend to understand,' Eustace said. 'Mr Crowe, I am sure, will offer a more satisfactory explanation.'

Arabella crossed the room to Mr Crowe's armchair. When he did not look up, she crouched beside him, taking his wrist and caressing it with her thumb. 'What is he saying? What haven't you told me?'

He glanced at her but said nothing. Freeing his hand from hers, he reached out absently to stroke her hair, then turned his attention back to the garden. She stared a moment longer at his face then shook her head in resignation. Lowering herself to the floor, she rested her head on his thigh.

Eustace got to his feet. 'I know what this will bring, even if I do not understand it. They will come to know of it. Is that not so? They will find out, and they will come.'

There was no answer.

'I will do what I can,' he said. 'I will make inquiries. If matters are in motion, it may be that some word can be had. We may yet have some allies in this.'

Mr Crowe nodded slowly, his expression faintly comprehending.

'You knew, then?' Eustace said. 'You already expect them?'

Still there was silence.

'Christ.'

He walked to the windows, surveying the untended parterre, the lank and unpruned roses. He remembered a masquerade ball that had been held one midsummer night. A string quartet had played where he now stood, while outside Mr Crowe held court, presiding over a parade of masked guests, of gilded porcelain faces.

'Not like this,' he said quietly.

Mr Crowe looked up at last, perhaps only because he had not understood. 'Not like what, Eustace?'

'Magnificent,' Eustace said. 'It was magnificent, once. We will not have it seen like this.'

'You propose to defend us with a spot of gardening?'

'Not only the gardens, Mr Crowe. If guests are expected, then nothing in our preparations will be found wanting. We are not done here yet.' He turned briskly from the window. 'I shall be giving instructions,' he said. 'There will be some expense. You will not find it unconscionable, I trust.'

Mr Crowe half-raised his hand. 'There is no great lack,' he said. 'Do as you see fit.'

'Very good,' said Eustace. He strode towards the door, but Mr Crowe called after him.

'A moment, Eustace.'

He turned. 'Sir?'

'Last night, Eustace. I'm afraid that I—' He slumped in his chair, scouring his cheeks with his fingertips. 'I acted in considerable heat, you see. I regret nothing of what happened, do not mistake me, but certain other aspects of my conduct, well . . .'

Eustace waited.

'I am immoderate, sometimes, in my behaviour. One is a prisoner of one's own nature, you see, and you will admit that you yourself were exceedingly trying.' Mr Crowe looked up, his expression strained and mournful. 'Still, it may be that I was intemperate in certain of my remarks.'

'I am sure,' Eustace said, after a long pause, 'that last night was very trying for us all. Now, I will speak first to Alice. We must see how things stand with the tradesmen.'

Mr Crowe looked away in weariness. 'How things stand?'

'Our accounts, sir, with those who have given us credit. Sooner or later, they must all be paid.'

Four

'*Of what does* a rose consist?'

Clara is startled by the question. She stops, looking up and down the darkened landing. It was the voice of a young girl, she thinks, but she can see no one. She continues in the direction of the stairs, treading with wary deliberation. It is then that she notices the mirror at the far end of the passageway. It rarely attracts her notice, though it is large and ornate; nothing in the house is unfamiliar to her, and her own thoughts preoccupy her, usually, as she makes her way among its rooms.

But her reflection. Her reflection is not moving.

She stops in mid-stride, tottering slightly as she draws back her foot. Her reflection is completely still. When she peers at it, her head set on one side, her mirrored self shows no such curiosity. Only when Clara herself becomes still does her image make the slightest movement, and then there is no mistaking it. Her reflection walks towards her.

As it approaches, Clara sees that it – that *she* – wears a nightgown just like hers; that she is of exactly her height and resembles her perfectly. She walks calmly along the landing, this other girl, until she is hardly more than an arm's length away, then she stops and repeats the question Clara heard. 'Of what does a rose consist?'

'I beg your pardon,' Clara says. 'Were you addressing me?'

Or rather, Clara does not say this. That is, she does not say it aloud. She cannot speak in her dreams, any more than she can while she is awake. In her dreams, however, the words she wishes a person to hear are somehow immediately understood.

The girl, her likeness, considers this.

'I suppose I was,' she says, 'though I hadn't meant to exactly. I was thinking aloud, I suppose.'

'I see.' Clara finds herself straining to be polite, though the circumstances make politeness seem faintly absurd.

'Still, here you are again,' her likeness says, 'though perhaps you are only a ghost. *Is* that what you are?'

The girl seems entirely at ease, if rather serious. If she truly suspects Clara of being a ghost, the prospect does not trouble her. Clara wonders whether she emerged, at the same moment she herself did, from a bedroom that is the mirror image of her own, whether she too was on her way to the kitchen to fetch barley water. It seems somehow unlikely, if only because she cannot quite imagine this girl wanting barley water.

Clara assures the girl that she is still living. 'At least,' she says, 'I believe I am. I certainly don't remember dying. Did you say *again*?'

'Oh, you would remember dying, if you had. Take my word for it. Well, then. I suppose you ought to manage it.'

'Ought I?' Clara says. 'To manage what?'

'Why, to answer the question, of course,' the girl says. 'Goodness. Are you sure you are not dead?'

'Quite sure, thank you. But I'm afraid I've forgotten the question.'

The girl sighs. 'Of what,' she repeats, 'does a rose consist?'

'Ah,' says Clara. 'Yes, of course. Well, let's see. A rose consists of a stem, of petals . . .' She trails off as she strains to remember her botany.

'Anything else?'

'A stigma,' says Clara carefully, 'and a pistol?'

'A pistol?' says the girl. 'Is that quite what you meant to say?'

Clara is struggling to make some sensible reply when she realises that they are no longer on the landing. They are in Eustace's room, standing on opposite sides of the bed where he lies asleep. The girl takes something from the nightstand and examines it idly. Only when she turns to face her again does Clara recognise it and draw back in alarm. It is a gun – one of the guns she noticed this morning.

'*This* is a pistol,' says the girl, gripping it with both hands. She raises it towards Eustace, tracing his sleeping form until it is pointed at his head. 'What do you suppose it's doing here?'

'*What are you doing?*' Clara hisses.

The girl brings the pistol to her own temple. Her expression is curious as she draws the hammer back. The sound it makes is dull and precise.

Clara lunges at her. For all her panic, she is horrified at the thought of how foolish she will appear when Eustace wakes to find her sprawled across his bedspread. Instead, she finds herself skidding on her chest across an expanse of polished marble. It is the floor of the ballroom, she realises, and it is strewn with a great quantity of white feathers.

Wincing a little, she pushes herself up, sitting with her back to a pillar as she catches her breath. The girl, her double, is sitting cross-legged in the centre of the enormous ballroom. Next to her is a great pile of feathers – it was these that Clara disturbed – and on her lap is what appears to be some elaborate piece of needlework. The girl looks at her in exasperation.

'Honestly,' she says. 'You've ruined hours of work.'

Clara is still disoriented, and does not immediately reply. She looks guardedly at the pile of feathers, as if the pistol might be concealed in it, and hunches forward so as to peer into the girl's sewing basket. 'I'm sorry,' she says at last. 'I don't know what happened. I didn't see you.'

The girl glances at her. 'You hardly ever do these days.'

Clara draws up her knees. The ballroom is cold at night. 'I'm afraid I don't follow.'

'And you are quite wrong, you know, about roses.'

'I'm not sure that I—'

'Stigmas and so on,' the girl reminds her, pinching a thread between her wetted fingertips. She is left-handed, Clara notices, just as her mirror image ought to be. 'I know that's what the books say, but it's not a question of anatomy. I've been trying to do roses, you see, so I've been studying them. You can't understand things by dissecting them, by cutting them into their parts. When you've dissected it, it isn't a rose any longer.'

To do roses. It is a strange thing to say, and Clara puzzles over it as she waits for the girl to continue. Her likeness, though, is intent on threading her needle and seems to have lost interest in the subject for now. Clara takes the opportunity of studying her more closely. She does not spend a great deal of time before the mirror, aside from washing in the morning and at bedtime, and gives no particular attention to her appearance. Still, the image of her own face is fixed somehow in her consciousness, as she supposes everyone's must be. She could not draw it, perhaps, but she could point without hesitating to where someone else's pencil had gone awry. This girl, though her manner is quite alien, is like her in every physical particular. If they were to stand silently one beside the other, she feels sure that even Eustace could not tell them apart.

'I'm Clara,' she says, extending her hand. 'How do you do?'

The girl looks up in mild surprise. 'Well, of course you are,' she says.

Abruptly, the girl puts aside her needle and her feathers. Ignoring Clara's outstretched right hand, she reaches instead for her left. She grasps it for a moment in both of hers, turning it over and stroking the palm with her thumb.

'You do not remember?' she says, releasing Clara's hand. 'No, I suppose not. You never do. I'm afraid I don't have a name, but it's very nice to meet you again.'

'Oh.' Clara is disappointed. 'Well, perhaps you can tell me how long you've been here, then. And what you do. I can't think why I've never seen you before.'

'Always.' The girl looks around the ballroom. 'I've always been here, just like you. And I make things, since you ask again. Like swans. I've made other things, but I'm fondest of those.'

'Gosh,' says Clara, struggling to think of a polite response. 'It must be terribly difficult.'

The girl smiles a little at this. She looks away, gazing absently at the frescoes on the ceiling. 'What about you?' she says, before yawning at some length. 'I'm so sorry. What do you do?'

'Do?' Clara is about to answer, but finds that she hardly knows what to say.

'You must do something, surely?' The girl is suddenly impatient. 'I should go mad if I didn't, wandering about this place for all this time.'

Clara stares down at her lap. 'Well,' she says, 'I write things.'

'Writing,' the girl says. 'Yes, of course. Letters and things. I'd forgotten. How nice for you.'

'No, I—' Clara presses her own thumb into her palm. It is warm still, the place where the girl touched her. 'It isn't just writing. I mean, they're mine, the things I write. I see them first, or dream them. It is a *little* like making things, though I suppose it's not quite the same.'

'Mmm.' The girl seems preoccupied, and says nothing for a few moments. She studies one of the fresco panels, a scene of clouds in which a man with the lower body of a goat is wresting a jug of wine from an angel. Something occurs to her. 'I could show you.'

'Show me?'

But the girl is already getting to her feet and smoothing down her nightgown. 'Come on,' she says. 'Give me your hand.'

They are in the Windbones then, standing among the reeds at the edge of the mere. It is a still night, under an almost full moon. The inky water, where it is disturbed, is creased with sapphire. It is very beautiful, if a little chilly.

'Do you like it here too?' Clara says. 'It's so odd that we haven't seen each other before.'

The girl studies her face for a moment, then glances in the direction of the house. 'It's such a pity. You could help them, you know, if only you remembered. You could help to put things right.'

Clara clasps her arms and shivers. 'What do you mean? Help who?'

'Never mind,' says the girl. 'Look.'

The swans are descending. As they near the water, each one arrests itself with a strenuous burst of wingbeats, pounding the dark surface and sending up bright detonations of spray. As they fold their wings and settle, this violence is effaced by a calm and noiseless grace. The lake beneath them is smoothed until each one tugs behind it only a gently rucked apron of silky water.

'They're magnificent,' Clara whispers.

'Yes. I suppose you'll want to dissect one.'

'What?' Clara is horrified. 'No, of course not. They're so very beautiful.'

'That's just as bad, you know. Being in awe, I mean. You'll never get anything done.'

'Thank you for your advice,' Clara says. She is beginning to find the girl rather rude. It occurs to her too that she has not yet seen her make anything. 'Weren't you going to show me how it is that you – how things are made?'

'I'm sorry, but I can't do that.'

'But you said—'

'I said that I would *show* you,' says the girl, 'not that I would show you *how*. I can't do that. No one can. Now watch.'

Searching the lake, she finds where the swans have settled and selects a spot a little way apart from the flock. Once she has chosen the place, she becomes quiet, staring intently at what appears to be clear water. It isn't, though, or it isn't quite. Now, there is a smear at the centre of Clara's vision, like ointment thumbed onto glass. It spreads as she strains to find some shape in it, an edgeless occlusion hardly more definite than the water itself.

Clara blinks, losing the place for a moment. When she finds it again, it has changed further. She can see fine details now, like the tissue of flaws at the core of an ice cube. For a while, it swells slowly, increasing itself in small surges. Then it branches and ramifies, taking on a spreading symmetry. And there is a pattern. It is *becoming* something.

'Oh,' she says. 'Oh, my.'

She sees them now, held high and tautly apart over the water: the supple bows of muscle and, arrayed beneath them in intricate translucence, the lavish spread of feathers. The stem of the neck, tense and elegant, is suddenly obvious, as if it had been there all along. It collapses its wings with soft emphasis, and tucks itself contentedly onto the lake.

'Oh, my,' Clara says again. 'Is that – is it real?'

The girl gives her an appraising look. 'What do you think?'

'It *looks* real,' Clara says. 'Will they notice, the others? That it's different, I mean?'

'I expect we'll see.'

Clara stares at her. 'Do you mean you don't know?'

The girl ignores her for a moment, her attention focused on the lake. Then she says simply: 'Watch.'

Clara follows her gaze. The flock is gathering, with unhurried grace, around the new arrival. A few individuals glide closer to it and begin to inspect it, arching their pliant necks as they peer at its plumage or sample the air around its tail feathers. The interloper is untroubled, puffing out its breast and regarding the others with preening serenity.

Clara watches anxiously. She has seen many such encounters among the swans and knows the signs to look for. The new bird, though, is unlike any she has seen. She cannot read the flock's intentions. She turns to the girl, and finds that she is whispering. 'Is this promising, do you think?'

But the girl's attention has been drawn by something on the water, her expression suddenly grave. When Clara turns back to the swans, she sees that two or three of those closest to the newcomer have drawn back their wings. In their postures, there is an unequivocal menace. They begin to circle it closely, issuing harsh, rasping whoops of denunciation. She has heard these sounds before.

'What is it?' she says. 'What's wrong?'

The girl speaks softly, her voice regretful. 'They are rejecting it, turning against it.'

'I know that. But why?'

'Of what does a rose consist?'

'Oh, for goodness' sake,' Clara says. 'Not that again.'

'I'm trying to tell you what's happening. It's a question of species recognition.'

'A question of what?'

'They do not believe it. They know it is not truly of their kind.'

'But it looks so perfect.'

'It isn't simply a matter of how it looks. It isn't a painting.'

'And what will they do?'

The girl stares at her for a moment. 'They will destroy it, of course. What else?'

Sure enough, two or three of the more aggressive males are taking turns now in rearing back and lunging at the impostor. It seems pathetically confused by their attacks, jerking its head from side to side and paddling in small, panicked circles. Clara finds it unbearable to watch, yet she cannot look away.

'But what is it that's giving it away?' she says. 'Can't you fix it?'

The girl shakes her head. 'It's a living thing now. It's finished.'

They have begun to peck at its neck, crowding ever more closely around it.

'It happens sometimes,' says the girl, turning to leave the shore. 'I'm sorry.'

'Wait,' Clara says. 'Can't you just—'

'Just what?'

'Just . . .' She is distracted by the increasing violence of the swans. 'Just make it like the others.'

'I've shown you,' the girl says quietly. 'There's nothing more I can do.'

But it is almost too late, and Clara is no longer listening. The newly formed swan is struggling to keep itself upright. It will not survive much longer.

What must be done seems so clear to her that she doubts herself. What could she possibly know that this girl does not? Yet it is so clear, too, that she cannot ignore it. It occurs to her like a possibility, but it is more than that. It is radiantly urgent. She can see what it is that must happen.

She is doing things, in the moments that follow, that she cannot fully account for. There is more of herself, of her mind, than there ought to be. She is here and she is out over the water. She is on the far shore and she is plunged into the violent cold of the lake. What she is doing – what is being done – is arduous and dizzying. She is filled with sensation, a torrent of it that floods her throat, surges into her skin. It comes to her, all of it: every barb of every feather, every lobe and thread of flesh, unravelled and palpated. She smells and tastes every hot and foul ounce of what is in them.

It is unlovely, this work of knowing, and it is hard. Every instant of it is an effort she feels has emptied her. But it continues, for how long she has no idea, glutting her so impossibly with feeling that she finds she can no longer locate herself in her own thoughts. Whatever is left of her is simply waiting, powerless and vacant, either to possess itself again or to vanish entirely.

Then it is over, and she is back on the shore. She staggers, her hands on her knees. The need for air torches her lungs. She thinks she will vomit. She wants, very deeply, to lie down. What steadies her, finally, and holds her upright, is the same luminous simplicity that drew her in. She is stupefied with weariness, but the thing she has done burns in her, like a filament in a bulb. She understands it only a little, but she feels certain of what she has glimpsed. There was no miracle or cataclysm, just a pushing aside of the last nothing where something needed to be.

She struggles to focus, and wonders dimly how it is possible to feel such exhaustion while dreaming. Out on the water, the thicket of whiteness is beginning to disperse. The other swans have lost interest, their ferocity no longer drawn by infelicities of scent or colouring. For a moment, Clara struggles even to identify the creature she has touched. Then she catches its signature: a ragged hollow at the base of its neck, and a bruised meekness, still, in the way it holds itself in the water. It is moving among the others now, nervous but unmolested.

Clara is anxious still, feeling a surge of panic when another bird, in a quick and fluid movement, dips its bill between the folded wings of the one she now thinks of as hers. But the other swan only snatches something away, a wad of sodden leaves that lodged there during the confrontation. It is an act of grooming, a small kindness.

For a while, it is almost silent. The swans return to their former disposition, their postures staid and downcast. They spread out in soft movements on the dark water, their poised glyphs alliterating among the dashes and ellipses of moonlight. Following no pattern that Clara can discern, they drift unhurriedly among each other, animated by such slight impulses that they seem almost without purpose.

She watches them for a long time, though she is shivering violently now and struggling to remain alert. It is growing light when she catches the first splash and flutter. At first, she thinks she has imagined it, but before long she sees it again. A single swan pushes itself proud of the surface and seems to test its wings, holding them tautly outstretched before refolding them. With a tattoo of quick pulses, it scatters the wetness from its wings, then seems to settle again. Soon, these movements are answered elsewhere on the lake as another swan repeats the sequence: the languorous splaying, the *staccato* beating of wings.

It is spreading among them, the idea of flight, taking hold as a fire does, gathering intensity until the first of the swans is compelled to leave the water. It hauls itself aloft with a rapid slicing of its wings, climbing stiffly as another bird finds its wake, shadowing it as they cross the grey fringe of the mere. Soon, the violet stillness is thronged with pale forms, keeping close to the water as they leave, passing out of sight in mirrored pairs and triplets.

Clara does not catch the new swan as it departs. It is among them, that is all she knows, and nothing marks it out. She sinks to her knees among the reeds, knowing that she cannot hold even that position for long, that she must allow herself to rest. She remembers, as the sky above her empties, that there was a question, that it was something about roses. There was something else too, something water-dark and older than words. She strains for it, for its particular shape and strangeness, but it slips from her thoughts, as if it is too delicate to be grasped.

When she looks for the girl, her likeness, she is gone. Clara searches the shoreline, straining to catch some small movement, but the morning is greying with approaching rain. In the distance, the pale grass folds under the wind, and she can no longer tell the water from the sky.

Five

The *Crouch brothers* seemed little changed.

They had waited in the stable yard as Eustace had instructed. The house overlooked it on three sides, allowing him to watch them at leisure before he emerged. They would see that they were placed at a disadvantage, of course, would feel themselves observed. That too was as he intended. He wanted them to understand their position, to be in no doubt.

They were less alike, if anything, than he remembered. Each had settled into his form, and they carried themselves with the candid laxity of men at the end of their middle years. John's heaviness, in maturity, had taken on a mournful emphasis. He could put himself to some use still, Eustace imagined, but a watchful idleness came easiest to him. He lounged against Gull's car, while Abel patrolled restlessly nearby.

The elder brother took care over his clothes, if not over his person. He smoked almost incessantly, and his gaunt face was sallow enough to appear sickly. He wore one of the suede jackets that seemed now to be in fashion, and beneath it a knitted garment with a high neck. None of it had come cheaply, Eustace guessed, but the whole gave him the appearance of a mildly threatening entertainer.

Though they had learned with age to give some gloss of subterfuge to it, both studied their surroundings with practised thoroughness. John surveyed the exterior of the house by means of squinting glances, his gaze skimming the roofline and the brickwork, alighting here and there on some fixture that caught his interest. Abel was less drawn to such details, but seemed taken with the scale of the place. He sauntered around the perimeter of the yard, pausing at the gate to frame a view out over the parkland, pacing carefully backwards from the west wing to take its measure in side elevation, halting only when his heel collided with an old iron boot scraper. He turned to inspect this, testing it on the soles of his own shoes. He was hunched over it still when Eustace chose to make his entrance.

'You put me in mind of other times,' he called out as he crossed the yard. 'That scraper has not been used since we last staged a hunt.'

John prised his haunches from the car on seeing him, but Abel did not immediately turn around. He made a show of working something from his sole.

'Italian, these are,' he said, looking up at length. 'Can't seem to keep them clean.'

'Business is good?' Eustace said.

'We're doing all right,' Abel said. He scanned what could be seen of the house and grounds. 'Up to a point.'

'Who's the big man, then?' said John. 'Duke of something? You never explained last time.'

Last time. When he had called on them last, the circumstances had been of his own making. His old life, by then, was already behind him, but he had not left it in the manner he might have chosen. There had been some unpleasantness, of a kind that might have given certain people cause to seek him out. The brothers had taken measures to make that difficult. They had provided certain documents, enlisted the aid of certain parties. They had allowed him to put his mind at rest.

'Mr Crowe is a gentleman of private means.'

'Well, excuse me. And you, you're the butler?'

'I perform many functions,' Eustace replied. 'And the arrangement we spoke of – if it interests you, you will answer to me.'

'It interests us,' John said.

'Yeah,' said Abel. 'No offence. You didn't exactly go into detail, though. About the arrangement.'

'We are attending to a number of matters,' Eustace said. 'Some of them are of a delicate nature, some less so. We wish to retain the services of professional men, men who are accustomed to the unpleasant necessities that occasionally arise in business.'

The brothers looked at each other, and then at Eustace.

'How unpleasant, exactly?' Abel said. 'You want someone to disappear?'

He gave a curt nod.

'Where is he now? It *is* a he, I'm assuming?'

Eustace inclined his head briefly, indicating the car.

John glanced behind him. 'The motor?'

'No doubt you have certain associates,' Eustace said. 'They are thorough in their work, I take it?'

'Very thorough.'

'Good. They must also be very discreet.' Eustace paused. 'We expect that everyone who acts for us will exercise the utmost discretion.'

'Goes without saying,' Abel said. 'The motor and the, er, contents we can take care of tomorrow. You won't have to worry about them no more.'

'I am glad to hear it,' Eustace said. He allowed a moment to pass.

'You mentioned a number of matters,' said Abel.

'Indeed.' Eustace looked up. It would be November soon. The swifts were gone from the eaves, and the air was sharpened with the first of the true cold. 'But please, let us discuss this further in the warmth. In this weather, I begin to feel my age.'

Entering by the stable yard door, he led them to a room near the kitchens that served as his office. It was from here that he oversaw the running of the household, though this function was somewhat diminished; Mr Crowe was content, these days, to live in a lesser style than he had once demanded. As he showed them in, they came upon Clara. She was at his desk, absorbed in a drawing. It was not unusual, but today he might have thought to lock the door. These two would have some business here, if only for a short while, but he intended to keep them as much apart from her as he could.

Her eyes, when she looked up, were smeared and tender, shadowed by some recent distress. She showed alarm, too, at the presence of the men behind him. Clara was an undemanding child. When she was not at her writing or her books, she roamed the house and grounds in contented solitude. She cherished her habits, though, and disliked any disturbance in her surroundings. She stood, tugging her sleeve across her eyes, and began gathering her papers.

'Your little girl?' Abel asked.

'As much as anyone's,' Eustace said. 'No, Clara. There is no need. We will find somewhere else to converse. Is something the matter?'

She lowered her eyes to the drawing on the desk. When Eustace approached, he could make no immediate sense of it. It showed a rough nest, in some deep hollow of reeds. It was strewn with rags and feathers, but was otherwise empty. He looked at her in bewilderment, then laid his hand across the table, palm upwards.

'Clara?' he said. 'What is it, child? Has something happened?'

She glanced at the men behind him, then shook her head. Whatever it was that troubled her, she would not reveal more while they were here. With her forefinger, Clara traced a quick sequence of shapes on his palm, the rudiments of letters. It was something she resorted to when there was some confidence that would not wait, or when her words were intended only for him.

Who?

Eustace clasped her hand briefly as he turned away.

'Abel and John Crouch, Clara. These men will be doing some work about the place. You have seen how wild the gardens have grown.'

Clara regarded them carefully as she considered this. Then, as if something had occurred to her, she took up her pen and a clean sheet of paper. Working quickly, studying them in shy glances, she produced a raw but skilful ink drawing. She slid it across the desk, indicating with a slight smile that she intended it as a gift. Abel looked it over without comment, though he gave Clara herself a look of careful appraisal. John was more taken with it, spreading it on the desk in wonderment, tracing his own outline with a blunt fingertip.

The brothers were roughly rendered, their faces shown in shadow under straw hats. But she had caught their postures and proportions, and they were recognisable enough. John was shown lazing at the foot of an old, spreading apple tree. Abel stood some distance off, loosely clutching some bladed implement. With his other hand, he shielded his eyes from the sun and stared, either at the viewer of the picture or out across the garden at something unseen.

Eustace took them down to the cellar. He would not have been inclined, at the best of times, to conduct these two around the finest rooms of the house. As it was, Mr Crowe would be entertaining Arabella, in what fashion he could hardly guess at from one hour to the next. It was not the time for those introductions.

He left the lights off, guiding them down the rough steps by the light of a single candle. They were ill at ease in the cellar, he could see, and not inclined by instinct or habit to be led into such a place. They talked to distract him from their discomfort, or to put it from their own minds.

'How many bottles, would you say?' John asked, ducking his head to pass under an archway.

'Some thousands,' Eustace said. 'I keep the tally in a logbook.'

'Don't worry,' said Abel. 'We weren't getting any ideas.'

They followed him into a low, vaulted chamber where cured meats were hung. The shapes suspended in its recesses were looming and obscure. Eustace set the candle down and gestured to a long bench, taking his own seat in an ancient, straw-cushioned rocking chair.

Abel sat down warily, peering into the surrounding darkness. 'Get a lot of spiders down here, do you?'

John looked on in amusement. 'Hates spiders, he does. You should see him when there's a big one.'

Eustace waited until they had settled themselves. 'We expect some visitors,' he said at length.

'I can see that,' Abel said.

'We shall be entertaining them, of course, but that was not my meaning. The guests we expect will not be entirely welcome.'

'Undesirables,' John said. 'We can help you with that.'

'Yeah,' said Abel. 'Providing they ain't of the uniformed variety.'

'We are taking care to avoid attention of that kind,' Eustace said. 'No, these will be men of breeding. One of them, at least, is a scholar of some distinction.'

They looked at him with frank scepticism. 'Come again,' said Abel. 'You mean, like a professor?'

'Like that,' said Eustace. 'He is much else besides, but I am telling you how he will appear.'

'This professor,' said John. 'Very dangerous, is he?'

Eustace sighed and leaned back. 'You are amused,' he said. 'You think, perhaps, that I brought you here for some entertainment?'

The brothers shared a brief look, and John raised his hands, his fingers spread in contrition.

'Very well,' Eustace said, appraising their faces. 'I will tell you what I can, and you must make of it what you will. Remember, though, that my need is for professional men, for men who approach their work with seriousness.'

Neither of the two spoke. If they saw any cause for amusement now, they kept it from their faces.

'In my master's profession,' Eustace continued, 'he has relied on a peculiar gift. There have been others like him, but only a handful remain. I am no judge of these things, but I have heard it said that none of the others could ever match him. Be that as it may, in using these gifts of his, Mr Crowe and those like him have been given great licence, but they have not acted entirely without restraint. Certain limits were placed on them by the – what might one call it? – by the order to which they belonged.'

'Order?' Abel said. 'What, like monks or something?'

'Like monks?' Eustace considered this. 'No, not like monks. I meant only that this order has survived for a long time. How long exactly I do not know. Centuries, at least. And it has grown powerful.'

'Vampires, then?' John said eagerly. 'Like that film with what's-his-name?'

'What?' Eustace looked upward and let out a long sigh. 'No, nothing like that. They are very much of this world, but they have – how can I explain it? They are gifted in the arts, let us say. Not in the ordinary way, but so much so that others seek them out. It is a service of an uncommon kind, and those who seek it do so secretly. It does not come cheaply.

'They live well, and very much as they please, as long as they stay within the limits I mentioned. If they do not – if they break certain rules – this professor, as you call him, is the one they must answer to. He is not gifted as they are, but has some power over them that I do not fully understand. In any case, his authority is absolute.

'I know how all this must sound to you. It sounded just as outlandish to me once. But I ask you to accept it, and to accept that I have seen with my own eyes what this man, this professor, is prepared to do to those who refuse to be bound by the rules. You are men of the world, and you have seen a great deal, but nothing in your experience has prepared you for this.

'Is he dangerous? Yes, he is dangerous. He is more dangerous than anyone else you will ever encounter. We are by no means defenceless, and we will not sit idly. We will take steps to ready ourselves for what is coming, but you can help us only if you accept my word in all this. If you do not – if you have the slightest doubt – then there is nothing further for us to discuss.'

For a long time, the Crouch brothers said nothing. Eustace simply waited. He did not expect them to believe all he had said, or even to understand it. They would decide, perhaps, that he had spent too long in this place, serving the whims of an unseen master with only a mute child for company. They might not be entirely wrong.

'We get the idea,' said John at last.

'Yeah,' Abel said. 'Benefit of the doubt, and all that. But here's what I don't understand.'

'Go on.'

'This professor. If he's like you said – dangerous and powerful and all that. What did you bring us here for? What are we supposed to do, cast a spell or something?'

'We are taking some elementary precautions,' Eustace said. 'To ensure our security.'

'You want us to come the heavy?'

'If necessary.'

'No, I mean heavy. With proper equipment.'

'Again, if necessary. You are professionals. I shall leave the question of tools to your judgement.'

'Right,' said Abel. 'But again – if he's all that, your visitor. If he's beyond the beyond, or whatever. What the fuck good is it going to do, us coming the heavy?'

Eustace looked down and massaged his temples. 'It is a fair question,' he said eventually. 'I can only explain it in this way. Certain things may happen here whose nature is hidden from you. You will see their effects, but not the events themselves. Do you follow?'

They said nothing.

'Be that as it may,' Eustace continued. 'Much will happen that is of the ordinary kind. What takes place in the world is of the world. Certain rules have no exceptions.'

'Meaning they ain't bulletproof.'

'Under most circumstances, no.'

John nodded slowly as he considered this. 'Looks like there might be a niche for our services,' he said.

Eustace rose and dusted himself off. 'I had hoped you would see it in those terms.'

Abel looked around the cellar as they made ready to leave. 'You mind if I ask you something?'

Eustace paused and turned to him.

'You talked about this other lot who been around all this time. You were pushing forty last time we saw you, and that was what – twenty-odd years ago? You don't look much more than forty-five now. What's your secret? Special cream, is it?'

Eustace did not immediately reply. 'There must be no trace,' he said at length. 'When you dispose of the car, of the man's possessions, nothing must be left behind. Come, we have work to do.'

He led them towards the stairs.

Six

Clara *pauses outside* the library. From within, she hears voices. The woman's she has come to know only in recent days. She has heard it everywhere about the house, though she and its owner have not yet been introduced. It is low and unrushed; sweetened somehow, if not quite sweet. Mr Crowe's is languorous but not, she thinks, intimate – her own silence makes Clara alert to the speech of others, even if it is not intended for her hearing. He is reading, perhaps, or reciting something, while the woman speaks only occasionally, in comment or reply.

Clara hesitates. Though she is often in the library, she would not usually think of interrupting Mr Crowe while he is there. It is silently understood by everyone in the house that he must not be disturbed while he is at work. Even Eustace is forbidden from doing so. Still, he can hardly be at work, surely, and at the same time conversing with this lady.

She raises her hand to knock. It does not come easily to her, entering a room where people are in conversation. She thinks of her writing table, and of the music box she keeps there. It was a gift, she thinks, though she no longer remembers from whom. It is a pretty thing, of bronze work and painted porcelain, and she has come to treasure it especially. It plays a Fauré melody, and there is something comforting in its sweet, declining sadness, in the halting pirouettes of the winged dancer. She longs for it now, for that comfort. The changes in the house have unsettled her, disturbing even her dreams. She longs for it, but knows it is a weakness. She must do this, even if she finds it disagreeable. There is something in the library that she needs.

She knocks quietly but firmly, taking care that she will not be mistaken for Eustace, whose company Mr Crowe seems lately to be avoiding. Eustace's knock is regular and unmistakable; three quarter-note beats, the intervals metronomic and unvarying. Clara gives hers a gentler pattern – five taps in a loosely decaying sequence – and chooses a place low down on the door, too low for a grown man.

Mr Crowe pauses in his monologue, then murmurs something in a speculative tone. There is a gentle surge of laughter, followed by a silence. When the door is opened, Clara looks up, her face prepared and contrite.

'Why, hello there, little one.' It is the woman whose voice she heard. She is wearing a fine evening gown of lucent, jade-like satin and seems to be adjusting it at her shoulder. 'What's the matter? Are you lost?'

Clara shakes her head. Reluctantly, because she had meant it for Mr Crowe, she shows the woman the card on which she has written her rather terse note of apology. She has not taken the time over it that she usually would.

Please excuse me. Something I need. On shelf near Racine.

The woman peers at her message. She is more intrigued, Clara thinks, by the piece of paper than by the words themselves. 'How very interesting,' she says. 'Is it a game?'

Clara shakes her head. She had not planned this. The woman does not know about her, and she has no means of explaining that is not somehow humiliating. She begins to wish she had not knocked. Mr Crowe arrives then at the woman's shoulder, wearing a velvet dressing gown. He has a book in one hand and, in the other, a capacious glass of some amber liquid. His expression, to Clara's relief, is one of bemusement, not of irritation.

'This little girl has a message for us,' the woman says. 'Something about racing.'

'Racine, you dreadful ninny,' says Mr Crowe. 'This is Clara, and she needs something from the shelf near Racine. Come in, Clara, darling. This is Arabella. She is very charming, generally, but I'm afraid the dessert wine has rather encumbered her abilities.'

'How dare you,' says Arabella, though she does not seem in the least indignant. 'Delighted to meet you, Clara. Shall I guess how old you are? You look terribly grown-up.'

Mr Crowe leans towards her and whispers something, most of which Clara hears.

Arabella presses both hands to her mouth. 'Oh, you poor thing,' she says. 'I'm so sorry.'

'Nonsense,' Mr Crowe says, returning to the armchair by the fire that he has evidently been occupying. 'Clara is entirely contented, and certainly not in need of sympathy. She is, though I hesitate to draw attention to it, a rather gifted child. Oh, yes. She will not thank me for saying so – look how pained she appears already – but it is Clara, you know, who is the true artist. Next to her, I am no better than the commonest of hacks.'

Arabella seems briefly taken aback. 'Is she – I didn't realise that you had—'

He laughs. 'No, no. Clara is not mine. None of my mistakes has had quite so delightful an issue. But she has been with us for what seems an eternity – have you not, my darling? We could scarcely imagine life without her.'

Clara smiles as politely as she can. It is true enough, she supposes, though she hardly ever thinks of it. They have been here for so long, the three of them, that the fact of it seems immutable. Still, she does not think of Mr Crowe as she does Eustace. Their bond is no less real, but they are each content, for much of the time, not to encroach on the other's solitude, and neither suffers greatly for want of the other's company. She wonders how well Arabella has come to know him, and whether she imagines that he would find her absence unthinkable.

Arabella studies her carefully. 'Yes, I'm sure she's a treasure,' she says. 'Children, I suppose, are a comfort I have learned to do without.'

'How lamentable,' says Mr Crowe. 'Clara, we must persuade Arabella of her error.'

Clara regards him doubtfully.

'Yes, yes. You shall dazzle her with your talents. And then, as your reward, you may take whatever it is that you so urgently require from the shelf near Racine. Here, come and sit at the desk. You may use my pen. It belonged to Shelley, you know. A fine chap, if a little wanting in composure. Used to go without shoelaces, half the time. And while he was at Eton, he once destroyed a willow tree with gunpowder, an achievement some would say he never surpassed. At any rate, he once found himself in need of certain favours.'

Clara complies uneasily, perching at the edge of Mr Crowe's large and sumptuous chair. The pen is certainly a beautiful object. It is made, she thinks, of finely carved bone, with an elegant gold nib, but it is far from comfortable to hold and she is fearful of damaging it. She dips it in the ink and makes a few preliminary scratches on the blotter.

'Splendid,' says Mr Crowe. 'Now, then. Arabella, would you be kind enough to choose a book from the shelves?'

Arabella seems sceptical. 'I'm sure Clara would prefer to find whatever it is she's looking for and be on her way.'

'Nonsense,' he replies. 'We've been shut up in here for days, woman. We have a visitor and we must make an effort. Come now, your first book, if you please.'

She approaches the nearest wall of shelves with visible reluctance. 'This is absurd,' she says. 'You might at least tell me the object of this game. What sort of book am I supposed to look for?'

'Well, any sort,' says Mr Crowe. 'That's the point, you see. Ah, but wait. We must be somewhat fair to poor Clara. There are manuals of animal husbandry and God knows what else. I'm afraid I have accepted rather too many job lots from booksellers in my time. Let us confine it, at least, to things of quality. Any novel, then, or book of poetry. Essays if you must, but strictly *belles-lettres*. Oh, and plays, of course. Nothing by Ibsen, mind you, lest the poor girl become too despondent even to hold the pen steady.'

Arabella wanders along the rows of books. It is a very large collection, and might easily seem bewildering. The volumes, for the most part, are handsome and finely bound, their spines lavishly inlaid or lettered in austere gilt. Though some belong to sets and form imposing and uniform arrays, they are arranged according to no particular order or system, and Arabella has almost nothing to guide her. 'What about the language?' she says. 'Quite a few of these are in French.'

'Well, indeed,' Mr Crowe says. 'And some are in Italian. Some are in Greek, for that matter, which is all to the good. Any language, damn it. Isn't that right, Clara?'

Clara widens her eyes.

'Well, any civilised language,' Mr Crowe concedes. 'Nothing in

German, for instance. Clara has never taken to German, which is much to her credit. It is as if a language had been assembled by a fanatical collector of consonants. There now, you have made your first selection. Let me see, what have we here?'

Arabella passes him a distinguished-looking book with a simple spine of walnut-coloured leather.

'Ah, *Troilus and Criseyde*. A marvellous choice. Chaucer, among his other distinctions, is the only poet to have been ransomed by an English king. Oh, yes. The French had taken him at Reims, the bastards, and Edward the Third forked out sixteen pounds, I think it was, to have him sprung. This was thirteen-sixty-odd, mind you, so sixteen pounds would have bought you a decent pub. Of course, he was worth every penny. But I digress. Clara, if you would, please – the first two lines will do, but feel free to carry on if you are so inclined.'

It is a parlour game he has called on her to play before. It began at dinner one evening, when he became irate with one of the guests, a member of parliament who beseeched him to 'do something' with his memoir. In his annoyance, Mr Crowe misquoted the opening lines of Elizabeth Barrett Browning's *Aurora Leigh* and Clara, to his great amusement, transcribed the first stanza on a napkin from memory.

She had not given much thought, before then, to this ability. It is something that comes easily to her. She is soothed, she finds, by the arrangement of words and characters on a page, by the fine details of their alignment and positions, paying attention even to the composition of the typeface. There are features, in an array of type – the way a serif nestles against a neighbouring stem, the peculiar interplay of proximity and balance – that are as distinct and recognisable as a person's face, as handsome or as plain. It is these qualities that Clara sees first in each page she reads, hoarding them without effort before she has even made sense of the words. There is no great labour in retrieving images from this store. It is a matter of selecting among treasures. Even so, it is not a feat that she enjoys performing for the amusement of others. It is a private act, and somehow an intimate one.

Clara sighs and begins to write.

The double sorwe of Troilus to tellen,
That was the king Priamus sone of Troye.

Mr Crowe peers at the page and claps. '*Brava*, Clara! *Brava*. Look, Arabella, and see for yourself how accurate she is.'

Arabella looks from the book to what Clara has written. 'Jesus,' she says, then catches herself. 'I mean, good lord. And how old is – how old are you, exactly, Clara?'

Clara is about to write something in answer, but hesitates.

'Oh, we never trouble ourselves about such things,' says Mr Crowe. 'What does a child's age matter, after all, unless she wishes to marry or come into an inheritance? Your next selection, please, Arabella. Shall we say three, altogether?'

Clara smiles weakly. Arabella is enjoying the game now, and scans the shelves eagerly. She returns after only a minute or two, carrying a book with a drab blue dust jacket. The title on the spine, Clara can see, runs from bottom to top in the French style. Mr Crowe takes it from her and looks it over.

'Zola?' he says. 'That miserable drudge? *Thérèse Raquin*, God help us. Have you bothered with this one, Clara? You have not? I cannot say that I blame you, child. It is an unmitigated misery from start to finish. *J'accuse*, indeed. It was this cheerless lackey who ought to have been shipped off to Devil's Island instead of Dreyfus. But never mind. Take Zola back, Arabella, and let us try something else. And don't be afraid to make it something else in French.' Arabella duly returns with an edition of *Madame Bovary*, primly bound in teal cloth. Clara picks up the pen again.

Nous étions à l'Étude, quand le Proviseur entra, suivi d'un nouveau habillé en bourgeois et d'un garçon de classe qui portait un grand pupitre. Ceux qui dormaient se réveillèrent, et chacun se leva comme surpris dans son travail.

Arabella again adjudicates, checking what Clara has written against the printed words. 'I'm afraid I only have school French,' she says. 'But it seems to be word for word. It really is quite extraordinary.'

'Indeed it is. We really ought to think about putting her in some sort of travelling circus. I am teasing you, my darling. We would never think of it. In any case, no one in the dispiriting age we now live in would pay to see it, unless you performed the feat while a man threw knives at you. Which is an interesting thought, is it not? But let us continue. Only one challenge remains, and then you may claim your prize. Onwards, Arabella.'

This time, Arabella again allows herself some leisure to deliberate. She pauses now and then as something catches her interest, laying her finger on the spine of a volume before changing her mind and moving on. At last, she takes something from an upper shelf. It is a heavy book, and clearly very old. It is bound in calfskin that age has stained and darkened to something like the colour of rosewood. The simple gilt title on its spine has been worn to an almost illegible faintness.

Mr Crowe accepts it from Arabella with unusual solemnity. 'We ought really to be wearing gloves,' he says. 'But to hell with it. It is not a museum, after all. And the gloves were off when these treacherous grave robbers got into the publishing business, I assure you of that. Old Bill's plays, Clara. The *First Folio*, as the dust mites and Casaubons insist on calling it. Do you know what they pay for these editions at auction nowadays? A fine choice, Arabella, and a fitting end to our evening's entertainment. But I fear you have missed your last chance to topple our champion. She has trodden this ground many times.'

Clara, in fact, has already taken up the pen and begun to write. She did so the moment Arabella took the book from the shelf. She pushes the page towards them with a slight smile. She cannot help but feel a little triumphant.

A tempestuous noise of Thunder and Lightning heard: Enter a
Ship-master, and a Botefwaine.

'Flawless, my dear,' says Mr Crowe. 'And look, Arabella, how she forms the long *s*. It is so much more pleasing in its italic form, don't you think? But come now, Clara. This is merely a stage direction. At least give us one of the choice cuts. Never mind the first page. You have earned the right to take your pick. Then, I promise you, you may claim your reward without hindrance.'

Clara sits back and folds her arms. She considers screwing up the page and running from the room. Then she glances at it, the thing she came for. Against the gloomy rank of leather spines, its soft lustre is unmistakable. If she leaves without it, she will hardly sleep tonight. She will have no choice but to come back tomorrow, when she may be forced to endure all this again.

She dips the nib and glares at Mr Crowe. She writes swiftly, then, and without hesitation.

But this rough magick
I here abjure: and, when I have requir'd

Some heavenly muſick, (which even now I do,)
To work mine end upon their senſes, that
This airy charm is for, I'll break my ſtaff,
Bury it certain fathoms in the earth,
And, deeper than did ever plummet sound
I'll drown my book.

She pushes the page aside and stands up, refusing even to look as they read what she has written.

Mr Crowe laughs then. It is a low and brief sound with no great amusement in it. 'Well chosen, Clara. Well chosen. Drown my book, indeed. You may be forgiven the urge. We have tried your patience, have we not?'

Clara meets his eyes for a moment, but makes no other sign.

'Go on, then,' he says. 'Take it, whatever it is. I trust you are not depriving me of something priceless.'

Clara walks with slow purpose to the shelf and takes down the opera glasses. She has coveted them for as long as she can remember. They are exquisitely made, their richly polished brass inlaid with lustrous mother-of-pearl. She has often held them for the simple pleasure of turning them over in her hands, examining the opulent iridescence of the nacre, watching as the delicate skeins of lavender and turquoise interleave and vanish. She still finds them marvellous, but wants them now for a rather more practical purpose.

Mr Crowe looks on in amusement. 'Opera glasses, eh? You are off to see *La bohème*, then? If I'd known it was such a trifling thing you were after, I should hardly have put you to all that trouble.'

'Oh, don't be so monstrous,' says Arabella. 'Let the poor child go, for heaven's sake.'

'Yes, you're quite right,' he says. 'I did promise, didn't I? Off you go, Clara, darling. Enjoy them with my blessing. They belonged, at one time, to Aubrey Beardsley, of all people. A gift, no doubt, from some besotted dandy. But I am wandering again. Pay no attention.'

Clara hurries out, clutching the glasses distrustfully. As she closes the doors behind her, she hears Mr Crowe's voice. He is reading what she has just written down, the words of Prospero's speech. There is something in his tone that she does not quite recognise.

She does not stay to listen. She is on her way, already, to a place in the upper part of the house. It is a place that only Clara knows about, and she has begun to keep things there. They are small items, for the most part, but each has a particular value or special purpose. Soon, perhaps, she will have to hide even her music box there, though she has always kept it near her. She can think of nowhere else now. It is the only safe place left.

Seven

At first, *Eustace* was not certain it was him. He appeared at the far end of the street, having rounded the corner, and stood for a moment in the gown of decaying light that hung beneath a street lamp. Eustace had been sitting in the Jaguar for some time, and the windscreen was blotted with rain. He squinted down the street, but the man had passed into the shadows, emerging only when he came to the next lamp post, this one about fifty feet away. Here he paused again. He wore a battered hat and a dark, rather shapeless raincoat. It was only when he raised his black umbrella – lifting it high above his head, as if to make himself unmistakable – that Eustace was sure.

He got out and crossed to the other side of the street. It lay almost entirely in the shadow of a disused railway viaduct, whose great arches had long since been bricked up. Some were featureless and vacant, while others had been occupied by obscure businesses or put to use as lock-ups.

'Would it be entirely too much to ask, Elias Cromer, that you establish yourself in a part of town where the cab drivers do not refuse to stop?'

Cromer touched the brim of his hat. 'A pleasure to see you too,

Eustace. I am fortunate, you see, in that I need open these premises only to those I choose, to old friends like yourself who do not depend upon the whims of cab drivers. A moment, please. My keys, as ever, have migrated to some region of my person where I have no recollection of placing them. Ah, here now.'

He busied himself at a large and forbidding door set into one of the bricked-up arches. It was drab and unmarked, but made of heavy steel and fitted with at least three locks. When Cromer turned the key in the last of these, it swung inwards with a low and resonant throb. He used his shoulder to push it closed again once they were inside.

Cromer flicked a number of switches. The lock-up, in the meagre light that resulted, was cavernous and oppressive. Though it was clearly of considerable size, it was filled almost to its entire extent by towering bookcases, like those of a library's stacks. Only the narrowest of passageways had been left between each row of shelves, and they rose in height at the centre so as to almost touch the highest part of the vaulted ceiling.

These were nothing like the ornate and burnished shelves that lined Mr Crowe's library. They were of sturdy metal construction and were painted a dull grey that conceded nothing to elegance. Few of the volumes they contained were even visible, since a heavy veil of some oilcloth-like material hung over the face of each bookcase. These huge and sombre curtains swayed almost imperceptibly in whatever small currents stirred the sepulchral air. From somewhere beyond the shelves came the indistinct thrum of a machine of some kind. It was used, Eustace guessed, to draw moisture from the atmosphere, which had none of the dampness that might be expected of such a place.

'It seems cheerier, somehow, than I remembered,' Eustace said. 'You have undertaken some renovations?'

Cromer smiled blandly. 'I should think of it, perhaps. At some establishments, I understand, one is offered all manner of inducements. A comfortable armchair by the fire. A cup of tea and a bun. That sort of thing.'

'You told me something once,' said Eustace. 'A man's arse, you said, is not an organ of learning.'

'Did I say that?' Cromer smiled at the thought. 'It was crudely put. But it is true, is it not? You did not come by your own wisdom while at leisure, as I recall. But come, this place is not entirely without comforts. There is whisky in the office, and the heater can usually be made to function.'

Eustace followed him along a passageway that ran between the rightmost of the stacks and the bare brick wall of the lock-up. It was no wider than any of the others, and it benefited least from the dim and sulphurous light. As he shuffled ahead, still wearing his black hat and raincoat, Cromer was all but absorbed by the gloom.

At the end of the passageway, a small office stood in a kind of clearing, an area perhaps as large as a railway station waiting room that had been kept free of bookcases. Here, Cromer dredged his pockets for yet another set of keys. When he had located them, and had undone the two further locks that secured the office, he showed Eustace in to the cramped and plainly furnished interior.

'I would offer to take your coat,' Cromer said. 'But you may prefer to keep it on for now. This contraption, I'm afraid, can be somewhat capricious.'

He worried at the controls of a gas heater until he succeeded, after two or three minutes, in eliciting a spark. This ignited three panels, which blossomed with a feeble, apricot-coloured incandescence but produced no discernible heat. Eustace sat on the hard, plastic chair to which Cromer had directed him and pulled his coat more closely about him.

Taking his own seat on the other side of a modest desk, Cromer rummaged in a drawer for a considerable time before producing a bottle. 'You will join me in a drink? It is a reasonable Scotch, but blended, I fear. I am no connoisseur of such things. It may warm you somewhat, if nothing else.'

Eustace declined with a brief elevation of his hand.

'No? Well, forgive me if I take some little sustenance myself. You have brought me out on a rather inclement evening, and the resilience of my youth has begun to desert me.'

'An imposition I regret, Elias. In normal circumstances, I would not have dreamed of putting you to such trouble.'

Cromer sipped his whisky and sat back a little, depositing his hat on the desk, where it obscured a hulking telephone. 'Think nothing of it,' he said. 'I gather, from your telegram, that the serenity of your great household has been disturbed.'

Eustace studied Cromer's face for a moment before replying. 'From my telegram?' he said. 'I made mention of it, yes, but you are nothing if not thorough, Elias. I suspect there is little you do not know of recent occurrences at my master's house.'

Cromer opened his palms and joined them again above his chest. 'He was my master once, remember. Some news has reached me, of course, but you know as well as I do how stories are told. Some fraction, always, is altered or withheld. Someone, you may be sure, has adulterated the liquor, has had his thumb on the scales.'

Eustace nodded. 'True enough. We are not chicks in the nest. We do not take every morsel we are offered. But what of my own account, Elias? Surely it is no more to be trusted than any other?'

Cromer drained his whisky and refilled it. 'I have known you a long time, Eustace. And the duties that are yours now were once mine. I know a little of your position, my friend, and you have good reason, I think, to be frank with me.'

'Indeed,' Eustace said. 'And I have no aptitude for storytelling. I will tell you what took place, that is all. And I will place my trust in you, Elias. You left Mr Crowe's service in good standing, and he remembers you with fondness.'

'When he remembers me at all,' said Cromer. 'But I am glad to have your confidence, Eustace. If it is within my power to aid you, I will do so.'

Eustace gave a deep sigh and stared for a long while into the gas heater's dismal and sputtering patch of radiance.

'Very well,' he said at last. 'I break no confidence, Elias, when I tell you that Mr Crowe has not for some time resembled the man we have both known. It has been years, as you know, since he worked in earnest on anything. His services, it seems, are not wanted as they once were.'

Cromer hollowed his cheeks as he considered this. 'Perhaps not,' he said. 'Or perhaps Mr Crowe no longer has need of the rewards.'

Eustace shook his head. 'It was never that,' he said. 'It was never the money. You remember how he was, Elias. He delighted in it, always, the thing that was peculiarly his, but when the great and the good were not seeking it out and enriching him for it, he gave it away to whom he would. You know some of the great works that were secretly of his making. They are among those shrouded on your shelves, I imagine. But he has seen fit to lend his pen to others too, to those without the means to pay the going rate. I never quite knew his reasons.

'Whatever it was that moved him, it has not done so lately. He was never a man to turn away from pleasure, if it was within arm's length, I do not pretend that. But when it was not before him, he was apt not to think of it. I have seen him go a week without so much as calling for a bottle.

'But he has changed. Whatever force it was that kept him, for all those years, from being consumed by the temptations that surrounded him, it has weakened. He sees no reason, now, why he should not devote himself to pleasure for every hour that he is awake.'

Cromer nodded at this, but rather absently. He tapped the side of his glass with a fingernail, as if thinking of something else.

'I am not wandering, Elias,' Eustace told him. 'This may seem a digression to you, and perhaps it is nothing that you do not know. If the truth be known, I am trying to account for it all in my own mind, for the decline that has led us to this. I have asked myself if it might have been halted by some word or action of mine.'

'What could you have done, Eustace? No one has been more faithful than you, but he takes instruction from no one. That much I remember.'

'You do not judge me harshly out of kindness, but I am not so sure. Still, it is idle to think of these things. I can change none of it now.'

Eustace broke off, staring for some minutes into the glow of the gas fire before resuming.

'Well, then,' he said at last. 'I must come to the incident itself, and to the events that gave rise to it. He returned late from an evening out, which is by no means out of character. He was in the company of a woman, a singer of some kind. She has had some training, I gather, but now performs at certain nightclubs. That too is unremarkable. Such are his amusements now.

'The woman was not married, but she had – we learned this afterwards – an attachment, let us say. She did not trouble herself much with the sanctity of this bond, of course, and nor did Mr Crowe. The young man in question, however, was rather more ardent in his feelings.'

Cromer raised his eyebrows. 'He rebuked her in a letter?'

'Do not tease me, Elias. You know the matter is grave. No, the young man followed her – followed them both – to the Estate. There was a confrontation in the avenue.'

'There was nothing that could be done to restrain them?'

'Perhaps there was. It was late. I knew nothing of what had occurred until I heard the shots from my bed.'

'Ah. *Un crime passionnel.*'

'Nothing so vulgar. He may be in decline, Elias, but he is not a hack. He was provoked, yes, and it is true that he acted intemperately. The young man raised his hand to the woman, you see. Mr Crowe's response exposed a want of caution, perhaps, but we may hardly condemn his instinct.'

'But he went too far?'

'Too far,' Eustace repeated the words with a small breath of weariness. 'It is one way of saying it, I suppose. You know what he is capable of, Elias, and why it is that people seek him out. It is no small matter, after all, to create something, to make it so only by setting down the words. We forget the magnitude, sometimes, of that miracle. I think, sometimes, that he forgets it himself. It comes too easily to him.'

'Easy come, easy go,' said Cromer.

Eustace hesitated. 'But it is more than that, sometimes. I have seen it on a few occasions, as you have yourself. He goes further, when he is greatly roused. Beyond the page, I mean.'

'I have seen it,' said Cromer quietly.

'But how, Elias? Was it always so with him?'

'For as long as I knew him. But not always, I think. That ability was something he came by.'

'Came by? How?'

A moth had been drawn to a lamp on the desk, and they both fell silent for a time, watching as its urgent tatters looped from the darker air to be beaten back, again and again, by the bulb's unbearable surface.

Cromer set his head on one side, his expression curiously intent. 'Remember, Eustace, that you guard more than one person. Remember it now, especially, for our friend may not have drawn attention only to himself.'

'Clara?' Eustace stared at him, unsure that he had understood. 'But she is only—'

'She is only what? Come, Eustace,' said Cromer. 'How long have you lived with them? There are things, surely, that you cannot have failed to notice?'

He slumped a little in his chair. 'I am not a fool,' he said. 'If I overlook things, in the child, it is for just that reason. She *is* a child, whatever else she may be. And I have come to feel – it is as if she were my own, Elias. I have no one else now.'

'A blameless weakness, if it is a weakness at all,' Cromer said. 'They say that children keep you young. And look at you – you are living proof of it. As am I, in my way.' He moved closer to the light, inclining his head so that deep shadows marked his face.

'You could return still. You would be welcome.'

'No, there is no going back. Not for me. But I think of it often enough. It is a place unlike any other. But come, let us return to the matter at hand. Let us see what may be salvaged from the situation. The incident you spoke of – it was unfortunate, though not unprecedented. One does not condone such excesses, of course. Some reparations could be made, perhaps? Some comfort given to the young man's family?'

'As far as I have been able to discover, there is no one. He has not even been reported missing.'

Cromer raised an eyebrow. 'How very fortunate.'

'It is curious,' Eustace replied. 'And I do not intend, of course, to rely on continued good fortune. I have taken steps to ensure that I am informed of unwanted attention.'

'Very prudent,' Cromer said, nodding gravely.

Eustace shrugged. 'It is no more than you would have done yourself. But it is not the police that concern me most.'

'Oh?'

'I have not yet told you everything. I mentioned that shots were fired. Mr Crowe was the worse for drink, and is no great marksman at the best of times, yet the young man we spoke of was gone when I reached them. He was gone, and there was nothing to be done. It seemed plain enough what had happened. I was sure of nothing, mind you, but it *seemed* plain enough. But when I examined him the next morning – his remains, you understand – I found bruises, nothing more. It was not the shots that killed him, Elias.'

Cromer nodded slowly, and gazed out through the small window of the office for so long that Eustace began to wonder whether he had heard. 'That does rather complicate matters,' he said at last. He reached for the bottle again. 'You had really better have that drink, Eustace.'

'Perhaps I will, after all.'

They drank in silence for a while. The gas heater sputtered out, and Cromer attempted, without conviction, to coax it back into service. When it produced nothing more than a faint clicking sound and a poisonous odour, he kicked it and returned to his seat.

'Nothing can be relied upon these days, it seems.'

'The world is much changed,' Eustace agreed.

'Much, but not entirely. Some things remain certain.'

Eustace looked up.

'I am thinking of death and taxes, Eustace. Equal and opposite reactions. The tendency towards disorder, and so on. That reminds me, I have come into possession of a delightful 1726 copy of Newton's

Principia. Only a third edition, mind you, but a notable one in this instance. He omitted Leibniz's name, you see, from the later editions, since the poor chap had obligingly died since the first publication and was therefore unlikely to object. Word had got about that Leibniz might have had a hand in calculus too, and Newton would have none of it. If I have seen further than others, it is by booting them off the shoulders of giants.'

Cromer seemed thoroughly satisfied with this witticism, and allowed Eustace a moment to savour it before continuing. 'At any rate, it was all rather unsporting.'

'I'll be sure to mention it to Mr Crowe.'

'Oh, he has a first. I procured it for him. The provenance was a little opaque, perhaps, but its authenticity is unimpeachable.'

'Well, then? I am tired, Elias. There is some message in this, I suppose, but I cannot decipher it just now. You must be direct with me, I'm afraid.'

'Forgive me,' said Cromer. 'I have acquired the habit of circuitousness. It is a necessity, sometimes, of my trade. I was thinking of the inevitable, Eustace, that is all. Of what is to come. It is a question that preoccupies you, is it not?'

'I think of little else. It was this question that brought me to you.'

'You wish to know what is in store for you?'

'You know them, Elias. The others of his kind, the one they must answer to. You know how they think, what weighs with them. You have some idea, perhaps, of what might satisfy or dissuade them.'

'Dissuade them? On that point, at least, I may offer you guidance. You will not dissuade them, my friend. They will not be put off, not in this instance. It is ludicrous, of course, this prohibition of theirs. "Any member who, in the exercise of his sacred gift, occasions mortal harm", and so on at very great length. A "cardinal misuse", they call it, yet they spend their lives planting knives of one kind or another in each other's backs. But such was the world in which they were formed. Secret societies with Latin mottoes, midnight convocations and so on. Hysterical and overwrought nonsense, all of it, but there it is. They have made a code of it, and if they do not defend it, they have nothing.'

Eustace considered this. 'I had thought there might be some token we could offer them.' He gestured towards the stacks outside. 'Some rarity, perhaps, that has come into your possession. We would compensate you more than fairly.'

Cromer shook his head. 'Your employer, Eustace, already possesses most of the true treasures that have passed through my hands. There are items on his shelves, you know, that would stop the traffic if they were ever to come to auction. And, who knows? Perhaps they will prove amenable to such tributes. Do not set much store by the hope, though. I speak as your friend – as your friend and his – when I say that the price they exact will be one that is not so easy for him to pay.'

'I know you are right in this,' Eustace said softly. 'It is the conclusion I had reached myself. And yet I felt I must ask.'

'Of course,' said Cromer. 'What if there were some means within your grasp and you had neglected them? You would have been remiss. But take heart, Eustace. It is not for nothing that Mr Crowe has come to occupy the place he holds. One does not simply call a man of his abilities before the headmaster. This will not go easily for anyone.'

Eustace tasted his whisky, felt the coarse flare of its heat at the back of his throat. 'His ability to empty bottles is all that has been in evidence of late. That and whatever displays of artistry he reserves for his soprano.'

Cromer opened his hands, regretful but benevolent. 'We cannot always be our finest selves,' he said. 'Do not despair of him. He has not been tested yet. And you, Eustace. You will not be found wanting.'

'I am not sure, Elias. I fear that I have been already.'

Something appeared to occur to Cromer then. He hesitated briefly before speaking again. 'I have some little intelligence, perhaps, that may be of use to you.'

Eustace set down his whisky glass.

'It will be Chastern himself who attends to this. Who else will accompany him I cannot say, but he will come.'

'I thank you, Elias, but this much I had surmised.'

'Yes, yes. But listen. Chastern is every bit as you will remember him. Age has not softened him in any way that I can discern. Quite the contrary is true. But he has not been quite untouched by the passage of time.'

'You will have to speak more plainly, Elias, if this is to serve me. I do not follow you.'

'He has begun to suffer, Eustace, from some affliction. What its exact nature is, those who talk to me do not know, but he contends with some diminishment of his strength. It is slow, they say, but it cannot be stopped. The day will come when it claims him entirely.'

'Claims him?' Eustace said. 'I do not understand.'

'They are not immortal, Eustace. They belong to a different age, of course, and the years have been long. They are not like you and me, I do not say that, but surely you did not think—'

'I am not an imbecile, Elias. There are certain questions, however, that I grew weary of asking a long time ago. Curiosity does not fit a man very well for the life we chose. This affliction of his – forgive my bluntness, but what does it profit us to know of it? Will it drive him towards one course or another? Is he bent on some purpose, now that he knows he is passing from this world?'

Cromer deliberated for a time before he spoke. 'I will say only this,' he said. 'Our friend's gifts hold a singular fascination for Chastern, and I cannot but think that he nurtures it in his decline. He envies those gifts, though he thinks it his duty to curb them. I cannot tell what he craves most. To possess them somehow? To put them to use in his own service? To discover their source? To destroy them? All of these, perhaps, even if that is impossible, for none of us is governed entirely by reason in the end. But listen to me, and to these extravagant suppositions of mine. I was more cautious once, and they do not amount to very much, I'm afraid.'

Eustace gave a small breath of laughter. 'There was no one else who could have told me so much. What do I have to complain of?'

'You might have wished for a softer chair.'

'But then I would not have learned so much.' Eustace smiled briefly. He rocked his glass, watching the light slide over the coppery dregs of whisky. 'Before I go, Elias, if I may – there are some other matters I wish to discuss with you.'

'Oh?' said Cromer. 'It is a pity, you know, that my services are no longer charged for by the hour.'

'It is in that former capacity that you may aid me. I do not know what lies ahead, Elias. There are certain arrangements I wish to make, eventualities that I must provide for.'

'I have not practised for some time, my friend. The law may be much changed. You would be better served, I think, by a man of more recent training.'

'In these matters, Elias, as in so much else, there is no one else I can trust.'

Cromer took a long breath, then rattled open one of the lower drawers in his desk. 'Very well,' he said, laying out a rumpled note-pad and uncapping his pen. 'How may I be of service?'

Eight

Clara pauses at the foot of the last staircase. She forces herself, while she counts to a hundred, to stand perfectly still and to listen. She hears nothing. The rooms on this floor were shut up long ago. Once a year, their doors are unlocked and their furniture unshrouded for spring cleaning. The only sound that reaches her comes from far below, where she hears the dim shudder of heavy furniture being shunted aside. Eustace left instructions that the floors were to be waxed.

The tower itself is not a secret place, though it is rarely visited by anyone but Clara herself. The staircase by which it is reached is steep and narrow. Eustace has pronounced it unsafe, and threatens on occasion to have it closed up, but she has so far managed to dissuade him. The chamber that forms the tower's upper storey is the highest room in the house, with views over the grounds from all four of its windows. It was used, at one time, as a map room and a large table dominates its centre with deep pigeonholes set into its base. The pigeonholes contain a great number of yellowed and tightly scrolled maps that Clara spreads out and studies in moments of idleness. The plans for most of the original gardens were laid out in this room, and designs were made – some of them fascinatingly elaborate – for additions to the house that never came to be built.

Today, she ignores the map table. She crosses without pausing to a narrow but finely carved bookcase set into an alcove in the east wall of the room. At its base is a cabinet, whose doors are inlaid with an intricate depiction of the Garden of Eden. The doors are flanked by elegant columns, each surmounted by a capital that has been carved, with great skill and intricacy, in the form of a dragon's head.

Approaching the dragon on the right, she eases her fingers with hesitant delicacy into the cleft between its jaws. As she probes more deeply, the polished jags of the teeth press against her wrist. The lever she is seeking is set into the roof of the dragon's mouth. To pull it, she must hook her finger backwards in a recess so narrow that she sometimes fears it will become stuck. No adult's hand, Clara is almost sure, could possibly operate it.

As she feels for the channel, her fingertips graze the dragon's palate. It is rough and grainy to the touch, quite unlike the polished outer surfaces of the head. The lever, when she finds it, is unmistakable. It is a slender peg, slightly hooked at one end, with the fine, easily warmed smoothness of ivory. It is like stroking a strangely contorted piano key.

Clara presses the hooked end towards herself. She must be firm, she knows, or it will not work. The hidden mechanism may be intricate, but it is not delicate. It yields, when she has exerted the right pressure, with a dusty click. She hears the groaning of taut wire and the muted knocking of heavy counterweights. Finally, the bookcase creaks free of the wall. The opening it exposes is just wide enough to allow her passage, and emits a breath of cold and faintly musty air. Clara squeezes through the gap and into the chilly cavity, heaving the bookcase closed behind her.

It is utterly dark, and the space is so shallow that at first she cannot even turn around. To do that, she edges further in, where the void widens a little into something resembling a large chimney. Here, Clara pivots to her right and feels for the first cold rung of the iron ladder. She does this slowly and tentatively. Once, when she reached for it, her fingertips brushed instead against the warm and coarsely furred pouch of some small body. It squirmed instantly from her touch and skittered away. Clara stood for half an hour in the dark before she could bring herself to move.

Once she is on the ladder, she climbs up six rungs and reaches above her head. Her fingertips skim cold iron until they graze the thick, rust-scabbed edges of the hasp. She pries it free and, with some effort, works the bolt from its recess. Now, at last, she can begin to push open the hatch.

At first, she raises it only by a few inches, so that she can peer out across the roof of the tower. It is absurd, she knows, to fear that someone might be out there, but she is growing ever more cautious in her habits. The roof is a mossy, stone-flagged square, enclosed by a parapet as high as Clara's waist. It is occupied only by a flabby and incurious pigeon, which is not in the least perturbed by her appearance.

Clara opens the hatch fully and climbs back down a rung. Now that daylight has been admitted to the shaft, a rough shelf is visible just below the level of the roof. From the back of the shelf, she pulls a chest. It is a squat box, sturdily made of walnut and brass. She used to store it under her bed, preferring to keep its small treasures close by her, but she brought it here some days ago. There are strangers in the house now. Her old hiding places are no longer safe.

She takes the opera glasses from her knapsack, polishing them with the old pillowslip she used to wrap them. In daylight, their mother-of-pearl surfaces are even more fascinating, their skeins of iridescence altered by the slightest tremor of her hands. It is like when, on a summer's day in the garden, a damselfly pauses on a halm of grass. With each minute twitching, it discloses a new sliver of astonishing colour, as if the fine blades of its wings have sliced open the sunlight itself.

She turns the glasses over. Between the barrels is a brass spindle that can be turned by a ridged wheel. It is used, Clara supposes, to adjust the focus. It occurs to her, as she toys with the wheel, that she ought to try the glasses out before locking them in the chest. After all, they may not have been used for years. They will be of no use to her if they have seized up, or if their lenses have clouded over with mildew. They will not help her to keep watch over the Estate, to see what might be coming.

She climbs out onto the roof of the tower, crawling to the battlement so that she cannot be seen from below. Even through her woollen stockings, the stone is frigid and damp. She props herself against the parapet and draws up her knees, positioning herself so that her head is inches from the nearest embrasure. From this side of the tower, the view is to the south, over the formal gardens to the maze of yew hedges beyond. At the centre of the maze is a large, perfectly square pond, where herons often stop to fish. A heron ought to be easy to focus on, standing in the water with that strange, martial stillness.

She is dusting off the lenses when she hears a shout from the garden. It is a man's voice, distant but harsh.

Clara presses herself against the parapet, keeping absolutely still. After a few moments, the man's voice is raised again. It is something about the maze, she thinks. His tone is impatient, hectoring. This time, another man answers. It is the Crouch brothers, the men that Eustace has put to work in the gardens.

Carefully, she inches towards the embrasure and peers through the gap. John, the larger and slower of the two, is near the centre of the maze, slipping in and out of sight as he paces along a corridor of yew. He calls out again, and Clara strains forward a little further.

His brother Abel has halted on the wide central path that bisects the parterre. Setting down his barrow, he cocks his head attentively. John calls out again, and this time Abel throws his head back in derisive laughter. He shouts back, giving some brief and jeering answer, and waits to hear its effect. When John bellows at him again, his agitation mounting, Abel sniggers in satisfaction. He picks up his barrow then, and continues on his way.

Satisfied that she has not attracted their attention, Clara shifts her position slightly to widen her view. Hesitantly, she raises the opera glasses to her eyes. To her disappointment, she sees nothing but a pair of greyish discs and, when she moves, a blurred disturbance of green. At the edges of her vision, she notices the spidery encroachment of her own eyelashes and realises that she is holding the eyepieces too closely. She experiments with this distance, and with the ridged brass wheel that adjusts the focus.

At first, she turns the wheel too far in one direction or the other, making everything seem smeared and amorphous. She is patient, though, and learns the tiny adjustments that must be made to bring clarity to the edges of objects. Gradually, she becomes accustomed to the stillness that is needed to locate things and keep them in sight.

She focuses on Abel, who is wheeling his barrow past a bed of greying lavender. The opera glasses do not magnify things quite as much as she had hoped, but Clara can make out details now that were not visible before. She notices that his jacket fits him poorly, and that his boots seem new and little worn. The barrow he is pushing is all but empty, containing only a spade and a hoe, yet he handles it awkwardly, making frequent corrections to his course.

There is another shout from John. His voice sounds clearer now, and sharpened with anxiety. Clara turns the glasses towards the maze, tracing its pathways until she finds him, his head protruding a little way above one of the inner walls. He has climbed a ladder, resting a pair of shears on the upper surface of the hedge. His face is glistening, pink with exertion and rage. There is something forlorn and a little comical about him.

Clara catches most of what he says, now that he is atop the ladder. He uses coarse words, some of them obscenities she has never heard uttered aloud, but there is no mistaking his meaning. John Crouch is lost in the maze.

He has gone in, she supposes, with the purpose of trimming the hedges – a job that might take him days if not weeks – and cannot find his way out. The maze, once you have navigated it five or six times, is no great puzzle, but John has never entered it before. He is weary from his day's work, she supposes, and the light is beginning to go.

She swings the glasses back to Abel, finding him on a bench seat at the centre of the parterre. He rolls a cigarette, listening with amusement as John's entreaties grow desperate.

'I'm off inside, mate. See about a couple of bottles of cider.'

John roars an oath in reply. Abel laughs, reclining contentedly to light his cigarette.

'I'll keep one here for you, shall I? And what about a bite to eat? There's pork pies in the pantry the size of dustbin lids.'

Clara turns her attention again to John, adjusting the opera glasses so as to bring him into clearer focus. He is slumped over the top of the hedge, resting his elbows on the foliage. She watches as he lowers his head onto his thick forearms, covering his face so that she sees only the sweaty tangle of his curls. He is a big man, and coarse in his habits. There is something abject, though, in his misery and humiliation. There are some advantages, she thinks, that he lacks. If his ingenuity is strained, he depends for aid on his brother, aid that Abel enjoys withholding.

She puts down the opera glasses and looks unaided at the maze. From her vantage point in the tower, its design seems absurdly simple. Still, she knows the traps and illusions that might have thwarted him: a zigzagging corner leading to a narrow aperture that is easily missed; an interlocking pair of spiral corridors that seem to curve endlessly inwards. She wonders how many attempts he made before giving up. She checks his position again, tracing the path that would lead him out. It is a simple geometrical figure, nothing more – a sequence of lines and vertices with no great complexity to it. To him, though, it is entirely mysterious. He might just as well find himself at the centre of some vast and unknown continent, without even the crudest of maps to guide him.

Clara takes out her sketch pad and begins to draw.

By the time she reaches the garden, it is half dark.

On the gravel paths of the parterre, even she cannot approach in silence. Abel looks up, acknowledging her arrival with a grudging upward flexion of his head, then his face settles into its habitual arrangement, an expression of watchful and somehow conditional tolerance.

'Nice evening for it,' he says.

Clara's answering gesture is slight and diffident. She raises a hand, but only to waist height. Her wave is quick, a four-note trill on the air. She looks away.

'Out with the sketchbook, is it?' Abel continues. 'You can do me if you like. Maybe take a bit of time over it. My own mother wouldn't recognise that other one.'

Clara pauses, surveying his features. The drawing she made, that day in Eustace's office, was a slight and unfinished thing. It was something she did almost reflexively, her way of registering the strangers' arrival. She studies him now, seeing not his face but an assembly of marks and shadows, the way it is made. For his almost colourless pupils, a hard grey, barely grazing the page, then hatch in the deeper shadows around the eyes. Note the bags beneath them, those loosely rucked declivities, with a few gathered threads of soft pencil. The taut smirk, finally: a clutch of seams and a thumbed rift of charcoal. There would be no great difficulty in it. She shakes her head then and walks on.

'No?' says Abel. 'Yeah, well. Maybe when the light is better, eh? Be dark soon.'

Clara ignores him, continuing briskly through the formal garden towards the maze. It is getting dark – Abel is right about that much – and the air is veined with cold. She was far too absorbed, of course, to stop for a coat. She folds her arms about herself for warmth, pressing her sketchbook to her chest.

In the maze, it is cooler still. It is not like entering a wood, where the sunlight is gently eroded as you pass from the edges into the shadowy heart. Here, the transition to shade is stark and immediate. There is a lulled hush, too, in the deep passageways, and even the wind seems drained from the air. Clara listens to her breath, to the quiet urgency of her own footsteps.

From outside, she hears Abel call to his brother, his voice deadened by the great mass of the yews. 'Hang on, mate. Cavalry's on the way, innit.'

Clara stops to listen for John's answer, but he says nothing. She hopes he will have the good sense to wait for her. If he wanders off again, now that it is growing dark, he will only blunder into some more remote corner. If she is to find him and lead him out, he had better stay put.

A sound comes from overhead, the abrupt smack and shudder of wingbeats. Looking up, she sees a barn owl cross the channel of pewtery twilight. It is plump but graceful, its underside spectrally pale. When it screeches, the sound is shrill and oddly coarse. Clara has heard it often enough, but to John Crouch it is sinister and unfamiliar. He gives a yelp of fright and begins roaring at Abel with renewed vehemence. He uses words that Clara has not even read.

Abel shouts something back, but it is lost to the quiet depths of the maze.

'Can't hear you,' John calls.

In Abel's reply, this time, Clara hears her name, and a skirl of taunting laughter.

'What you saying?' John moans. In his voice now, there is something helpless and disconsolate. He falls silent again.

When Clara finds him, he is exactly where he was, though he has climbed down from the ladder and sprawls on the grass at its base. His head is bowed in dejection, and he stares at some bright object on the ground between his knees. Occasionally, he reaches down and fidgets with it, or wipes his nose with the back of his hand.

Clara coughs.

'Mother of Jesus,' says John, hauling himself upright as quickly as he can manage. He stows the bright object in his pocket and stares down the dim passageway to where Clara is standing.

'Is that – you're the little girl? Claire, is it? No, hang on. Clara? Clara.'

When his shock has subsided, she approaches him more closely, greeting him with a brief smile. On some impulse, she reaches out and squeezes his forearm. John looks at her with embarrassment.

'I was just – well, I was giving the hedge a bit of a trim, and the time must have got away from me. When I looked up, it was getting dark and that.'

Clara nods gently.

'So, I was having a quick sit-down,' John says. 'Just to catch my breath, like. Then we was going to call it a day. I expect you heard

Abel. Yeah, we was just about to head for the kitchen. See about a bite to eat.'

Again, Clara reaches towards him, brushing the furred clump of his knuckles where they hang at his side. She passes him the folded paper, pressing it softly into his grasp.

He unfolds it hesitantly, keeping his broad thumbs to the edges. Stretching out his arms so as to hold it clear of his own shadow, he studies the carefully rendered pattern of the maze, the thread of soft pencil leading from its centre.

'A map, eh?'

Clara nods.

'And this is where I am? No, hang on. There's a "J" and everything. I get it.'

She offers him an encouraging smile.

'Well, that's very nice of you, miss. Very thoughtful, I'm sure. Only you didn't have to go to no trouble.'

Clara points back along the passageway.

'Of course, if *you're* leaving,' John says, 'I'd better keep you company. Getting dark and that.'

Turning from him, she begins to retrace her steps, taking care not to walk too quickly. When she looks back, John Crouch is following at a small distance. He has not stopped for his ladder.

Nine

The flowers had come while Eustace was away. They were white roses, as always, and in no mean quantity. Two or three dozen had been arranged in a crystal vase and placed on a table in the entrance hall. Alice, it did not surprise him to learn, could give no exact account of when they had arrived.

'Well, it won't have been Sunday, of course, so I expect it was yesterday or the day before. No note or anything, and the chap who brought them didn't have two words to say for himself. Foreign, I think he was. Are they for you, then?'

Eustace was impatient. 'Listen to me, Alice. Those who sent these flowers could have seen to it that they came on Sunday. They could have seen to it that each of them was borne up the avenue on its own satin cushion by a pageboy. I must know when they came, exactly when. It is of the utmost importance.'

'Well, really, Mr Eustace,' Alice said. 'That's all fine and well, but it's not as if you left me with nothing to do. There have been all these preparations of yours to see to – nectarines, and such like. I've hardly drawn breath this last week. And if that wasn't bad enough, each way I turn I am tripping over these new staff you have insisted on, which I don't mind telling you—'

'The roses, Alice. When did they come? The day and the hour.'

She drew herself up, her lips crimped with indignation. 'I'm sure I don't know, Mr Eustace, why it is that I put up with being spoken to in this way. I could put my coat on, you know, and walk right out that door this minute.'

'Do please feel free,' said Eustace. 'Before you leave, however, I'm sure you will do me the courtesy of acquainting me with the books of account you have kept for the kitchens. We must ensure that they are kept in good order in your absence.'

Alice did not pursue this point any further. Deciding that it was in her interest to seem amenable, she was induced to say – even to affirm with some vehemence – that the roses had come on the morning of the day before. Eustace could see, though, that it was only to satisfy his insistence. It was clear enough, from the confusion in her answers, that her recollection was uncertain. He noticed, too, that she seemed at pains to keep some distance between them. When she spoke, she averted her face from his.

He took a step towards her. 'You seem much put upon, Alice. If the arrangements I have called for seem out of the ordinary, it is because the occasion calls for it. The guests we expect are men of a certain rank. They are accustomed to certain luxuries, and I will not have us found wanting. It is a matter of some importance that brings them here.'

'I daresay,' Alice replied. 'Though you would hardly know it to look at our master.'

Eustace allowed a moment to pass in silence, then stooped towards her ear. 'As for our master's business,' he said, his voice hardly more than a whisper, 'you will, God knows, have little enough to do with it, but if you cannot be called upon, while it is being conducted, to do as you are asked, if you cannot keep your nose out of the bottle and wits enough about you to tell one day of the week from another, then you will not, I assure you, ever again be troubled by his appearance. Is all that plain to you? I have not burdened you with too much?'

Her face was bunched and mottled, but she managed to govern herself. She gave a prim nod, her eyes fixed on the staircase behind his head.

'I'm afraid I would have you answer yes or no,' he said. 'I wish to avoid any further confusion. Is that plain, Alice?' He drew back to have her look him in the eye. Her voice, when she answered, was kept small and grudging.

'Yes, Mr Eustace. Quite plain.'

'Very good,' he said. 'Now, I am going to see Mr Crowe. If it does not tax you beyond endurance, perhaps you would be kind enough to ask the Crouch brothers to wait for me in my office. You need not bother, at least, about telling one from the other. I wish to speak to them both.'

Eustace had the leisure, as he followed the sluggish progress of the ball, to inspect the job the Crouch brothers had made of mowing the croquet lawn. The best that could be said of it was that the hoops were no longer entirely hidden by the grass. They had gone about the pretence of gardening with more energy than he had intended.

He raised his foot and lowered it again, trapping the ball beneath it with a soft tap. Mr Crowe looked up. He had been hunched over Arabella, the better to guide her application of the mallet, though the resulting shot seemed to benefit little from his intervention.

'Eustace,' he said. 'Thank God you are back. Look what those navvies of yours have done to the croquet lawn. One might just as well play on a field of barley stubble.'

Eustace glanced at the champagne bottle that listed in an ice bucket at the far edge of the lawn. 'I do see,' he said, 'how it might be found unsatisfactory by players of your ability. I shall give it my attention, I assure you, when the present matter is behind us.'

Mr Crowe brought himself upright and leaned on his mallet. 'The present matter?' he said.

Eustace approached them, tossing a single white rose so that it landed with gentle ceremony at their feet. Mr Crowe regarded it bleakly for a long moment before crushing it, with some thorough-ness, under his boot.

Arabella was amused. 'I must remember that you dislike roses.'

'I have a garden full of roses,' Mr Crowe replied. 'Should I be de-lighted that someone has sent me more?'

'I suppose it depends,' Arabella said, 'on who it is that sends them. Was it some secret admirer?'

'It was a gentleman of Mr Crowe's acquaintance,' Eustace said. 'You will have the opportunity of meeting him.'

'How soon?' said Mr Crowe.

'I cannot be certain,' Eustace replied. 'A day. Two days, perhaps. Alice cannot recall the day on which they arrived. I don't suppose that you or Miss Arabella . . . ?'

Mr Crowe waved the notion away. 'We have been much occupied.'

'Of course,' said Eustace. 'I would not usually think of asking. And I am afraid I have another unusual request. I must take the liberty, in fact, of asking a small favour of Miss Arabella. If it were not a matter that requires a lady's judgement, I would attend to it myself.'

Mr Crowe had begun to issue some rumbling protest, but Arabella cut him short. 'I'd be delighted to help,' she said. 'What's the matter, Eustace? Are you in love?'

'We shall be entertaining them, the visitors we have spoken of. It will be an affair of some formality.'

'Oh, I'm afraid I'm no good at that sort of thing,' said Arabella.

'Choosing menus and so on. It's one of the many gaps in my education.'

'It is nothing of that kind. The child, Clara – she will need something suitable to wear. Something—'

Arabella laid her hand on his arm as he sought the word. 'I understand perfectly,' she said. 'It will give me a way of making amends. I'm afraid a certain someone has been teasing the poor child horribly.'

Eustace tensed briefly at this. 'Clara does not spend a great deal of time in adult company,' he said. 'She does not much concern herself with fine gowns and ribbons. She prefers to dress for the outdoors, and somewhat in her own manner. It is something I confess I have rather indulged.'

'She does seem quite the little eccentric,' said Arabella. 'But terribly pretty. In the right frock, she'd be perfectly adorable.'

'Perhaps,' said Eustace. 'But she has never wished, as far as I can tell, to play at being a princess. Whatever you devise for her – and I do not doubt the delicacy of your tastes in these matters – do not make her unrecognisable to herself. Her nature makes her susceptible to such things, and I would not have her made unhappy.'

Mr Crowe emptied a champagne glass with an indelicate gulp. 'Listen to yourself, Eustace,' he said. 'Little girls enjoy dressing up, man. And Arabella knows her way in and out of a nice frock, I can assure you.'

'Alice will help you to find her,' Eustace continued, addressing Arabella. 'Tell her that it is something I have asked you to do, for she may well be reluctant – and that she must make haste, that we all must.'

Arabella glanced at Mr Crowe before turning back to him. 'You wanted me to do this right away?'

Eustace inclined his head. 'I would be very grateful indeed. You will find Alice in the region of the kitchen, if she has not encountered some new difficulty since I left her. There are certain related matters, in any case, that I must discuss with Mr Crowe.'

'Of course,' said Arabella. Before proceeding towards the house, she stooped to retrieve the disfigured rose from the grass at her feet, raising it to her face to savour what remained of its scent. A bruised petal, its whiteness unrecognisable, detached itself and tumbled gently to the ground.

'Perhaps something in white,' she said, rising to leave. 'Yes, I'm sure white is her colour.'

The Crouch brothers had made themselves comfortable while they waited. John was seated at a small round table, toying with the elaborate device at its centre. Abel slouched at the window.

'You will find it difficult,' said Eustace as he entered, 'to replace that item from the fee I am paying you. You would be well advised to treat it with care.'

John lumbered to his feet. 'I was only saying to Abel,' he said, 'how it was a nice little piece. I come by antiques now and then, so I take an interest. What do you call it, then?'

Eustace examined John's features as he took his seat. 'I was not aware,' he said, 'of these scholarly interests of yours. It is called an orrery. It demonstrates the motions of the planets.'

'Funny name for it. It don't look horrory,' said John. 'It's fascinating, really. The stars and that.'

Eustace contemplated him frankly for a moment. 'The device is named for the Earl of Orrery, who commissioned it. This one was not his, but it is by the same instrument maker, a Mr John Rowley. Of course, you may know all this, given your interest in such things.'

John nodded. 'You must have piles of this stuff.'

'Myself, no,' said Eustace. 'Mr Crowe is the great collector. This was a gift from him, in recognition of an early service of mine.'

'You must have done something right.'

Eustace used his cuff to rub a smear from the orb representing the sun, then gently pushed the Earth a little way along its orbit. 'You yourselves have been busy in my absence, I see. The croquet lawn is now visible, which is a great relief to us all. And the parterre has taken on a pleasingly abstract character.'

Abel chose this moment to interject, shoving himself upright and pacing towards the middle of the room. 'Most of what we been doing ain't quite so visible.'

'Naturally not,' said Eustace. 'And it is those arrangements I am most interested in. As for your labours in the garden, let us maintain the pretence, at least. If someone is passing, by all means clip something. You need no longer trouble yourselves with the work itself. I will see to it that someone else is engaged.'

'Whatever you say,' said Abel. 'We never made out like we was Capability Brown. We need to have a word, though. About those other arrangements.'

Eustace leaned back in his chair. He made a slight gesture towards the other side of the desk. The brothers took their places, and Abel leaned across the desk.

'Those other tools,' he said. 'The heavy equipment. It's all here.'

'Where, exactly?'

'One of the outhouses.'

'A locked outhouse?'

'Of course, locked. But it's all in this outhouse. My point being,' Abel went on, 'there's nothing in the house, which obviously we was thinking of safety. Children about the place and what-have-you. All the same, it means they ain't exactly within easy reach, if the need arises.'

'Most of it may stay where it is for now,' Eustace said. 'But you are right, it would be prudent to keep a small number of items in the house. I will show you a place.'

Abel nodded. 'Smaller items, I'm assuming.'

'Just so. And you have something, I imagine, that may be kept about one's person without arousing suspicion?'

'One or two things. This is my person we're talking about?'

Eustace nodded. 'When our guests arrive, you will be introduced in some domestic capacity that allows you to be much in attendance.'

'A butler or whatever.'

Eustace scrutinised him frankly. 'As it is, you will persuade no one that you have been long in service. Do not take it amiss, but we shall have to give you some instruction.'

Abel shrugged. 'My feelings ain't hurt. What about him?'

'We need another man to keep watch over the grounds, to observe anyone that might come or go. There will be certain tradesmen, deliveries to the kitchen and so on. I will have Alice make a list of these, but you must treat others with suspicion. John will have access to the larger items, should they be needed. You may also be called on if we should need to prevent our guests from leaving, if for some reason they are reluctant to depart empty-handed.'

John brought his stout fingertips together in a gesture of ease and assurance. 'Just say the word,' he said, 'and they won't depart at all.'

Eustace toyed with one of the outer planets. 'Let us be vigilant,' he said. 'But let us not be too eager to use force. Our business may well be concluded with civility. If you are to stand guard outside, we shall need a signal of some kind, some means of letting you know that matters have deteriorated beyond remedy. It is something to which I must give some thought.'

He fell silent for a while. Abel occupied himself by trimming his fingernails, snipping fastidiously at each one until he judged its curve acceptable. John nudged his thigh with the heel of a boot.

'Here,' he said. 'Disgusting, that is. Give it a rest.'

'What you talking about, disgusting? Good grooming is what it is.'

'It's that sound the clippers make,' said John. 'That little *snick*? Oof.' He gave an elaborate shudder.

Eustace rose from the desk and crossed to the orrery.

'Do you know your planets?' he said.

They shared a brief, consulting glance. 'Not massively,' Abel said. 'Don't come up much,' John confirmed.

'The plough,' Abel said, as it occurred to him. 'Is that one?'

'What do you see?' Eustace said. 'Never mind the stars. They do not figure. What do you see, when you look up? Day or night.'

Abel flexed his neck. 'There a point to all this?'

'What do you see?' Eustace asked again.

John spoke, stretching his limbs to dispel his embarrassment. 'Sun, moon and stars, innit.'

'Never mind the stars,' Eustace said again. He gestured towards the orrery. 'They are beyond our scope here.'

'The sun and the moon, then.'

'The sun and the moon,' Eustace repeated.

Abel shook his head and sank back in his chair. John looked from Eustace to the orrery, but could offer nothing further.

'What we are discussing,' Eustace said at last, 'are details of business. Important details, but details nonetheless. I want you to keep the sun and the moon fixed in your thoughts.'

They said nothing.

'Mr Crowe and Clara,' Eustace continued. 'Look to them, above all. Seek my guidance in all else, but if they should be threatened with any harm that it is in your power to stop, you must not hesitate. Do you understand?'

Abel sat upright again. The brothers looked at him almost without blinking. Each of them lowered his head. The gesture was curt and emphatic.

'The fees we have discussed,' Eustace continued. 'These are guaranteed in any event. But your rewards, if one or both of you should be forced to take such an action, will be far in excess of those. I have seen to it that this provision will be honoured even in the event of my death.'

'What about you?' Abel said, after a long pause.

'What about me?'

'If they cut up rough, you don't think they might have a go at you?'

'I am of no consequence. I am from nowhere, as you gentlemen will recall.' Eustace drew the dust cloth over the orrery. 'I no longer exist.'

At a quarter before midnight, Eustace put on a heavy overcoat and let himself out by the stable yard door. He crossed the yard and slipped out into the west lane. It had been used, at one time, by servants coming in from the town. Where it passed through the gardens, various contrivances of landscaping kept it from the sight of those in the house. Further on, its course ran through the beech woods all the way to the edge of the grounds.

The night was cold, and the wind was gathering a strength he had not seen since the previous winter. Already, the lane was strewn with skittering claws of dead wood, and worse would be done before morning. Eustace found himself glad of the air, however unquiet it might be. Having extra hands about the place did nothing to lessen his own burden. When he had not been concealing firearms about the living quarters, he had been showing some dead-eyed scullery boy which end of a rabbit was its arse. He could not remember when he had last rested.

Half a mile or so from the house, where it passed through the thickest of the woods, the lane was partly blocked by an old holly tree. The night was almost lightless, with only a faint blade of the old moon remaining. He was almost upon the tree when he saw it, the great twists of its dimly silvered limbs looming from the darkness like a sea monster.

Eustace ran a hand over the holly's bark, idly gauging its girth. It was no sapling – he put its age at eighty or even a hundred years – and it had come down in the last hour or two. A tree of even a quarter of its size could have killed him. The thought did not disturb him greatly. There was a simplicity in such a death, an innocence almost. There was nothing that could be done.

Still, he cursed softly. It would have to be cleared in the morning. It would make him no easier in his mind to know that the way was barred on the safest road from the Estate. It was yet another thing to think of. He knew, too, that before he set someone the task, he would first have to show him the way to the tool shed and instruct him in the use of a saw.

He could leave the tree where it lay. He could carry on past it, all the way to the west gate. He could pass through without stopping to the roads and the country beyond, walking until the sky showed the first sweetness of dawn, until the sun coloured unfamiliar fields. He would stumble then into the yard of some inn, in a town whose name he didn't know. It was nothing he had not done before.

Mr Crowe had encouraged such excursions, at one time, to remind him that he had chosen his life freely, that he could do so again. It had been years since he had made such a journey, but he remembered the levity of being on the road, the clean ease of the stainless horizon. He remembered how real it had felt, that liberty. He might go anywhere; he might never return. He had known, though, that it was an illusion. He had always known.

The car was parked in the lane just outside the west gate, a battered Wolseley of indeterminate colour. Its engine had been silenced and its lights switched off. Eustace approached the passenger door and knocked – three taps, quick and even. The door was opened, and he lowered himself wearily in.

Cromer consulted his watch. 'It is after midnight, Eustace,' he said. 'I'm afraid I shall be forced to impose a charge for unsociable hours.'

'I apologise, Elias. There was much to detain me. And a tree had fallen in the lane.'

'*Per aspera ad astra*,' Cromer declaimed softly. He coughed, seeing Eustace's look, and dropped his theatrically raised hand. 'You have brought the documents? And signed them in the places I had marked?'

Eustace reached into his coat and drew out the envelope. He checked the seal and stared down at it, stroking the brown paper with his thumb. He passed it to Cromer, who deposited it in a briefcase he had left open on the back seat.

'You set me a melancholy task,' Cromer said, after a slight pause. 'Although I am obliged to add, in a professional capacity, that it is prudent to make such provisions.'

'It is a matter I had neglected. I am not as young as I look, after all, and none of us knows now what faces us. I must think of—' Eustace paused, bringing his hand to his mouth.

Cromer glanced at him, then decorously bowed his head.

'I must think of those who depend on me,' Eustace said at last.

'Of course,' said Cromer. 'To say nothing of your new employees. Well, the arrangements have been made final and binding. You have informed the beneficiaries?'

'Yes,' said Eustace. 'All but one.'

Cromer paused. 'You are aware of my advice in this matter.'

'You know their identities,' said Eustace. 'If I should be unable to give you further instruction, you may proceed to make contact with them in the manner we discussed.'

'It is preferable, as a rule, if all the beneficiaries have been informed.'

'Your advice is noted. The circumstances, as you know, are unusual.'

'You understand, also, that when we have concluded our business here tonight, the arrangement becomes irrevocable. If for any reason you are unable to attend our next appointment, I will expedite matters without further consultation. I – or my duly authorised delegates, should I myself be incapacitated – will take the actions we agreed.'

Eustace stared out the window.

'I understand the arrangements, Elias. They are my arrangements.'

'Forgive me, Eustace. A professional habit.' He extended his hand. 'Until our next appointment, then.'

Eustace shook his hand and climbed out.

'Go,' he said. 'Stop for no one. It begins now.'

Ten

The changes are everywhere in the house. Clara senses them almost from the moment she wakes. It is no longer quiet, even in the dark hour before she dresses and goes downstairs. She is disturbed, at her writing table, by unfamiliar sounds, by the indistinct commotion of activity that fills the house below. Alice, she knows, has been joined in recent days by other servants, and Eustace has ordered all manner of preparations. By seven o'clock, the ovens are at work and the grates are being scoured and made ready. In the scullery, the boards are being pounded and there is a dim but constant clatter of crockery.

On the landings and stairways, Clara encounters a procession of unfamiliar maids. Charwomen gossip in the unshuttered rooms, straightening unsmiling portraits and beating the drapes until the sunlight is slow with dust. They chatter among themselves as she passes, and she turns to find them staring after her. They murmur as if in disapproval, as if it is she who is the stranger.

The Crouch brothers too have changed. Though they arrived only recently, Clara had begun to accommodate herself to their peculiar presences. She had become accustomed enough to their movements, to the places where they might be found, that she could avoid encountering them for much of the time. When she did, she no longer felt her habitual discomfort, the small pressure of unease amid her ribs. For John, who has treated her with bashful deference since she led him from the maze, she had begun to feel something almost like fondness.

Now, she sees him only at a distance. He has been given duties, it seems, that keep him always about the grounds and often far from the house. She has glimpsed him from the tower with the opera glasses, trudging along the west lane towards the beech woods, returning much later from the direction of the front gates, passing from tree to tree as he skirts the margins of the avenue. He carries something, always, slung over his shoulder or gripped warily at his side.

Yesterday, at dusk, she saw him sit down to rest at the edge of the fountain. He seemed utterly weary, slumped with his back to one of the dragons and staring into the dark and undisturbed water. She watched as he lowered his knuckles to the surface of the pool, grazing it gently at first, then smashing his fist into the stillness.

Abel, for his part, is usually to be found about the house, dressed now in sombre domestic uniform, though his official function is not clear. When Clara goes down to breakfast, she finds him in the entrance hall. He no longer lounges against walls or mantels, but stands with an oddly self-conscious uprightness. Though he notes her arrival with the same laconic adjustment of his features, he no longer follows her idly with his gaze. Instead, he stares straight ahead as if he were a sentry.

In the dining room, Clara crams a buttered roll into her pocket. She goes to look for Eustace, though he too has come to seem unlike himself. She sees him less often now, and is conscious, when she does, that his attention is strained by other matters. He takes care, as before, to make some mild enquiry as to how she has spent her day, to remark on some detail of whatever scrap of manuscript she has most recently set out for him. Though he is diligent still in reading through to the end, she does not believe that he finds amusement in it as he once did. She can no longer imagine his face as he reads, his expression softening as he lingers over a particular line.

Clara tries not to think of it. He is preoccupied, she knows, by whatever business it is that has brought about the recent changes in the house. She is more circumspect now in what she shares with him, and feels she ought to trouble him less with idle diversions. Still, she could not bear to abandon their customs altogether. She cannot believe he would wish for that either.

And it is not only that. Not all of what she shows him, she has begun to feel, is inconsequential. She reads what she has written, sometimes, and feels a peculiar weight of certainty. So it was with today's pages, which came to her unprompted just after she awoke. They were written all at once, with a strange, unthinking compulsion. It was only when she read them over, half an hour later, that she set them quietly aside. She marked them with Eustace's name, so that she would not forget, and underscored the title.

The Song of the White Nightingale

Once, in the far north, there was a dying king.

He was prodigiously old, having reigned for the better part of a century. Although he was not greatly loved by his subjects, his time on the throne had been for the most part untroubled. His youngest son had been born a simpleton, it was true, but neither of the others displeased him especially. The eldest was quite of age, and eager to take up the sceptre if that burden should fall to him. Indeed, he scarcely left the palace lest he should fail to hear the cough that announced his father's passing.

For all this good fortune, the king was enraged by the prospect of death. He railed against the cruelty of the gods, who would visit such suffering on a man left unready by many decades of comfort. He cursed the uselessness of physicians, of whom he had put so many to death that there was no one left at court who would admit to the slightest acquaintance with human anatomy. When he offered an immense reward to anyone who might possess a remedy, not a single soul ventured to come forward.

At last, his most trusted counsellor took him aside, a man who was himself widely feared in the kingdom. The counsellor confided to the king a story that he had heard as a boy. In a forest at the borders of the kingdom that was known to be enchanted, there lived a nightingale. It was no common nightingale, he said. Its plumage was as white as Arctic snow, and its eyes might have been beads of purest sapphire. What set it truly apart, however, was its song. The song of the white nightingale was of such bewitching loveliness that it was said to cure any ill, no matter how grave. Hearing it, even a man lamed from birth would spring from the woods like a deer; an infant that had slid cold and still from its mother's belly would climb pink and mewling to her breast.

For all their wondrousness, such miracles were vanishingly rare. The white nightingale had been spoken of for a thousand years or more. Countless afflicted souls had braved the forest to seek it out, but no more than a handful had been so fortunate. It was not for the counsellor to say that it was beyond hope. That was for His Majesty alone to contemplate.

In this counsel, the king heard only what he wished. At once, he dispatched his youngest son, choosing the simpleton first on the pretence that the boy might have his wits restored into the bargain. Hardly a week had passed when news reached the palace that the idiot prince had been drowned while fording a river.

Again, the king wasted no time. He ordered his second son to ride out, forbidding him to return without the white nightingale. Within days, a letter was received from the prince himself. He had renounced his title and his birthright, he said, and had fled to a neighbouring kingdom. He was betrothed to the daughter of a swineherd, and would swallow poison before he would return.

It was with some weariness, then, that the king turned at last to his eldest son. He dispatched the crown prince, who protested fiercely, on the morning of winter solstice. Already, as he watched him gallop into the blizzard, hope had grown dim in his heart.

A month passed, and in that time the old king had grown so ill that he could no longer rise from his bed. The counsellor entered his chamber one evening with grave news. His eldest son, he said, had been slain by bandits just outside the city gates. They had stolen what he carried, the counsellor said, but he himself had pursued them. He had returned with their heads, which were mounted now on pikes outside the palace, and with the prize he now unveiled: a birdcage, most exquisitely gilded and ornamented, and within it, serene on its perch, the fabled white nightingale, its snowy feathers and sapphire eyes more magnificent than any story could have conjured.

The bird was placed at the king's bedside, where it was served with the finest of sweetmeats. It was given nothing to drink but freshly fallen dew, collected each morning in a jewelled goblet. But the nightingale would eat or drink nothing. It would not so much as turn to face the king, however he beseeched it, and it refused to utter a single note of song.

Other songbirds were brought to the king's chambers, in the hope that the bird might be moved to imitate them. Musicians were ordered to perform before it, to coax it into song with delicate melodies played on flutes and piccolos.

It was all in vain. The bird would not be enticed from its silence, and the king grew ever closer to death. Seeing this, his counsellor urged him to try another course. If the bird would not be induced to sing by kindness, he said, it must be compelled to do so by other means. The king gave his assent, for he knew now that each hour might be his last.

Opening the gilded cage, the counsellor held a burning torch to the bird's white breast.

'Sing or burn, little one,' he said. 'You have exhausted our hospitality. You shall sing now, or you shall burn.'

And indeed the bird did sing then, and its song was of such extraordinary beauty that the frail king sat up in bed for the first time in months, thinking himself restored to health. But it was not the king that the bird had healed. It was a lioness, a lioness whose pelt had lain before the hearth in the king's bedchamber since the day he had taken the throne. That lioness was roused now, made whole by the bird's song, and quite as powerful and sleek as if she had just stolen from among the parched grasses of the Serengeti.

She felled the counsellor, tearing out his entrails while the torch he had held set fire to the king's bedding, the flames rising quickly to consume him. When she had sated herself, she paused beneath the cage and allowed the nightingale to alight on her shoulder. The bird had broken off its song, and was silent once more as the lioness bore it from the burning palace.

Many people marked the passage of these two strange creatures, as they paraded calmly through the streets of the city. In the stories that were afterwards told, it was said that they were greeted with rejoicing, for the blood that dripped to the snow from the lioness's maw was taken to be the king's. It was usually remarked, at the conclusion of these stories, that the next king had the good sense to die when his turn came, by which time he had decreed that in all the length and breadth of that kingdom, no songbird should ever again be caged.

*

She finds Eustace in his office, the nib of his pen suspended intently above a document. Without looking up, he raises his other hand to indicate that she should wait. When he has satisfied himself on some final point, he signs the paper briskly and deposits it in a drawer. Only when he has locked the drawer does he raise his eyes to greet her.

When he does, however, Clara is surprised. The changes she has seen in Eustace have not been undone: there is a tautness about his posture still, a weariness that seems to have settled beneath his skin. But there is an ease in him today that she has not seen for some time. He has even cleared away his deepening drift of papers, restoring the desk to its customary order. She arranges her own pages unobtrusively as always, squaring them away in one corner.

'Thank you, Clara. I look forward to studying today's dispatches, though I'm afraid I don't quite know when I shall find the time. But come in, do. I have been much absorbed by business in recent days, and I have neglected you. Let me look at you. Have you been taking your meals? I have asked Alice to ensure that you do.'

Clara produces the roll that she took from the sideboard. She might have forgotten about it if Eustace had not mentioned it, or fed it to the ducks in the ornamental pond.

'Well?' he says. 'A roll that is still in your pocket hardly helps your case. Look at you, you are skin and bone. You must care for yourself.'

He grasps her wrist, holding it with the faintest of pressure, as he might a finch that he found tangled in a net. Clara offers him an unfelt smile and drops her gaze. She has spent much of the last week alone. In itself, it is not unusual, and she is accustomed to solitude. But it has been days, too, since she and Eustace exchanged more than a few words. She cannot remember when this last happened.

Eustace grazes her cheek with his flexed fingers. 'Clara?'

She shakes her head and turns away, sinking into a chair by the orrery. He scans her face as he takes the opposite seat. Some moments pass before he speaks. 'I am sorry, Clara. I have not—'

She looks away in discomfort. Absently, she tinkers with the moon.

'There are things I have not—' He weaves and unweaves his fingers. 'Things have not been as I might have wished.'

She works at the stiff handle that protrudes from the base of the device. With a squeak of complaint, the small bulb of the moon pivots on its fine mechanism.

'This house, this place,' Eustace says, looking about him. 'You have been here all this time. You have made your way in it, I suppose. You have woven your stories about it. But you have not had what a child should have. I have done what I could, but I am not—'

He pauses, lowering his head. He studies the back of his hand, traces the thwarted course of a vein with his fingertip.

'You are no ordinary child – it is not that I do not see it, only that I have never understood it. And all that I can offer you is of the ordinary kind. But you are cared for, Clara. That much I hope I can say. You are very much cared for. And will be always, even if I should—'

Clara releases the handle and looks up.

'I mean only that you must not worry,' says Eustace. 'I have seen to it that you will want for nothing. You do understand, don't you? But these matters were hardly foremost in your thoughts. There was something else, perhaps, that troubled you. I have a notebook you may use if yours is not to hand.'

She shakes her head.

'Listen to me,' he says. 'I am talking like an old fool. Eustace, you old fool. Oh, yes. You are being polite, Clara, for my sake, but I may say it.'

She leans across the table towards him, resting her hand on his.

She traces the prominent vein with her fingertip, finding and losing its yielding rope of warmth.

'It will be over soon, Clara, this business. Perhaps it will be time, then, to think of how we ought to live, all of us, whether we shall go on as we have. I know, of course, of your special attachment to this place. No one cherishes it, I think, quite as you do. But there are other places, surely, that you might wish to see. Not the fusty hotels that we have dragged you to, but places of your own choosing. In the universities, I gather, there are many young women now. Your curiosity would not be thought unusual there.'

She turns his hand over so that his palm faces upward. So much has been hidden from her that she hardly knows what to ask. She draws a simple shape with her forefinger: the crook and tittle of a question mark.

Eustace folds her hand in his. 'I have kept things from you, Clara, I will not say that I have not. And it will do no good, I suppose, to tell you that I have shared far more with you than was ever shared with me, when I was your – well, when I was young.'

He looks away for a moment, and gives a brief and almost bitter laugh.

'No, it does no good. If you find it a poor answer, you are right to think so. Let me say this instead, then. If I keep things from you, it is not from any want of confidence. If all those around me had a tenth of your wits, Clara, my hair would not be as grey as you see it now. Even Mr Crowe might be considerably improved by looking to your example. Oh, it is true.

'And you have given me your confidence, after all. Why, every day you entrust to me some new secret about the world that no one else could have revealed. Today, I am to learn about' – Eustace leans towards the desk, peering at the pages she left for him – 'the song of the white nightingale. Now that is a singular and charming creature, by the sound of it, and one I have never encountered in my field guides.'

Clara manages a brief smile, but shifts uneasily in her chair. They are not charming at all, these pages, but strange and unsettling. Why must she show him such things, when he must have come to dread the sight of them? Why did she not destroy them as soon as she read them? *Drown them. I'll drown my book.*

'Do not think I accept these gifts lightly, Clara. One day, perhaps, I will show you some measure of my gratitude. It is not right that I should ask you to wait, that those who are less deserving should continue to be put before you. And yet I must ask, Clara. I must ask you to wait while I attend to these last matters, that you give me a few days more to put our affairs in order. Will you do that for me?'

She fishes out her notebook, hesitating as she takes up her pen. She has known almost nothing beyond this place, and she cannot guess at the nature of these affairs that so preoccupy him. She knows only that they are encroaching on the borders of her world, and yet he keeps them secret from her. There are a hundred questions she might ask, but she writes nothing. She rests the pen on the empty page.

'I knew I could depend upon you,' Eustace says. He leans towards her, studying her intently. 'And it will not be so very trying, I promise you. These guests we are expecting. They will not stay, I should think, any longer than two or three days. It will be rather dull for you, and our conversations with them may seem unusual, even a little unsettling. They spend too little time among people, and they are poor company for children – even for such a child as you.

'But be patient, I beseech you. Show them courtesy, that is all, and watch how I behave. You will find it all tolerable enough, and we shall have them out from under our feet before the week is out.'

Something occurs to Clara. Decisively, she takes up the pen

again. She writes swiftly and forcefully, not caring much for her penmanship.

I would find it more tolerable if I were not wearing that silly dress.

Eustace reads with puzzlement at first, but winces slightly as he takes her meaning. 'I had almost forgotten,' he says. 'You disapprove, then, of Arabella's choice? I feared as much. But look at me, Clara. Look how I must dress, in dark suits always and persecuted by stiff collars. I am condemned to the appearance of an undertaker. It is only the starch, mind you, that keeps my back straight. Otherwise, I should be a hunchback by now.'

She laughs at this, though it does little to persuade her. Eustace, she has always thought, looks rather dignified in his suit, and appears rather younger than his years.

'These costumes serve a purpose, Clara. They protect us, you know. They protect us by making us appear as we choose. Never doubt how much we are shielded by such things.

'And I ask you to wear it because I would have these visitors see that they are addressing a young lady of whom they must take account. You are a person of consequence, Clara, and I will have them take account of you. Do you understand now why I ask this of you?'

Again, she writes quickly and firmly.

Just this once.

'Thank you, Clara. We shall be allies, then, in this encounter. And afterwards, if you like, I'll help you to burn the dress. Now, forgive me, but I still have much to do. We shall muster at dinner to face our enemy, eh?'

Eustace gives her a fond look as she gets up, then returns his attention to his papers. Just as she is closing the door behind her, he calls out to her. When she turns, he seems uncertain, as if measuring out what he must say.

'You spend your days, sometimes, among invisible things, in the world of daydreams. There is no great harm in it, and God knows I would not try to alter what is in your nature. But you must keep your wits about you, if only for a few days. The man who is coming, Clara – he wishes to settle a disagreement with Mr Crowe, but that is not quite all. He covets something that Mr Crowe has. He would covet it, I think, in anyone who possessed it, even in a child. I do not mean to frighten you, and no doubt half of these dangers are only my imaginings. Promise me, though, that you will be wary. Will you promise me that?'

In reply, Clara holds up her palm. The gestures are slight: a wreath of small and inkless ciphers. It is a word, nonetheless. It is her word.

Eleven

They arrive in the last of the light.

Clara is in the tower when the car appears at the gates. It is large and sleek, its feline greyness gilded by the November dusk. Silently, it passes along the avenue, the frayed shadows of the limes slipping from its polished surfaces.

She is standing, not taking care as she usually does to keep out of sight. It is almost dark, and she has dressed for dinner. The ridiculous white gown that Arabella chose was not made for crouching behind battlements. She ought to hide, she knows. The urge to do so tugs at her – to drop to her knees and scramble out of sight. Yet something prevents her; something keeps her rigid and unmoving, her eyes fixed on the car. It is halfway to the house.

She presses her fingernails into her palms.

Get down.

Move, she must move. These are the very people from whom the tower must be kept secret. She must move, but she cannot. She follows the quiet progress of the car, her breathing clotted and shallow. In her thin dress, she feels the cold insistence of the wind. Her bare arms are growing numb.

Get down. Get down.

Wolves. Clara thinks of wolves. They are alert, she has read, to movement above all else, to even the slightest tremor at the edge of their vision. Your best hope, finding yourself hunted to the edge of some Siberian forest, is to keep perfectly still, to stand at the dark eaves of the woods as they draw closer, stifling the longing to run even as they paw at the ground all around you. It is stillness that will keep you safe, stillness and the gentle obliteration of snow.

The car draws up outside the house. There is a soft disturbance of gravel, then silence. Nothing happens for some time. No one gets out of the car. Its doors are not even opened. At last, Clara sees Eustace emerge from the house. He is followed by Alice and four other servants, who arrange themselves at either side of the front door.

Get down, get down, get down.

The driver's door is opened. The man who steps out is tall and very lean. His dark hair is cropped closely, and his beard is carefully groomed. He circles the car to the rear door and holds it open, his movements purposeful and smoothly assured. There is an alertness in him that Clara has never seen in anyone. There is not a single moment when his eyes are not at work, settling attentively on each of the faces assembled before him, scanning the house, window by window.

The passenger emerges much more slowly. He is partly concealed at first, as the tall man helps him into an overcoat, passing him a dark cane with a silver handle. The driver steps back then, and she sees a much older man. He is gaunt and slightly stooped, resting both hands on his cane. His grey hair is swept severely from his forehead, and his skin, above the dark velvet collar of his coat, has the unsettling paleness of something drawn up from deep water.

Unlike his driver, the passenger shows no interest in his surroundings. He glances up at the reception party and lowers his head again with something like a shudder. As Eustace detaches himself to approach him, offering him a bow and some brief formula of welcome, he looks on with apparent resignation. When these formalities are concluded, he seems to sigh. He glances impatiently at his attendant.

It begins to rain. Clara shivers, clamping her arms to her sides. Still she cannot move. The slightest stirring now will be seen. *He* will see it. The flicker in the changeless snow. The sudden bolt of lush fur.

The driver addresses Eustace, gesturing curtly towards the house. Eustace regards him for an instant, his expression carefully void, then nods his assent. He directs some final courtesy towards the passenger, who ignores him and waits to be conducted to the door. As the party begins to move, the driver slips fluidly to his master's side, shielding him with a dark umbrella.

They proceed slowly, their pace governed by the passenger. His gait is slow and deliberate, marked by a limp he tries to mask. When they reach the steps, Eustace and the servants file into the house and out of Clara's sight. The passenger pauses on the topmost step, perhaps while he waits for the doors to be held open. He plants his cane in front of him, cleaving the fan of light that spreads from the hallway.

The driver pauses on the step, pivoting smartly to fold the umbrella. As he does so – dispelling its skin of droplets with a sharp quarter-turn – he looks out over the grounds, receding now into the twilight. From the beech woods, off to the west, his gaze crosses the parkland to the avenue, continuing methodically eastwards to where the lawns make their banked descent to the formal gardens.

Clara is so cold now that she can no longer be sure that she is keeping still. Her hair is drenched, and clings in cold ropes to her face and neck. She wishes for warmth now more than secrecy. She thinks again of her music box, which she has just stowed in the walnut chest below the hatch. If she were in her room with it now, she would stroke its lid to feel the particular coolness of the porcelain. When she opened it, the dancer would right herself with a little stuttering lurch, with that faint tremor, always, of her delicate satin wings.

She looks down again at the porch. The tall, lean man has folded the umbrella. He stands with his back to the doorway, leaving his face almost entirely in shadow. Clara cannot tell the direction of his gaze, but something has caught his attention.

He has become perfectly still.

Mr Crowe turned from the fireplace in the entrance hall, a heavy cocktail glass in his fist.

'Chastern, you desiccated old mantis,' he called out. 'What a delightful surprise.'

He wore the suit that Eustace had set out, and had consented the day before to the attentions of a barber. Arabella had not yet come down, and his attention for now was complete. He faced the room with something of his former intensity, with the almost incandescent composure that Eustace had so often seen. He thought of the salons and drawing rooms that Mr Crowe had held in fascination, of all those that had been lulled by that voice. He remembered princesses, smirched and abandoned on starlit terraces. He remembered the dogs barking behind them as they ran, and the morning coming, pale and forgiving.

'Next time, though, you must let us know to expect you. We have a telephone, you know. You do know about telephones?'

Chastern did not immediately reply. He glanced at Mr Crowe as if he were a newspaper vendor who had bawled some distasteful headline, then began a slow and methodical circuit of the hall, peering sceptically at wall hangings and items of furniture. Eustace and his retinue were left to stand in awkward formation opposite Chastern's driver, who remained impassively watchful.

The visitor paused to examine a bust of Voltaire, drumming his fingers lightly on its protuberant crown and smirking at some interior pleasure. He struck a brass umbrella stand with his cane, as if unconvinced of its robustness. Abel flinched at the resulting clang, suppressing a slight flexion of his right arm. The driver studied him with calm curiosity.

When Chastern reached the fireplace, he took considerable care over the selection of a chair, seating himself at last with a long exhalation. He regarded Mr Crowe briefly, then closed his eyes as if in pain. 'Crowe, Crowe, Crowe. How I have missed the sweet salve of your wit.'

'And I the Arctic summer of your charm. Join me in a drink, Chastern, before part of you peels off.'

'Where is that splendid little Poussin? It hung, I believe, where you are now displaying that ludicrous trophy.'

'I keep the splendid little Poussin in my private chambers. Had I known you cared for it, I might have moved it to the henhouse. This is why you must make the effort of writing a few lines.'

Chastern resumed his survey of the room. 'I rather think of that,' he said, 'as being your proper province. It has been some time, though, since my attention was last drawn to something bearing your mark. Have you folded up your tent, perhaps? Has that particular circus animal deserted you?'

'On the contrary, it is a creature that refuses to be banished. Speaking of the circus, your young understudy looks as if he has thrown a knife or two in his time.'

'Nazaire?' Chastern glanced around at his attendant. 'I'm afraid I wouldn't know. It is not a skill I thought to enquire about when he entered my service. It is boorishness of that kind, Crowe, that makes you unfit for the academic life. Disparagement of any kind is discouraged, you know. It is rather a bore, but one becomes habituated.

And as for slighting remarks directed at a chap of Moorish extraction – are you Moorish, Nazaire? In some degree, at least?'

Nazaire considered the question. He rocked his long, elegant fingers in a gesture of equivocation. 'Ish,' he said.

'Well, there you are,' said Chastern. 'No, it isn't done, Crowe. It is considered – if you will forgive the locution – rather beyond the pale.'

Mr Crowe was dimly amused. 'What makes me unfit for academic life, Chastern, is my lifelong affliction with talent. It is my tragic propensity for enriching the human store of beauty.'

'Hmm.' Chastern looked away, raising his cane to indicate the crystal vase near the foot of the stairs. 'You received the roses, I see.'

'Were those from you?' said Mr Crowe. 'I assumed Arabella had an admirer.'

'They are no longer at their best, I'm afraid. It is the time of year, you know. All beauty passes from the world, does it not? All beauty, and all its admirers.'

Eustace stepped forward. 'The gentlemen have had a long journey,' he said. 'Perhaps they would care to be shown to their rooms so that they may refresh themselves before dinner.'

'You do look a little travel-worn,' said Mr Crowe. 'We are lodging you in the primrose room. Cromwell once passed the night in it, while on one of his progresses about the country.'

'Which Cromwell?'

'The less convivial of the two.'

'I shall endeavour,' said Chastern, rising, 'to honour its illustrious past.'

'Crouch will see to it that your baggage is brought up,' said Eustace.

'Do not trouble him,' Chastern replied. 'It has been a consolation to me, in my senescence, to discover quite how modestly one may live, how few of our accustomed comforts are truly indispensable. I do not burden myself with a great deal of baggage when I am abroad. Nazaire will bring up what little I need.'

'As you wish, Dr Chastern.'

'Do you hear that, Crowe? He is punctilious, your man Euston.'

'Eustace, sir.'

'Eustace, of course. I do beg your pardon. He is punctilious, Crowe. He attends to the details of propriety.'

'Oh, he is a paragon of correctness,' said Mr Crowe. 'Knows which side of a countess to start with, that sort of thing. I can never keep it straight.'

Chastern looked Eustace over. 'Yes, I have no doubt,' he said. 'I'm sure he thinks of everything.'

Eustace acknowledged this with a slight bow. 'If you would be so good as to follow me, sir, I will show you the way. Everything is ready for you.'

Clara hurries along the landing, clutching her prim leather shoes by their ankle straps. Her limbs are stiff with cold still, but she barely pauses at the head of the stairs. There is no time now, and anyone who might see her is in the hallway far below. She reaches the second floor, running the entire length of its L-shaped landing. The back stairs are the quickest way to the laundry room.

On the ground floor, she must pass by the kitchens. By now, it will be almost five o'clock, and preparations for dinner will be underway. Her wet hair and clothes will not go unnoticed, even if no one guesses where she has been. Alice, she feels sure, would have a great deal to say about them. She inches forward as she approaches the kitchen doors, pressing herself close to the wall. She listens to the humid clatter of the busy kitchen, alert to any inflection in the noise, any sign that someone might emerge.

No one comes, and Clara slips quietly past, rounding the corner and coming to the end of the passageway. In front of her is the door to the stable yard. To her right are the dimly lit steps that lead down to the laundry.

Clara does not touch the light switch at the top of the steps, which serves both the stairs and the laundry itself. Though the laundry is in the basement, its single window looks out onto the stable yard. The light would be visible to anyone who happened to be outside, and would be unusual enough, at this hour, to arouse curiosity. She hesitates for a long moment at the head of the staircase, clenching and unclenching her fists. Below her, the steps recede into a void that seems almost perfectly black. Slowly, she lowers her foot to the first step.

The stairs to the laundry are made of rough stone. Beneath her stockinged feet, their surfaces are pocked and uneven. An iron rail set into the wall serves as a banister. Clara grips it so tightly that her palm begins to ache. The darkness, once she has gone seven or eight steps down, is complete. She knows she has reached the bottom only when she seeks the next riser with her toe and stumbles forward into nothingness. At the foot of the stairs, she knows, there is a short passageway that leads to the door of the laundry. Here, there is nothing to hold on to.

Clara is not especially afraid of the dark. She is often about the house on some private errand long after everyone is asleep. But the laundry, even in daylight, is a room she enters only when she must. It is cramped and dungeon-like, little more than a boiler room that has been fitted out with crude appliances. Its bare stone walls are veined with sclerotic pipes, its ceiling covered with spreading, tea-coloured stains. It is oppressively hot when the boiler is running and frigid when it is not.

This evening, since it is November and guests were expected, the boiler has been at work for some hours, though the results will be felt only unevenly about the house. When she finds the door, at last, and enters the laundry, the heat envelops her instantly. Clara has a peculiar horror of intense warmth. It is inseparable, for her, from a sense of suffocation. Even in midwinter, she sleeps with her window open. She turns back, gripping the door frame and pressing her forehead against the cool stone of the wall. Her urge is to climb the stairs again, to throw open the stable yard door and gulp the clean air of the autumn evening. But it is the heat, after all, that she has come for. The sooner her dress is dry, the sooner she can go upstairs.

She pushes herself away from the door and looks around her. However brutal the heat, there is at least the faint light from the high window. Clara sets down her shoes and strains to undo the buttons at the back of her frock. She manages only two before growing impatient, bunching the dress instead around her chest and, with some effort, wrestling its sodden coils clear of her shoulders.

She drags a clothes horse closer to the boiler and arranges the dress over one entire side. To make room, she moves a number of small garments, taking care not to examine them too closely. When their shapes are unmistakable – like the cloven flag of a pair of long johns – she plucks them fastidiously from the rung and, with a small shudder, drops them to the floor.

She stands for a while in her shift, grateful to be free of the dress. Even in the insistent heat, there is a faint pleasure in the weak currents of air that reach her skin, but she finds she cannot be still for long. Restlessly, she casts around for some small distraction, even attempting to study the instructions on a box of soap powder. When the moonlight proves too feeble to read by, she begins to wander around the dim room, idly examining the few dull items that come to hand. She is reaching for a tin of starch when her foot collides with a mop bucket.

The bucket tips over with a violent clang, rocking on its rim before settling at last under a work bench. The noise floods the small room, reverberating against its bare stone walls. In the silence that follows, Clara stands helplessly. The disturbance was loud enough, surely, to be heard upstairs. She glances down at herself, awkward in her thin shift, and begins looking for a place to hide.

Set into one wall is a deep bay of airing shelves. The lower three or four are stacked with piles of linen, but the topmost shelf – too high, she supposes, to be of use to the charwomen – is thinly stocked. There, if she keeps herself pressed against the wall, she will be hidden from the view of anyone below.

She clambers up quickly. Compared to the ladder behind the bookcase, the slatted shelves are an easy climb. Hauling herself onto the top shelf, she finds the space cramped, but not unbearably so. It is open, at least, on one side and high enough that she can look out onto the stable yard. From below her rises the scent, faint but wholesome, of freshly laundered linen. She slides towards the wall and lies still.

The room just above her is the scullery, she thinks. Its sounds, when her breathing settles, are strangely intimate: the knock and scuff of heels; a voice, then others, coalescing in a fug; the scrape of utensils, water-dulled or bright. The other sound – regular and percussive – is inseparable at first from the working of knives against boards. Soon, though, it detaches itself, grows near and unmistakable.

It is the sound of footsteps, brisk and sharp, approaching along the passageway from the kitchens. Someone is coming.

The footsteps draw closer, nearing the end of the passageway and the top of the steps. Clara presses herself against the back of the alcove. She cannot be seen, she feels sure. Even if the light is turned on, whoever it is will do no more, surely, than glance about the room and go back upstairs.

She takes the smallest possible breaths, flaring her nostrils so that each inhalation is almost soundless. The footsteps cease, just as she expected to hear them on the steps. Someone is looking for the light switch, perhaps.

Or someone is already on the stairs, shoeless now and silent.

How many steps? Clara tries to remember. She counts with a fingernail on her palm.

. . . *six, seven, eight, nine* . . .

A door slams. The sound, after such a long silence, is colossal, but she realises, the flare of panic fading in her chest, that it came from above her. The stable yard door, then. The footsteps resume, slower now and more deliberate as they negotiate the uneven cobblestones. Clara unflexes, takes a long, rich breath. Outside. Someone is outside in the stable yard, though for what purpose she cannot imagine. The footsteps come and go, crossing the same short distance, over and over.

Very slowly, she works her way back to the edge of the shelf, straining upwards a little on her elbows. It is uncomfortable, and the view is constricted by the deeply recessed window, but she can see a swathe of the stable yard that stretches almost to half its width. The rain has stopped, and the cobbles have the muted gloss of eel skin.

Clara sees her then – the woman. She wears fine stockings and high, gleaming shoes. Her scarlet dress, or the lower part of it, is of a sumptuous fabric. Because the laundry is in the basement, its window onto the stable yard is almost level with the ground. Above the woman's hem, Clara can see nothing.

Even so, she is sure. It can only be Arabella. The guests can be excluded, since there are no women among them. The servants are all occupied elsewhere, and none of them is likely to possess such clothes. It is Arabella. It must be.

Brightness sweeps across the stable yard then, followed by a smooth and resonant rumble, close enough for Clara to feel it in her chest. The car surges into the yard, the one she saw from the tower. It seems even larger now, more forbiddingly grey. She tenses, retreating slightly but unwilling to give up her view.

The engine is stilled and the light vanishes. The driver steps out, fluidly unfolding his height. As he does so, the woman crosses quickly to the car, coming fully into view. It is Arabella, just as she knew it must be. She wears a fur over her red dress, and pulls it closely about her as she waits, holding herself stiffly in the cold. She is beautiful, Clara supposes, as Mr Crowe's companions always are. The tall man does not immediately acknowledge her. Instead, he scans the buildings that encircle the stable yard, intent and methodical as before. Clara recoils, even in the darkness of her hiding place, as his gaze passes over her window.

He turns to Arabella and they begin talking immediately, as if resuming an earlier conversation. They exchange no obvious greetings, addressing each other in a way that seems familiar if not intimate. It is possible, Clara supposes, that they were introduced in the house just now. Mr Crowe may have presented Arabella to the guests as they arrived in the hall. It is possible.

But Clara sees none of the propriety and deference of those recently acquainted. If anything, Arabella seems to become agitated as the conversation continues. They are not strangers, these two. They are something else, something Mr Crowe knows nothing about, though he is always so certain of everything. It is strange to think of. Arabella listens as the tall man says something, then shakes her head. When he repeats it, she makes an emphatic, slicing gesture and turns to leave.

The driver moves to intercept her. With shocking swiftness, he brings his hand to her throat, pushing her back against the car. Arabella holds herself still, straining upwards slightly to relieve the pressure on her neck. He leans over her and speaks carefully into her ear. Though his arm is held inflexibly, his posture is otherwise relaxed. His expression, visible to Clara in profile, is smoothly composed. Though she cannot turn her head, Arabella's eyes flicker towards him as he speaks. He relaxes his grip, studying her as she nods in response to what he has said. Finally, he releases her, inspects her briefly and moves to the back of the car.

He busies himself at the luggage compartment for some time, though he removes from it only a single small valise. He works calmly, showing no further interest in Arabella. She turns unsteadily to examine her reflection in the car window, touching her throat with disbelieving gentleness. She huddles in her fur, eyeing him nervously, until she has persuaded herself that it is safe for her to leave.

Clara hears the door slam upstairs. From the passageway, she hears Arabella's footsteps, more rapid now than when they were approaching. She listens until they recede beyond hearing. Keeping her eyes fixed on the driver, she retreats again into the shadows at the back of the shelf.

She lies as quietly as she can. He is out there still, the tall man, and the house is full of strangers. Nothing is as it seems. It is not only Mr Crowe who is being deceived, but Eustace too. There are dangers he keeps from her, she knows that much, but what if there is something worse? What if something threatens them that is hidden even from Eustace?

She keeps still, and tries to calm herself. She listens, straining outwards into the darkness, for the familiar intervals, for the cadences of the secret world. She threads the dead veins of fallen leaves, tests each frail filament of spider silk. She combs every seeded drift of air, touches every cell of the silence. She is weightless then, beneath or between the darkness, where everything is as she remembers it and nothing can do her harm.

Twelve

I n *the dining* room, Eustace attended to the last things.

Slowly, he made a final circuit of the great dining table, inspecting each place setting for the slightest imperfection. He paused to lift a claret glass to the light, gently cradling its bowl with his white-gloved fingers while he effaced the ghostly striations of a fingermark. Elsewhere, he made a minute correction to the alignment of a dessert fork, reversing an adjustment that he himself had made a few minutes before.

At the head of the table, he allowed himself a moment to contemplate the scene in its entirety. In the gloom of the grand and dark-panelled chamber, the immaculate white field of the tablecloth, crowned at either end by magnificent, seven-branched candelabras, seemed to be held aloft amid the surrounding shadows. The sideboard, running almost the entire width of the opposite wall, had been arrayed with fruit in accordance with Mr Crowe's peculiar custom. As always, Eustace took satisfaction in the richness of their colours. The nectarines, of course, in swollen clutches of ruby and sienna; the densely jewelled quarters of pomegranate; the varnish of the cherries, that intimate and perfect red.

It pleased him, the finished tableau of his preparations. It had been a weakness of his, from the first days of his service, to take pleasure in the ordering of fine things in great rooms, to savour the grace and symmetry of their arrangement in the last moments before they were put to use. It was a part of his training that he had taken to with a strange zealousness, a tenderness almost. In these rituals, in the unrushed arraying of beauty, he had felt his new life enclose him. It was a world of weight and permanence, of things that could not be taken away.

Eustace turned to the huge, gilt-framed mirror that hung to one side of the dining table. He leaned towards his reflection to examine his dark collar and lapels. He undid and carefully reknotted his white tie. After studying his out-thrust chin from a number of angles, he concluded that another shave would not be necessary. He touched the slightly prominent bone of his temple, traced its stark bracket of shadow. His cheeks, too, had come to seem more deeply hollowed. His pallor, like the whiteness of the tablecloth, appeared almost spectral against the darkness of the background.

Still, his age had not marked his face as it might. Was it the face – as Abel had said – of a man twenty years younger? Had he gone so much unchanged? Perhaps he had. There were judgements a man could not make about himself. Although his position obliged him to attend to his appearance, he studied his face itself as little as he could. He saw it – as he saw so much else that he could not account for – and yet it went unseen.

He turned from the mirror. Only one task now remained. It was one he had taken care to leave until last. He lit a long taper from one of the candles on the table and carried it to each of the two large windows in turn. The curtains were not drawn, in spite of the darkness, and an ornate candlestick had been set in each window.

Eustace lit the candles and stood back. The effect, on the whole, was rather pleasing. It was a slightly unusual arrangement, perhaps, but with so many other candles about the room, it would not seem especially incongruous. The candlesticks were silver, well-made things and handsome in their way. Each had an ornamental base, fashioned to resemble a heavenly body. One was in the form of a splendidly radiant sun. The other had a simpler elegance, and was made in the slender shape of a crescent moon.

When Clara wakes, the darkness is complete. There is a lurch of incomprehension as she struggles to recall where she is. She presses her hands against the cold surface that prevents her from sitting up, believing herself, for a few horrifying moments, to be buried alive. It is only when she reaches beneath herself and grips the slats of the airing shelf that she recognises the place, that she remembers what she saw.

Her impulse is to climb down immediately, to take her things and go upstairs. She forces herself to lie still and listen, to make sure it is safe. As she does so, she tries to recollect all that has happened, to explain it to herself. She has been asleep, for how long she has no idea. It seems strange to her that she should have fallen asleep at all, in such circumstances. She is not quite well, she thinks. Her throat is constricted and behind her brow there is the faint thrum of fever. She caught a chill, perhaps, standing on the tower in the cold for all that time.

Clara props herself up on her elbows. She hears nothing now, from outside or from the passageway above. Whatever it was that she witnessed in the stable yard, it is over. They have returned indoors, Arabella and the driver; to dress for dinner, she supposes, as she is expected to be doing. Or perhaps dinner has already been served. It may be nine o'clock, for all she knows. It may be midnight.

As quickly as she can, given the darkness, she lowers herself from her hiding place. The dress, when she locates it, is perfectly dry. How long would that have taken? An hour? Two, maybe? Irritated, she pulls the dress on, smoothing it down with rough and careless strokes. There is a distinct and potent discomfort in waking with no way of knowing the time. She makes her way to the stairs, almost tripping over her shoes.

In her room, at last, Clara can check the clock. She *is* late – it is almost a quarter to nine – but her movements, as she dashes around the room, are urgent yet aimless. She has no particular idea, she realises, of the preparations she ought to make. She has dressed for dinner before, but never on occasions when her efforts were likely to be noticed. She has read enough, of course, to know that young debutantes would be rouging their cheeks and dabbing scent behind their ears. She has been aware, without feeling the slightest urge to possess them, of the accoutrements that girls are expected to delight in. She does have a hairbrush, at least, and makes do with applying it to the more disordered parts of her hair. Feeling that she may have neglected something, she inspects her teeth briefly before the mirror and splashes some water on her face.

On her way downstairs, Clara encounters Alice, who has been dispatched to look for her and is labouring up the stairs with a sternly pursed expression. 'Well, there you are, Miss Clara,' she says. 'What can you be thinking of? The guests have gone in to dinner, and I'm sure I have enough to occupy me. Mr Eustace is most anxious, and I can't say as I blame him. Honestly, child. I sometimes think you're in another world entirely.'

Clara follows her to the dining room, where Eustace is called out to present her to the company. He looks her over brusquely, clucking with disapproval at the appearance of her dress. 'I was becoming concerned,' he says. 'You are all right? You are not unwell?'

Clara shakes her head impatiently, taking hold of his wrist. Even as she does so, she realises that she is not at all sure how to explain what it is that she has seen. She does not understand what passed between Arabella and the tall man, only that it reveals something even Eustace does not know, something that places all of them at a disadvantage.

Eustace pulls his hand away, reluctantly but firmly. 'There is no time, Clara. You must tell me later. Think how rude this must appear. Did I not ask that you help me in this? That you show them some small courtesies?'

Before she can respond, he turns and re-enters the dining room, holding the door open for her to follow. Alice prods her when she hesitates. 'Go on, child, for heaven's sake. You've caused quite enough of a fuss as it is.'

In the dining room, Clara's eyes adapt again to darkness. The faces of those seated around the table loom as if suspended in noth-ingness. She struggles to focus as Eustace introduces her.

'Clara, this is Dr Chastern.'

He indicates the elderly passenger she observed from the tower. He and Mr Crowe have been seated at opposing ends of the huge dining table, each partly obscured by a constellation of candle flames. It is absurdly formal and somehow unreal, like a banquet for ghosts.

'And this is his associate, Mr Nazaire.'

Twice now, Clara has watched this man while she herself re-mained unobserved, yet she is almost persuaded that the opposite is true. He studies her with such consuming deliberation that it seems impossible that anything might escape his attention. She looks down, unable to meet his gaze, and hurries to the chair that Eustace has pulled out. She glances at Arabella as she takes her seat – she is leaning towards Mr Crowe to hear some private aside – but quickly looks away again. Nazaire, she knows, is observing her every movement. He sits at the edge of her vision, still and vigilant, seeing everything.

She clasps her hands in her lap and looks straight ahead. The curtains have not been drawn, she notices, and a candle flickers in each of the windows. She thinks again of John Crouch, looking in from the cold. Even Abel is inside in the warmth, standing with stiff decorum behind Mr Crowe's chair. Alice brings Clara a bowl of the soup that the others have just finished. She is not hungry, but sets about it diligently, grateful to have something to occupy her.

'You must forgive Clara,' Mr Crowe says, breaking the silence. 'She is a great adventuress, you see, and finds the tyranny of regular mealtimes to be insupportable. In this, as in so much else, we share a certain kinship.'

'How delightful,' says Chastern. 'My own acquaintance with children, alas, has been no more than what I have glimpsed in books. In literature, of course, one scarcely notices dutiful children. It is only when they are thrust upon the world by some contrivance of circumstance that we may tolerably fix our attention upon them.' He speaks slowly, and with a jaded languor, as if he takes pleasure in it but finds it somehow effortful.

'A death, usually,' says Mr Crowe.

'Well, quite,' Chastern says. 'But death is hardly a contrivance of circumstance.'

'It is when Dickens does it,' Mr Crowe replies. 'Some pallid and virtuous mama is usually required to die in childbirth so that our sturdy little hero, before he has so much as uttered his first word, is adequately furnished with woe. No, Dickens never dispenses a teaspoonful of misfortune when a ladleful will do. Still, it is no great fault. It is no more objectionable, after all, than the irruption of outlandishness that brings young Jim Hawkins into possession of Captain Flint's treasure map. And what of it, if it gets the job done?

He may be a cheerful and dauntless little urchin, but we shall hardly put up with him rinsing out piss pots for three hundred pages. Get things moving, that's all that matters, and do not trouble yourself at occasional creaking from the scenery. Get his arse out the door so that things can happen to him.'

Chastern considers this with a look of distaste. 'A vulgar formulation, though I must defer to you, I suppose, as a master practitioner. And we must concede the principle, of course. Every tale must have its *casus belli*, its abducted Helen. Miss Clara, of course, finds herself in rather more agreeable domestic circumstances than did young Jim, but even such fine places as this may occasionally be visited by the agents of fortune.'

'*Et in Arcadia ego,*' says Nazaire. His voice is soft and measured. There is something unignorable in it.

Clara raises her eyes from her soup. Both he and Chastern are looking at her as if awaiting her response. She toys with her spoon, the heat of discomfort rising in her face. Eustace, standing attentively at the sideboard, clears his throat and fixes his eyes on Mr Crowe, who seems after a moment to realise that he is expected to intervene.

'Clara finds her voice on the page, gentlemen. Like me, she is devoted to the written word. If she had pen and paper to hand, and if we were not at the dinner table, I assure you that you would find her responses dazzling. She does not speak, however. It is a mark of singularity that she has always carried, and for which we cherish her all the more.'

'Yes, of course,' says Chastern. 'It is a detail of which Eustace took care to apprise me, but I confess that it slipped my mind. I'm afraid my age begins to betray me. You must forgive us, Miss Clara, if our indelicacy caused you discomfort. The hopes and prospects of the young, you see, are intoxicating to those of us who have entered our declining years. So much awaits you in the world beyond this place.'

Eustace comes to the table and leans over Clara, taking up her plate and adjusting her napkin. His arms shield her from Chastern's view.

'There is time enough to think of such things,' Mr Crowe says. 'She is a child still, and will be a comfort to us for some years yet. Besides, she does not want for amusement here. She has the run of this house and all that lies about it. She knows my library, I often think, better than I do myself. There is room enough here for any child's adventures.'

'Indeed,' says Chastern. 'We do not forget, Crowe, how grandly you have established yourself. How ought one to describe the style of the house? It seems to have Elizabethan notions, among others.'

'The house?' Mr Crowe says. 'The house has been added to by every age.'

'There must be many rooms,' says Nazaire, looking unblinkingly at Clara. 'One could lose oneself.'

She feels a cold pressure, as if something were coiling itself about her neck and chest. Eustace interrupts the conversation to announce the serving of the next course while Abel replenishes the wine glasses. When the food has been served, Mr Crowe begins to relate an anecdote involving a tsarina and a pearl necklace that he was somehow instrumental in restoring to her. Clara has heard the story several times, and does not give it her full attention. There is some joke in it, she thinks, that is intended to be obscure to her.

'Splendid,' says Chastern, when Mr Crowe has finished. 'How splendidly you have lived. And you see, Clara, Crowe was never content to have his own adventures bounded by the walls of a house, however magnificent it might be.'

'I was young, Chastern. It is a common condition, though you yourself managed never to succumb to it. This was long before I came into any property.'

'Indeed,' says Chastern. 'But you have not quite lapsed into blameless senescence, have you? Even now, though you find yourself lord of the manor, with all the cares of your great Estate to weigh on you; even now, you contrive to find amusement for yourself, do you not? You do not want for the consolations of beauty.' He looks at Arabella, who inclines her neck uneasily. Clara can see no marks on it, but she holds herself as if in some mild discomfort.

Mr Crowe takes a mouthful of wine. He swills it for a moment, his head to one side. 'What would you have me do, Chastern? Pass my evenings at the cribbage table? As long as there is life, there are pleasures to be taken.'

'Just so,' says Chastern. 'As long as there is life.'

Nazaire finds some obscure amusement in this observation. He laughs to himself as he cuts his meat. Like his voice, the sound is at once smooth and forceful, seeming calibrated to achieve some precise effect. Mr Crowe scowls and glances impatiently at Eustace, whose answering look is carefully restrained.

Mr Crowe and Chastern continue to spar in this manner, expounding some high principle of art before returning, by an elliptical path, to Mr Crowe's personal history or the affairs of his household. There is an elaborate formality to their exchanges, though Mr Crowe lapses occasionally into coarseness, and a refined if rather sour wit. There is no warmth or ease between them, it is clear, and even Chastern's extravagant politeness seems to conceal something unpleasant. It makes Clara think of the jewelled handle of some gleaming and deadly implement. And at the periphery of the conversation, always, is some cloaked and unmentionable subject, something that is almost but not quite said.

More courses arrive. There are tender morsels of pheasant and pigeon, blazoned with a sweetly piquant sauce. An elaborate confection of lobster is served, for some reason, in crystal goblets and garnished, astonishingly, with flecks of gold leaf. The arrangement of finely sliced beef that follows seems to Clara to be raw, though it has a delicate fragrance and is tender enough to be cut with the edge of her fork. Most of these dishes she pushes away untouched. She feels unmistakably feverish now, with a diffuse ache that has spread to her limbs.

Nor is she the only one whose appetite is poor. Arabella, she notices, takes only a distracted mouthful of whatever is put before her. Nazaire consumes a portion – never more than half – of each dish before decorously setting down his cutlery. Chastern, meanwhile, examines everything that is brought to him with puzzlement or horror, and appears to find the very notion of food vaguely outlandish. Only Mr Crowe eats with relish, savouring every bite with a contented indifference to those around him.

When Eustace announces dessert, Chastern raises a hand in theatrical protest. 'Forgive me,' he says, 'but I must forgo any further indulgence. It is wrong of me, I know, to spurn such immoderate hospitality, but my constitution is no longer robust.'

'Nonsense,' says Mr Crowe. 'Take something sweet, Chastern. It cannot but do you good. Look at you, you have the complexion of a scorpion.'

Chastern does not immediately reply. 'Perhaps I do,' he says, at length. 'It is the outward manifestation of what is now my nature. I have grown melancholy, you see, as age and infirmity stalk me, and I find myself beyond the consolation of sweetness. But the rest of you must continue, of course. I would not dream of depriving you of your – what was it, Eustace?'

'A sorbet of passion fruit and *eau de vie*, Dr Chastern.'

'Truly?' says Chastern. 'How very peculiar. Nonetheless, do carry on, all of you. I shall observe, as it were, from the gallery.'

Mr Crowe screws up his napkin and drops it on the table. 'I won't hear of it,' he says. 'In any case, it will do none of us any great harm to abstain. We are all sufficiently glutted, I think, with the fruits of passion. But I trust, Chastern, that you will stay to take a liqueur with me. And a cigar, perhaps, if your physician has not ruled it too great a hazard.'

'Perhaps I might manage a thimbleful of something,' Chastern says. 'I seem always to be troubled, of late, by one thing or another. It would be a comfort to me to discuss certain matters with you, to assure myself that our views are consonant.'

Mr Crowe gives him a bleak look. 'I wonder if you do not confuse me with someone else,' he says. 'But let us talk, by all means. Arabella, my love, would it be altogether too Edwardian of us to ask you to wait for us in the drawing room?'

'As a matter of fact,' Arabella says, 'I haven't been feeling quite myself this evening. I think I may be coming down with the flu. It's very rude of me, I know, but I'm afraid I may have to retire early.'

'You poor lamb,' says Mr Crowe. 'Will you manage, do you think? Shall we have Alice help you upstairs? Eustace has cut off her rations, I think, and she appears remarkably steady on her feet.'

'There's really no need,' says Arabella. 'Alice has been run off her feet all evening. Perhaps Clara could be a darling, though, and help me to find something in the library. You'll all think me ridiculous, I know, but when I felt poorly as a child, I used to curl up in the bottom bunk with *Jane Eyre*. It was probably awful of me, but I used to find it somehow comforting that Jane was having such a rotten time. Would you mind terribly, Clara? I couldn't possibly find it on my own.'

Clara smiles weakly. She feels feverish herself, and more fatigued now than she can disguise. She had hoped to escape upstairs alone as soon as she could be excused. Still, she can hardly refuse without appearing rude, especially in view of her late arrival at the table. She stands and waits for Arabella to precede her. The gentlemen rise too, and Chastern, as she passes him, stops her and takes her hand. His fingertips are parched and fibrous, with the peculiar softness of rice paper.

'My dear creature,' he says. 'It was delightful to meet you at last. I had taken the trouble, on learning that Mr Crowe's household was gladdened by the presence of a child, to discover some little about you, but I must admit that I did not expect to be quite so helplessly beguiled. I do hope it is not long before we may be reacquainted. I so look forward to witnessing these gifts of yours for myself.'

With as much politeness as she can summon, Clara withdraws her hand. She glances at Nazaire, who looks on with placid and un-wavering attentiveness. He bows elegantly, holding one hand across his shirt front. The smile that accompanies this gesture is shallow and colourless. Clara curtseys awkwardly in response, her movements thick-limbed and graceless. What she wants, more than anything, is to bolt from the room and race to the kitchen door. She wants to slip outside, as she has done so often, not heeding her fever or the November cold; to feel herself vanish in the darkness of the laneways, among the faint disturbances of the woods. She wants to be gone.

Eustace tried the light switch again, though he knew it was fool-ish. The cellar's cavernous central vault remained unlit. It was illuminated, normally, by bulkhead lights fixed at intervals along its ceiling. They were sturdy fixtures whose bulbs he seldom had to replace. This evening, it seemed, all three had burned out at once.

He glared for a long moment into the darkened vault, tapping the plate surrounding the light switch with a fingernail, then turned and stalked back upstairs. From the pantry, he took a candlestick and a box of matches. He knew the cellars well enough, and could make his way quite passably by candlelight. Still, it irked him, after the pains he had taken, to be put to this trouble. It was not by any omission of his. He had brought up, in ample quantity, any wine that might reasonably be called for, given the evening's menu. Of the claret he had chosen – a Margaux widely considered to be un-impeachable – four bottles remained, two of them already decanted. He had taken similar care with the port and the Armagnac.

It had been Chastern who forced him to return to the cellars, referring in one of his lengthy and preening anecdotes to a 1928 Chateau Pétrus that had been served by the Master of Balliol College. Mr Crowe, of course, had felt obliged to demonstrate the parity of his own cellar, insisting that he possessed 'seven or eight' bottles of the same vintage and urging Eustace to bring one up.

Eustace muttered disgustedly at the recollection. He strode through the vault now, guarding the candle flame behind bracketed fingers. Mr Crowe, of course, had hardly helped matters. He knew better than anyone what faced them this evening. He knew – even if he did not care to enquire into the details – that Eustace was oc-cupied with much more than the niceties of hospitality. Yet even now he could not check himself. He was so long accustomed to the indulgence of his whims that he rose to Chastern's bait without an instant of reflection.

At the heart of the cellar was a storeroom. It was used to hang cured meats and to keep the whole cheeses before they were cut. Along the walls, there were rough benches that had once done duty as pews in a chapel. In the centre of this low-ceilinged room was an old tasting table. From one of its deep drawers, Eustace lifted out the logbook, a wide and heavy ledger that was wrapped in oilskin to protect it from the damp.

The log had been kept since long before the cellar had come into his custody, by Cromer and his predecessors. The earliest pages were faded almost beyond reading. Though a 1928 wine would have been laid down by Eustace himself, it was far too long ago for him to recollect. As he turned the coarse and yellowing pages, his forefinger descending column after column of meticulous entries, he hardly recognised what he himself had written. It was like poring over an ancient register of births and deaths, kept by some long dead and unremembered clerk.

Still, he found the Pétrus before too long. There were two bottles of the 1928 – there had never been more – and the location of each was exactly as the log recorded. He could be thankful, at least, that Mr Crowe had not ferreted them out during some long-forgotten and undocumented debauch. Eustace checked his watch in the candle-light. He had been away from the dining room for fourteen minutes. Fourteen minutes, in spite of the care he had taken to ensure that he need not leave at all.

He drew out one of the bottles, handling it gently so as not to upset the sediments. He stroked the dust from the label with a thumb, checking the particulars of the vintage. With a clean flannel, he polished the rest of the bottle. He did not intend, if it could be helped, even to decant it, yet there were proprieties that he would not sacrifice. He would not have it said.

Reaching the stairs again, he paused with his hand on the rail. He stood for a moment, his head bowed and his eyes closed, then straightened again. Briskly, he dusted his own cuffs and collar with the flannel. He cleared his throat, so that he would not be forced to do so in the dining room, and hawked up a bolus of dust-thickened phlegm. Holding the bottle at the correct angle, he climbed towards the light.

*

Arabella stops and looks around, her heels snapping to a halt on the polished tiles of the hallway. 'There you are,' she says. 'You're such a quiet creature, aren't you? I don't mean— oh, I'm sorry. I was worried that I had lost you, that's all.'

Clara pauses too, preserving the distance between them. She hears the strenuous cheerfulness in Arabella's voice, the mild and patient exhalation as she waits for an answering smile. Clara does not look up. She is feverish, her thoughts dull and humid, her legs growing more silted and ponderous with every step. She wants only her room now, a few minutes at her desk. She will lock her door and open her window. She will not have her music box – she remembers this with a small pang of sorrow – but she will be able to lie still at least, to feel the cold spilling from beneath the curtains.

'Yes, well, I'm sure you're very tired,' Arabella says, turning and walking on. 'Poor thing. This won't take long, I promise.'

A little further along the hallway, Arabella stops again, pivoting this time towards an ornate mirror. She inspects herself with brisk dissatisfaction, bunching and distending her lips as she applies a rich slick of raspberry-coloured polish. 'How perfectly monstrous I look,' she says quietly. She glances at Clara with a lopsided smile. 'You mustn't think I'm always like this. It's just that I'm not quite feeling myself.'

At the doors of the library, Arabella produces the large brass key that Mr Crowe entrusted to her in the dining room. She examines it distractedly, seeming embarrassed as she turns again to Clara. 'I suppose you've read it lots of times? *Jane Eyre*, I mean. Or isn't it considered serious? I really don't know very much about these things.'

Clara nods hesitantly. She has read *Jane Eyre* many times, never giving any thought to whether it is serious or not. The books she loves most are those that seem somehow complete, their worlds proximate and habitable. There is an ease in entering those other lives, in feeling herself enclosed by another consciousness. It is strange, that unruptured intimacy, like possessing a second skin.

'Well, now you know,' Arabella continues, sliding the key into the lock. 'My secret is out, for better or worse. You won't think badly of me, will you? We shall have the chance to get to know one another better, when all this is— well, when the time is right. You'll show me all the things I ought to have read, and I'll introduce you to some of my favourite music, though that's probably disreputable too.'

Arabella sighs with impatience and jiggles the key in the lock. Clara wishes she would let her try. There is a trick to it, a slight upward pressure that must be exerted as the key is turned.

'Oh, for goodness' sake,' she mutters. 'It's like breaking into a bank vault. Yes, you must let me introduce you to jazz. You'd adore it, I'm sure you would. We'll become the best of friends, you and I. You'll see that I'm not so awful.'

Arabella rattles the lock as she speaks, her voice lurching from gaiety to exasperation.

'I'm sure it's a bore for you,' she says, 'having all these strange grown-ups descend on your home. And grown-ups can seem terribly caught up in their own world, can't they? Doing things for all sorts of odd reasons. But you'll see— ah, here we are at last.'

Arabella holds the door a little way open. Beyond it, the library is in darkness.

'Would you mind if I waited here?' she asks sweetly. 'I'm sure you'll be much quicker if I'm not in your way, and then we can both be off to bed.'

Clara peers into the unlit room. Arabella smiles fixedly, holding open the heavy oak-panelled door. She holds the key in the lock with her other hand, gripping it so tightly that her fingertips have whitened against the brass.

The certainty comes to her with a strange ease and finality. It is like the disorienting relief of recognising a face that has seemed for a long time familiar. For a strange, suspended moment, Clara stares at the key, at Arabella's tensed and blanching fingers.

Then she runs.

Nazaire was gone.

He had replaced his chair carefully after vacating it, and someone – Alice, Eustace assumed – had cleared his place. Chastern, meanwhile, had taken the chair next to Mr Crowe's. He spoke to him now in a low, confiding voice while Mr Crowe stared into his wine glass, listening with grudging attention.

In deference to the privacy of this conversation, Abel had withdrawn a little way from Mr Crowe's chair. He shook his head fractionally when Eustace consulted him. He had seen or heard nothing beyond what was evident. It was hardly surprising.

Eustace approached with the wine, which he presented with a modest flourish. 'So good of you, Eustace.' Chastern reclined in his chair. Regretfully, he caressed the label of the Pétrus. 'I'm afraid, however, that we have put you to needless trouble. Our visit, alas, must be cut short, though we had only begun to savour your hospitality.'

'I am sorry to hear it, Dr Chastern. It is nothing untoward, I trust, that has forced this change in your plans?'

'Oh, it is nothing of the slightest interest. I am called away on college business. Such is the lot of the humble scholar.'

'Humble my arse,' said Mr Crowe. 'Aren't you the dean of something? Surely there are lackeys?'

'It is a matter of sensitivity,' said Chastern. 'And there are few enough functions, in my office, that I am called upon to exercise. No, I must not complain too bitterly, and Crowe and I, at least, have had leisure to discuss a matter that had been troubling me. It relieves me greatly to have had his confidence.'

Eustace paused. He was not expected, he knew, to believe this story. Since it could not be questioned, no great care had been taken over its appearance of plausibility. Something eluded him, though. Something in the mechanics of it.

'It is very regrettable,' Eustace said. 'Did the news reach you this evening? I was not aware that anything had arrived.'

'By telephone,' Chastern said. 'A wretched instrument that I myself refuse to operate. Nazaire was good enough to speak to the other party when your housekeeper advised us of the interruption.'

Eustace set the bottle down quietly. 'Alice?'

'I'm sure that's right, Eustace, though I don't believe you introduced us.'

'Of course.' He turned to face the table. 'Mr Crowe has no doubt expressed our dismay at your early departure. You will let me know, of course, if I may be of service as you make ready to leave.'

'You are kindness itself, Eustace.'

'I'm afraid I am made of rather coarser stuff than that.'

He offered a curt bow, but Chastern had returned his attention to Mr Crowe. While they resumed their private dialogue, he busied himself with small tasks about the table. When he was satisfied that his actions were unremarked, Eustace approached one of the windows, taking up a small brass douter that lay next to the crescent moon candlestick. He hesitated a moment, releasing a long, silent breath, then snuffed out the flame.

For a minute or two, he waited at the window. In the darkened glass, his own face had an almost lunar pallor. Eustace proceeded to the kitchen door then, addressing Abel calmly before leaving the room.

'I must attend to one or two matters about the house. You will see to everything here?'

Abel glanced at the window, and then at Eustace. He nodded, briefly and without emphasis. He said nothing.

On the stairs, Clara stumbles. She tries to catch herself, but the fever has coarsened her movements. The steps bite into her ribs, into the tender underside of her outstretched arm. Glancing downwards, she sees Arabella at the foot of the staircase. She has made herself wide-eyed and solicitous. She does not wish to seem hurried.

'Why, Clara, darling – whatever is the matter? Aren't you feeling well?'

Clara rights herself, sitting up to tug off her shoes. She frees one foot, then pushes herself up another four or five steps, still seated. She struggles with the tiny buckle of the other ankle strap, her fingertips blunt and easily thwarted.

Arabella mounts the first step. 'Clara, dear. Come back down. You must tell me what the matter is. We'll fetch some paper from the library.'

The strap gives way. Clara grips the banister and lurches upright, scooping the loosened shoe from her foot. She clutches it for a moment, breathing thickly as she scans the hallway below. For now, no one else is coming.

'My darling, please.' Arabella climbs to the second step, clasping her throat and extending a beseeching arm. Clara tries to wring some sound from herself, some grunt or shriek of rage. The impulse wells uselessly in her nape, but nothing comes. She hurls the shoe. It catches Arabella's thigh and skitters across the tiles.

Then she is turning, lunging up the stairs again. She takes them in twos and threes, slipping again as she nears the first landing, but scrabbling to her feet without stopping. She will not stop again.

*

Eustace pulled off his white gloves as he strode down the passage-way, thrusting them at the porter who stood aside as he passed. He flung the kitchen doors open, startling a scullery boy whose stack of greasy plates slid from his grasp into an empty and echoing sink. A maid paused above the blood-glutted board she had been scrubbing, sleeves bunched at her elbows, fouled soap sliding from her arms.

Alice was at a broad work table, plucking the shreds of meat from a slumped carcass. She wiped her fingertips on her apron.

'There's a racket, Mr Eustace. Whatever's the matter?'

'You,' Eustace said, approaching her. 'You stay. The rest of you, out.'

At first, none of them moved. The maid turned to Alice, her face slack and uncertain. He took up a utensil and examined it. It was a meat tenderiser, a sturdy wooden mallet with a serrated face. He hurled it at a dresser, shattering one plate outright and sending two others crashing to the floor.

'*Out, I said! Out, or you will wish you were never here!*'

When the others had fled, he turned again to Alice. She had re-treated from the work table and was standing now with her back to a sink, holding her forearms upright and looking around for some-thing to clean them with. There was alarm in her face now. Her eyes were alert, evasive. She no longer mistook him.

'Mr Eustace,' she said. 'What's all this about?'

With one foot, he hooked the leg of a chair. He pushed it out into the middle of the tiled floor. 'Sit,' he said.

Without taking her eyes from him, Alice lowered herself onto the chair. Making do with her apron, she worked the clots of grease from between her fingers, the darker, syrupy residues. He paced around her in a slow circuit.

'Mr Eustace, I—'

'There was a telephone call, is that correct?'

He circled her again. Twice. Three times.

'For Mr Chastern, yes—'

'For Dr Chastern.'

'For Dr Chastern, I mean. While you were in the cellar, this was, or I would have left it to you, of course.'

'Of course.' Around her again. 'The telephone rang in the hall, then? And yet you heard it from here?'

'I was in the passageway, Mr Eustace. Goodness, you're like the police. I was in the passageway, on my way from the dining room.'

'I see. And the caller, he or she said what, exactly?'

'He, Mr Eustace. A very well-spoken gentleman. A university man, I suppose, like Dr Chastern. He asked for Dr Chastern, that was all. Said there was something urgent, some college business, and would I be so good as to call him to the telephone.'

Eustace stopped behind her. 'There was nothing else?'

'No, not that I— no, I believe those were his words.'

From an inner pocket, he fished out the twist of wire. Reaching over Alice's shoulder, he dropped it into her lap. 'This will be familiar to you, perhaps.'

She picked it up hesitantly, turned the coil in her lap. 'I'm no good with all these electrics.'

'It is the telephone wire, Alice. It belongs to the telephone in the hall.'

She followed him with her eyes as he circled her, glancing over one shoulder and then the other. 'I don't understand. What have you brought it in here for?'

He leaned towards her ear. 'I brought it here from a drawer in my office, where it has lain these last eight months, since I found it bitten through by mice.'

Her shoulders lapsed. Like her ears, they were flushed and pink. 'Mr Eustace, I don't understand—'

He stepped away, drew his leg back and kicked the chair from beneath her. Alice came down on her hip. With a scandalised gulp of fright, she shunted herself across the tiles.

'There was no telephone call,' he said. 'There have been no telephone calls for eight months, as you might have known, you drooling halfwit, if you had kept your snout from the bottle for even half the day.'

'Mr Eustace, please, I must have made a mistake.'

She worked herself into a corner, between the range and a stack of copper kettles. He lowered himself on one knee in front of her. 'Yes, Alice, you have made a mistake. You have made a grave mistake. And now you will tell me the nature of that mistake, and how it was that you were persuaded to make it. You will tell me everything, and you will do it quickly, before someone comes to harm.'

Alice sobbed. Eustace took her mottled chin between his finger and thumb.

'Did you think you knew me, Alice? You did not, and you do not yet. But understand this. If any harm comes to the child – if she is so much as touched – then you will know me. Then you will come to know me very well.'

The house is coming apart.

The hallways are too long, receding to vanishing distances or folding upon themselves, their geometry all undone. The walls slide in opposite directions, like the rose-patterned hulls of gigantic ships, and the carpet sinks as if laid over a swamp. The shape of everything is wrong, the distances impossible. She cannot reach the ends of things.

It is the heat, Clara thinks. The heat of the fever. The walls are not viscous to the touch, the picture frames not sagging like ropes of molten gilt. But no, it is more than that. She can feel it. Beneath her feet, behind everything, an absence is deepening. Everything she knows, all the quiet and the dust. It is coming apart.

Still she runs, runs or stumbles. On the last landing, she crawls. She is sure of nothing now, trusts nothing to bear her weight. There is no listening now for sounds from below, no turning and looking behind her. She keeps her eyes on her own splayed fingers, on the carpet whose whorled and ancient flora dissolve beneath her knees.

She drags herself the last telescoping yards, grasping at collapsing table legs. When she reaches out, there is nothing. She grasps only the heated and vacant air. The shapes of things are wrong, their lines dog-legged like sticks in water. Like what light does. The bend from true. The colours too are failing, even the whites distended, pulled down the octaves of lesser heat, like the falling away of galaxies.

She slumps near the end, grasps at something but cannot quite. A vase tumbles across her back, and on the floor is broken where her hands. When she. The inside bones of it, the shell of everything gone thin. And a small blood now, the jewel tear. But quiet. What if they. All the broken noise.

In the tower, and still she hears nothing. The scrape of breathing only. The blood mutter dark and constant, her own red noise. In her rusted lung. Her seized-up heart. There is no waiting. Only inside, and she will be safe. In the place behind, the where she kept secret. In the dragon's mouth. If she can just— but it is deeper between the teeth, and harder to— her fingers knit and swell, a tongue in the wrong mouth.

Open. The dark is open at last, and she is. Here is her, in the safe. She is in the cold unseen, in the hidden everything. Here, no one will. She is the only one who. No one will. She could sleep, even. With the small wings dancing, the long-ago music.

She is almost, then. It is somewhere in the near dark, the snakes and ladders. Just a small unclimb to the. It is where she. In the rosewood, her treasures. A small gleam in the locked heart. And sleep then. No long ago, but only now.

'Little one.'

The hands. They are from the other dark. Behind her where she cannot. And how did they, those long fingers. How did he.

'Little one.'

That voice. And held now, so she cannot. Butterfly held, and the crushing heart unwinged.

'Little one, we are going on an adventure.'

Eustace moved without thought.

They had not been in the library. The door was unlocked, but there was no sign that they had entered. He looked for Arabella, but she too had vanished. Later. He would find her later. He would make her answer.

But Clara. Clara.

She was not in her room, or in any of her usual haunts about the house. She might have gone out about the grounds, though it would by now be bitterly cold. She did so often enough, even when nothing troubled her. And she was troubled, of course. All that had changed in these last weeks, the strangers coming. It had unsettled her. He had seen it and done nothing.

Mr Crowe was gone from the dining room. Abel too, though he had given the signal before leaving. Both candles were out now. The sun and the moon.

His office, then. He could go without his overcoat, his hat and gloves. But the item in the locked drawer beneath his desk – he would need it now. He would put it to use if he must. He moved without thought. There was nothing to think about. Nothing was left.

A car, from the stable yard. A car starting.

He was running, hurling himself along the passageway. Skidding at the corner, his shoulder slamming against a wall. Seconds to the stable yard door now. He could do it. He was close enough, could reach the garage. The Jaguar would not be found wanting. Abel had serviced it, and they had locked it away. It could not have been touched. He could do it.

But the door, the door would not give. Not the lock – there was weight against it, he could feel it when he shouldered it, the heft piled low down, like sandbags. He swore again. Brutal words, a thick bolt of them. Words he had not used in years, words from before. Matters were simpler now. Sacrifices must be made.

By the kitchen door, then. It cost him a minute and a half, two minutes maybe. He would make up for it. Leave the locks – he and Abel had used two on the garage door. Leave them, there was no time. With a half-brick from the yard – the crude heft was welcome in his fist – he put the window in, blunted the standing shards. He hauled himself inside.

The ignition flickered only for an instant. With a violent snort, the Jaguar was running. He coaxed the motor to an urgent pitch and reversed it, slamming it against the garage wall. A workbench collapsed in a spill of clattering tools. Paint cans crunched and spat. He felt for first gear, throttled deeply before releasing the clutch. The wheels spun but he clawed for traction, in second gear even as he hit the doors, one arm braced across his eyes. He felt a moment of strain, then the staves burst apart like skittles. The hasp of the lock screeched across the bonnet. The windscreen held.

From the stable yard, he tore across the north lawn. The grey car was on the avenue, a little beyond the fountain and running without lights. If he cut across the grass, kept it flat out, it would put him close. It could be done.

From the house, on his left, he caught a small incision of brightness. The front door open, and Abel running towards him, one arm upraised. His gun was drawn and he limped slightly. Eustace did the reckoning. He could slow for him, but not stop. Let him take his chances.

He dropped from fourth to second, veering out from the shallow curve he had plotted. Leaning over, he thumped open the passenger door. Abel sprinted to close the distance, his injured leg buckling twice. He clamped a hand over the knee to brace it, forced himself upright. When he was close enough, he lunged for the door, scrabbling for grip on the passenger seat. Eustace took hold of his belt and surged back up to speed. By the time Abel bundled his legs in, they were passing the fountain at over sixty.

Eustace glanced at him. The bruise was succulent, lush as an orchid. It spread from cheekbone to temple. Something broad and flat had done it. An iron or the blade of a shovel. He gave him a minute to breathe. 'Where is Mr Crowe? What did you see?'

'They put me out. Never felt nothing. I woke up, he was gone. No one could have done different.'

'You snuffed the candle? The sun?'

'Like we said.'

'And you saw no one else, after you came round?'

'You're the first.'

Eustace said nothing. Ninety. A hundred. He strained forward in his seat, trying to pick out the car in the darkness. There. A narrow scratch of incandescence, then the sound of the shot.

'Those our guests in the car?'

Eustace shook his head. 'Chastern is already gone.'

'How?'

'A butcher's van. He had help – a rat in the kitchen.'

Abel hissed in disgust. 'Well, John's at the gate. He'll put manners on the other one.'

Eustace glanced at him, growing impatient. 'The child is in the car.'

'Eh?'

'*The child*,' he snapped. 'The child, Clara. Have you listened to nothing I said?'

The grey car had come to a halt just short of the gates. Eustace braked and wrenched the wheel, hurling them aside from the avenue. He braced himself hard, sure they would roll, but the back drifted outwards on the frosted grass. For a strange, somnolent moment, there was quiet, then the momentum found them, spun them twice. A young birch stopped them, the rear wing splintering its barely whitened trunk.

John Crouch stood in the avenue, bringing his gun level. It was his warning shot they had heard. Eustace hauled himself out, but Abel could not move. Something held him in the passenger seat.

Eustace shouted, unrestrained. '*John! John, the child is in the car! Clara is in the car!*'

John raised a hand to acknowledge that he had heard. He braced the rifle again, checked his sight. 'The sun and the moon, Mr Eustace. The sun and the moon.'

'Eustace,' Abel called after him. 'My ankle's caught in something. Get me out.'

There was movement from the grey car – the driver's door opening, Nazaire bringing himself slowly upright. He held Clara, his left arm bracing her narrow chest against him. She held her head weakly. Her feet were limp beneath her soiled hem. Eustace felt a breach in himself, a cold insurgence. He drew his own gun.

'We are going on an excursion,' Nazaire said. He did not raise his voice. Not even here, amid all this. His words were addressed to Eustace. 'A little drive. She will be returned, of course, once your master has done as Dr Chastern asks. He has work to do, I believe. A manuscript to deliver.'

John cocked the rifle. 'No one is going nowhere,' he said.

'Eustace,' Abel called again. 'Get me out. This needs all of us.'

Nazaire looked for Eustace, blinking in the Jaguar's headlights. 'Talk to him, Eustace. She is skin and bone, this child. I can feel every rib. The slightest pressure would— well, let us not be uncouth. It will not end well.' He kept his right hand unseen, somewhere close to her.

Clara stirred, hearing his name spoken. Feebly, she lifted her head to search the darkness. From her nose, a stripe of blood crossed her lips, spreading in a grubby delta over her chin. Eustace raised his own gun.

'No one leaves,' he said.

Nazaire sighed and stood clear of the door, keeping Clara pressed to him. He stepped backwards, towards John. 'You are not lucid, Eustace,' he said. 'You will not fire, not with the child between us. Will he? The fat one with the rifle? Perhaps he will.'

'You stay where you are,' said John. 'You stand where you are and you let her go, or I will put you down like a fucking dog.'

Nazaire ignored him, treading carefully backwards. Clara's legs swung helplessly. 'Yes, perhaps he will. He will need no luck,' he said. 'At this range, he could take my head off. But what would happen then? Men move violently as they die. It is electrical, or so I have read. I can feel her every rib, Eustace.'

'You stand fucking still,' said John. 'You said it yourself. I'll take your fucking head off.'

'Eustace,' Nazaire said. 'I was told you were a man of reason. You disappoint me.'

'*Get me out of the fucking car!*' Abel's voice was taut. There was urgency in it, and pain.

Eustace held his gun steady, advanced towards them. 'A man may lose his reason.'

Nazaire lowered his head and gave a long sigh. He took another step backwards, so that his neck almost touched the barrel of John's rifle. Still holding Clara, he pivoted swiftly, lowering himself as he spun and halting slightly, as if wresting himself free of something. As he came fully about, he rose and stepped neatly aside. Behind him, John had lowered the rifle, held it loosely apart from him. He stared down at himself, his expression wondering. The cut was a foot long, and gaped like a pillowslip. From it, his bowels peeked, unspooling in plump tangles. He made to cover the place with his hand, but could not bring himself to touch it. Thicker coils slipped from the wound, their weight unsettling his balance. He shifted on his drenched legs.

Abel screamed and pounded at the window, but Eustace ignored him. He watched Nazaire pick his way back to the car, Clara struggling to twist from his grip, to see over his shoulder. He pinned her more firmly, but she saw. As he folded her into the back seat, she jerked her head free for an instant. She saw.

John sank to his knees, the rifle slipping from him. He looked at Clara – open-mouthed, as if she were an apparition – and at himself again, staring in perplexity at the lush knots that spilled from him.

Clara's mouth gaped. She wrestled from Nazaire's grip as he pulled the door closed, clawing at the roof of the car. He gathered her thin wrists, wrapping them in one hand, and shoved her onto the back seat. He was behind the wheel, and the car was somehow in motion. The door was slammed shut.

Eustace paced rapidly towards the car, the gun raised in his tensed arms. Clara was clear of him now. He need only sight him clearly.

An instant would be enough. But the windows were darkened. The Jaguar's lights made mirrors of them. He saw himself only, shadowed and desperate, his tie coming undone.

The car surged forward, swerving around John. He lowered himself gently to the ground, curling sleepily around the ruins of himself. The lights were turned on only as it reached the gate. Eustace raced towards them, out onto the lane.

He ran for as long as he could see the tail lights. They seemed tauntingly close at first, haloed with drizzle and malignantly red. They slipped from him quickly, though, the gulf of distance deepening beyond crossing. Still he ran, long after running was senseless. He ran until he could no longer separate them, until there was a single mote of radiance that stuttered among the trees and was gone.

II

A Whiteness

Thirteen

The boy comes from nowhere. He comes from the end of the world.

He knows this because his father tells him so. He tells him one morning, when they have gone out into the marshes to fish. For a long time, his father stands without moving, his line a bright curl that lazes on the water. The boy grows restless and tugs at his coat, but his father clips his cheek and sends him running. He has no use for him yet; he must wait until he is called. Climb that tree, his father says, and tell me what you can see.

And so the boy climbs the tree, a willow whose limbs rise in a close splay from among the reeds. He climbs as high as he can, making a seat for himself in the narrow crook of two boughs. From here, he has a clear view in all directions. He looks upstream first. It is winter, and the reeds have the pallor of old parchment. Beyond the marshes, and as far as he can see, the country lies flat under the colourless sky. Nothing rises from it but a scattering of ash trees, a clutch of willows as grey as his own. In the distance, there is nothing.

The boy looks the other way. The town is downstream, but it lies mostly out of sight. Even their home, which is nearby, is hidden by a bend in the river. On the estuary, the wind is up, and close to shore the weather roughens the water. The waves are edged with the clean grey of new ash and darken to the silver of beech bark.

They came to the town because his father is to run the ferry boat. He paid good money to the aldermen for his lease, and he will get his due from it, whatever the men of the town may say. They are fishermen, his father says, and think they are masters of all boats. In truth, they are only farmers in oilskin coats who would not have wits enough to run a ferry boat. They would fill it with mackerel and send it to the bottom.

His father talks often of the men from the town. At night, when the boy has been put to bed, he raises his voice and slams his mug down on the table. They do not trust strangers in this town, his father says. They are superstitious, and know no more of the world than savages. They spend their time out at sea, talking to mermaids and Dutchmen; they must have four or five sons each when they might keep one alive by teaching him to swim.

The boy has heard such things many times. He doubts that the fisherman have spoken to a real mermaid, but he believes the rest. He is a stranger now too. Every day, in the small schoolroom above the excise office, he is asked where he comes from. He is asked his name, and he gives the one his mother chose. They laugh at him and call him a pansy. It is no name for a boy, they tell him. Have they no boys' names where you come from?

'Where do I come from?' The boy repeats the question to his father.

'This is where you come from now,' his father says. He gestures towards the town with his free hand, keeping himself otherwise still. He keeps very still when he is fishing. 'We have made our home in this place, though some don't like it. You come from here now, you may tell them.'

The boy looks towards the town again, where those houses that can be seen are crouched and drab among the fading reeds. 'But what is it called?'

'This place?' His father glances up at him. 'Ask your mother, she'll tell you.'

The boy looks towards their house, not understanding. His father gives a low laugh.

'The end of the world, she says. This place is the end of the world.'

In the evenings, when Eleanor has settled in her crib and his father is still on the river, the boy sits with his mother at the kitchen table. She is skilled in dressmaking, and comes by a little work in the mending of clothing and oddments. It is a low occupation, she says, and hardly worth her trouble for the pennies it brings in. There is better work, sometimes, making blouses and fine gowns for the few ladies of the town who can afford such things, and this she keeps aside for the evenings.

The boy spreads his primer before him on the oilcloth. While he reads aloud from that day's lesson, his mother opens the lacquer workbox in which her sewing things are kept. The bobbins of thread are neatly arrayed by their affinity of colour, and little cushioned compartments keep every thimble and pair of scissors in its proper place. She is watchful even while she is about her work, and chides him if his attention falters. Still, he is often distracted, his eye drawn especially to the silks and laces his mother uses, to the intricate gauzes and lavish velvets. The richness of these materials seems extraordinary to him, next to the plainness of their home and belongings.

His mother was used to such fine things at one time, and does not find them strange. She knows their proper names, and how to judge their quality. She bargains ably with the draper, though he is well established in his trade, and the boy has heard her complain of his ignorance. Half of what she needs for the better garments, she says, cannot even be had in this place.

Though she seldom speaks of the life she knew as a girl, the boy's mother abides by certain customs. She keeps a small garden outside the kitchen door, though she says it is a bad place for it, for the plot is full of silt and given to flooding. Still, she has made something of it. She grows herbs there, and a rose plant she brought with them when they came here. Its flowers are the colour of cream, welling from a small pinkness like the corner of an eye. Once, when the river was in spate, half of all she had planted was swept away in the night. It is a curse and a nuisance, she says, but she will not give it up. She has few enough consolations in this place.

On summer evenings, the boy is free of schoolwork and his mother has fewer commissions to occupy her. From the garden, they gather petals for rosewater. When they have filled a shallow basket, they crush the petals in tender fistfuls before dropping them into a pan of simmering water. When it has been passed through muslin, the rosewater is set out to cool, and the scent that rises from it threads every part of the air.

It is a fragrance that seems to the boy to belong elsewhere, and it is entwined with his faint images of his mother's childhood home. She has told him only a little, but he knows that she lived in a house with a piano, and that there was a sitting room where two birds were kept in a golden cage. She was not sent to school, as he is, but was taught at home by a lady with a small dog.

'It is strange,' he says as he breathes it in. 'It makes me think of other places.'

She looks at him for a moment, her head inclined to one side. 'Then you must remember how it is made,' she says at last, 'so that you may keep some by, and have it always – for you must always think of other places.'

Later, while she waits for his father to return, the boy is sent to his small cot by the range. He lies awake for as long as he can, and together they listen to the sounds that remain. There is the thin song, now and then, of the sandpipers on the marshes. There is the slow disturbance of the fragrant water, and beneath that always the deeper labouring of the river.

If it is late and his father is not yet home, she sings to him sometimes to send him to sleep. Her voice is not strong, but it is pure and warm. It has a way of filling the air without disturbing it. He turns to face the wall and pulls the blankets over himself, closing his eyes so that the world recedes from him. There is a softening of all he knows and remembers. Things come unfast from their proper places and come to seem other than they are. He may see the boys from his school, but perched in the willow tree. They call him names and tell him to go home to the mermaids. His father catches them with his fishing rod, and tosses them one by one into the near-black river.

He and his father drift home on the skiff, floating into the house through the open window. They find a well in the middle of the kitchen that his father says should not be there. It must be knocked down, he says, and goes to fetch his tools. While he is gone, the boy leans over the lip of the well and looks in. On the surface of the water, far below, are rose petals and crushed herbs. His mother's voice rises from the deep, swirling in the dark, scented air. Before he knows what he is doing, he has climbed over the lip of the well and finds that he is held by nothing, that he is falling. It is a strange, slow kind of falling and the boy is not frightened. He falls and falls, the song rising about him, and he is not afraid of reaching the bottom. He waits for the emptying shock of cold, for the dark water to close over his skin.

*

One evening in August, the boy goes out with his father after supper. He is older now, and the way his father talks to him has changed. There is something he wants the boy to see. He follows him along the shore to the ferry house, struggling at times to keep up. His father is in high spirits and strides eagerly ahead.

On the slip before the ferry house is a new boat, much larger than the old skiff. His father has been putting money by, he explains, though he expected to bide his time a year or two longer. It was no more than luck that he came by this one. A passenger he carried one morning had been in the same trade, a Company waterman thirty years on the Thames. A palsy had afflicted him that put him off the river. He was dissatisfied with his pension, and bore a grudge against the guildsmen. He wished to see the boat go to a man from out of the city, a man who was beholden to no Company and paid his own way. He did him no favours with the price, but that was no crime in one whose living was gone. He did enough in letting the boat go out of town.

His father moves around the dark hull as he talks. He hauls away tarpaulins and brushes at flakes of creosote. He will have room enough for eight passengers, he says, or for two men and their horses. Even the farmers bringing their animals to market will come to him now, unless they are fond of the eight miles they must drive the cattle to the bridge. This boat will establish them, his father says, no matter who in the town might begrudge it. It will put him in the way of handsome money too. They will live in a better style than they have put up with until now. On Saturdays, the boy will have sixpence of his own to do with as he pleases. He will have the price of a silk ribbon for his sweetheart.

As his father talks, the sun sinks beyond the reeds. The water is sluggish and glazed with amber. Midges throng the unmoving air.

It comes to him that he will not be going back to school, that this is what his father is telling him. He touches the boat himself, twisting a fine splinter from the stern. His father lays a hand on his wrist, for a moment only, and the warmth of it is coarse and sure.

The news causes him no particular sadness. He will not miss the schoolroom, or the children of the town. He is a stranger among them still. When the day's lessons are over, they disperse in twos and threes to fish for dab or flounder. They hunt for birds' eggs in the hour of liberty before they are wanted at home. He no longer asks if he may go along.

His mother makes him practise his letters still. She gives him verses to learn, on scraps of paper that she wraps up with his bread and cheese. He is helping his father for as long as he is needed, she says, but he must not think it is to be his life. The boy does his best, but they no longer have the time for lessons that they once did. It is Eleanor who occupies his mother's evenings now, for she has long outgrown her crib. She is a sweet-natured and curious child, always chattering somewhere in her mother's wake. She sleeps now in the small cot by the range that was once his, and there is no hour of the day or night when the house is entirely quiet.

He is put to light work at first. The luggage is too heavy for him still, and he must find his river legs before he can be taught to pole the boat. At dawn, when the river is streaked with lavender and steel, he and his father make their way along the bank to the ferry house. There is a sanctity in this first quiet passage of the day; neither of them speaking needlessly, each still half sunk in the secrecy of sleep.

While his father checks the caulking and readies the strongbox for the takings, the boy sets to scrubbing the decks and thwarts. There can be no muck or bird soil in any place where a passenger might sit or lay a hand. Elsewhere, to keep it from taking in water, he rubs the wood with pine tar and turpentine. The mixture has a smell unlike anything he has known. There is a fierce, resinous sweetness to it, and beneath that a dingy musk that makes him think of railway yards and sawmills, of tanneries and quayside inns. It is the smell of rough work, of the places where only men gather.

It stays close to him for days, banishing all other scents. He can no longer tell, in the evenings, when his mother has been making her rosewater. The boy's bed now is in the small lobby between the kitchen and the garden. Eleanor has taken to sleepwalking, and at night he props his bed against the garden door to keep her from wandering from the house. Even here, with the roses beneath the open window, he can smell nothing but the coarse odours that cling to him from his work.

He learns to tie up the boat, to jump to the pier as his father brings the stern around, looping the lines swiftly around the pilings so that the boat will not be brought up too hard. When they are moored, he sees the passengers ashore, then guides those waiting aboard. If a lady is nervous, he will hold the line taut to close the gap. He will offer her his forearm to steady her as she climbs down. The gesture is less familiar than putting out his hand, which is seldom entirely clean. Some ladies will refuse his assistance no matter how it is offered, but most take it gratefully enough. Some tell him he is a fine young man, and whisper to their husbands that he must have a penny for himself on the far bank.

One morning, Alderman Swaine is crossing with his wife and two nieces. Swaine is harshly spoken and contemptuous, and it is said that he has put more than one man in the churchyard in coming by his wealth. Still, his is one of the town's handful of fine families, and Lucy and Eliza are spoken of as great beauties who will marry well beyond this place. They are travelling to London, a journey few in the town have the means or reason to undertake, and are outfitted with great elegance. The coach that awaits them on the other side is Swaine's own, sent ahead of them by the longer road that they themselves would be spared.

When they have been settled and their bags and boxes stowed, the boy frees the lines from the pier. He takes his place in the bow with an easy leap as his father pushes off. His task, for most of the crossing, is to watch the water ahead. This stretch of river is restless and shallow. The currents shift ceaselessly, stirring new masses up from the bed and gouging channels where before there were none. In the mornings, especially, it is common for them to find a new spit of sand, lying across a course they plotted through clear water the evening before.

His eyes must be unresting, skimming every part of the surface, reading it for signs of what is hidden beneath. Where it is freely running, there is an ease and delicacy to the forms it makes, the water coursing in supple ribbons, gathering in gentle braids and pleats. What he looks for are deeper disturbances, where the current meets some hindrance and builds in slow and unseen coils. In such places, the surface bears other marks – flexing rucks, deep and knife-bright creases – or is pulled as taut and innocent as kidskin.

The boy has learned vigilance, and does not forget himself. Still, he cannot keep from looking back at the passengers. Alderman Swaine and his wife have seated themselves so as to face the stern, but Lucy and Eliza are side by side on an opposite thwart, talking in low but excited voices. They are sixteen or seventeen, he guesses – older than him by some years – and have the appearance of creatures no closer to his own kind than mermaids.

They are dressed, beneath their travelling cloaks, in richer fabrics than even his mother can have seen, in gauzes and silks as exotic as the bodies of dragonflies. About their wrists and at the margins of their skin are intricate adornments of lace, and these in turn are constellated with tiny pearls. It is not only their clothes that captivate him. They themselves seem fashioned with a delicacy that is not ordinary.

It is to Lucy, though, that his gaze returns most often. He has never seen such tender skin. It is like the tissue of a new blossom, something that has been kept safe even from the light. His urge to look at her is like nothing he has felt before. When he tries to summon a need that matches it, he can think only of thirst, of ice in muslin pressed against fevered skin. But it is not like either of these things, not truly. They come to him only because she is as bright and perfect as water.

She glances up, and he looks quickly away. Her face, in the instant before he turns back to the river, is not disdainful or mocking. There is a puzzlement, perhaps, in the press of her lips, but her eyes are merely alert, even amused. At the edge of his vision, he sees her lean towards Eliza and speak to her behind her sleeve. They whisper intimately, coming together in a glistening confluence of laughter. Alderman Swaine and his wife shift in their seats to look for its cause. The boy fixes his eyes on the far bank, the heat climbing in his cheeks.

Their amusement passes soon enough, and the passengers fall silent. The boy's attention is drawn by something in the water ahead. He motions to his father to slow their progress. He keeps still as they approach it, saying nothing until he is sure, then calls back for a change in their course. It is a mound of slag, dumped onto a sand-bar by a coal boat. Her crew were obliged to take it on, he guesses, by some foreman at a forge or a shipyard. They cursed him, most likely, and kept it aboard only until they were out of sight. There is no telling how much more is piled beneath the waterline, or in which direction the spill lies. To be sure of clearing it, they must go downstream, following a channel alongside the bank until they reach deeper water and can push back to their favoured course.

In this more open water, they are alert and hushed. It is further downstream than they like to cross, and the poles must be driven deeper to find purchase. They feel the breeze more keenly here, and must work harder against it to right the boat. The boy and his father are quiet and watchful, only sparse words of warning or guidance passing between them. When they can, they signal changes in speed and bearing with their hands. It is quicker and surer, and does not alarm the passengers.

It is some minutes before they round the downstream end of the sandbank. The Swaines too have fallen silent, noticing the change in course or sensing that there is some unspoken concern. He wonders if Lucy is watching him at his work. It is very far beneath her own occupations, no doubt, but he is showing himself capable. He is keeping her safe.

Behind him there is a soft exclamation of distress. He snaps around in time to see Lucy's pale blue hat scud clear of the starboard side and settle on the water. He watches it to see what the current will do. If it has come down on fast water, it will be gone in moments. Lucy rises from her seat, her eyes wide with alarm. The breeze prises a gap beneath its brim, and the hat tumbles a little further away, but the water beneath it seems still enough. It is a pool, most likely, in the lee of a wide spit.

The boy raises a hand and the boat slows to a halt. His father would not normally think of stopping for such slight cause, but for the Swaines he must show willing. 'It may be lost, miss,' his father says. 'We've no pole long enough to fish it back.'

Lucy raises her fingertips to her throat. 'It is my very best hat,' she says. 'Even the flowers are silk. What shall I wear to Covent Garden?'

'Such empty-headed nonsense,' says Alderman Swaine. 'Did I not say that you had no business wearing such things while travelling?

If it had not come off here, it would have come off on the road and been trampled by the horses.'

Lucy sinks to her seat. A blush has risen on her neck, and in her anxiety she pushes out her lip, exposing a lush sliver of its inner surface. The boy stares at her for a long moment, and the impulse that comes to him cannot be governed. He stands on the gunwale, tenses himself and dives. He hears his father shout something, but it is cut off as he breaks the surface. The water is brutally cold, but he is swimming before it grips him. He judged the current rightly, and the going is not hard. It could have been otherwise, he knows, and his father will have something to say about his foolishness.

He reaches the pool in thirty strokes or so. On the way back, his progress is slower because he makes do with one arm. With the other, he keeps the hat awkwardly aloft, unsure of how such a thing should be held. He feels strangely apologetic, though he has gone to such trouble to rescue it, as if in touching such a precious and intimate possession, he has trespassed so far that no effort or kindness can redeem him.

He hauls himself aboard and dries himself as well as he can with one of the flour sacks that are offered to passengers as rough cushions. Wordlessly, his father passes him his own coat. As the boy puts it on, his father shakes his head and sends a pulse of spit out across the water. When he has governed his shivering enough to hold it steady, he carries the hat to where she sits. There is silence as he approaches. Alderman Swaine watches him with bladed eyes, a thick hand clamped over his jowls. The girls' faces are intent, disbelieving. In Lucy's, there is gratitude, he thinks, but it is guarded and uncertain. It is as if he has accomplished a miracle that is stained somehow with disgrace.

As the boy draws near to where they sit, Alderman Swaine holds out his cane. It is heavy and ornate, with a polished ferrule at its tip.

'Leave it there, boy,' he says. 'I shall hand it to her. We don't want you dripping all over their gowns to add to the day's calamities.'

The boy stops short and looks down. The tip of the cane is inches from his chest. He covers it carefully with the hat and takes a step back. Lucy regards her uncle with horror, but he passes the hat to her by the same means and she accepts it without protest. As she takes its sodden brim in her hands, she looks again at the boy. He is much closer to her now. Her eyes are like nothing he has ever seen.

'For shame, Charles,' Mrs Swaine says. 'What will they say of us? The boy is half dead from the cold. You will be civil, Mister, and give him a shilling for his trouble.'

'I'll do no such thing,' says Alderman Swaine. 'For that price, we might have bought the girl a new hat altogether. I'll not be held liable for every lunatic child that jumps into a river. He may have thruppence, and no more about it.'

'Thank you, sir, ma'am.' The boy is speaking before he had thought of doing so. The cold presses his chest. His voice is weak and constricted. 'I am obliged to you, but your fares have been paid.'

He glances again at Lucy. 'Miss,' he says, and lowers his head briefly. He takes his place again in the bow, though the cold has seized him with force and he must clamp his hands on the sides to keep himself steady. He scans the water again, straining to regather his wits. The boat drifted a small way while he was in the water, and he takes a moment to regain his bearings. He gives a deep, sodden cough and loosens his voice in his chest. He raises a hand to signal his father. 'Ten or fifteen more as we were,' he calls back. 'Then about to port.'

There is a slight lurch as his father releases the poles bracing them in position. Then they are away again. Before him, the estuary spreads seaward, gilded in the rising morning. It widens in seams and flukes of brightness to the open water, where the light is an obliterating scatter of white gold that forces him to look away.

*

It is Easter when the boy next sees her. He leaves the house early, intending at first to fetch his rod and line from the boathouse. The morning is peaceful, though, and he wanders only a little way along the river road before finding a place to sit in the shade of an ash tree.

He watches the water for a while, but finds that he cannot do so and remain at ease. He has spent too long searching its surface for the signs of danger. Instead, he takes from his pocket the last verse his mother pressed on him. It catches something in him, this poem, and he is so absorbed in it that he hears the girls approaching only when they are almost upon him.

They are returning from church, strolling at leisure in the company of a lady who keeps a little way behind them. He fixes his eyes on the small scrap of notepaper; his mother uses carefully quartered pages, so as not to waste whole sheets, and chooses verses that will fit. The boy stares at the lines, seeing nothing. He waits for them to pass him by. Though his Sunday clothes are scarcely different from those he wears on the boat, he has it in his head that he will not be recognised.

'There, you see,' Eliza exclaims. 'It *is* him, Lucy. I am seldom wrong about faces, you know.'

The boy looks up. Getting to his feet, he takes his cap off, as much to conceal what he is holding as to show the ladies courtesy. He ought to offer some words of greeting, but he can think of none that seem adequate.

'How shy he is,' says Eliza. 'You must tell us your name, young man, for we never learned it, you know. Lucy and I you know already, and this is Miss Avery. She has just returned from Lausanne, where she was engaged by a very fine family, until their terrible loss. What was it, Miss Avery, that poor little Amelia died of?'

'A wasting disease, Miss Eliza.'

'A wasting disease, yes, of course. Isn't it unbearably sad? Poor, poor Amelia. And now Miss Avery is going to teach us French, and all the most exquisite pieces by Schubert. Do you know Schubert? Oh, but I'm forgetting – you were about to introduce yourself.'

The boy looks away, squinting in the direction of the town. He mutters his name.

'How charming and unusual,' Eliza says. 'And quite befitting a young hero. He dove into the freezing current, Miss Avery, just to rescue Lucy's hat. Didn't he, Lucy? And we never had the opportunity of thanking him.'

The boy glances at her, at Lucy. The hat she wears now is a pale rose colour, held in place by a ribbon of cream satin. She puts her hand to her face as she speaks, to check a slip of hair that the wind has caught. It is a moment before the boy makes sense of the words.

'What is it you are reading?'

'Miss?'

'You were reading something as we approached. I expect it's a love letter.'

Love. Her lips part as she speaks the word, and her tongue darts for an instant beneath her teeth, glistens and recedes.

'*Un billet-doux*,' says Eliza with satisfaction. Miss Avery gives a brief and embarrassed smile.

'It's a poem,' the boy says.

'How perfectly romantic he is,' Eliza says. 'Who wrote it?'

'My mother.'

Behind her silk glove, Eliza's face crumples with laughter. Lucy glances sternly at her. 'May I read it?' she asks him. 'If it isn't private, I mean. I should very much like to.'

The boy uncovers the piece of notepaper, stowing his hat under his arm. He smooths it out on his palm, and for a moment he is uncertain.

'Perhaps we ought to leave you in peace,' says Lucy. 'We must seem terribly rude.'

'No, please— here, do take it. I don't know if it's a good poem. It seems so to me.' He passes it to her, fumbling as her gloved fingers touch his. He takes a step backwards, looking away as she reads.

'Bright star—' Lucy hesitates, as if surprised by some intimacy in the words. 'Would I were as steadfast as thou art.'

'Keats, I believe,' says Miss Avery with a gentle cough. 'It is by John Keats.'

Lucy scans the rest. Her lips move now and then as she reads. Unthinkingly, she thumbs her wrist, as if in search of her own pulse.

'The moving waters at their priestlike task,' she says aloud. 'That is a strange thing to put, though it has a delightful sound. *Are* they priestlike, do you think? You must know them very well, after all.'

The boy reflects for a moment. 'Sometimes they are,' he says. 'But they're like all kinds. That's the way, with the river. It can be like anything.'

Lucy considers this. 'I expect you're right,' she says. 'May I keep it, this poem? It's so very lovely, and your mother has such a pretty hand. But, of course, if it's precious to you—'

'Please,' the boy says. 'Please, it's yours.'

'Well, it was very pleasant to make your acquaintance,' Miss Avery interrupts, 'but I do think we ought to start for home.' She returns to the road, where she turns to see if the girls are following. Eliza links Lucy's arm and begins to lead her away.

'Goodbye, then,' Lucy calls to him. 'And thank you, though I really ought to thank you twice. I shall treasure your gift.'

'Honestly, Lucy,' Eliza says. 'How very forward you are. Isn't she, Miss Avery?'

They take a few more steps, and Lucy turns again. 'We shall look forward to seeing you on our next crossing,' she says. 'We must hope for priestlike waters.'

Eliza puts up a parasol, so that Lucy is half in shadow. Still, for as long as she can be seen, the boy stands and watches. He worries at his wrist, in imitation of her habit, feeling for the knot of quickness, the hidden seam of heat.

The summer brings a run of flood tides. On the third night, the boy and his father haul the boat all the way up the slip and into the ferry house. It takes them an hour and a half, all told, and will cost them the same again in the morning. Better that, his father says, than to find it has been carried out to sea trailing half the pier.

The boy stays behind when his father leaves for home. The lines must all be retied for high water, and will need more oil in case they are lying under. If he does not finish tonight, he will sleep in the boat and rise early. His father teases him. It is some little miss from the town, he says, who is coming to oil his rope. There is some more hospitable place, surely, to bring her courting.

The boy says nothing, and his father leaves him be. He is content, the boy thinks, to see him stay. He takes it as a sign that he is settling to the work, that he is coming to see the worth of what will pass to him. His father is seeing only what he wishes to, though the boy says nothing to contradict him.

The work has a simplicity, it is true, a smooth grain of purpose that gives ease to his thoughts. It keeps his mind from prospects that can only taunt him. Though he finds a quietness in the ferry house that he now finds nowhere else, he makes no other use of it, whatever his father may think. He spends his nights there alone, not courting. There is no one who comes from the town. The one he wishes for will not come.

He keeps his thoughts from her when he can, though they come to him sometimes with a force that cannot be suppressed. Against the dreams, too, he is helpless. When the dreams come, it is better that he is not in his narrow bed in the lobby. He fears what he might say while he sleeps, the secrets that might slip from him.

He works at the lines until his arms ache. He takes a small supper of bread and mackerel, then lies awake and listens to the river. When a swell is coming, there is a change in the music of the water. The notes are deeper, and strain against each other. Its pulse is slow but unresting. His sleep, when it comes, seems shallow at first, but envelops him wholly. There is nothing then, or he does not know what comes.

When he wakes, a little after dawn, he pulls aside his rough cover of sacking and looks down with unease at his own body. He feels strained and soiled, as if he was about some rough work even while he slept. He dresses wearily and goes out onto the slip.

Already, the day carries the promise of heat, but for now the air is cool enough. He crouches at the edge of the water to wash. It rose again during the night, and the bank is strewn with the small things that were carried in the surge. He walks idly along the shore, lifting odd pieces of flotsam with his toe. Most of it is worthless; shreds of net and boat timbers smashed to kindling, rusted spoons and gutted purses, a ravaged and tongueless boot. He finds a silver comb that will polish up well, half hidden beneath a splayed razor shell.

As he stands and slips the comb into his pocket, his eye is caught by something a little way ahead. From a dense stand of reeds that juts out into the river, a nap of pinkish cloth spreads out onto the sand. The boy saunters towards it to see if the fabric is serviceable. He has been taught to put such things to use, even if it is only as rags.

He is mid-stride, nearing the reeds, when he slackens and halts, a coldness blooming beneath his ribs. Behind the rough stalks it has snagged on, the cloth is rucked over a pale spindle of flesh. It is a child's leg, thrust oddly askew. The boy urges himself onwards, though something bitter seeps into his muscles. His movements are cramped and lurching. His father has found bodies more than once. He will not tell him that he saw this and turned away. His life is on the river now, and the river brings such things.

The body lies almost entirely on the shore. Only the heel and ankle of one leg are still submerged. The limbs are bluish but unswollen. It was not under for long, the boy thinks. The face is concealed by the clotted tangle of the child's hair, and by the silt that has gathered on the upstream side. He will not look, he tells himself, until he has lifted her. He will wash the filth from her and carry her to the ferry house. He will cover her for decency, and to ease the shock when they come to see her.

He crouches above her and braces himself. He drives his arms into the yielding muck beneath her back and lifts her free of the reeds. He walks slowly and looks straight ahead, her faint weight pressed against his chest. Her limbs are stiffening and will not lie easily across his arms. He staggers twice, his breathing coarse and urgent, but forces himself onwards. He tugs the ruined hem over her frail knees.

He does not look, not at her face. He does not look because there is no need. He knows her small shape and her fading colours. He knows the nightgown that was made from offcuts. It is ruffed at the wrists and adorned at the hem with a simple pattern of flowers. His mother thought first of roses, but Eleanor pleaded for daisies. Daisies were always her favourite.

Fourteen

Whiteness.

Only
whiteness, all this time.

Such a long, deep time to be. In a taken world, and all the bright things gone. To hold like this, in touchless waiting. Such a long time. Hard even to feel, lying like this. All faraway, ungathered. With the other always, quiet and coiled under. Remember it. The clutched, red thing, the careful hurt.

Breathing small to gentle it.

It is night, the first time.

Dark too, the pain, while she is still. Dark rust. She knows it, all its colours. The voice of it, the scritch and split. She remembers.

Not yet. Wait for light, for seeing. Wait.

The snow. She sees it first, sees nothing else. Some whitened place. A spread of hushed fields, shaded oyster near the sky. The clean falling, a throng of smudges. Quiet air, and everything edgeless.

She sees, in the morning. She begins to see.

The room first, all that whiteness. And the bedclothes. The blankets are a sickish colour. Whey or old wheat. Bones in weather.

She looks at her fingers, their weak stirring. At her arm, a sallow stalk in its cowl of cotton. The threads of veins, the hollows. And at her wrist, a garland of bruises. The colours tender somehow. Like sweet peas.

Waking again, she finds changes in the room. Couldn't miss them, in all this bareness. The blank, limewashed stones. The landscape, uncurtained. No softness anywhere, or ornament. The room as white and empty as the fields.

Two armchairs have been set out before the vacant fireplace. A small table draped with a simple cloth. At its centre, there is a slender vase. A single rose, though even that is white. And water. Near the edge, there is a glass of water.

She moves without thinking. Some quick urge stirs her. It is only a little. An inch or so, and only on one side. But the pain, all at once. It blazes, flares from hiding. Her arm, still beneath the covers, glows in it like an iron.

She sinks back in it, in the flooding heat, and she can't. It is too much. A lightness comes. A drift.

She tries again. But not like before. Not the way she remembers: sitting up, pushing the covers aside, swinging out her legs. Rising to her feet. No thinking in it. Her limbs fluid, her body as simple as water. But not now. She can't, can't move like that. There are spaces in her, intervals that her intentions will not cross. Parts of her have gone dark.

She searches herself, for the untouched places. Slowly, gently. She maps herself, in small throbs. In flickers. She finds other ways. Threads the maze.

She must turn first, so that she is face down. This will be easiest. She can rest again, afterwards. If it is dreadful, the pain, she can lie still. A reward. But it is slow, so slow. She guards her useless arm, and can't roll the way she wants. She levers herself instead, pries herself onto her side. She cradles the injury, letting her weight take her over.

She is not face down, when it is done, but wedged against the wall. She has kept her right arm shielded, but must work it now from under her. She is careful, shunting first her hips and then her shoulders, but she is too weak. She feels it happening. And the pain again, the completeness of it. The blunt incandescence, trapped beneath her. Everything else gone.

She lies still at the edge of the bed. She is afraid now, afraid to move. When it passes, the agony, she will sleep. The thirst will be worse, when she wakes again, but she will wait. She will sleep again, keep sleeping. Until it stops.

But it is not sleep that comes, only a fading. The greyness again, like spent weather. She watches the wall, the changes in the light. Dreams come to her, or half-dreams. Shapes tread the air, pale as watermarks. A whispering quickens to noise. She lets the day darken, thinks of nothing. And it fades, the pain. Slowly, just enough.

She moves, the tiniest increment, then stops. She pants in fear, waiting for new pain. But nothing comes, nothing yet. She starts again, pivots on her hips; a fraction, not even an inch. Still nothing. Again, and stop. Again. She reaches the edge of the bed. She tries to be careful, to ease one leg over first, but feels them both slide. Like a foal, veiled and helpless, spilling from a mare. She almost laughs.

She waits again, feels pins and needles. A swarm of stray heat. She tests the muscles in patient sequence. She tenses, flexes. Hardens them against the numbness. She works her left hand under her chest and spreads her fingers. Carefully, in small and graded urges. She pushes herself up.

It surprises her, at first. The ease of it. She judged it rightly. Her weight is square above the floor. She strains outwards, keeps the pressure small. Attends to her momentum. Not too much, or it will carry her too far. She will come back too hard. Down on the arm. She cannot think of it, of the pain.

She does it by eighths, by sixteenths. The slightest nudges. Until she stands, upright at last. Draws her left hand from the bed. Delicately, rocking slightly on her feet. Finding the centre, the equilibrium. She waits for it, waits to be sure, still trying her weight. She turns then, towards the room. Takes a shuddering step.

And does not lurch, does not fall.

She takes a breath. Sways slightly, snakes her arm out. Waits for balance. Another step then. And another. She reaches the end of the bed, lets herself pause. The glass is there still, on the table by the vase. It was not a mirage, something dreamed by her thirst.

Gently, so gently. Like urging a paper boat across a pond. She pushes herself, outwards and away, steps forward. It is wonderful, for a moment. Just to stand free, to move.

For a moment, then she feels it going. She is unstrung, slackening to dissonance. Her body is distant, a long ago faintness. Where there was heat once, was starlight.

Her head is slam the dark taste.

Nothing nothing nothing.

She feels him in the room even before she is fully awake. He has been close to her in darkness before, next to her without her knowing, but that can no longer happen. He was the beginning of this. In the dragon's mouth, in the dark. He was the splintering, the red cataract of pain. He was the rope.

Clara opens her eyes. She is in the bed again, lying on her back. There are pillows beneath her, raising her slightly. Her right arm has been dressed with bandages and bound in a sling. The pain has dimmed to a dormant ache. Her throat feels abraded and tender, but the thirst has eased.

He was this too. He did all this. He bound her arm while she slept. He made her drink somehow, gave her something. She wants to retch herself clean. She wants to stitch her lips closed.

'Little one,' he says. 'You seem always to find a way to come to harm.'

He has arranged himself in one of the armchairs by the fireplace. A fire has been lit, and its glow touches the edges of his dark clothes. She turns her face to the wall.

'Dr Chastern was most concerned,' Nazaire says. 'We have done what we could to make you comfortable while you slept. You will find, I hope, that the pain is less. If it returns, you must let me know. I will give you something for it.'

Clara does not move. She stares at the whitewashed stones. She tries to think of nothing.

'You are distrustful still,' he continues. 'It is forgivable. I regret that such force was needed, but I assure you that I did only what was necessary. We are not such monsters, little one. You will see that, now that you are to be our guest. You will be offered every kindness. In return, we ask only that you too behave with civility, and that you observe certain rules.'

She tries to lie perfectly still, to give no sign that she has heard. But his voice. She cannot keep it out, cannot stay empty. She is there again, on the back seat. Eustace runs at the car, his face gone white and hard. And John. John Crouch on the ground, bending to touch where he is undone, where he is spilling.

'In time,' Nazaire says. 'In time you will come to forget. And there will be time, you know. You will be with us for some time.'

There is a soft scrape as he rises from his chair. Clara watches the quick seep of his shadow as he crosses to her bedside. His footsteps are purposeful, unhurried. She hears him set something down.

'We brought a nightstand,' he says, 'so that you may keep things within your reach while your strength returns. There is water now.'

The footsteps retreat again. He does not return to his chair, but continues towards the door. He stops for a moment. Clara takes slow and shallow breaths. When Nazaire speaks again, it is in his softest voice. She feels it against her nape, like the wings of a moth.

'No more accidents, little one,' he says.

The snow has stopped falling, though it lies heavily on the ground. Now that she is raised a little in the bed, Clara has a better view. It is high country, a whitened moorland massed under a hushed sky. A march of dark pines crosses one flank, but the higher ground is otherwise sombre and featureless. On the lower slopes, if she strains her neck a little, Clara can see blanketed fields, the shadowy knit of crouching hedgerows. No roads are visible from where she lies. She sees no sign of dwellings, of other living souls.

The water glass at her bedside is replaced while she sleeps. Clara drains it, though it repulses her to take anything he has touched. There is sugar in the water, she thinks, something that is meant to restore her strength. She wakes for longer now, for hours at a time. She watches a pair of buzzards, scoring the vacant air in long, clean arcs. She begins to feel hungry.

Nazaire comes again. This time, he brings food. He sets a tray on the table before the fireplace and lifts the cover from a soup plate.

The smell reaches Clara almost instantly. She turns away again, clutching her stomach to silence it.

He approaches the bed with the soup. 'You must eat,' he says. 'We brought you here only to demonstrate our convictions to your guardian. We intend to treat you well.'

It is chicken broth, Clara thinks. There is a delicacy to the aroma too, a thread of fragrance. Tarragon, and sweet bay.

'Come,' says Nazaire. 'You do not like me. You think I am not your friend. Perhaps you will come to think differently of me, perhaps not. But I am afraid you must tolerate my presence. It will be me who sees to your needs, while you are here. Come, you must eat.'

Clara turns slowly and looks up at him. He is elegantly dressed, as always. He has folded a napkin over one arm in a way that reminds her of Eustace. He holds the soup plate on one upturned palm, his arm unfailingly steady. With the other hand, he half-fills a spoon. He dabs its underside on the napkin, then holds the spoon to Clara's lips.

'You must eat,' he says.

The silver handle gleams in his smooth fingers. He was the hidden hand. He was the knife.

She opens her mouth very slightly. In her chest, there is a choking coil of panic. She tries to slow her breathing. She closes her eyes and feels him rest the warm blade of the spoon on her lower lip, feels the broth spread over her tongue. The spoon is taken away. Clara closes her mouth and opens her eyes.

Nazaire has withdrawn the spoon and is waiting, alert and patient, for her to swallow. His hands are entirely still. She cannot see even the flicker of his pulse. She takes a sharp breath. With all the force she can summon, she spits the soup at his face.

It is a thin broth, and only weakly coloured. Most of it, she thinks, has spattered over his collar, though some reaches his ear and hangs from the lobe in a glutinous thread. His stillness is almost undisturbed. Setting the soup on the nightstand, he takes a handkerchief from his pocket and unfolds it. It is starched and spotless, bearing a discreet monogram in one corner. With unhurried care, he blots his skin and clothing. He shows no more agitation than if he had spilled soup over himself.

When he has cleaned himself, he folds away the handkerchief. He takes up the soup plate again and brings the spoon to her lips.

'Little one,' he says. 'You know you must.'

The next day, Clara eats by herself. When Nazaire brings her soup, accompanied this time by a small piece of bread and butter, she shakes her head and points at the nightstand. He sets the food down and takes a step backwards, watching without comment. Since she cannot hold the plate, she leaves the soup on the nightstand, reaching out with the spoon and lifting each mouthful laboriously to her lips. She is weak still, and her hand trembles. Much of the broth is spilled on the bedclothes, and it takes almost an hour for her to finish. Nazaire does not move or speak until she at last drops the spoon onto the empty plate.

'There,' he says. 'It is better for everyone this way. I have no great gifts as a nursemaid.'

When she has finished, Clara sinks back onto her pillows. Eating unaided has exhausted her, but there is something else. She had forgotten the comfort of rest and food, the simple warmth of well-being.

'You have been well cared for,' Nazaire says after a moment, 'by your Eustace.'

She looks at him warily.

'Crowe is your guardian, yet it is Eustace who seems most attentive to your needs. And there is a fondness between you, is there not?'

Clara swallows and clutches at the sheets.

'You miss him, no doubt, and you find me a poor substitute. But I will show you, I hope, that he and I are more alike than you think. I have been in service, like him, since I was young. And like him I have devoted myself to a great man; to order, and to duty. I have made sacrifices, just as he has. Perhaps you will come to see our resemblance.'

She presses her lips together and tugs her sleeve across her eyes.

'Forgive me,' he says. 'You feel his absence keenly still, and it was thoughtless of me to mention it. It is enough, for now, that you begin to accommodate yourself to your circumstances. Through that door there you will find a washroom, where you may refresh yourself when your strength returns. When you have recovered sufficiently, there will be other comforts we can provide. A desk, perhaps. Paper and pens.'

Clara looks up at him, still blinking.

'Oh, yes,' he says. 'We do not forget how you value such things. And you have questions, perhaps, that you would like to put to us. You will have your chance, and we will answer frankly, within reason.'

She studies the even contours of his face. He wishes to appear reasonable, and has allowed his expression to soften slightly. When he continues, the softness vanishes. It is smooth and complete, like the erasure of chalk marks.

'You must know, little one, that this is *une arme à double tranchant*. You know this expression, yes? If you do not behave with courtesy, then there will be difficulties. If you do not accept our hospitality until it is time for you to go home, if you try to return without our leave, then there will be difficulties. Grave difficulties. You understand?'

Clara glances at him and turns to the window. Above the moors, one of the buzzards is hunting alone.

'Very good,' says Nazaire. 'The view is not what you are accustomed to, perhaps. In winter it is not so cheerful. I assure you, though, it is one of our better rooms. There are rooms downstairs with no windows at all. With not even a light to read by.'

The buzzard idles above something unseen. Tracing a steep but graceful curve, it slips towards the snow.

The next afternoon, Nazaire brings Clara a lamb chop for lunch. He offers to cut it up for her, but she insists on doing it herself. Straining with her left hand, she presses the knife into the leathery surface of the meat. With no fork to hold the chop steady, she cannot saw with the blade. It is awkward and tedious, but she persists.

'I have been telling Dr Chastern of your progress,' Nazaire says. 'He is very pleased. He looks forward to visiting you when you are well.'

Clara does not look up. She has positioned the chop in the centre of the plate. Her wrist trembles as she bears down on the knife, rocking it slightly to coax apart the fibres of the meat.

'You will be agreeable, I hope,' he says. 'As you have been with me. Dr Chastern would be most upset if you were not. He was not pleased when you were injured. He is a man of learning, you see, while I— well, my education has been wanting.'

She grips the knife in her fist so that she can exert more pressure, but the chop is hardly tender. Whatever his other abilities, Nazaire is an indifferent cook.

'I will tell you a story, little one. Dr Chastern was travelling once in a country that was at war. It was not called a war, but that is what it was; that or something even worse. When he returned to his lodgings, he found the lady of that house dead in her chambers. Her daughter lay beside her, also dead, and on the floor lay a soldier; an irregular, as they are called. A boy stood over him, holding the soldier's rifle. He was the only one in that room who was still living, this boy, but he was holding the rifle's bayonet to his chest. When Dr Chastern questioned him, he said that he had killed the soldier. He had killed him to avenge his mother and his sister, who had – I must choose my words carefully, since you are only a child – who had been defiled. He had killed him, and had waited for someone to come so that the truth of what had happened would be known. His mother and sister were gone, the boy said. He had released them from their shame and suffering. Now he too wished to die because the memory of what had been done that day would make his life unendurable.'

He pauses. *He had released them.* Clara holds the knife still as she waits for him to continue.

'Do not be alarmed, little one. I will not distress you by saying more about what took place that day. Indeed, I *cannot* tell you more, because I do not remember. Dr Chastern possesses certain skills, you see, and wished to see the boy freed of his torment. There was a way, he said, to cleanse him of those memories. It was an act of kindness that placed the boy in his debt.'

The blade screeches across the plate, sending the chop skidding onto the nightstand. Breathing hard, Clara raises her eyes to Nazaire's face. She tightens her fist around the silver handle. He watches with amusement, making no movement to take the knife.

'Have I not persuaded you, little one? Do you wish to take your own revenge? If so, you must choose your moment more wisely.' He glances at the lamb chop, which is marked but largely intact. 'And you will need a sharper knife.'

*

He brings the writing table three days later. She wakes to find it positioned at the window, a scuffed and unadorned bureau with an ill-matched chair. Clara pushes herself to a sitting position, wincing at the discomfort in her neck and ribs. She is sore and tender in several places still, but can get out of bed without too much difficulty. Shuffling to the window, she lowers herself carefully into the chair.

She spreads her fingertips over the surface of the table, startled at how consoling it is. Beneath the thinning varnish, she feels the coarse muscle of the oak, how readily it is warmed by her touch. She began her days once with this small ceremony, all the days she remembers.

The desk is bare, its shallow drawers empty. Nazaire has left no paper or ink. She is coming to know his ways, his fondness for withholding as he gives. He squanders nothing. With each reward, he reminds her who has granted it, how easily it may be taken away.

Clara sits calmly at the desk. Her longing to write is deep and mournful, but she is content for now with this much. She looks out over the white and untouched moors, their poor scattering of marks and adumbrations. It is a desolate place, yet it fills her with a strange sense of intimacy. She feels close to herself, to the life that was within her life.

That too began with a whiteness, with a tremor in the sinuous flux of ink. She feels them even now, those other pulses. They throb beneath her fingertips, somewhere deep in the sinews of the oak, waiting for the emptiness of the page.

Fifteen

After Eleanor is gone, the boy's mother falls silent.

Even in the first days, when the child has yet to be buried and they are making what small arrangements they can, she speaks only when she must to make her wishes known. She does not reproach the boy's father for bringing them to this place, where the river rises almost to their door. She does not blame the boy for sleeping at the ferry house, or for the empty bed that might have kept his sister from wandering.

She gives no opinion of the casket that the boy's father makes from boat timbers. Some of these have been oiled already, and the air of the tiny parlour where Eleanor is laid out is syrupy with the stench of pine tar. The handful of townspeople who come to see her clutch handkerchiefs to their faces and leave the room almost as soon as they have paid their respects. The boy's mother stands by the stopped clock on the mantel, making no reply to their expressions of condolence. She meets their eyes and allows her hands to be pressed but looks down again without uttering a word.

Only on the matter of Eleanor's grave clothes does the boy's mother speak forcefully. In this, she will defer to no one and will be kept from no expense. Though the cost is almost a week's takings, the boy is sent for a bolt of the best linen. It has the simple whiteness of stitchwort, and its weave, when it is laid across the counter, is fine and even. The draper, knowing its purpose, wraps it in black crepe. The boy carries it home with slow reverence, as if it were the body itself.

From the linen, his mother makes a simple gown. It is long enough, when Eleanor is laid in it, to cover her almost to her toes. It fits loosely, and conceals the skew in her legs, which cannot be made to lie flat. The boy thought to join her fingers upon her chest when he brought her to the ferry house, and about them his mother arranges a small garland of daisies.

It is while she sees to this, adjusting Eleanor's cuffs and tucking the stems under the bluish nubs of her fingertips, that his mother makes the only sound of grief the boy has heard. She bends slightly and clutches herself, and the sound that escapes her throat is a clotted gulp, as if something in her chest is torn. She stays a moment longer, her palm pressed against her child's interlaced knuckles, then stumbles from the room. She shuts herself away until the casket is covered and the undertaker's carriage is brought to the door. It comes on the morning of the third day, among the first thick gouts of the rain, drawn by a poorly fed mare whose hindquarters are streaked with her own filth.

Afterwards, the boy and his father keep themselves from the house when they can. They stay late on the river, making crossings even after dusk. When they tie up for the night, the boy's father makes his way towards the inns on the quays. He has taken to spending his evenings there, though his suspicion of the men of the town has not lessened. Nor has his misfortune done anything to soften his manners. In the mornings, he comes reeking and sullen to the boat, his cheek thickened sometimes by bruises. He drinks alone, the boy suspects, in those places where his money is still taken, and stops only when it runs out.

His father speaks of Eleanor only once, and even then his meaning is almost hidden. He pauses one evening as he is leaving the ferry house. The boy is at the workbench, cleaning a tarbrush in a pot of spirits, and looks up to see him in the doorway. His father is working at the loop of his purse, which he has just filled, and his face is shaded and wary.

'You will see that the doors are locked?'

The boy gives a slight nod. 'I will see to everything.'

'You are a steady lad,' his father says. 'It is a comfort, after all that has happened.'

The boy puts down the brush, wiping the heels of his hands on his apron. 'I am only waiting,' he says.

His father looks down the slip to the boat. 'It will come to you soon enough,' he says. 'The river has wearied me before my time, I think, and you are almost of age.'

The boy shakes his head. He walks past his father to the slipway.

'I am not waiting for that,' he says, watching the slow water. The river, in the evening light, is a dull skein of rust. 'I do not know what I am waiting for.'

When his father has trudged away, the boy goes back inside. He has not returned to his old bed since the day he found his sister. He sleeps in the ferry house now, and sees his mother only when some necessity brings him to the house. It is he who keeps aside enough of each week's takings to ensure that she is not left wanting. He climbs to the roof if a slate has been loosened by the weather, or chops the firewood for the range, stacking it neatly against the gable.

If they sit down to eat, he speaks to her of small and practical matters. She answers his questions briefly and quietly, rarely looking him in the face. When the boy can think of nothing else to say, they eat in silence.

She brings in no herbs or flowers now, and the kitchen is no longer perfumed with mint and rose petals, with chamomile and sweet bay. The flood that took Eleanor came higher than before, sweeping away even the rose with blush-white blossoms that she brought to the house when they first came. She has planted nothing in its place. She no longer sets foot in the garden.

The spring comes, or a semblance of it. For a full fortnight, they are visited by a succession of storms, each one seeming to recede before gathering violence out at sea and returning as if some act of retribution had been overlooked. There are days when the boy and his father can make the crossing only once or twice. There are days when they do not dare even to take the boat down the slip.

At any time, this slackening in their trade would be unwelcome. Now, it threatens to ruin them. Two or three days, the boy thinks, is all that keeps them from the mercy of their creditors. In better times, his father had been more provident. When the boat had first come to him, when he still spoke eagerly of the coming changes in their fortunes; in those days, a portion of every fare they took was put aside for wintering. It was not that they did not cross at all in the darker months, but what they brought in between November and February could not be depended on to feed a family, still less to keep a ferry boat in trim and tackle.

Now, his father leaves the ferry house every evening with all of the day's takings but the handful of coppers the boy has kept back for his mother. Sometimes, when he has spent all he had by ten o'clock, he will come back even for that pittance. The boy bars the doors and waits. If he has had his fill already, he will fall soon enough into a stupor. If not, he will slouch back to the town or give up and go home. He does not demand money from his wife, even on the worst nights. For all that he has turned from his duties, there is that much decency in him still, or there is something in her that forbids it.

By the time the worst of the weather has passed, the pier has suffered so much damage that they are forced to shorten it by almost a quarter. With the timber they cut from it, they repair what remains. The job is passable, and will see them through to the autumn, but the shorter pier does nothing to ease their lives. The character of the river is changing as the mouth of the estuary widens. The bank they are licensed to put out from is silting up, and it grows harder now with each landing to keep from running aground.

If any good comes of this, it is that the boy is left more and more to run the boat alone. He is more adept at these short landings now, and has come to know the water better than his father ever did. It means he must do the work of two, poling the boat and navigating the channels, but he likes it better all the same. He steers his own course now, making each correction as soon as he sees cause. No time is lost conferring with a skipper who knows no better – or whose judgement is blunted by last night's whisky – but who cannot keep from offering some contrary view.

One day in March, when a mist as thick as muslin lies on the river, the boy leaves a pair of surveyors on the far bank. He is making ready to return when he hears a man shout for him to wait for a passenger. It is a common enough occurrence, but today he does not at first see who it is that hails him. At length, a coach emerges from the mist, the driver standing with the reins and calling again for him to hold ashore.

'Hold up, ferryman. Gentleman here on urgent business.'

The boy loops a line about his elbow and returns to his checks. 'I am not weighing anchor for Tasmania. You need not cause a stampede.'

'If you want the gentleman's business, you little river monkey, you'll keep a civil tone.'

The boy does not pause in his work. 'There's me or there's the bridge. Seventeen miles or so, the round trip.'

The coach has come to a halt now. It is some ten or twelve yards off still, and the boy sees only a dark hulk in the mist. The driver, by the sound of it, is helping his passenger down and putting himself in the way of a tip. The boy sits on the stern and watches.

The man that approaches is tall, but his shape is so indistinct in the mist that at first the boy can tell no more. Soon, though, his dark hat and cape can be seen, and the man's voice reaches the water. For a moment, the boy thinks that he is calling out to him, in some language he does not understand, but it is not that. The man in the dark cape is singing as he strides towards the boat. He carries a cane, though his gait is strong, and swings it at his side as he walks.

It is a kind of singing that the boy has heard only once before, when a travelling show came to the guildhall. On that night, a man in a coat of crimson velvet climbed to the platform, his face powdered like a woman's. He sang in just this way, with a great force and heat in his voice. The song was in another language, its melody voluptuous and extravagant. It was like watching a glass blower, who begins with no more than a slug of red-hot crystal but coaxes from it a graceful and fluted vessel.

The man breaks off his song as he nears the water. He raises his cane in salute. 'You must forgive my driver,' he says. 'They are apt, in that profession, to succumb to piles, a complaint that has likely taken the lustre from his manners. It gave me a pain in my own arse, I may tell you, listening to his soliloquy of misery all the way from London. You do not suffer from piles yourself?'

The boy stares at him and slowly shakes his head.

'Splendid. And this thing.' The man raps the side of the boat with his stick. 'It is entirely seaworthy, or riverworthy, as I suppose one must say?'

'We keep it in good order, sir.'

'Who is we, boy?'

'It is my father's boat, sir. He is in the town about some business.'

'Is he indeed? I have business there myself. There is someone I am most anxious to see. I would take it most kindly if you could arrange for an immediate departure.'

'You have no baggage, sir? Nothing you would like me to fetch from the coach?'

'Nothing, my young friend. I carry all that I have to commend me here in my breast.'

The boy stands on a thwart and offers his forearm, but the man reaches instead for his hand, grasping it warmly.

'I am particularly delighted to make your acquaintance,' he says. 'My name is Mr Crowe.'

Unlike other passengers of high station, Mr Crowe does not keep himself apart from the boy's company during the crossing. He takes a seat opposite the stern and keeps him so much in conversation that the boy becomes anxious that he will miss some hazard in the water ahead. As they talk, Mr Crowe looks about them with interest, turning frequently towards the town, though little enough of it can be seen from the river. The guildhall and the fine buildings about the square are no more than a nest of shadows in the mist. Above the dark juts of the quays, gulls rise in dim scatters, passing through bends of fraying smoke.

'I fancy,' Mr Crowe says, 'that the true beauty of this place lies hidden.'

The boy gives a small laugh. 'It may be for the best.'

Mr Crowe regards him with amusement. 'You do not greatly love your home?' he says. 'It is an understandable sentiment, and common enough in a young man. You feel, perhaps, that you are not fitted for this place, that it keeps you from the life that should be yours?'

The boy looks at him carefully. Beneath his dark cloak, he is richly dressed. His face, though there is a small skew in its line, is strongly made and marked by the ease of his place in the world. Whatever life this Mr Crowe leads, he feels no great lack in it. And yet the boy sees no mockery in his face. Whatever he means by asking this, it is not to show his disdain.

'This place was not always my home,' he says. 'I don't remember anything before, though. My father brought us here to run this boat.'

'And you have not taken to it?'

The boy shrugs. 'There isn't much to take to. You can see for yourself. We call it the end of the world.'

Mr Crowe laughs. He looks out towards the estuary, but today even the sea is lost to the mist. 'It is a poor enough prospect,' he says. 'I assure you, though, that the world is not so distant. France lies not so far in that direction. You have travelled to France?'

The boy shakes his head.

'And this morning, before I called upon the services of our mutual friend the coachman, I woke up in London. You have been up to town, at least? No? A day trip on the train?'

'The train does not come here. They are surveying the land for it, but it is too marshy, they say.'

Mr Crowe makes a snorting sound. From an inner pocket, he produces a silver cigarette case. He holds it open before the boy. The cigarettes are retained by a black ribbon. Each one is perfectly made, the paper as fine and white as cotton. The boy shakes his head. He is struggling to work the pole free of an embedded lobster pot.

'And yet you have made something of it,' says Mr Crowe. 'You have applied yourself to your trade. Your father entrusts the boat to you, though you are not quite of age. You will forgive my saying so, I trust. All this is to your credit.'

The boy shrugs. 'I will not sit idly, even in such a place as this.'

Mr Crowe lights his cigarette and narrows his eyes against the smoke. 'That is all very well,' he says, 'but what good will all your industry have done if you totter from this deck in fifty-odd years to smoke your pipe in a place that is every bit as miserable as it was when last you looked up? A boy who chooses not to sit idly might do so anywhere in the world.'

The boy rests a moment on the stern as the current takes them through a channel. 'And you, sir?' he says. 'Did you begin in such a place as this?'

'I?' Mr Crowe worries at his cigarette and gazes off towards the east. 'I hardly know, my young friend. It was not today or yesterday. Is that the pier ahead? I had it in my mind, for some reason, that this would be a long crossing.'

'We had it easy today,' the boy says, struggling to bring the stern about before the shortened pier. 'The water was with us.'

'Now, now,' Mr Crowe says, rising from his seat. 'You do yourself an injustice. I saw how skilfully you worked. It is like a labyrinth, that stretch of river.'

'You might keep your seat, sir, until I have tied up.'

Mr Crowe ignores him. He plants a boot on the gunwale and launches himself onto the pier. 'You need not fear for me,' he says, looking himself over and dusting down his travelling clothes. 'I have had cause to leap from more than one boat in my time.'

The boy joins him on the pier and kneels to tie a bow line. As he rises, Mr Crowe takes his hand and shakes it with both of his. The boy feels the impress of a thick coin.

'I look forward to my homeward crossing,' Mr Crowe says. 'So that we may renew our acquaintance. Now, there is one last service I must ask of you. My business here is of a tender kind. There is a young lady, you see. We met in London, and something remained unfinished between us when she was compelled to return home. I will not strain your patience by saying more. There is a lass who waits for you, I have no doubt, who gives some salve to your misery when you are ashore.'

The boy looks down. He says nothing.

'I ask only that you set me on the right road to her house. She is a ward of her uncle, I am given to understand, a man who laid great stress on his standing in this place when I had the misfortune of making his acquaintance. The girl's name is Lucy, Miss Lucy Swaine.'

The boy makes ready to leave.

It comes to him suddenly, the knowledge that this is what he must do, and yet the thought does not feel new. It is like a pebble that he has kept for months in the same pocket, that he has turned in his palm countless times without any consciousness of doing so, only to take it out one day and examine it, to find it faultlessly smooth, as warm as his own skin.

He goes to see his mother. He busies himself for a short while with a loose slate, then comes in and sits by the range. He thanks her, but tells her he will not stay and take a bite of supper. There is a gentleman from London, he says, who may have need of an early crossing. There is much to be done before he goes to bed. His mother accepts this with little comment. She prepares her own meal in silence, and seems content to have him sit and watch as she does so. She gives no sign, at least, that she wishes him to leave. She makes no enquiry as to the business of the gentleman from London. She asks nothing about the day's trade or how he found the crossings.

The boy looks around the kitchen. There is a coal bucket now in the corner by the range where he and Eleanor slept in their turns. The old oilcloth is spread over the table, but it is otherwise entirely bare. His mother stands at the stone sink, where a small window looks out over the river. She keeps her eyes down. With her thumbnail, she prises the scabs of shell from a hard-boiled egg. Her hair is arranged in a coarse knot and sheathed in a scarf.

He approaches her and touches her arm. Next to where she works, he sets down an old syrup tin. 'There is a little more I have kept aside,' he says. 'There are tips, still, though I am getting too old now. And he is only there half the time. He does not know about this. It was to be next year's wintering.'

She pauses in what she is doing, but his mother does not turn around. She glances at the syrup tin and takes a long, halting breath. She releases it softly. It is not quite a sigh. The boy rests his hand on her shoulder. She lowers her head to one side as if considering something. The boy closes his eyes for a moment, then withdraws his hand.

He closes the door quietly as he leaves.

He goes next to the churchyard, though it is no time for such a visit. It is growing dark, and the lanes are veiled with mist. He will be thought mad by anyone who sees him. Someone will tell the story of how the ferryman's boy crept into the churchyard, of how he lay all night wailing on his sister's grave. More will be said than was ever seen. He has heard how they talk. The boy does not concern himself with the thought. He no longer cares to have their good opinion.

On the way, he gathers daisies. It is early in the year still, and even the grass is only beginning to thicken. Some of the flowers have begun to close against the oncoming night, so he picks two or three in each place and moves on. In the end, he finds two dozen or so that are fresh enough to be used. It does not seem a great number, though so many daffodils would make a fair posy. They are frail in his cupped hands, seeming to amount to nothing.

He sits on a stone bench under an ink-dark yew. He cannot remember whether he has ever made a daisy chain before, though of course he saw Eleanor do it. He takes to it quickly enough, splitting the tender fuses of the stems with his thumbnail, making sure that the fissure lies along the centre so that one side or the other does not weaken. He takes care, when threading each flower, to tug gently all the way along its length so as not to rupture the preceding link.

When he has finished, the boy takes the garland to where Eleanor lies. There was no money for a stone, so the grave is marked by a simple wooden cross. He tries hanging the daisies from this, but is not satisfied with how it appears. It occurs to him, absurdly, that they will be beyond her reach. Instead, he lowers himself on one knee and arranges them in a loose ring on the turf, as if to hang them about her shoulders. He places a kiss on his fingertips, and lays them on the cool and darkening grass.

The boy spends his last night in the ferry house. He sweeps it out and sets the workbenches in order, tying the loose lines in neat coils and stowing them in the rope locker. He oils the tools and hangs each one in its place, ranking them by size so that they gleam on their nails like the pipes of the church organ. If his father notices any of this, it will be in exasperation. He will want something and will not know where to look for it. As he hunts for it, he will disturb everything else. Within a day or two, the ferry house will have fallen into disarray. A week after that, the boy thinks, his father too will be gone. He no longer has the heart or the patience to do this alone.

He leaves the boat on the slip when he locks up for the night. At first light, he will haul it down and make the crossing alone. He has carried his last passenger. He does not care to think of what business this Mr Crowe might wish to conclude with Lucy Swaine, but if he should return here in her company, he will find the boat tied up on the far bank. The boy will not await their pleasure.

Still, he thinks of her before he sleeps. The longing is dry and pleasureless now, but he cannot keep himself from it. He wishes he could make himself proof against her, caulk himself like a hull, but he is as helpless as he has always been. She seeps into him from beneath. His skin is stretched over skewed ribs, and the dream finds every fissure. He is sinking, his body bucking in the brackish surges, slowing in the clouded shallows and at last becoming still.

When the noise wakes him, the boy thinks it is thieves. He hears the deep, shuddering scrape of the keel being dragged down the slip, making a greater racket than is needed. They have wandered down from the quays, he thinks, a trawler crew on shore leave who can find no better entertainment. He rises quickly and goes to the small window above the workbench. He slept in his clothes so that he would waste no time when daybreak came.

They have it in the water already. The boy swears, reaching for an old axe handle, but sees his mistake even as he does so. His hand goes still on the haft. The man who was pushing from the stern loses his footing as he tries to board. As he rights himself, he turns towards the ferry house and the boy sees his father's face.

He has been to the town and is much the worse for drink. It is why he made such heavy work of pushing the boat from the slip. When he manages at last to climb into the stern, the man already aboard confers with him and claps him on the back. That man is Mr Crowe, and as his father shoves off and the boat settles on the dark water, he takes his seat beside Lucy Swaine.

The boy loosens his grip on the axe handle, allowing it to slide to the floor at his heel. On the boat, they are making preparations that at first he fails to understand. Lucy scrapes her hair back and secures it with something roughly knotted. His father hands her his dark cap, which she pulls low over her brow. They are disguising her, or something simpler; they are keeping her from sight.

He watches as Mr Crowe stands to unhook his own black cloak, enfolding her with laughing ceremony. She looks up at him, raising her hand to where his rests on her shoulder. They are making distance already, receding into the gauzy darkness, but he sees the line of her upraised chin, the white flame of her throat. Mr Crowe lays a finger on it, on that whiteness. She turns to him then, and he no longer sees them clearly.

The boy will not watch this, he will not stand still. The boat is gone, and with it the small means that were left to him of marking his own passage. He will leave by the road, with no trace or flourish. It matters only that he goes, that he walks until he almost sleeps on his feet, that when he lies down he is weary enough that no dream can taint his rest.

He is lacing his boots when he hears the horses. Two, at the very least, and they are being ridden hard, approaching along the lane from the town. The riders can be heard too, with one voice to the fore, bellowing oaths and giving orders. The horses are slowed to a canter as they near the end of the lane. They round the ferry house, their hooves deadening as they leave the road. The boy returns slowly to the window.

Alderman Swaine dismounts almost before he has pulled up his horse. He is a bulky man, and unused to such strenuous movement. His thick back heaves as he marches to the water's edge, roaring with renewed energy. The boat is almost halfway across, and will soon be gone from sight. Swaine turns and directs his rage at his companion, urging him to make haste. This other man ties up the horses and joins Swaine at the end of the slip, carrying something the boy cannot see.

'*Crowe!*' In his rage, Swaine can barely keep himself from wading into the river. He strains to see who is aboard the boat. '*Crowe, you whoremaster! Where is she? Do not think to come back for her if she is hidden ashore! I will find her, by God, if I have to raze every kennel in this town.*'

Swaine turns from the water and stalks up and down the shingle. He is looking wildly about him, and for a moment the boy thinks he has been discovered. Swaine, though, is consumed by his pursuit. His eyes are all but unseeing.

'*Crowe!*' he bellows again. '*What have you done with my niece? Have you cast her off now, after blackening her name? You will not acquit yourself so easily, you son of a tinker's bitch!*'

Swaine issues a snarled order to the man with him, who stoops for a moment to retrieve something. When he stands, he is shouldering a rifle. At his master's sign, he steadies himself and takes aim. Though he moves with urgency, there is a practised ease in his stance, in the way he knits his body around the path of the sight. The boy pushes himself from the bench, lurching in the slow darkness. He hunts for the axe handle.

The first shot is so loud that he feels it in his chest and throat, a suffocating clot of pressure. He has the axe handle now, and runs for the door. When he pounds it open, the rifleman has pulled back the bolt. He shifts his stance by a careful fraction. When the second shot comes, the boy is already on the slip. He staggers, a halo surrounding all that he hears. He glimpses the boat, stalled on the water. There is a third shot, and a fourth.

The boy stands in the strange, gaping quietness. A furl of smoke thins above the rifleman's shoulder, and the river has the blue darkness of mussel shells. From the water, which seems almost still, a voice rises, a great moan of anguish. When he sights the boat again, it has drifted a little way downstream. He strains to make something of the shapes that can be seen.

His father is slumped in the stern, his head lolling over the gunwale. The pole he had been using juts from the water, almost upright in the silt. He must have clung to it as he went down, driven it into the bed. And Lucy – Mr Crowe stands with Lucy clasped tightly to him. The cap has fallen from her head, and the cloak hangs open about her pale form. He keeps her on her feet, as if he will not accept that there is no strength left in her. When he is not roaring at Swaine, he leans and speaks to her, caressing her hair and clutching at her clothing. As he does so, surely, he can see what the boy can, even at this distance – the drenched and glutted silks of her bodice, and near her heart the seeping nest of ruin.

Mr Crowe settles her weight on one arm. With the other he points to the shore, where Swaine watches mutely. The alderman's fists are limp at his sides. He is hunched slightly, and his body heaves with his subsiding rage. Mr Crowe fixes upon him, his hand outstretched. He is possessed by fury, but also strangely intent, shouting something beyond the boy's hearing.

And then Swaine is gone. He is simply gone, and a strange silence settles.

What the boy sees, in the moments that follow, is slow and skewed. His senses seem somehow disordered, so that he hardly trusts that he is truly present. He stumbles to the end of the slip, to the place where Swaine was standing only a moment before. The air above him is ruptured by a maw of unaccountable heat, and the quietness envelops him. He watches the horses tear themselves free of their post, but finds that he cannot hear their hooves as they gallop away along the shore.

He rouses himself and approaches the rifleman, who has turned from the water and is staring at the place where Swaine stood. His lips move as if he is figuring a sum in his head. The boy looks into his eyes for a moment, then does the first thing. It is the first of the things he must do.

The act itself is neither hard nor easy. The rifleman does not go down with the first blow, but stands wondering at this new puzzle. He touches his jaw where it is torn open. The boy puts him down and does not stop until there is nothing that can be recognised of a living man. He hears himself say that it was for his father, but that is only because he cannot say her name.

Lucy. It was for Lucy.

When it is done, he throws the axe handle aside. Let them find it here. They would pull it from the river anyway. He stoops and picks up the man's rifle. In a pouch on his belt, he finds a magazine. He stands for a moment to look around himself, to form some memory of the place he is leaving. Beyond the ferry house, he sees almost nothing. It is not quite light still, and the town is only a daub of shadow in the early mist. He sees the eaves of his home, or thinks he does, a little way upstream. Perhaps it is only the reeds, crossing and shivering in the greyness before morning.

The boy goes to do the next thing. He goes after Mr Crowe.

Sixteen

C lara *begins to* write with her left hand. It is a matter of necessity, at least at first. Her right arm, when she is allowed at last to have paper and pens, is still bound in the sling, braced stiffly against its splint. She cannot so much as pick a pen up in the way she is used to.

She looks on coldly while Nazaire sets the writing things on the desk. When he has finished, he steps back with a small flourish, gesturing towards the gleaming ink bottle. In answer, she glances down at her injured arm.

'Ah, yes,' he says. 'It will be some weeks more, I am afraid, before the splint and dressing may be removed. Do not think of removing them sooner. It is a slender bone, and will be vulnerable still, especially so in a child.'

He is calm and precise, as always. He might easily be mistaken for a doctor, by someone who knew no more of his nature. It might not have occurred even to a doctor to wonder which hand she wrote with, but it is not a detail that Nazaire would overlook.

Clara glares at him, keeping her face set hard, and takes her seat at the writing table. She takes up the pen with her left hand, her fingers gathering hesitantly as she grasps the shaft. She adjusts her grip slightly, tracing a broad scribble in the air, but her movements are effortful and clumsy. It is as if she has never held a pen.

When she puts the nib to the page, Clara is even more dismayed. She labours over even the crudest of shapes, forming letters that are scarcely recognisable. No matter how deliberate her movements, what she writes is a grotesque distortion of her intentions, of the graceful succession of marks that she sees so clearly in her mind.

When she attempts the descending curve of a *g*, it becomes a hideous barb, like the leg of a smashed spider. The loop of an *h* is clownishly contorted. Even for a simple *e*, she manages only a sprawling and unclosed curl.

Nazaire approaches the desk. Clara stiffens in discomfort, but forces herself to continue without looking up.

'My first language,' he says quietly, 'is written from right to left. You have seen it, perhaps, in your guardian's great library.'

Clara sits upright for a moment. She picks up the page she has defaced with these first efforts and tears it fastidiously down the centre. She folds the pieces, tearing them in turn into quarters. She repeats this until the page is little more than confetti, then pushes the pile to the edge of the desk.

'When I was taught to write in French,' Nazaire continues, 'I struggled just as you do now. It seems a simple thing, and yet it defeats you. You work against something in yourself, as if there were a grain in you.'

Clara resumes her efforts as if she has not heard. She begins in the simplest way she can think of, writing the letter *a* over and over again, filling an entire line. She repeats this doggedly until its shape, at least, is unmistakable, achieving no particular elegance. She moves on to the letter *b*.

'I too was resolved,' Nazaire says. 'I sat for long hours, doing exactly as you now do. Your progress, if I remember well, is easier than mine was. You learn quickly, little one.'

Clara gives no sign that she is listening. She tears the page up, just as thoroughly as she did the first, and begins again. Nazaire laughs softly and moves towards the door.

Clara writes. She writes until her left hand aches, its muscles protesting at the unaccustomed strains. She writes at all hours, in the greying light of the winter afternoons and, when dusk comes, in the sickly radiance of the room's single bulb.

She sets herself tasks, transcribing fragments from the store of books whose pages she can call to mind. She is strict with herself, completing even the most arduous of these exercises, and yet she chooses carelessly, not caring what it is that she happens to recollect. She copies nursery rhymes over and over, or the names and reigns of kings and queens. She conjugates French verbs, puts the common names for plants against their Latin ones. She lists all the white things she can think of, then all the red things. In all of this, she is concerned only with the mechanics of what her hand must accomplish. The words themselves may just as well mean nothing.

She writes, but it is not writing as she knew it. There is nothing in it that comes from herself. She no longer begins her days as she did, her pen struggling to keep pace with the receding fugue of her dreams. The inventions of her sleep have been darkened by her circumstances. It is inhabited now by things she prefers not to record.

Still she writes. She forces herself to continue, to sit before each blank page and set herself some new piece of drudge work. Wearily, she reproduces passages of Jane Austen, of Stendhal or George Eliot, hearing nothing of their voices, trudging sightlessly among their thronged and opulent rooms. It matters only that she keep going, that she urge the cramped bundle of her fingers onwards, coax from them the next curve, the next ragged stem.

At first, she tears up each page as soon as she has filled it. If a fire has been lit in the grate, she burns even the shreds. After a few days, however, she looks down at a line of George Herbert that she has copied out over a dozen times. It seems to her, though she doubts herself for thinking so, that there is some small improvement. She can manage no more than a scrawl still, but there is a scattered evenness to it, a straining towards symmetry.

She cannot be certain of this, since she has kept none of her initial efforts. Nor does she have with her any sample of her usual handwriting, though that perhaps is for the best. From now on, she decides, she will keep one page aside for each day of her progress. She will lay them face down so that they do not distract or discourage her while she is busy with other exercises. When a few more days have passed, a week perhaps, she will turn them over and place the first of them side by side with the last. She will know whether she imagined it.

Clara's strength begins to return, though that too goes unnoticed for some days. It occurs to her, one day at about noon, that she has been sitting at the writing table since dawn. Though she has stopped many times to rest her fatigued left hand, she has not been forced – as she was so often in her first days here – to return to her bed, stupefied by weariness. That pain too has slowly ebbed from her. She no longer needs the phials that Nazaire brought to ease it, the tinctures that lowered her into dreamless darkness.

When Nazaire brings her meals, she begins to take them at the small table by the fire. She eats quickly and without any urging on his part, anxious to return to the writing table, but finishing everything, forcing herself to swallow every dull spoonful of porridge. She needs her strength now for what she must do.

Nazaire, once he has satisfied himself that she no longer eats under protest, does not stay to watch over her as he used to. He leaves her food and water on the table and waits only for her to take her seat. He remarks, in his blandly intent way, that she is making progress. He assures her that Dr Chastern takes great interest in the course of her recovery, that he is pleased she has chosen to make fruitful use of her time. And he looks, of course – he is always looking. Even if he spends only five minutes in the room, he surveys it minutely. He makes clear, though he remains almost expressionless, that there is a reason for his scrutiny, that not the slightest alteration or disturbance will escape it.

Clara is unconcerned by this. Aside from the writing table, there is not a single thing in the room to occupy her attention. When she was first given paper and pens, and when she had the means at last to scrawl a simple message, she thought that she would ask immediately for books. The lack of them seemed the most desolate thing about the bare room in which they keep her.

She did not ask, and the urgency of that wish faded. Reading belongs to the other life, to the place she was taken from. There is the room now, and there is the white weather on the changeless moors. There is nothing else, nothing but the work. And the work is the same, day after day. To scratch at the whiteness. To start again.

Clara writes.

Chastern comes at last to see her. Clara is at the writing table when he arrives, and at first she does not even look around. She is accustomed now to Nazaire's comings and goings, and often continues to write until he has set down her tray. In this way, she can continue in her practice until the last possible moment before she must stop to eat. It spares her, too, from having to meet his eyes.

It is Chastern's tread that makes her turn. Nazaire's is discreet but brisk, unvaryingly even. These footsteps are slow and laboured. When Clara turns from the desk, he is arranging himself in an armchair. He is wearing a richly patterned crimson housecoat, and he pulls its velvet collar more closely about him as he takes his seat. His appearance, in daylight, is less imposing than when she first saw him. He seems frail, and slightly shrunken.

He raises his hand lightly. 'No, child,' he says. 'Do not allow me to disturb your work. Nazaire has told me of your progress, and of how you have been diverting yourself at your writing. I came only to assure myself that you are recovering well, that you do not want for anything.'

Clara shifts uneasily in her chair, but makes no move to return to her exercises. When Nazaire enters with a tea tray, she is almost grateful for his arrival. Chastern glances at him as he sets out the cups, then stares distractedly into the fire. He appears, as he did the first time Clara saw him, to be faintly disappointed with all that he sees. She feels a profound discomfort in his presence, a sense that beneath his pellucid skin there is some unrecognisable creature. He makes her feel cold.

'I'm afraid I have rather discommoded our young guest, Nazaire. Perhaps it would be better if I took tea in my study as usual.'

Nazaire straightens. He examines Clara's expression, then appears to consider something. 'The child is unused to company,' he says. 'And she is not yet at home in this place. I think, though, that there are questions she wishes to ask.'

'Questions?' says Chastern.

'I have explained only that we were forced to act as we did. It was not my place to say more. No doubt there is more that she wishes to know, now that she has the means to ask.'

'The means?' Chastern says. 'Ah, yes, of course. How obtuse of me. Well, I should be delighted, if it would be of some comfort to the child. Come and join me, Clara, do. Bring your writing things, for we must alleviate some of this mystery that so oppresses you.'

Nazaire pulls out the chair opposite Chastern and sets a place for her at the small table. Chastern watches her as she hesitates. His grey eyes do not settle on things as Nazaire's do, but pass over everything with the same disdainful weariness. She has no wish to be any closer to him than she is, but it is true that there are things she wants to know. There are things that she wants.

She makes her way slowly to the other armchair, carrying herself with a little more delicacy than is needed, adjusting her injured arm carefully as she sits down. While Chastern sips his tea, Nazaire makes his customary survey of the room, then withdraws without another word. When they are alone, Chastern falls silent for a long while. He gazes absently about the room and taps the lip of his teacup with a fingernail. He sighs periodically, as if contemplating some sorrowful but dimly remembered occurrence.

'Well, my dear,' he says at last. 'You are making do, then, in your reduced circumstances? You must forgive the rather brutal character of these lodgings. I live elsewhere, as you might imagine, but this place offers a degree of tranquillity. And seclusion, of course. You will have noticed that we are not much troubled by visitors here. One need not fear the intrusion of the person from Porlock. You are familiar, perhaps, with the anecdote?'

Clara grimaces slightly as she takes up her pen. Though she can now manage a laborious cursive, her left-handed efforts are still coarse. She finds it almost unbearable to show them to him, and writes no more than the first couplet.

In Xannadù did Cubla Khan
A stately Pleasure Dome decree

Reluctantly, she pushes the page towards him.

Chastern picks it up and peers at it. 'How delightful,' he says, returning it to her. 'I had forgotten about your rather singular ability. It is the Crewe manuscript, perhaps, that you reproduce here. You are greatly privileged, you know, to live among such treasures. Your guardian is less reverent, of course, towards the priceless things that he has gathered. Familiarity breeds contempt, and his familiarity is especially intimate.'

Clara is uncertain of the point of this observation, and decides that she need not respond to it directly.

I cannot yet write passably with this hand. When my right arm has healed, I will show you.

Chastern examines the page. He glances at her bandaged arm with obscure regret, as if he is only approximately aware of how it came to be injured. He folds the paper and fans himself with it, sighing as he does so.

'It is all very unsatisfactory,' he says. 'Nazaire has told you, perhaps, how displeased I was at your misadventure. I do not see, even now, why it could not all have been accomplished with less unpleasantness. But then, I am a mere scholar. I am unaccustomed, I assure you, to such practices. It gave me no pleasure to find myself put to such extremes.'

Clara takes a fresh page.

Why did you bring me here? When will you let me go home?

Chastern glances at these questions and returns the page with impatience. 'Yes, yes,' he says. 'I will come to that presently. You will understand, I'm sure, that it is not a simple matter. Someone of my kind does not lightly act as I did.'

I don't understand, Clara writes. *I don't know who you are.*

'They did not tell you?' Chastern says. 'Your guardian and Eustace? No, I suppose they did not. They hoped, perhaps, that it might be avoided, that you could be entirely spared. Well, I shall spare you what I can, but since you have asked, let me answer you in this way. Do you know who your guardian is? Do you know, Clara, who Mr Crowe is?'

She stares at the page. She begins to write, then falters. She crosses something out.

He is a writer.

Chastern laughs weakly. 'Well, quite,' he says. 'Is that all he has told you? That he is a writer? And is that truly what he seems to you to be? You do not suppose, surely, that all writers come to live as he does, that they may choose to seclude themselves in quite such a place as your home? He is a writer, yes, but not at all of the usual kind. You will have heard it said of some authors, no doubt, that their careers have been long and distinguished. It is an odious cliché, of course, but that need not detain us. Mr Crowe's career has been long – very long indeed, in fact. It has not been distinguished, however, or not in the usual sense.'

Chastern taps his teacup again as he talks. Clara waits for him to resume, knowing that she need ask nothing further. Whatever it is that he is telling her, she can see that it exercises him. There is much more that he wishes to say.

'It is not the work itself, of course. Mr Crowe's work – that is, the work he has had a part in – has never been other than luminous. There is no one living or dead, in fact, who has given us so much that is unquestionably fine. No, the work has never been in doubt, but he *himself* enjoys no distinction. He has – how might one put this? He has *originated* many of the most sacred works we have, and yet he has remained unacknowledged, except by those he aided.'

Fixing his fingernail on the corner of her page, Chastern turns it and draws it towards him. He reads the lines of 'Kubla Khan' with what appears to be dim amusement.

'"A person from Porlock", indeed. Yes, he has been nothing if not discreet. But did you never wonder, my dear, why there was not a single volume among all those in his library that bore his own name? Did you think, perhaps, that his modesty restrained him? If that were so, I must tell you that it would be a thing without precedent among the authors I have known – and I have known, I assure you, a great many. Indeed, some are so enamoured of their own progeny that they can hardly bear to cede their shelves to anything else.

'No, I'm afraid Mr Crowe has not quite told you everything, Clara. He is a writer, certainly, but he is rather more than that. If he were merely a writer, he would be no different from the countless thousands of tinkerers who covet that name, who may contrive, after six or seven hours of arduous nudging, to produce a tolerably beautiful sequence of words and who lack any conviction, even then, as to what duty those words might have in the world. No, Mr Crowe is not merely that.

'What he is, my dear, is the thing that writers wish for. He is what they pray will visit them as they crouch in their bedsitters and fetid box rooms, labouring over pages that have yellowed before they even see the light of day. He is the one they seek when they leave behind the screeching of some inconsolable infant and descend at midnight to the street. They would give anything, on such nights, to possess some little of what is his. And sometimes, Clara, sometimes that is just what happens.'

Chastern pauses and sits back in his chair. He puts down his teacup and seems to be catching his breath. She takes the opportunity to put down another question.

Do you mean that he writes other people's books?

He glances at the page, but pushes it aside.

'That,' he says, 'is a rather inelegant way of putting it. He is not a *ghost writer*, as we must now say; nothing so coarse and mercenary.

He is not some journeyman who turns out squalid memoirs to order. And they are not other people's books in anything but name. When he chooses to lend his aid – which is seldom now – his patrons must take what they are given, though they are invariably glad to do so. But you are right in supposing that the works are by his hand. And they are of a preternatural brilliance, of course, for that is why he is sought out.'

Chastern sips minutely from his teacup, returning it to the table with an air of displeasure. He seems to hesitate before resuming. 'Of course, that is not quite all,' he says at length. 'It is not merely upon the page that your guardian achieves the miraculous. But come, let us return to this subject on another occasion. I have already taxed you, I fear, and you may find the rest somewhat abstruse.'

Clara writes quickly, disregarding the appearance of the letters.

I read everything. Tell me.

He studies her for a moment, then gives a cold, sceptical laugh and reaches for his cane. He rises with some difficulty from his armchair and crosses slowly to the window. 'You must think it a dreadfully bleak place,' he says softly, 'coming here in winter as you have. If you had come in June, you might even have found it to your liking. I keep a garden here, you know.'

Clara turns in her chair. He is looking out, not at the white barrenness of the moors, but towards the walled enclosure immediately beneath the window. Since it too lies under a quilt of snow, she has paid it no particular attention.

'There is a much more splendid garden, of course, attached to my house at the college. But that one is maintained by the university's own gardeners, and I am scarcely listened to when it comes to what is planted there. One of my predecessors, you see, was excessively devoted to dahlias, a vulgar passion that has been immortalised, God help us, as an article of tradition. At any rate, the garden at this house, whatever its shortcomings, is of my own fashioning. It is here, for instance, that I indulge my fondness for roses. The weather is hardly propitious, of course, but one may keep even tender specimens with high enough walls.

'I favour the old garden roses, naturally. Gallicas, damasks, bourbons – even the names are exquisite, don't you find? In the matter of colour, I will countenance certain pinks and very occasional pale yellows. No reds, and certainly not the barbarous apricots that are now tolerated. It is white roses, though, that are my truest passion. In them, nature has achieved her most inexpressible perfection.'

Clara remembers the white roses that were delivered to the house, how agitated Eustace was to find them there.

'What is it, do you suppose, that such perfection consists of?'

She looks away, distracted by a small tremor of recollection. There was a dream once, a dream that ended with swans.

'The question may be profound or facile,' he says. 'Or rather, the answer may be so. In any case, it is a question that all art must answer. Every work of art, if it is to be of value, must give us its account of that perfection. It is not a matter of explication, of course. That is the domain of science. What art must do is attempt, as nature has, to assemble the tissues of beauty for itself. It must construct its own rose from the raw air, endow it with its colour, its small weight, its tender volutes – even its scent. Art must set this thing before us, must assert its reality in the void of our disbelief. It must make it live.'

Clara strains against the impulse to yawn. She is thankful that she has never been made to go to school. It is this sort of thing, she supposes, that children must endure in classrooms all the time. Chastern now seems only to be explaining something that she has always found luminously obvious, something that must be obvious to anyone who has ever read and loved a book. And he has still not answered her question.

'We may only approach the rose, Clara,' he says, turning from the window. 'In art, that is all that we may achieve. It is a limit as inviolable as our own mortality. We may approach the rose, sometimes so closely that we are sated, for an instant, by the illusion. But then it is over, and we move on. We stand before the next painting, we listen to the next string quartet, we trudge towards extinction.'

Clara thinks of holding up the pages on which she has written her questions. She resists the urge, glancing towards them instead in what she hopes is a pointed manner.

'In his art, Mr Crowe does not merely approach the rose.' Chastern looks intently at her. He grips the handle of his cane. 'I can give you no better explanation than that. He is not limited as others are. On the page, there is almost nothing he cannot achieve, and he has crossed even that boundary on a few occasions. Oh, yes. Not often, and it costs him great effort, but he can do it when he is greatly roused.

'That, I confess, is a puzzle to me. It is something that none of his fellows have ever accomplished. He knows of my curiosity, of course, and delights in keeping it unsated. Still, I am not entirely benighted. I have developed certain conjectures. Do you know what I think?'

Clara shakes her head solemnly.

'I think that there is someone else, someone whose gifts are greater still. This person has remained hidden from me, though not, I think, from Mr Crowe; someone, perhaps, who has remained hidden even from himself – or from herself – whose gifts lie undiscovered, but whose proximity has proved nourishing to your guardian.

'For that person, I rather fancy, there is no boundary at all. Nature and its image permeate each other without hindrance, and anything is possible. The rose itself, Clara. Life and death. It is a remarkable thought, is it not?'

Clara looks down. She fixes her eyes on the page as if she is contemplating this answer, but that is not it. She is no longer thinking about Mr Crowe.

'In any case,' Chastern goes on. 'Whatever the nature of these gifts, their exercise, as you might imagine, is attended by grave duties. There is a covenant, you see, that binds all those who do this work. They may destroy what they have themselves created – they do so routinely, indeed, in quest of perfection – but they may not undo what nature itself has wrought. They may not destroy what is living. It is a prohibition that binds Mr Crowe as much as any other, and even he will not lightly be pardoned for breaking it. It is in such matters that I have a certain authority. I am a mere superintendent, of course; no more than a functionary. Nonetheless, when such a violation occurs, it falls to me to restore order.'

Clara considers all this, then takes up the pen again. *How? Can you do what they can? Why would they listen to you?*

Chastern receives the question with a look of chilly amusement. 'You may well ask,' he says. 'My own gifts, admittedly, are rather more modest, but they have proved sufficient to the small office that I hold; they have allowed me, when I must, to bring sanction against those who offend our covenant. What is it, do you suppose, that is craved by those who produce artefacts of beauty? Fame and acclamation? In some degree, yes, but there are those – Crowe is one such – who enjoy no fame whatever, except among their peers.

'No, what they desire most, even those who work from the shadows, is memory. If a thing of beauty goes unremembered, it is as if it never existed. If all they have done is forgotten, they may come to feel – even those as prodigiously gifted as your guardian – that they themselves have been abolished. And it is memory, too, that is drawn upon in the act of creation. It was Mnemosyne, after all, who was mother to all the muses. The rose, you see, is not simply beheld when its likeness is made; it is beheld and cherished, and its image is treasured along with all those the artist has ever seen or touched. Memory is the very fabric of their art. If it is taken away, they have nothing. Even Crowe, for all his prodigious abilities, is susceptible in this regard. He is sentimental at heart, you know, and excessively attached to what little he remembers of his youth. Memories can be so very fragile, don't you find?'

Chastern has become agitated in the course of this speech. He pauses now to catch his breath, with both hands folded upon the handle of his cane, his chin raised in satisfaction.

'That, at any rate, is why they listen to me. That is what I can take from them. Your guardian has offended our covenant in the gravest manner. He has done so more than once, in fact, and although the last time was long ago, it remains unaccounted for. I have offered him an amnesty, but only in return for an act of reparation on his part. There is something I wish for myself, Clara, something that will scarcely strain his gifts. I have acted more moderately, I believe, than was warranted by his offence, and yet I fear he will prove too indolent, too heedless, to do me this small service. It is for this reason that you have been brought here, and you will go home, to answer your other rather terse question, when that small thing has been done. Not before.'

She reaches for the pen and begins, with awkward urgency, to write another question. Chastern, though, is making his way to the door. He glances with cold distaste around the plainly furnished chamber, but does not look at her as he passes.

'I do hope,' he says, 'that you continue in your recovery. I will see to it that Nazaire brings more paper.'

She leaves a word unfinished on the page. Chastern has closed the door behind him, and is gone.

What happens in the garden begins almost without her knowledge.

All morning, Clara has been at the writing table as usual. For her first exercise of the day, she has chosen verses from the Old Testament. She has not read very much of it, and can recall only the pages of the Book of Genesis with clarity. Still, it suits her purposes, since many of its verses are of a length that allows her to write them on one line, and to fill an entire sheet with her repeated attempts.

She has copied a particular verse perhaps half a dozen times when she finds herself imagining the scene it describes. This is something she has not done since she began these efforts. She has been alert, until now, only to the shapes she must imitate, seeing the page of the King James Bible, with its crabbed trains of black letter, as if it were open in front of her. Clara pauses to read the verse.

And the LORD God planted a garden eastward in Eden; and there he put the man whom he had formed.

Her left hand is cramped, but not yet so badly that she would normally consider allowing herself to rest. For no reason that she is aware of, she rises from her chair and goes to the window. She looks down at Chastern's garden, absently opening and closing her aching fingers. Beneath its undisturbed crust of snow, she can guess at little of its appearance in summer. A central path can be discerned, leading towards the high wrought-iron gates. On either side of this path are traces of the garden's symmetry, of geometrical shapes whose outlines are indistinct beneath the white drifts. On the high stone walls, she sees the stark tracery of what she takes to be his roses, snarled and colourless now, without the tiniest insurgence of green.

She returns to the desk with no particular thought, with no intention other than to resume her exercise. She copies out the verse another six or seven times, achieving a regularity in her script that she finds mildly satisfying. But she finds, without being conscious of the transition, that she is writing something quite different. The pen – in spite of the discomfort the effort causes – is crossing the page in trembling surges. The words are her own, she thinks, but scrawled in such rapid profusion that she struggles to follow their sense. She sees the word *child*.

The word *rose*.

The sensation is one she has experienced before only on the periphery of sleep, when her thoughts are warm and motile. She is aware only of a gentle subsidence, of lapsing into something that is not quite thought. She sees nothing, at first, or nothing that is clear to her.

It begins with the cold. She feels a dense and clutching cold, pressing on her from above, and knows somehow that she must push through it, must drive upwards. This is slow work, and she is hampered by how little she knows of her shape and nature. She has no fingertips now, no nails to claw with. She cannot brace her knees beneath her. She searches outwards, pushing through dark matter in minute surges. She threads her way, from the faintest of her fibres to the places where she thickens, the ropes of her joining and massing against the blunt teeth of the stones.

She is no longer only mute. She is blind now, and deaf also, but discovers things by other senses, by a quiet seeping of pulses. She knows the knit and clutch of what surrounds her, finds where it is weak, where it is leavened with air. She learns the light without seeing, senses its cadence and flux, its coming richness. She pushes upwards.

The white cold is easier, after the deadening burden underneath.

She has gathered strength now, her urges bundled and intent. She is a closed fist of veins, and near its crust the whiteness yields in a crush of softness. She is in the light then, the limitless depths of it. It comes to her from everywhere, inundates her. She is free and golden. She is above.

She labours upwards still, and outwards now too, finding nodes of tenderness along her stiffening spine. Through these she pushes urge after urge, splitting and twisting, finding new ways to be everywhere in the light. She claws at it, lusts for it. Hungers for its syrup.

It is slow, this new spreading, but nothing like the slowness beneath. In the light, she is glutted with splendour. She swells and bursts, is splayed and ramified, repeating herself over and over. She wants to be more, to go on devouring the radiance, to deepen her pulse of sugar.

She does not know what she has climbed towards until she finds it, a flourish of undiscovered notes in the rising song of growth. She chances upon them at her junctures, finds them suddenly everywhere at her limits, beads of lushness in threes and fives, lolling with new density. She gives them everything, urging sweetness to them through the vast spread of her vessels, lavishing their cores with tiny folds.

They fatten, these capsules of pursed softness, until she feels herself sag under their sumptuous heft, their intolerable fullness. She is pervaded, slowly but entirely, by the need for their release, by a vast and luxuriant desire that is threaded dimly with fear, with the distant chill of extinction. She trawls the darkness beneath her, tugging wetness from the cram of filth, combing it for the clots and grains that nourish her.

She needs it, this dredged strength, to force the buds open. The light is not yet high and long enough; there is not enough heat. To gather it, she must push through narrow and incomplete channels, must insist on a great violence of distension and fissioning. It cannot be done without injury. She feels sluggish rivulets of panic, returning to her from her ruptured places.

She disregards the damage, finds other ways. She is thousands, she is uncountable millions. She is a monstrous instrument of motes and filaments, of sacs and membranes. There is no part of her that cannot be remade, no part she will not sacrifice. She will have her way, will have this done even if there is nothing afterwards that can be saved.

When the blossoming begins, its shocks are so gentle, so scattered, that at first she fails to realise it is happening, that the calyces are splitting, furling clear as their interiors overwhelm them. It gathers pace quickly, though, and soon it is unmistakable, each bud disclosing itself in a meticulous spasm of delicacy, unclutching its treasure of softness.

It is beyond her then, driven by its own inexorable pulse; the same extravagant coda repeating at her every extremity. At its height, when it demands no more of her effort, it becomes ecstatic. She is multiplied beyond measure, a constellation of blossom. She is vast and intricate, drunk with light and fashioned from the living air.

She lets herself recede then, knowing that it is finished. She sinks in contented exhaustion, becoming contiguous again with her own body, and realises that she is lying on the cold floor in the litter of what she has written. She is feeble and vacant, unable to move. She tastes blood in her mouth.

None of it matters, not anymore. She is untouchable now. She has done the last and unsurpassable thing.

She has flowered.

Seventeen

'**M**r Eustace?'

The boy, Jonah, knocked three times always. Eustace had the same habit once, but now he no longer knocked on doors. He awaited no one's pleasure.

'Mr Eustace?'

The knock came again, but it was hesitant still. Jonah was meek by disposition, and Eustace had given him reason, more than once, to approach his door with caution. He brought himself half upright in the narrow bed. Through the stained and uneven drapes, he tried to read something of the character of the daylight. It was after midday, if not later. Jonah knew better than to trouble him before noon.

'What, damn you?'

'Sorry, Mr Eustace. I wouldn't have disturbed you, only there's two bills wants paying.'

Eustace levered himself to a seated position on the edge of the bed, wincing as he did so. He had come by some new injury, this time just to the right of the small of his back. He lifted his shirt, twisting himself to inspect it. This time, he swore aloud. A tear in the muscle, if not something worse.

'I paid Mrs Haim for a month in advance. Tell your mother that nothing is owed for another week. Leave me in peace.'

'They ain't our bills, sir.'

'Well, put them under the door, boy. Where are your wits?'

'Sir, they ain't—'

Someone was with him. Eustace heard them now, in muttered conference. He crossed to the rough dressing table, where the washbowl held an inch or two of greying dregs, and picked up a spotted mirror. He used it for shaving, though he did so now at irregular intervals. In the month that had passed since he left the Estate, he had not often felt inclined to study his own face. He glanced at one shadowed half of his jaw, then shoved the glass across the dresser, face down.

'Look, Mr Eustace,' Jonah called again. 'Might be best if you let me in for a bit. Got Mrs Fraser here with me wants to have a word.'

Eustace closed his eyes, spanned the ache behind them with his thumb and forefinger.

'Let me dress,' he said.

Elspeth Fraser gave no sign, in her manner of dress or conduct, of the nature of the business she kept. Eustace had known enough women of her kind, but those he remembered had never troubled to strive for decorum. They had announced themselves with certain excesses of ornament, with jewelled fans and florid silks. Mrs Fraser was compact and clean-skinned. With her grey suit and pleated blouse, the strict arrangement of her hair, she might have been a governess with a prominent family, a widow of means who devoted herself to good works.

Jonah retreated after admitting her, closing the door behind him. Mrs Fraser walked to the only chair in the room, but did not sit down. She brushed its upholstery with her fingertips and drew them quickly away.

'I will open the window, Mr Eustace, if that would not trouble you.'

He raised an open hand. 'I am troubled only by your appearance here. The window you may do with as you wish. You will take a drink of something?'

'Thank you, Mr Eustace, but I do not drink liquor.'

He took an enamelled cup from the nightstand and filled a third of it with whisky. 'You will change your mind, I suspect, when you see the view.'

She drew the curtains briskly, dusting her hands against her skirt. The sash window did not immediately yield when she tried to raise it. From a handsome leather purse, Mrs Fraser produced a small pocket knife. She worked it carefully into the crack beneath the lower pane and succeeded, after some minutes of effort, in prising it a little way open.

Eustace sat at the end of the bed and looked on. 'You have done more already than I have in all the weeks I have been here,' he said. 'I mean to find better lodgings, of course, when I am less occupied.'

She remained near the window, taking a long breath as she folded away her pocket knife. 'Your lodgings are your own private business, Mr Eustace. It is not my practice to come to gentlemen's homes.'

Mrs Fraser looked at him keenly, as if to ascertain whether he had understood some unspoken point. She was waiting, perhaps, for him to enquire further. Eustace took a slug from his whisky, holding the cup between his knees while he fastened his cuffs.

'It is not out of deference to your privacy, Mr Eustace. I keep an orderly house, and give no one any cause to look into my affairs. On a Friday morning, by rights, I should be on the train to London. An aunt of mine in Kentish Town has no one else in the world.'

'When I was a boy,' Eustace said, 'the train did not even come here. Fifteen years it took them, out on the marshes with theodolites.'

Her cheek flickered. She was irritated, perhaps, or it was a nervous habit. 'I would not have chosen to come here, Mr Eustace, and I'd as soon not prolong the visit.'

'You managed the window well enough, Mrs Fraser. The door should give you no trouble.'

'Oh, I'll not keep you, Mr Eustace, but there is a matter of business we must discuss before I go. You did not leave my house peacefully last night, and your account was not in good standing.'

Eustace went to a drawer in the dresser. 'Was that all, Mrs Fraser? An oversight, merely. The girl herself had as much champagne as I did. I will be happy to put matters right.'

'If it were only that, I need not have put off my trip, Mr Eustace. I would have reminded you on your next visit, of course. It was not only champagne, by the by. There was a bottle of single malt also.'

He folded four bills and passed them to her. 'I do not doubt you, Mrs Fraser. This will settle the account, I trust, and recompense you for your trouble.'

'I would not have put aside my plans, Mr Eustace, for an unpaid slate. As I said, you did not leave peacefully. A doctor had to be called for the young gentleman. Doctors, in my experience, will be followed by constables. It is a thing I will not tolerate, and nor will my landlord, for that matter.'

Eustace put his hand to the tender place at the base of his back. 'You must forgive me, Mrs Fraser, if I do not recollect the incident in all particulars, but I wonder why it is my rest you are disturbing, and not that of the man who had half-strangled your own employee when I came upon him.'

Mrs Fraser looked away briefly. Again, there was a small disturbance in the muscle of her cheek. 'If the girl had not already told me the same story, Mr Eustace, I would not be here, and you would no longer be welcome in my house. The boy was rough with her. It has happened before with other girls. We deal with these things in our own way.'

Eustace drained the enamel cup, allowing the whisky to pool for a moment beneath his tongue. He could feel a new ulcer there, livid and precise. 'Your way has made little impression on him, it seems.'

'The boy's father is a magistrate, Mr Eustace, and our way has kept him from looking too closely into how his son spends his evenings. As I told you, I keep an orderly house.'

Eustace went back to the dresser and set down his cup. He stared for a moment into the open drawer, then slammed it shut with the heel of his hand. 'Let him come to me with his price,' he said, turning to Mrs Fraser. 'Let his father come with his. I will give them my answer in person.'

She consulted a plain but finely made wristwatch. 'I must go, Mr Eustace. It is not a question of money, I assure you. Mr Gill wishes only that you make your apologies before those who were present last night.'

'That is all he wants?' said Eustace. 'What good will that do him, or anyone else?'

Mrs Fraser looked away in distaste. 'I cannot think, Mr Eustace. Perhaps he wishes to restore his dignity before those who saw him humiliated. Perhaps he wishes to act the part of his father, calling people to account before him in the court. It is as near as he will ever get. The good Lord did not greatly burden him with gifts.'

She began buttoning her jacket and pulling on her gloves. 'In any case,' she said, 'he visits us on Thursday evenings, as a rule. It need not be next week, since it will be only a few days past Christmas, but it must be soon. If you do not come, Mr Eustace, and make this small concession to him, I will take it that you no longer wish to be a visitor at my house. That may not concern you, perhaps, but I will not stop there. I will take the girl's belongings from her room, and I will burn them. I will turn her out on the coal quay, where she will find some occupation, I'm sure, though she may be without some of the comforts that she is used to. You will find her there, if you are heartsick when she is gone. She will be delighted to see you, I'm sure, and to hear how you defended her honour.'

'Jonah,' Eustace called. When there was no answer, he picked up the enamel cup and flung it at the door. 'I know you are there, you imbecile. I did not hear you go down the stairs.'

The door was opened quietly, though Jonah felt it prudent to keep himself from view.

'Show Mrs Fraser out, Jonah. And be so good as to admit no more visitors.'

Eustace had asked for a room that did not overlook the river.

Mrs Haim, who kept the boarding house, was quick to point out that he would save himself nothing by forgoing the view. There was just as much work in it for her, whatever a guest might look out on, and she took it as a very bad sign if money was quibbled over at the outset. Eustace paid her for a month in advance. The rates were hardly in proportion to the limited comforts of the accommodation, but he assured her that they would not be disputed.

The room that was found for him was cold and cheerless, its faded wallpaper stained with damp. It was at the top of the house, its walls curtailed on two sides by the pitch of the roof. A single sash window was set into a gable wall and looked over a side street to the gated yard of an abattoir. The slaughtermen, Eustace found, took no particular pains to disguise the noises of their labours. A lorryload of pigs arrived during the first week of his stay, and the first of them to be gutted could be heard screeching even while its fellows were being herded across the clattering yard. On most days now, Eustace left the curtains closed.

He spent little enough time in the room, in any case, that the view from his window was a matter of indifference. His habits kept him apart from his fellow guests. He rose so late, sometimes, that the winter dusk had already begun. Mrs Haim served meals at strictly observed hours, in a dining room as dark and narrow as the interior of a mail train. Eustace went down for dinner only once, and was joined at the table by a single other guest, a man in a brown suit whose skin was profoundly yellowed by jaundice and who muttered incessantly between mouthfuls of soup, as if to some unseen confessor.

He ate elsewhere and infrequently. Though he usually left his room not long after waking, he was often too sickened by the ale and whisky of the night before to contemplate food. But it was not only that. At mealtimes now, no one came in by the kitchen door, smelling of woodsmoke and sorrel. No one slipped to her seat with ink-darkened wrists and untended hair. He had only his own nourishment to think of. It no longer seemed pressing.

He bought bread rolls from a bakery, but brought them untouched to the modest public square in front of the guildhall. There he sat on a bench under a cherry blossom of the kind that flowers even in the dark months. He chose this place because it was opposite a fountain where small songbirds gathered. If the weather allowed, he would stay and watch them until it was almost dark, the sparrows and finches dipping hesitant wingtips, scattering the water from themselves in brief convulsions. He tore the bread patiently, dispensing the tiny morsels one by one as the birds approached in tentative, stitching leaps.

When it grew dark, he went to the Grey Swan. It was a place, unlike the more reputable establishments in the centre of the town, where a man could drink alone and be left largely in peace, where he could go unremarked even if he had not been fastidious in his grooming, his history and occupation attracting no enquiry. It was a place, Eustace thought, where he would not be recognised. Indeed, there were nights now when he scarcely recognised himself.

The Swan was presided over by Rosie Ennis, who had lost half her leg to polio and had not reconciled herself to the prosthesis that replaced it. Rosie was a handsome woman, possessing a natural authority of demeanour. She seated herself usually at the end of the bar, where the two stools on either side of her remained vacant by strict convention. She tended for the most part towards vigilant restraint, intervening only against the most flagrant disorder, or when her arbitration was directly appealed for. In all cases, Rosie made her wishes known by way of Viking Boone, whose stature and magisterial beard had earned him his nickname, and who kept the bar and fulfilled most other practical functions at the Swan.

Rosie's tolerance did not extend to excessive curiosity. It was she who enforced her establishment's indifference to the private affairs of its patrons. This Eustace discovered on one of his early visits, when he attracted the scrutiny of a querulous old drunkard, a man in perhaps his middle eighties who wore the brass-buttoned regalia of some minor and long-relinquished office. The old man peered at him with undisguised suspicion, and exclaimed several times that he knew his face. At length, he tottered to where Eustace sat, his face set in an inquisitorial leer.

'I knew it'd come to me,' he said. His breath was hot and sour. 'That's what they says about me, you see. Bill don't forget nothing. Might take him a while, but Bill don't forget *fucking nothing.*'

'You have mistaken me for someone,' Eustace said. *I am not myself.*

'Nah, nah,' said the old man, jabbing the air with satisfied certainty. 'No mistake. There's not many remember it now, what happened to that poor Swaine girl, out on the river. Her uncle tried to save her, so they say, but he weren't never seen again. Long time ago, that was. They never found the ferryman's boy neither, who done Swaine's man. Or maybe he done them all. They said they found him, in the papers. Some headcase up in Pentonville copped to it, they said, before he swung for knifing a postmistress. Said he was him and changed his name. But that don't mean much, does it? Confessions from headcases up in Pentonville ain't exactly hard to come by. Nah, he run off, the ferryman's boy, and you'd have thought he'd have the sense to stay run off.'

'You are mistaken,' Eustace repeated. He stared fixedly at his glass and gripped the counter in front of him. The old man raised his finger again, and was about to resume his interrogation when Viking leaned over the bar and took hold of his wrist.

'Rosie says to leave the gentleman be.'

'Ain't no gentleman, this one,' said Bill. 'You don't know the half of what this little river monkey got up to when he—'

Viking moved his grip to Bill's upper arm, pulling him closer to the counter. 'When he what, Bill? How long ago was it, all that business with the Swaines? Forty years? Even if that headcase didn't do it, this gentleman here don't look much over forty-five. What's he supposed to have done, bashed their heads in with his rattle? Now piss off home, Sherlock Holmes, before I take you outside and crack your fucking case.'

This drew a murmur of amusement from the Swan's patrons, though most took care to disguise their interest, keeping their eyes fixed on their drinks.

Bill retreated, licking his lips in thwarted vindication. He finished his drink and lurched away, raising his finger from the door in a final denunciation. Eustace had no idea who he was and had no inclination to ask, but he knew the story of the hanged lunatic well enough. The Crouch brothers had done him more than one service, all those years ago. The confession they had procured had satisfied those who mattered, whatever this creature might believe. The boy the drunkard remembered was dead. He lay in an unmarked prison grave.

Eustace murmured his thanks to Viking, then looked to Rosie Ennis. He raised his glass slightly in acknowledgement and gave a brief and courteous nod. Rosie's answering look was knowing but disinterested. She joined her hands and separated them, as if in absolution.

Eustace did not go to Mrs Fraser's house on the Thursday that followed. He went instead to the Grey Swan.

It was not long after midwinter, and already the low sun was dissolving in the dregs of the sky. He stopped at the bakery, but a cold and insidious rain had set in by the time he reached the square. He disposed of the bread and continued towards the quays.

He had walked perhaps a quarter of a mile when it came to him that he was being followed. He stopped to cross the market square, where the traders had begun to pack up their stalls, the rain spilling from the edges of their awnings. Behind him, the street was busy, but most of those Eustace could see were trudging back towards the town, clutching sodden paper bags against their raincoats. The man moving against the crowd was thinly built, and not particularly tall. He wore a loosely fitting cap, whose peak he had pulled down so as to obscure the upper part of his face.

In a side street, Eustace stood to check his watch in the light from a shop window. When he glanced around, the thin man had stopped too. He patted a jacket pocket, as if to satisfy himself that he had remembered his wallet. As he walked on, Eustace reached into his own coat, a movement that had recently become habitual, but his fingers met with nothing. He had left the gun at the boarding house. He did not take it with him when he went out at night, though he often felt the urge to do so. He acted with excess, on occasion, when he had been drinking. It was better, at such times, that he was without easy means of doing harm.

Eustace kept his hand in his coat, making sure that he could be seen to do so. He walked on, taking care not to alter his pace, not to be seen to hurry. When he reached the doorway of the Swan, he looked back once more. The thin man halted halfway along the street, making no show this time of having a reason for doing so. Like Eustace, he kept one hand out of view. For a long moment, neither of them moved. The street was otherwise deserted, and the only sound was of the rain, insinuating itself among the cobbles. A van emerged from a gateway and sat idling between them. When it moved off, the thin man had vanished.

Eustace took his hat off and shook the rain from it. He stepped inside.

He found Julie early on. Or rather, he looked for her. He had gone a long time without such comforts.

It was not that there had never been women, far from that. In the early years especially, when Mr Crowe had shown him Paris first, then Granada and Tangier, Buenos Aires and St Petersburg – in those days, it had gone unquestioned. He had approached them all – the garlanded parlourmaids, the silent duennas – with the same simple adoration. He had been young enough still to shed himself entirely before those creaking cots, to feel nothing but that unmeditated heat.

Later, though, his duties had grown solitary. In those long years at the house, there had been time enough to keep company with the old dreams. In the end, there had been nothing else. It had been years.

He had visited Mrs Fraser's house twice before, and had told himself that he would not return. He was sickened by it, by how cold their skin was to the touch. A fire was kept lighted only in the room downstairs, the one they referred to as the *salon*. In the warren of bedrooms, there was softness without comfort. Satin cushions were piled on the raw sheets and draughts crept from every crack.

She undid herself briskly, the girl who came to him first, and set impatiently about him with her fingers. Her knuckles were raw, as if she had scrubbed them with carbolic soap, and the flesh between her breasts was pale, stippled by the chill. He could hear a soft, clotted rattle when she breathed. Eustace pushed her hand away and excused himself. He had taken too much to drink, he said, and felt unwell.

It was true enough. He was sickened, and yet the need persisted in him, a particular need that could not be met by the girls he had been shown. It was a matter of speaking frankly to Mrs Fraser, of setting out the special nature of the requirement. He stayed late at the Swan, on the night he went back. He had not made himself senseless, but he had drunk more than enough. When he spoke, at least, he did not listen in revulsion to his own voice. He imagined, afterwards, that he remembered how she had looked at him, as he spoke to her of certain preferences, as he wondered if there might be someone of quite that description. But he had avoided her eyes, for all the time that he talked. He had stared at his hat, which he had placed on his knees, or he had closed his eyes. With his eyes closed, it was easier to remember.

Mrs Fraser rose and asked him if he would care for something while he waited. There was someone, she said, who might fit the bill, with a little attention to her hair, with certain other refinements. It was not uncommon, she assured him. Gentlemen often expressed a fondness for girls of a certain appearance, though most were not quite so particular in their requirements. There was someone he had known, perhaps, and he wished to be reminded of her. That too happened often enough, but he must take care not to mistake one thing for the other. The girl would come to him when she could, but he must not think of her as especially beholden to him. When he was not here, she would earn her keep as before.

An hour passed, perhaps even longer. Eustace was drowsy from the whisky, and had dozed off when Mrs Fraser returned. She showed him to another room on an upper floor. He would find it more comfortable, perhaps. A fire had been set, since he seemed to feel the cold so keenly, but he would appreciate that such luxuries could hardly be provided at no cost.

The room, when he entered, had been lit with candles. The gentler light, he supposed, was to maintain the illusion, to soften the infelicities of resemblance. Other comforts had been provided, and some effort had been made in the matter of clothing. A quilt of some kind had been found, and had been turned down as if by an attentive chambermaid. The gown was far less fine, of course, than the one he remembered, and the ribboned straw hat did not even approximate his description.

But the girl herself – what Eustace felt was like the moment of dislocating levity when you are standing below decks and find that your ship is underway, when the permanence of the world is briefly suspended. She was not identical, of course. One girl could not be the miraculous twin of another, of a girl who was long dead and whose face, at last, he might remember less intimately than he could bear to admit.

There was a consonance, certainly, in the line and set of the features; they had the affinity of cousins, if not of sisters, and her skin had the same peculiar quality of tenderness. But the eyes – the eyes transfixed him just as hers had done that first day on the water. They were charged with the same alertness, with the proximity of laughter. They were wide and soft-lashed, almost extravagantly lucent. Disbelievingly, he brushed her cheek with his fingertips.

'Here now,' she said. 'You'll have me going in a minute. I cry for nothing, I do.'

'Forgive me,' said Eustace. 'You have seen many old fools like me, I suppose, with their lost loves. You must think us worse than the rest.'

'I ain't been here for long, but I've seen a lot worse than you. You must have loved her something awful.'

'I loved her. Or I wanted to, but— something awful, yes. Something awful.'

'What was her name, then? I suppose you'll want to call me by her name.'

Eustace could not say it, could not speak at all. He lowered himself slowly to the floor and laid his head in her lap.

'Here now,' she said again. 'It can't be as bad as all that. Hush now. Shall I tell you my name, then?'

'Please,' he said at last.

'Julie,' she said. 'My name is Julie.'

Eustace did not look for the thin man when he left the Swan. It was late, long after midnight, and he had taken more whisky than he had intended. He could not go to her, to Julie, until he had done as Mrs Fraser asked, so he had tried to put himself beyond the reach of even that longing. He had asked Viking for the bottle and had emptied it steadily, in even and pleasureless doses, but the peace he sought would not come to him. What he wanted could not be darkened by stupor.

He walked to Mrs Fraser's house; he could not make himself do otherwise. Even if he could not go in, she could not prevent him from passing the door. The house was on one of the better streets, not far from the guildhall. It was handsome and well kept, indistinguishable from the doctor's surgery next door with its brass plaque and gleaming black railings.

The light was on in the room at the top of the house. It was the smallest of the bedrooms, and was always given to the newest girl. She would be there – he could not help but imagine it – waiting or not waiting. No fire would be lit tonight, and it would be as cold as the other rooms had been. He gripped the railings and hung his head. He must not mistake one thing for the other.

Eustace turned away from the silent house.

Silk must be touched, above all. His mother had taught him this, and the lesson had stayed with him. There were other ways to tell the good from the bad, but touch was the most important. You looked for softness, of course, but softness of a quite particular kind. Even inferior silks were hardly rough to the touch, but the texture of the finest could not be mistaken. The surest way was to touch the fabric from beneath.

'Lay it out, please,' Eustace said.

He had spent only three nights with Julie when he ordered the fabrics. Even in that time, they had talked for longer than he had with any woman he had known. She would tell him nothing of her own life – Mrs Fraser forbade it – but she asked him things that no one had. Was he kind to his little sister, before she went, or did he tease her? Had he tried to find his mam's people, who sounded so fine? What did they wear in those days, young ladies going up to Covent Garden?

The draper set the bolt on the counter and pulled a yard or so free. Eustace slid his left arm beneath it, choosing a place a few inches from the roll. Keeping his forearm straight, he raised it clear of the bench, so that the silk spilled from it evenly. Very gently, he ran the fingertips of his right hand along its underside, taking care to keep them flush with the weave, exerting only the faintest upward pressure.

'You'll find it's top-drawer, sir,' the draper said. 'Siamese mulberry silk, just like you ordered. The chap we deal with in London, he got it in special.'

You allowed it to pass freely over the pads of the fingers. Its movement must be frictionless and sinuous, the delicacy of the fibres unchanging even over great lengths. The most desirable silks were woven from a single, continuous strand, the unravelled interior of the silkworm's cocoon. Such threads could be a thousand yards long, and without the slightest defect in their surfaces.

'It is acceptable,' Eustace said. 'But barely.'

'Acceptable? Sir, I'll have you know—'

'See here.' Eustace turned the fabric over and held it to the light. 'That unevenness in the way it reflects the light? The weave is imperfect, and there is some slight flossing. Here, do you see? And again here.'

Julie had asked him about children too. He looked old enough to have had two or three, she said, but he needn't tell her what they were called. He had made light of that, or tried to. Did he look old enough only for children, and not for grandchildren?

'Is that so, sir?' the draper said. 'Know a lot about this sort of thing, do you?'

Eustace regarded him in silence for a moment. 'If my requirement for these items were not so urgent, I would send this back. As it is, it must be tolerated. How soon will I have the finished garments?'

'Well, we are doing our best, sir, but it's them old-fashioned designs. We had to get a dressmaker in who had the patterns from her mother's time. Then there's that lace you were so particular about, which ain't come in yet from— where was it?'

'Brussels. How long?'

'Three weeks, sir, with a fair wind.'

'You have a fortnight,' Eustace said. 'And I expect a discount of at least ten per cent on this silk.'

She had laughed when he told her he would show her, when he said that the clothes would have suited her. She had laughed, but there was no unkindness in it. She would look like Lady Windermere, she said. Like Lady Windermere gone dotty, still getting done up the same way after all these years, going off to tea at the Ritz.

He had not known that brightness either, when a woman laughs as you make love. It was like unclasping a locket to find that it held sunlight.

Eustace found himself at the head of the coal quay, though he had wandered there with no particular destination in mind. He had been conscious of no intention, as he walked, other than a wish to be away from the better-lit streets, a wish to go unseen. The quay had fallen into dereliction when the trains came. No boats tied up there now, and by day it was entirely deserted. At night, it was no more welcoming. It was open to the water, the wind coming harsh and untempered from the North Sea. The streetlights were indifferently maintained, and what little light there was came from the doorways of abandoned warehouses, some without even their doors, that at night were put to other uses.

Eustace kept close to the wall as he picked his way among the filthy cobbles. The rain had thickened now to a sleet that clawed at his face and neck. Even in this weather, there were those who offered their comforts unsheltered. One woman tottered towards him from the shadow of a blank doorway. A child watched her from the step, a tin cup in her frail fingers. The woman wore what had once been a fur coat, though it lacked an entire arm and was matted and filthy almost beyond recognition. She opened the coat to uncover a sodden nightgown, its bodice torn almost to her belly. From this gape, she plucked the famished skin of her breast, then grasped at his sleeve to tug him towards her.

'Josie's got something for you, darling. Come see what Josie's got for you.'

He spun free of her grip and hurried on, keeping himself well clear now of the alleys and doorways that he passed. The disused warehouses gave way, after a little distance, to a stretch of waste ground that was intermittently hidden by hoarding. In the glimpses that came to him through the gaps, Eustace saw scattered clutches of men, some gathered around rough bonfires. One such fire had been set beneath an archway that was the only standing remnant of a warehouse vault. Here, another gang had set dogs to fighting, and one man stood in silhouette at the periphery of the fray. He held his own beast on the taut radius of its leash, bawling in delight or disgust at the savagery closer to the fire.

Beyond the waste ground stood a squat terrace of what might once have been shipping offices. Their lower windows were boarded up, but some of those above glowed dimly through the rough canvas that had been stretched in place of glass. Their doorways, like those of the warehouses, stood open to the quay. In the first of these, a heavyset man in a labourer's jacket had taken hold of some unwanted patron. The smaller man squirmed from his grasp and leaned against the door jamb, where he vomited explosively against an interior wall. The doorman howled an obscenity and dragged him out onto the cobbles, where he kicked him until he no longer moved.

The man standing guard at the next door slammed it shut when he saw Eustace approach. He had been made wary, perhaps, by the disturbance outside the neighbouring premises, or admitted men according to some code that Eustace could not guess at. He walked on, passing two houses that were entirely derelict, their doors boarded as well as their windows. Beyond these was the last lighted door of the terrace, a house that stood almost at the end of the quay itself.

At this doorway, no one stood guard – no one, at least, who could be seen from outside. As he drew near it he caught sight of the child again, slipping from shadows and disappearing inside. It was her, he felt sure; it was the beggar girl he had seen huddled behind the old whore, though he could not fathom how she had crept past him unseen.

Eustace approached the house cautiously, with no clear intention that he could name. He was deeply tired, he realised. It had worked at him, beneath the ebbing warmth of the whisky. It had carried half of him away. In the hallway – it seemed almost homely, in such a desolate place as this – a light bulb burned beneath a pinkish shade, and paper of an ancient floral pattern adhered in places to the walls. He leaned in and knocked on the open door. The courtesy was faintly absurd, but he was not inclined to provoke anyone by his presumption. He counted out a minute in silence, then knocked again.

This time, when no one came, he crossed the threshold.

Julie loved the boxes in which the clothes were packed. They were powder blue, and carefully secured with ribbons of ivory-coloured satin. Even these he had ordered specially, taking care that the colours complemented those of the items within.

'Ain't they just the most beautiful things?' she said. 'That's real satin, that is, even on the little hatbox.'

'I was afraid you might think all this a little off-putting.'

'Well, you won't catch me wearing them to the pictures. Still, though – do you think I could keep just the little one? The box, I mean. I wasn't saying the clothes, because God only knows what they're like.'

'They were made for you,' Eustace said.

'She'll kill me for asking,' said Julie. 'But the little one, I can hide that in the locker. She gives us a little locker, one each, even though she probably has the key.'

'They are yours, all of them, if you care to keep them. They were made for you, though I'm sure it does me no good to confess such a thing. I cannot think how I must appear to you.'

She looked up from the boxes and drew him towards her, narrowing her eyes as if in appraisal. Her fingertips climbed his back, making an accounting of its muscles. 'You keep saying that. Maybe you don't look as bad as you think,' she said. 'You scrub up all right, though you ain't been looking after yourself.'

Reaching his neck, she pulled his face towards hers. 'And these suits of yours. Some of the girls don't like all that, but I do. A man who looks serious, like he has an important job.'

Eustace averted his face. 'A man who has nothing now. A man who failed.'

'Here now.'

Julie took his chin between finger and thumb. She pressed herself to him, applying the softness of her midsection until she found his heat, his shape. 'Here now,' she said again. 'I have a job for you, and you ain't failed at that yet.'

When she kissed him, he no longer thought of the light on the river. What he felt was no longer old.

He would go upstairs first. He had reasoned it out, or thought he had. It had worn him away, this weariness, had left him diminished. He was no longer sure of himself. He would climb the stairs first, though the upper part of the house was dark and soundless. The child was light on her feet; if he were to look in the lower rooms first, she might easily slip downstairs again, and out onto the quay. She would go back to the woman then, or to whatever brute had power over them both. She would be put to some use, given scant protection in return. He could not think of it.

The stairs were skewed, and grew yielding and unsound as he neared the landing. The last step but one was missing entirely. He sought it with his foot and staggered, finding only a cold vacancy. He thrust his arm out for the post at the head of the banister, and for a time he could go no further. He grasped the post and closed his eyes, persuading himself of his own stillness.

I am not myself.

It was the damp, no doubt, that had rotted the timber. He had caught the odour when he came in, a fetor that thickened as he ascended. The lower rooms were lit, at least, and had not been entirely abandoned. They were used by squatters, perhaps, who set fires when they had the fuel. The rest of the house might have gone unwarmed for years.

Eustace edged slowly along the unlit landing. He could give himself no reason for going on, knowing that half its floorboards might be rotten. He could not account for it. At the Estate, he had declared the tower unsafe for much less. He knew better, or he had once. He thought of himself, in his office near the kitchens, of the ordered desk, the polished orrery. The planets in their proper circuits.

The sun and the moon.

What good had he done, in all that time? He had seen to the starching of the cloths, to the upkeep of the silverware and the cornices. He had kept the roof in good repair, so that they would not be deluged in their beds. He had tended to them, in his unseen black and grey, had fussed and chided, flattered and pleaded. He had warned them. And they had gone on, the master and the child; they had continued in their grand and heedless orbits. It was useless, all of it. It was foolishness.

To have thought he might tame such a creature. That he might keep her safe.

He came to the first door on the landing. It was shut fast, and lacked any kind of knob or handle. He thrust his shoulder against it, not knowing when it might give. He thought of stumbling, as he had on the stairs, but plunging this time into some dank and lightless void. He thought of the dead cold, of water threaded by eels. He waited for the dread to seize him, to press him back. Nothing came, and the door did not hold for long.

He called out to her as he lurched into the darkness.

He left Julie's room while she dressed. When he returned, she was standing with her back to the door. She had put the hat on last, and had turned to the mirror to fasten the ribbon under her chin. She reached back to make a last adjustment, and a barb of her hair slipped free of its ravel, spilling brightly onto her nape. He did not know he had made a sound until she responded.

'You like it, then? I was worried I'd do it up all wrong.'

He put his arm about her waist and lowered his head to kiss her there, in the tender recess at the base of her neck.

'Let me show you.'

'Is there a trick to it, then?'

'A miracle,' he said. 'It is like a miracle.'

He lit a match, when he had collected himself, and cradled it as he looked about the room. The walls were streaked with filth. At their margins, mould bloomed in dark profusion. Above him, one half of the ceiling was swollen and buckled. The remainder hung in ragged slabs from the joists. From the attic above, with the spilling cold, came small ticks and scratches, steady and industrious. Jackdaws, maybe. Or rats.

The next room was worse: it was desolate, like the first, and a rich stench had coiled in its stale air. Some meagre carcass – a cat, maybe, or a fox – lay splayed and sunken in one corner. From an exposed beam hung a lank curl of rope, cropped a foot or two from the ceiling. Beneath it, on the floorboards, some message had been daubed with a fingertip. He could make nothing of it; the letters were dark and crudely formed, and his matches lasted only moments.

The last door on the landing had seized in its warped frame. He heaved at it without much heart before giving up. It was beyond his strength, and no famished child could have forced it open. She had not come up here. Had she entered the house at all? He slumped against the door, doubting even what he had seen.

I am not myself.

It was a common enough form of words. It was what people said of themselves at such times as these. Perhaps it was not so much out of the ordinary.

But the words were not right, not for this. It was a worse thing than becoming someone else, a more awful thing. There was a *lack*, when he sought himself, an incompleteness. He reached inward and found absences. He felt it when he tried to right himself, stumbling on a skewed board; the heft gone at his centre. *Derelict* – that was the word. He was derelict, or would be soon. He would stand day and night in the unseen weather, sheltering nothing living.

Returning downstairs, he trudged among the lower rooms, animated now and then by some dim panic, but forgetting for long stretches what he had come for. In the ruined kitchen, the rain dribbled from the shattered lip of an old sink, spattering the refuse beneath. The room had been flooded. The floor, afterwards, had been swept indifferently to its edges, leaving drifts of muck and broken things that rose almost to knee height. He lit the rest of his matches and puzzled over the oddments: a scoured paintbox; a colourless stocking; a knave of hearts, torn perfectly along its axis.

He went last to the room at the front of the house, off the hallway whose light had first drawn him in. A bulb hung here too, but the light it gave was feeble and halting, hardly brighter than an ember. As in the hallway, the wallpaper survived in mottled swatches, marked in places by deeper stains. It had been ivory-coloured, he thought, or primrose yellow. It was patterned with songbirds, and might have been pretty once, when the lamps were lit. Perhaps this had been the parlour, when the house was lived in, the room where occasional callers were entertained. Perhaps the children had been called to the hearth to sing. He tried to think of it.

There was not much else, once he had taken in the rags of burgundy curtain. There was the mirror frame – empty but for a few jags of brownish glass – that leaned against the chimney breast. And there was— he proceeded slowly towards it, making no sense of its shape. It had been laid atop a pair of seatless dining chairs before the fireplace. The arrangement was deliberate, even ceremonial. On the mantel, a wooden cross had toppled and rested on its spar.

What other purpose could it have, an oblong box of those proportions? It was roughly made, but some pains had been taken over its painting. It was plain and clean, like nothing else in this place. Why else would it have been laid out in just this way, its lid left discreetly askew, as if for the paying of respects? He slowed as he approached it, finding himself unsteady. The box was white, and a little more than five feet long.

Behind him, the bulb flared and dimmed.

Outside on the waste ground, the fires had burned down, abandoned by the dogs and their keepers. The doorways he passed were darkened now, and no light came from the upper windows.

He turned away again, moving now towards the quayside. The exhaustion had all but consumed him. He could walk barely ten paces without stumbling. The ache in his temples pressed against his consciousness, darkening the borders of his vision. He could see the water now, an unmoving skin beneath the darkness.

The cold alone would do it. It would not take long.

When the blow came, it seemed a simple and ordained thing. His fatigue had saturated him, or he had suffered a stroke. It had been coming. He came down on his knees, watching the calm lurch of the glistening stones. The shadow slipped from behind his back, becoming a steady presence. He forced himself to focus, to decipher the pattern of the shoes. He looked up.

The thin man, Abel Crouch, and the gun in his face. Hard and scratched, this close. That unreflecting darkness.

'What were you doing in there? You look like you seen a ghost.'

'Nothing, empty. There was nothing.'

'Yeah? You sound disappointed. I'm disappointed too. You left before our business was finished.'

Abel waited for him to speak, but he could not. There was nothing.

'Your friend in the nice suit, he paid me a visit. Said he had my money. You know what I told him?'

Shaking his head. No.

'I told him to keep it. I said, my brother getting killed, we never talked about that. That wasn't what we agreed. He said I'd have to take that up with you.'

I am not myself.

'So I come here to take it up with you.'

I am not myself. All my love, everything gone. The river always.

'Eustace?'

The barrel of the pistol nudged his cheek, cold and perfect. He brought his lips to it, tasted oil and smoke.

Eighteen

When *Clara wakes*, they have taken her pens and paper.

She is lying in the bed again, but it is not like before, when she was so much suffused with pain that her body seemed hardly to belong to her. She feels only an ebbing exhaustion, like the strained tenderness that follows long exertion. Her right arm is still in its sling, but it lies comfortably across her chest. She lifts her left arm from the covers and looks at it with vague wonder. She flexes and curls her fingers.

It is strange, this tiredness, softened by an unfamiliar plenitude. She takes pleasure even in the light, its cool acuity on the white-washed stones. Above the moors, a tear of clean sky has opened in the weather. The buzzards prowl at its apex, then swoon in graceful helices through the clarified air. The snow has begun to melt, perhaps, and they have sighted something living.

She registers the bare surface of the writing table without alarm. She does not understand what she did with the roses, not fully, but she senses its magnitude. She knew, somehow, that this would be among its consequences. It is tiresome, this new cruelty, and yet she is untroubled. She has learned something new, a language almost. It is full of blood and earth, of dark profusion. She sleeps again, and dreams of it, of the red and secret alphabet.

She is sitting in the armchair when Nazaire enters. She has been there for some time, gazing contentedly at the changing complexion of the sky. Another week has passed, and it must now be a little after midwinter. The days are no longer waning. He glances at the bed, and at the bare writing table. His manner is composed, as always, his movements unrushed, but he studies her more carefully than usual. In his expression, she thinks, there is the faintest inflection of curiosity.

He sets a modest fire in the grate and puts out the tea things, arranging the cups and saucers with his customary precision. 'Dr Chastern will be joining you,' he says. 'He was concerned by your behaviour. There are other matters too that he wishes to discuss with you.'

He inspects the table, plucking a minute crumb from the white cloth, then turns to address her directly.

'It is disappointing, little one. I believed we had reached an understanding. That was why we continued to reward you. Now we must take these rewards away. It is a pity, no?'

Clara holds a sugar lump on her spoon and lowers it slowly beneath the surface of the tea, watching the slowly spreading stain. She looks up at Nazaire and smiles distractedly, then returns her attention to her cup.

When Chastern arrives, he is dressed for the outdoors. He wears a tweed suit, and at his throat is an olive-green cravat. The effect is incongruous, even a little comical. As he takes his seat with effortful ceremony, Clara raises her teacup to cover her mouth. He looks at her as he waits for his breath to return, clutching and releasing the handle of his cane. His expression is indignant, and faintly disbelieving.

'The winter,' he says eventually. 'It has not yet relinquished its hold. In the weather, we have not yet seen the first glimmering of clemency.'

Clara selects a chocolate biscuit and nibbles at its rim. She offers Chastern a mild smile and brushes crumbs from her lap.

'Yet in the garden certain changes are already evident. Some of the roses, for instance, have convinced themselves of the arrival of summer. It is a remarkable thing. You had noticed, I suppose?'

Clara looks away, as if considering the question. She takes a pensive bite from her biscuit.

'It is charming, in its way, but one is always disquieted when such things happen other than in their natural course. It rarely ends well, I'm afraid.'

She puts her teacup down and looks at him attentively.

'The word "precocious", you know, has precisely this original sense. From the Latin *praecox*: that which ripens too soon. Oh, I have seen it often enough, the premature flowering that follows a few days of brightness. But it is illusory, of course. Winter does not surrender quite so easily. The frosts return, my dear, and all those pretty petals shrivel and die. Sometimes, the entire organism will succumb. It has overreached, you see. It has expended too much of itself to outlast the cold.'

Clara gets up and goes to the window. The snow lies deeply still over the garden, but the morning sunlight is sharp and pure. The new roses glisten perfectly. She smiles.

'We were becoming concerned, my dear, that you were tiring yourself. You were quite insensible with exhaustion when Nazaire found you. You had to be carried to your bed.'

A little bird – a blue tit, she thinks – alights on one of the rose's upper branches. It picks at the tender stems in tiny, stuttering movements.

'At any rate, we felt it was prudent to take away your writing things, if only until you have been given proper instruction. It is entirely for your own good, of course.'

Clara puts her head on one side as she watches the flickering bird. It is a negligible creature, no more than a palmful of bright feather, but there is something dauntless in its colours, its ardent flushes of blue and yellow.

Chastern is still talking. 'It is a blow to you, no doubt, but you will find other amusements. You will see, in time, that it was for the best.'

The bird flits from its perch, darting somewhere out of sight with the morsels it has taken, as if it were nesting. But it is too early, surely, even for blue tits. There cannot be enough food yet.

'Still,' says Chastern, 'you mustn't be too gloomy. There is some good news.'

Clara turns from the window.

'I had written to your guardian, you see, to assure him that you are well. I mentioned my business with him also, and it seems he has become convinced of his best course. He assures me that he is working in earnest on the item I commissioned. I must leave shortly for the college, since the new term is about to begin. There I will await further news from the Estate, and I look forward to travelling there to oversee the completion of the work.'

She waits for him to continue, uncertain what all this may mean.

'It was my intention, as you will recall, to arrange for your return once I had satisfied myself that Mr Crowe had done as I asked. And yet . . .'

He adjusts his cravat, looking away as if vaguely occupied. Clara remains completely still. She breathes slowly.

'I confess,' he says at last, 'that I have never found children to be especially absorbing of my interest. One is aware, of course, that they are generally cherished. One is even persuaded, occasionally, by certain Pre-Raphaelite depictions – some of Millais' children, for instance, are quite enchanting, and so very decorative. For the most part, though, I have been contentedly incurious about the young. That, at any rate, is how I must account for it – for having overlooked you until so recently.'

He pauses, but does not look towards her. He stares vaguely still, and appears unsatisfied with his own explanation.

'It was an unforgivable lapse,' he says, resuming abruptly. 'But you must rest assured that I have seen my error, that you have had my attention for some time. Of course, it was necessary to wait for some manifestation of your abilities – one doesn't wish to appear foolish, after all. And how lavishly you have rewarded my patience. What a great deal we shall have to talk about, when I return. It would be such a great shame, would it not, if we were to squander our only chance at becoming acquainted?'

Clara stares fixedly ahead as Chastern labours from his chair and makes ready to leave. 'Yes, yes,' he says, 'a very great shame. And so I trust that you will not find it too great an imposition if I ask that you remain here, if only until I return. We shall have leisure then to decide what is best. In the meantime, of course, Nazaire will see that you are kept entirely safe.'

At the door, he pauses and turns to her. 'Goodbye, my dear. You will remember our chat today, won't you? You will take care that you do not endanger yourself by your exertions?'

Clara raises her left hand in a parting wave. She flexes each finger in turn.

Ordinarily, it is something Nazaire would not have missed. It has occurred to Clara, for instance, that she might keep aside a piece of cutlery, even a teaspoon. In the event, she has always thought better of it. His attentiveness, much of the time, takes the form of habit.

As he leaves the room, especially, he performs each task scrupulously, and in unvarying order. After Chastern visits, he returns the tea things to the tray, arranging the teacups neatly on the stacked saucers, their handles nestling one inside the other. The cutlery he arrays in perfect symmetry, forks aligned at the centre, then the knives, each with its blade outwards. At either end, he places a teaspoon, so that the sequence resembles a palindrome.

The tiepin, however, has no place in Nazaire's methodical housekeeping. It was Chastern who brought it to her room, who set it aside as he adjusted his cravat and brushed it from the table as he stood to leave. When Clara finds it, she conceals it first in a gap in the floorboards. If he misses it and returns to her room to look for it, it is a place where it might easily have fallen without her knowledge.

She waits until the evening of the next day. The urge to retrieve the pin grows so strong that she can think of almost nothing else. She distracts herself by watching the blue tits. She has seen the pair now, diligently scouring the fresh shoots of the climbing rose, returning tirelessly to their hidden nest. Nazaire enters the room while she watches them. It is the last of the three visits he makes each day, and he conducts his inspection quietly, not addressing her until he is about to leave.

'You have grown quiet in your habits, little one. I wonder what it signifies.'

She watches the birds. They are losing the light, and there is an urgency now in their foraging.

'Never mind,' says Nazaire. 'It is in my own nature to be silent. We shall enjoy the tranquillity, both of us, until Dr Chastern returns.'

Clara waits for ten minutes after he leaves. It is as long as she can manage. She kicks her shoes off and crosses the room in her stockinged feet. Crouching above the crack in the floorboards, she prises the tiepin from its narrow recess. Its shaft is delicately ornate, and at its head is a pearl in a silver clasp.

She returns to the window. Over the moors, the sky is a wash of sombre violet, fading towards dusk. The birds are no longer visible. She presses the tiepin against her palm, the pearl warming easily against her skin.

When the feather falls, swooning gently onto the table, a moment passes before she notices. It is slender and white, settling noiselessly by her wrist and trembling with each slight disturbance of the air.

She looks up. The window is shut, and it cannot have drifted from the chimney, since a fire has been lit. Approaching the desk, she finds that its colour is softened by a gentle greyness. The line of the shaft, a little way from the centre, is strong and faultless. With the utmost gentleness, she traces the soft edge of the vane with her fingertip.

The surge of recognition is so forceful that for an unbreathing instant she is no longer here. It is long ago, and she stands by the dark water, in the place where things were first made. She waits, knowing that she must be patient.

But she remembers. Clara remembers.

Nineteen

Eustace vomited the moment he awoke, spattering the floor beside the washbasin. Abel Crouch pushed the bowl closer with his heel.

'The dead arose,' he said. 'Sleep well?'

Eustace wiped his face with the sheet and slumped onto his back.

'I had no wish ever to wake again. Why did you not end it?'

'I still might, you play your cards right.' Abel got up and crossed to the door. He opened it and called down for Jonah. 'But like I said, you left before our business was finished. There's other bastards I want to kill worse than you.'

Jonah, when he entered, was more nervous than usual. 'Everything all right, Mr Eustace? He said he was your friend, and you was in a bad way.'

'He's all right,' said Abel. 'Clean that up, there's a good lad. And see about getting a bit of breakfast up here. Mr Eustace has a busy day ahead.'

'Mr Eustace?'

'It is all right, Jonah. Do as he asks. I am unwell, that is all.'

Jonah swabbed the sour muck from the floor. He brought clean

260

washing water and fresh linen and towels. When the room was habitable, he trudged downstairs, returning after twenty minutes with toast and kippers, a pot of tarry coffee.

'Abel,' Eustace said. 'Will you give the boy ten bob? You will find money in that dresser.'

'I already found money in that dresser. That's how come we're sitting here all nice and cosy. You want to be more careful, you know. You used to know how to look out for yourself.'

Eustace waited until Jonah had left. 'You see how it is with me. There is nothing left now for me to protect.'

'I noticed you didn't seem that perky. Anyway, be that as it may, you've got something to live for now, ain't you?' Abel took his pistol out, gestured with it towards his head. 'So eat your fucking kippers.'

Eustace shaved for the first time in days. He combed his hair and put on one of the freshly laundered shirts that Jonah had brought. The coffee was foul, but he managed two cups with milk and sugar. He ate a mouthful of toast.

'That's better,' said Abel. 'I almost didn't recognise you before.'

'I no longer recognised myself.'

Abel finished his breakfast and lit a cigarette. 'How long you been here? The whole time, since what happened?'

Eustace nodded.

Abel shook his head. 'You didn't even look for her?'

He lowered his face into his hands. 'Do not think to judge me, not about that.'

'Yeah, well. Not my concern. Don't look right, though.'

'You think it did not occur to me? That it does not torment me? What do you think they would have done, even if I had found them? You saw for yourself how easily it comes to them. Should I have played at being a hero, even if it put her in the way of more harm?

No, they have named their price, and only my former employer can pay it. I could not stand by and wait for him to bestir himself.'

'So, what? You go to the seaside for a bit?'

Eustace lunged from the bed and took him by the throat. Abel had drawn the gun before he reached him and shoved it against his belly. 'Shoot me if you are going to shoot me,' he said. 'But do not question me in this, or I will leave you with something to remember me by.'

Abel's voice was a harsh croak. 'Don't fucking tempt me.'

Eustace released him, returning wearily to the edge of the bed. 'I came here,' he said. 'I came back here and I poisoned myself, I lowered myself into filth, night after night, to make it stop. I am sorry, Abel, for what happened to your brother. Truly I am, but what would you have had me do? I can offer you nothing. Not without her. Not without the child.'

'You want her back,' Abel said. 'And I want them, them who took her. We both have a dog in this race. I told you, that's why I'm here. That's why you ain't dead.'

'What of it? What difference does it make that we have common cause? What can we do that I could not have done alone?'

'Shut up and listen for a minute. I been keeping an eye on things, while you been off having a nervous breakdown. I have a few ideas, but there's things I don't know. That's where you come in.'

'Go on.'

'I stayed around for a while after it happened. We had a lot of stuff there needed taking away, and I weren't exactly sure what I was going to do next.'

'He did not question your presence there? Mr Crowe, I mean?'

'Him and his soprano, they went off the rails a bit after it happened. More than usual, like. I don't think they'd have noticed if I'd parked a tank on the lawn.'

'I expected no better.'

'Yeah, well. I'll come back to that in a minute. Anyway, a few days after it happened, this bloke turns up, says he's been engaged by you. Bit shabby looking, he was, but talked the talk all right.'

'Cromer. Elias Cromer.'

'That's him. Like I told you, he tries to pay me off. Says you've left instructions. I tell him where to shove it. I want to deal with you in person. He says you're unavailable, but he *notes my wishes*. He goes on like that a lot. Bit like you, as a matter of fact.'

'It was Cromer who trained me. But his own training was in law. It was among the reasons I sought his services. He is thorough, and he can be trusted.'

'That a fact? He looks like he ain't got the price of a cup of tea. Anyway, after he's had his little chat with me, he goes in to see his lordship. He's in there about an hour, and when he comes out, I have another word. See what I can find out. Now, at first he won't say nothing, he's on about client confidentiality and all that. So I get a little bit agitated due to my recent loss, and point out that I'm the only one seems to give a toss about making things right.'

'And?'

'Your boy Cromer, he still don't say much, but he gives me the *broad strokes*, as he calls them. Says our mutual friends ain't bringing the little girl back until Crowe discharges certain obligations.'

'That much I knew before I left. Is that all?'

'He don't go into detail, and I ain't really all that interested. Like I said to him, all I want to know is whether Crowe's going to give them what they want. And if he is, when's it going to happen. Because if he's got something for them, they've got to come back for it, ain't they? Or he's got to bring it to them. Either way, I want to mark the occasion. Make my presence felt.'

'What did Cromer say?'

'Not much, except what I can see for myself. That Crowe ain't doing much in the way of discharging. That he ain't even compos mentis half the time.'

'Again, that much was evident even before I left. It is why I saw no hope.'

'It don't look good, granted. So anyway, Cromer goes on his way. Says he's got other instructions from you. Next day, I get our stuff packed up and leave. See if I can't move matters forward by myself.'

'How did you propose to accomplish that?'

'By finding the cunts. How else?'

'That was foolish,' Eustace said. 'You did not succeed, I take it, and if you had, you would have put the child in danger.'

'No, I didn't succeed. Oxford ain't exactly home turf for me, not that he was ever likely to be there. So I decide to move down the list. Come looking for you, in other words. But before I do, I go back to the Estate.'

'Why?'

'Same reason I stayed in the first place. The more I know about what's going on, the better my chances of being in the right place when the professor and his mate turn up.'

'You might have saved yourself the trouble. My former employer was much as you left him, I take it?'

'I didn't expect much, but it turns out there's been a development.'

'What kind of development?'

'Well, I can see right away that he's taken himself in hand a bit. Him and the bird ain't spending all day every day arseholed. I see him shutting himself up in the library a bit. Don't get me wrong, he ain't become a monk or nothing, but you could say he's keeping regular hours. He took a day off for Christmas, which is how I got in there.'

'In where?'

'Into the house. Into the library.'

'And you discovered something?'

'I don't know.' Abel took a carefully folded page from an inner pocket and handed it to him. 'You tell me.'

'What is this?'

'I had to copy it out so he wouldn't notice. I probably ain't spelled everything right. And I couldn't copy the flower, obviously.'

'The flower?'

'A white rose, pressed or whatever you call it. All dried up and flattened, it was, and folded into the original letter. The letter's *about* the rose, far as I can tell.'

Eustace unfolded it. It was from Chastern to Mr Crowe, and was dated the 22nd of December.

My Dear Crowe,

I write to thank you for your recent hospitality, and to assure you that we strive in our lesser fashion to accommodate your young charge in comfort. Though I fear she finds her circumstances rather austere, she has the resilience that one envies in the very young. She possesses a faculty of inventiveness also that we have remarked on as somewhat beyond the ordinary, and we note with relief that she seems always to devise some means of amusing herself.

It is in this latter connexion that I enclose a keepsake, one that I do not doubt will provoke the sentiments of pride and affection that are proper to a guardian. The flower you find enclosed is from a cherished specimen in my own garden. Though I have, I hope, been assiduous in my husbandry, I have never induced it to flower – as it has done in recent days – while the garden lay in repose under the midwinter snow.

The serendipity of this occurrence became more forcefully

apparent to me when I discovered that our young guest had, in a
passage of writing, devoted considerable imaginative effort to the
same rose.

What a treasure you have kept from me, Crowe – what a rare
and lucent treasure. I see now why you guarded her so zealously,
and you must have no doubt that I shall do likewise. This will
comfort you, I hope, until the day comes when she may be
returned to the tenderness of your custody. That day, of course, will
be entirely of your choosing.

I trust, in the meantime, that you keep well and that you
continue to find some tolerable occupation for your own estimable
gifts.

I remain, as ever, your admiring friend

Chastern

Eustace folded the letter and passed it back. He stood and went
to the window. Outside the abattoir, a boy sluiced blood and filth
from the yard with two or three desultory bucketfuls of water. When
he judged his efforts satisfactory, he sat on the upturned bucket to
smoke a cigarette. The effluent coursed around his boots, thick with
grease and darkening to sienna.

'What's he saying?' said Abel. 'How come Crowe's sat up and took
notice?'

Eustace spoke quietly. 'The sun. She was the sun.'

'Eh?'

'The sun and the moon, remember? She was the one I should
have guarded most closely. There were many such miracles, and yet
somehow I did not see.'

'The flower, you mean? How's that a miracle? Remember I ain't
exactly got green fingers.'

'It is not important now. You left the Estate then, after you found the letter?'

'Well, it looked like the professor had only just lit a fire under your boss, so I reckoned I had time. Thought I'd pay you a visit.'

'How quickly could we get there, if the need arose? Do you have a car?'

'Funny you should ask. I have yours, as a matter of fact. Or his, I suppose it is. I fixed the Jag up. Reckoned it wouldn't hurt to be able to get somewhere in a hurry.'

'There are some small matters I must attend to here before we leave. In particular, there is an appointment I must keep on Thursday evening. It is something I ought to have done last night, in fact, but I was— well, you saw how it was with me. You have no objection?'

Abel considered this. 'One condition,' he said.

'Namely?'

'I'm keeping you company. If we're going to be held up for another week, I want you coming out in one piece.'

'It is a matter of some delicacy. An intimate matter.'

'More intimate than dying?'

Eustace stared down at the slaughterhouse. The boy had abandoned his bucket and his spreading delta of waste. The gates to the street had been locked for the evening, but inside the lights continued to burn.

Twenty

O n the stones, the words cannot be made beautiful.

It is rough and indelicate work, more scratching than writing, but Clara no longer frets over her clumsiness. Her right arm will be free of its sling soon, and before long it will be strong again. Even then, she expects no great improvement in her technique. The words on the stones are not exercises. She is no longer practising.

To begin with, there is the question of space. The marks she makes on the stones cannot be erased. She is confined, therefore, to the twenty-four stones that are hidden from view. Twenty-four stones: she counted them the first time she crawled under the bed, contorting herself in the musty darkness to touch and memorise each of them in turn. The characters she etches with the pin are crude and angular. No more than two hundred, she has found, can be crammed onto each stone.

Twenty-four stones times two hundred. It would amount to fewer than a thousand words, hardly enough for even the shortest of stories. But what she writes will not be a story; it will be like nothing she has written before. It is another kind of making that she has begun, with its own rules and possibilities; with even its own alphabet, though it is older and stranger than any other she has known.

It contains only a handful of crude tokens, and these must be assembled in clusters of three. They are not like the words she is used to, these triplets. There are hardly more than a few dozen, all of them recurring over and over. These are dull patterns, taken alone, with none of the music or grace of true words, nothing to soften the labour of scratching them out. It is only in the entirety of the sequence, she knows, that its secret grandeur is expressed. Its beauty is hidden in its cadences, in its unseen treasure of colours: its amber and ochre, its opal.

What she makes will be hidden too, once she has seeded it. It will swell in silence, like chalk or bone, like a tulip bulb or a tusk of quartz. It will be beautiful, in its way, but it will not be perfect. There will be mistakes – not many, but just enough; of just the right kind. If she gets the sequence exactly right, the rest will unfold by itself. The thing she makes will nurture itself. It will quicken and flourish in silence, like something waiting to be born.

It will be beautiful, but only if she gets it right. This is why she takes no chances, why she writes nothing – scratches nothing – until she has recited it inwardly hundreds of times, until she can envision the chain of marks with such familiar clarity that she feels she could etch it in her sleep. She does this, most often, while standing at the window, where she looks out, only half-seeing, at the thawing landscape and its patient insurrection of colour.

In this way, too, Clara assures Nazaire that there has been no change in her habits. He is accustomed now to finding her always at the window. He no longer remarks on it, having had little cause since Chastern's departure to speak to her at all. He is watchful, as always, and has abandoned none of his meticulous precautions, but she gives him no new cause for concern. Perhaps, like her, he is simply tired of this. Perhaps he wishes it to end.

Her long vigils at the window have another advantage. Standing for hours in complete silence allows her to listen, to detect the faint and infrequent sounds that Nazaire makes while he is elsewhere in the house. They are small clues, of course, and she is careful not to place too much trust in them. She does not forget his preternatural stealth. As long as she can hear nothing, he might easily be just outside the room.

Still, there are certain domestic necessities that even he must attend to. She hears the ragged and shearing cracks as he chops firewood for the stove, the subdued gurgle of plumbing after he bathes or uses the lavatory. She even comes to recognise those occasions, at least once a day, when he leaves the house. He goes to buy provisions, she assumes, and the nearest village must lie a few miles off. He is never gone for less than an hour.

Clara wastes none of this time.

The bed is old and sits on a squat frame, leaving a gap that is barely high enough for Clara to squeeze through. When she does, it is like crawling into a collapsing and desiccated mouth. The aging mattress sags between the slats, and the coarse bulges press against her back as she squirms inwards. She feels, by the time she reaches the stone wall at the far end, as if she has been swallowed.

She is hampered still by her injury. She must crawl into position under the bed using only one of her elbows, keeping her right arm clear of the floor. Twice, she has slipped while twisting to face the wall, trapping her splinted forearm under her torso. She did no serious harm, she thinks, to the healing bone, but even the smallest flaring of the old pain is enough to fill her with dread.

She is careful not to rush, taking four or five minutes to work herself into place by the wall. She is wary, too, of spending too long in the act of writing itself. While she is under the bed, she has no way of marking the passage of time. Instead, she sets a limit on the number of letters she allows herself to complete. The tiepin was not made for such rough work, and the whitewash makes a poor and flaking surface. Even the simplest shapes can occupy her for long and agonising seconds.

She counts these seconds, though, and arrives at an average. In twenty minutes, if she encounters no unusual difficulties, she can complete two stones. Allowing five minutes each for crawling in and out gives a total of half an hour. Even if she is confident that Nazaire will be occupied for longer, half an hour is as long as she dares to stay hidden.

It is maddening, this restriction. An entire day may pass between one opportunity and the next, and her progress seems absurdly slow. Still, she resists the urge to linger. She cannot allow her caution to lapse. If her secret labour is discovered, she will not have another chance. She knows enough of her captors now to be certain of this much. If they find her out in this, they will spare no cruelty. The next punishment will be worse.

Nazaire coughs.

At first, Clara pays no attention. She is standing at the window while he clears away the remains of her lunch. In the days since she first crept under the bed, the thaw has continued steadily. As she studies the emerging landscape, she touches her right arm. She has been free of the sling for only two days, and it feels no less lumpen and unfamiliar. It is her left hand still that she uses to work on the stones.

He coughs again, and Clara looks around. He has set down his tray and raises his hand to cover his mouth. It occurs to her, though it seems preposterous, that he has never so much as cleared his throat within her hearing. He picks the tray up and returns his attention to the table, only to put it down again a moment later. He places his hand lightly against his abdomen. His expression is displeased, yet faintly curious.

'Excuse me, little one. I feel unwell.'

She watches closely as he moves towards the door. His movements are fluid, as always, but slightly hurried. It is out of the ordinary, as is the coughing, but by themselves these things may mean nothing. It is only after he closes the door that Clara notices the most unusual thing.

The lunch tray is still on the table.

Twenty-One

A bel parked the Jaguar in a side street opposite Mrs Fraser's house. The place he chose was in the shadow of a plane tree, and gave them an oblique view of the front steps, of the lighted windows of the salon.

'Tell me again about this Gill.'

'He is a magistrate's son. His father, as far as I can see, has not troubled him with seeking any occupation of his own. He devotes himself, therefore, to his own pleasures.'

'Likes his booze, you mean? And the ladies, obviously.'

'Young women are among his pleasures. There is no liking in it.'

'Yeah, you mentioned he weren't exactly gentlemanly.'

'I am not like some, Abel. I do not lightly excuse such things.'

Abel looked away, and did not respond immediately. 'We had a sister, me and John. I ever mention that?'

'Not that I recall.'

'Lily was only seventeen when she went. Threw herself under the Southend train.'

Eustace looked at him, but said nothing.

'Which, that was my old man's train. He was the driver, I mean.

Wasn't until we found the note that we knew why. I did my first stretch for that, for what happened after.'

Eustace waited, but Abel did not turn towards him. He kept his eyes on Mrs Fraser's house. 'I am sorry, Abel.'

'I don't lightly excuse such things neither, but we ain't going in there to set the world to rights. You're going to make things right with this Gill fucker, and you're going to say please and thank you, even if he starts giving you lip. You're going to take a moment with this bird you're fond of, set your affairs in order or whatever, and then we're coming out here and we're getting back in the car. No complications, no loose ends. Agreed?'

Eustace closed his eyes. He took a long breath. 'I do not mean to confront him. That is not my plan.'

'Worst comes to the worst,' said Abel. 'I'll be maintaining a discreet presence, as your driver for the evening. I've got the equipment, so you can leave any unpleasantness to me.'

'Abel,' said Eustace. 'Everything has been agreed.'

Abel turned and studied his face for a moment, nodding slowly as he did so. 'You coming back for her, this bird? When it's all over, I mean? Is that what this is?'

Eustace looked straight ahead, his arms resting in his lap.

'Come,' he said at last. 'There is much to be done.'

It was Mrs Fraser herself who greeted them at the front door.

'Mr Eustace,' she said. 'I am delighted that you could join us. I was not aware, however, that you intended to introduce another gentleman. I prefer, as you know, to make certain inquiries before inviting new clients.'

'Mr Crouch is my driver,' said Eustace. 'I have business elsewhere, and will be leaving for the country after this engagement. He will wait for me in the hall, if you have no objection.'

She admitted them without further comment, though she subjected Abel to candid scrutiny as he took his place by the coat stand. 'Mr Gill and the rest of the company have already gathered in the salon. The girls have begun to come down. We have lit the fire, you will be pleased to hear. I know how you feel the cold.'

Mrs Fraser showed him in, not withdrawing as she usually did, but finding an unobtrusive place by the mantelpiece. Gill sprawled on a sofa that gave him a view of the door. Over his rolled-up shirt-sleeves, he wore a garish waistcoat. He had seated one of the girls on his thigh and was inducing her, as Eustace entered, to hold a match to his out-thrust cigar.

'Mr Eustace,' he called out. 'There you are now. We thought we might have to go out looking for you. I says to Michelle – what did I say, Michelle? I says, our Mr Eustace has got himself into a bit of bother. He's got form, I says.' Gill laughed forcefully, and was joined by the two men on the opposite sofa. They appeared younger than him by some years, and remained as yet unaccompanied. Like him, they had peeled their shirtsleeves from their forearms and splayed their legs as widely as the furniture would accommodate.

'Mr Gill,' said Eustace. 'You are seated quite comfortably, I am relieved to see. I was concerned that some irreparable damage might have been done.'

Gill plucked his cigar from his mouth and licked his lips. 'Aren't you going to have a seat yourself, Mr Eustace? You haven't even taken your coat off.'

'I regret that I cannot stay long. I have been called away on pressing business.'

'This business of yours, Mr Eustace.' Mrs Fraser took up a poker to agitate the fire's meagre bank of coals. 'Forgive me, gentlemen, for interrupting. Your business will not keep you from us for too long, I hope.'

'His business is his business,' said Gill. 'He's come to say his piece before he leaves, that's the main thing. Let him have his say, Mrs Fraser.'

She joined her hands across her hips and looked at Gill with her lips slightly askew. She turned to Eustace again. 'Julie would be most upset, I'm sure, if you were not to return soon.'

'It is hard to say,' said Eustace. 'It is a difficult business. It has occupied me, already, for quite some time.'

'She will be joining us later, I'm sure,' Mrs Fraser said. 'Go and let her know Mr Eustace is here, Michelle. You need not rush. The gentlemen wish to discuss a private matter. You will excuse her a moment, Mr Gill?'

'Don't mind me,' said Gill. 'Gives Mr Eustace room, if he wants to have a seat. I haven't seen him for a fortnight. We've got lots to talk about.'

'Thank you,' Eustace said. 'I prefer to stand. And Julie will not be joining us.' He crossed to the fireplace and stood opposite Mrs Fraser. She wore a suit of robust and autumnal tweed, and smoothed the trim of her jacket as she watched him.

'Is that right?' she said. 'She did not think to inform me. But you will take a small drink, in any case? There is some of that single malt still. You have paid for the bottle, so you might as well have the benefit of it.'

Eustace turned to the mantelpiece and reached into an inner pocket. The envelope was heavy, bearing an elaborate seal. 'I shall leave these documents with you,' he said, 'so that you may look them over at your leisure. They were prepared by the firm of Curzon and Howlett, which acts now for Julie.'

Mrs Fraser glanced at the envelope. 'Indeed?' she said. 'Has she such great affairs to manage?'

'She has interests now that must be protected,' Eustace said. 'Your own affairs will not be greatly affected, if certain conditions are met. The firm will advise you further.'

Gill pumped his thigh with impatience, flinging a moist scrag of cigar into the coals. 'What's the matter?' he said. 'That tart giving trouble, is she? I told you, a girl like that wants a firm hand.'

Eustace turned to him. As he did so, he saw Abel, an attentive shadow encroaching on the doorway. 'Your father, Mr Gill. He is a magistrate, is he not?'

Gill leaned back. 'She told you, did she? I says to the boys when we heard you coming in, I says, I wonder how she put manners on him. What did I say, boys?'

Eustace waited until their hilarity had abated. 'You need not look far, then, to seek advice in regard to the offence of trespass.'

'Trespass?' Gill brought himself upright on the sofa. 'Forgive us our trespasses, is that it? That's what you came here for, Mr Eustace. You're not forgetting your lines, are you?'

Mrs Fraser took the envelope from the mantelpiece, patting at her clavicles for the chain on which her reading glasses were suspended. Putting them on, she broke the seal carefully and drew out the wad of documents. Abel was fully visible at the doorway now, alert to every current.

'I have no training myself,' Eustace continued, 'but I am given to understand that ignorance of possession is no defence.' He watched Mrs Fraser straighten quietly, fumbling with the chain of her spectacles as she took them off.

Gill bunched his fingers on his thighs. 'I hate to trouble you, Mrs Fraser, but is this what I was supposed to hear from this clown? Did we not have a little chat about your circumstances?'

'Mrs Fraser's circumstances are largely unchanged, as I mentioned,' said Eustace. 'The new proprietress, I gather, will seek no review of the terms of her tenancy. Your own circumstances, Mr

Gill, are rather less certain. It is no defence, against a charge of trespass, for the tinker to say that he thought he had put his horse to graze on land that was in commons.'

Gill stood, approaching Eustace with his paunch out-thrust, his arms spread. 'I'm giving you a chance,' he said. 'You fucking get me, Jeeves? I'm giving you a chance.'

Mrs Fraser spoke. 'Go home, Mr Gill.'

He looked from her to Eustace. 'Come again?'

'Or for the son of a magistrate to claim—' Eustace paused. 'Do you have any occupation of your own? I never thought to ask. The law, in any case, is clear. The son of a magistrate may not claim licence to occupy on the grounds that he has had his limp cock felt on the same premises for several years, and was unaware of any change of ownership.'

'Eustace,' said Abel from the door.

'If a trespasser has been informed of his violation,' Eustace said, 'and does not vacate with reasonable haste, the rightful possessor is granted considerable freedoms by the applicable case law. Again, I speak as a layman. Your father, I am sure, could advise you more competently.'

'Eustace,' Abel repeated. He entered the room now, approaching the fireplace with a quiet tread.

Gill took a step towards Eustace, leaned closer to his face. 'You're a whoremaster now, is that it? Your very own doll's house, just like you always wanted?'

'I am only a messenger,' said Eustace. 'The house belongs to Julie now, and you are no longer welcome here. Abel, would you be kind enough?'

'Not that big a step for you, eh?' Gill's breath was moist and sour. Spittle had curdled at the cusp of his lips. 'From them dressing up games you like. I heard you asked for—' He twisted as the forearm wrapped itself around his neck, becoming still again as he recognised the pressure between his shoulder blades.

'I heard about you too, big boy,' Abel said. 'I heard what you like doing. So now you and me, we're going to play a little game of our own.'

Twenty-Two

Nazaire *stumbles as* he is leaving her room. He has caught himself when Clara turns from the window, but leans uneasily against the door frame. He clutches his abdomen and holds still, as if waiting for something to subside. She realises that she can hear his breathing. He begins coughing again – the sound is coarse and sodden – and it is some time before he can suppress it. When it eases, he takes his hand from his mouth and examines it.

He pushes himself upright and turns to find her watching.

'What do you find so interesting?' he says. 'Go back to your birds, little one.'

He slams the door as he leaves the room. She shudders slightly. It is the loudest sound she has heard in all the time she has been kept here. And his face, his anger. It is something she has never seen in him. Even when the worst things happened, his actions were measured and exact. In all the time she has been here, he has done nothing that betrayed recognisable emotion. Not rage, not pity – not even irritation. Not until now.

Clara clenches her left hand and turns back to the garden.

*

That night, she is woken by dim noises in the lower parts of the house. At first, she fails to recognise them. They are sounds she has heard before only by day. She sits on the edge of the bed, tense and unmoving, straining to catch the slightest disturbance. For a long time, there is silence. She is on the point of going back to sleep when she hears it – the muted scrape and snick of an outer door.

He has left the house. Clara gets up and crosses to the mantelpiece to check the time. A quarter past two in the morning. She cannot think what might have called him out so late, and she has no idea how long he might be gone. For a long time, she stands and claws at her palms, unable to bring herself to move. It is not a risk she would usually take, and yet it can hardly be a brief errand if it takes him out at such an hour.

She takes the tiepin from its hiding place.

It is cold under the bed, and she is wearing only her nightgown. The floorboards gnaw at her bare knees and a splinter pierces her palm. It is so dark, when she has dragged herself into place, that she can barely see the surface of the stone, much less the signs she scratches on it. Still, she perseveres, using her right hand to guide the movements of her left. She writes for the allotted time as always, completing her tally of four hundred characters and finding that she has reached the edge of the stone.

Clara pauses. She has been consumed by the thing she must write. It has been days since she thought of her progress, of how much remained to be done. She allows herself a minute or two longer to count the remaining stones. She has worked methodically, beginning at the foot of the bed and continuing towards the corner, working her way across the shorter span of wall before returning to the beginning and starting on the next course of stones.

She has reached the head of the bed again, and is nearing the rightmost stones of the lowest course. She feels in the dark for those that remain, stroking their surfaces lightly to assure herself that they are unmarked. When she reaches the end, she repeats the count, then shunts herself hurriedly back out from under the bed. She restores the tiepin to its hiding place, glancing once more at the clock before returning to bed.

She lies awake and allows herself to think of it. Six stones. There are six stones left. Twelve hundred letters. She makes the calculations, counting out the opportunities she will need. She wonders if she might relax her own strictness even slightly, if she might allow herself a few more letters on each occasion. Even if she does not, even if she continues just as she has, the task that remains seems small enough now that she almost savours it.

She is nearing the end.

He comes and goes without ceremony. Though he maintains his regime as before, bringing her meals and conducting his inspections at predictable hours, nothing is quite as it was. The food he offers her now is simple and crudely served. In the mornings, he may bring only porridge and a glass of milk, at lunchtime nothing more than bread and cheese. He no longer makes his meticulous inventories of cutlery and crockery. Often, there is only a single cup and plate to clear away.

His rituals are abbreviated now. He does not stay as long as before, and makes only brief circuits of the room before leaving. There are changes in him too, though it is some days before she is sure she has not imagined them. He is slower now, and his gait is disturbed by hesitations. His skin has grown pale and oddly glazed. His breathing is almost always audible.

Clara tries to ensure that her own habits seem unchanged, that she is at the window when he comes in, occupied by some inconsequential novelty in the garden. She makes her observations as

inconspicuously as she can. In the evenings, she can watch his reflection without turning around. Once, she sees him lower himself
into one of the armchairs, his forearm clamped across his belly. She
listens closely, conscious of the effort he is making to keep silent.
When a weak groan slips from him at last, she turns to face him. She
is careful to reveal nothing in her expression.

He looks up. 'I see you, little one. Do not think I do not see you
watching. It is a small ailment, and it will pass. Do not hope for too
much.'

Clara feels an urge in the fingers of her left hand. She clamps it
with her right, joining them in front of her.

'I have sent for someone,' Nazaire says. 'You think, perhaps, that
you will find me senseless one morning, that you will step over me
and be free. Yes, I see what you are thinking. I have sent for someone. Soon, all will be as before.'

He leaves the house again that night. Clara works for ten minutes
and returns to bed. She lies awake for an hour, and still she hears
nothing. Before she can stop herself, she has crept back under the
bed. When she lies down again, it is nine in the morning. She is
exhausted, taut with panic and elation. Nazaire has not returned.

She is watching the birds when she hears him on the stairs. She fears
for them now. It is her rose they have been feeding on, scouring the
tender shoots for aphids. Already, those young stems are growing
dark and brittle. In the cold, the blooms are greying and growing
frail.

Nazaire fumbles with the lock and almost falls into the room. He
is pale and dishevelled, gripping the door frame to steady himself.
He is clutching something. She sees a pair of dull metal rings, a loop
of chain.

'Little one,' he says. 'There is something— I must leave for a time.'

He takes a step towards her, but lurches immediately to one side. He clutches the edge of the table, almost toppling it, and falls to his knees. He grips the arm of a chair and braces himself against it, unable for now to go any further. He paws at his stomach. It is hugely swollen, straining his grimy shirt. The skin of his hands is blotchy, strangely discoloured.

When he heaves himself to his feet, he grunts in pain. He looks down at himself, spreading his fingers over his distended shape. His breathing is laboured now, and it is some time before he can speak again. When he does, his voice is weak, distorted by a viscous rattling.

'I will be gone only a day or two,' he says. He shows her what he is holding. It is a pair of steel cuffs, linked by a chain. 'You will allow me to make you secure while I am away.'

Clara folds her arms closely around herself. She edges slowly from her place at the window, keeping herself pressed against the wall. She could run, she thinks. He has not locked the door behind him. If he comes closer, she could get around him. He cannot move as he once did.

'Little one.' He takes another shuffling step. 'You know you must. You know I cannot allow—'

He begins to cough. It is prolonged and violent, worsening the discomfort in his abdomen. He bends at the waist, clutching his gut with one hand and struggling with the other to keep his mouth covered. When the coughing subsides, he lowers his palm to inspect something he has expelled – a quivering slug of crimson tissue. He looks up at her.

'I see you,' he says. 'I see you watching, keeping your secrets. You have hidden something from me, but I will find it. I will—'

The coughing seizes him again, and he sinks to his knees by Clara's bed, clutching at the quilt for support. He retches, bringing up stained fluid and another bolt of glistening pulp. When he raises his eyes again, he strains to focus on her.

'The body,' he says. 'The body keeps its own secrets, though they come out always, in the end. It is like a serpent, little one, a snake in my own guts. Is that what it is? But you cannot tell me, can you? You cannot say.'

He sways on his knees, his mouth gaping. Blood dribbles over his chin, and his breathing is clogged and syrupy. He bends, clasping his midsection, and vomits. It bursts from him in great surges, drenching the bedclothes and splashing noisily on the floor. It is watery at first, but thickens with darker matter, spongy shreds filmed with mucus.

Clara paces carefully along the wall, keeping clear of the spreading pool. Her eyes never leave him, but he does not look up again. He slumps forward as the convulsions weaken. He tries to prop himself up, but sprawls on the slick floor and lies still as his ragged breathing fades, facing the void beneath the bed.

The house surprises Clara with its plainness. The rooms she passes through are as bare and cold as hers was. The windows are curtainless, the white walls unrelieved by ornamentation or colour. Not a single painting or mirror hangs anywhere. In the large but comfortless drawing room, there is no piano or gramophone. There is not even a bookcase.

For all its austerity, there are signs in the house of increasing disorder. Flies cluster on a plate of untouched food. A broken glass lies in a yellowing puddle of milk. There are fingermarks on walls and tabletops, on banisters and the edges of doors, in glancing smears or clustered darkly like grapes. On a sideboard, she finds one of his monogrammed handkerchiefs, its centre richly bloodstained. On some impulse, she picks it up. Touching only its edges, she folds it away.

She ransacks the kitchen for provisions, though there is little enough to choose from. She finds half a stale loaf and a wedge of crusted cheese. From the back of a cupboard, she takes a tin of sardines. Nazaire's own meals must have been no less dismal, in recent days, than those he brought to her. She bundles the food in a tea towel and knots it at the top.

The kitchen door, when she tries it, is locked. She ought to have expected it. Nazaire was scrupulous about such things. The key is likely to be somewhere on his person; in his pocket, perhaps, or on a chain. To look for it, she would have to go back upstairs. She would have to creep towards his still form, picking her way through that darkening film. She would have to touch him.

She searches the kitchen, her agitation growing as she upends jars and rummages in drawers. She climbs onto the counter and tries the window, which seems wide enough for her to clamber through. The handle, though, has seized shut.

She moves with quiet urgency as she makes her way back through the downstairs rooms. When she reaches the tiled hallway, she tiptoes along its length, glancing up the stairs as she passes them. It is absurd, perhaps, but the fear is undiminished. She would feel it, she thinks, even if she had seen him hanged.

She is looking back even as she tugs at the hall door. It is the air, cold and pristine, that makes her turn. Simply and unaccountably, the door has opened. She stands, in a slow hiatus of disbelief, as the latch slips from her hand, as she blinks in the widening light.

Outside, in the walled garden, the snow is beginning to melt.

The day is clear and cold. She opens the garden gate and steps out onto a lane. It is open to the moors and scoured by a harsh breeze. She ought to be wearing a coat. Eustace would want her to wear a coat.

She walks quickly for warmth, and to feel the cottage recede behind her. She has no idea where she is, or how far away the nearest house might be. She chooses a direction simply because it takes her slightly downhill.

She has gone only a few hundred yards when the noise of a car makes her start and turn. It has pulled up on the verge a little way off, large and black and slightly shabby. She looks anxiously from one side of the road to the other. For as far as she can see, there is nothing but the sombre barrenness of the thawing moors. There is nowhere she can run. The driver, a man in a dark and tattered raincoat, steps out and takes off his hat.

'Clara,' he calls. 'Am I so much changed that you do not know me?'

She stares at him, gripping her cuffs and shivering.

'It is Elias, Clara. Elias Cromer. I have come to take you home.'

Twenty-Three

The boy leaves by the river road.

He does not look back, once he has turned from the water's edge, at the still heap that was Swaine's man, and he finds that there is no hesitation in him. He must take the river road as far as the bridge, and so he steals a good horse from the stable of a coaching inn, laming two others that look quick enough to be used in pursuit. The mist has ceded to rain, and he rides with his clothes soaked to his skin. When his hands grow so cold at last that he can no longer grip the reins, he hitches them instead around his wrists.

When he chances upon the one he is following, making camp in a copse of ash and hazel, he has no idea how far he has ridden, only that he has come some way along the Dover road. Mr Crowe is in the company of another man, a fellow of shrewd appearance, though he is indifferently groomed. They have set a small fire and are well-enough provisioned to have taken a meal of some kind. They are passing a brandy bottle between them and show every sign of good cheer.

The boy walks into the clearing and stands facing them across the fire. He lifts the rifle and takes aim. Mr Crowe raises the bottle, gesturing towards him.

'Ah, now there he is, Cromer. That is the young man I mentioned to you as we rode.'

Cromer regards him mildly, the rain spilling from the rumpled brim of his hat. 'Indeed?' he says. 'I must confess that the promise you spoke of is not immediately apparent to me. It was his name, perhaps, that impressed itself upon you?'

'I regret to say,' Mr Crowe says, 'that I neglected to ask it. Will you divulge your name, my young friend, so that we may invite you to join us?'

'I had a name,' says the boy. 'I had a name, but it is gone.'

'I am sorry to hear it,' says Mr Crowe. 'A boy should not be without a name, no more than should anything in this world. Never leave a void where something may be written.'

'I have no name,' the boy insists. 'I won't need one, where I'm going.'

'Nonsense,' says Mr Crowe. 'What do you say, Cromer? Does he look like a Holloway to you? A Morley, perhaps?'

'Neither quite hits the mark, in my estimation. He has a certain quality, this boy.'

'Well, quite. That is just what I tried to convey to you. He is not a Fairfax, exactly, or a de Vere, though I fancy it is something in that region.'

The boy cocks the rifle. 'I have no name.'

'Give me a moment,' says Mr Crowe. 'It will come to me.'

He fires, or means to, but the rifle has seized in the incessant rain, or the trigger thwarts his numb fingers. He cannot tell, and never afterwards knows. Mr Crowe looks down, as if in politeness, only raising his eyes again when the boy has lowered the rifle to his side, when he feels his right leg buckle under him and sinks staring to one knee.

'Come,' Mr Crowe says. 'Come and warm yourself while we

deliberate on what we are to call you. It is not a thing that may be rushed, after all. A name is like a shoe, you know. Nothing is so irksome as one that is ill-fitting. Sit with us, there's a good fellow. Take a slug of this brandy before you pass entirely from the world. Cromer, where is that cutlet you were eating?'

'I gave it to you, Mr Crowe.'

'Well, cook another one, man. The boy is at death's door.'

'I thought to keep some portion aside for tomorrow. We have a long road.'

'And what earthly good would that do, if the boy does not live to see it? Sufficient unto the day, Cromer. Sufficient unto the day.'

The boy sits before the fire and is wrapped in a horsehair blanket. Silently, he eats and drinks what they give him. He keeps the rifle at his side, and neither man moves to take it from him. Indeed, they seem to forget that he has it at all. When he has warmed himself, when his strength returns, he will finish it. He will do the next thing, the last thing, and he will be finished.

When he wakes, they are readying their horses. The air is cold and damp, scented with woodsmoke and coffee. He throws off his blanket and searches with his flattened palm. The rifle lies where he left it. As he sits up warily, Mr Crowe looks around from his saddlebag.

'*Bonjour, mon jeune ami. Tu as bien dormi? Tu as faim?*'

The boy looks away, unwilling to show that he has not understood.

'French, old chap. The language of Flaubert and Baudelaire, and of seduction, as you have no doubt heard. When you speak to a woman in French, it is as if your tongue were applied directly to her most intimate heart. The education of a young gentleman is not complete until he is proficient in conjugation.'

The boy gets up, keeping the rifle slung at his side. He circles the remains of the campfire, toeing the last of the warmth from its embers.

'We sail at— what time do we sail, Cromer?'

'Four o'clock was what we agreed, though it all rather depends on our associate's luck in finding a suitable beach.'

'Four o'clock. There you are, my friend. You have until teatime to shoot me. If no opportune moment has presented itself by then, you will have to accompany us to Paris and shoot me there at your leisure.'

'That may be difficult,' says Cromer. 'Lavoisier will not have guns aboard, not after the incident at Deauville.'

Mr Crowe snorts. 'How particularly tedious he is, even for a Frenchman. No widow could have been more handsomely provided for.'

The boy stalks off into the trees to relieve himself, stooping afterwards by a stream to wash. On his hands still, minutely seaming his fingertips, is the blood from what he did to Swaine's man. It has darkened now to umber. They are mocking him, with this levity. They are mocking him, and he ought to silence them. He ought to return to the clearing with his gun raised, to finish what he came to do.

Instead, he trudges back without a word. He sees to his horse, the one he took from the coaching inn, making his own preparations to leave. Cromer hands him a canteen of water and a buttered roll, and the boy accepts them without a word.

When they are a mile or so along the Dover road, Mr Crowe turns in the saddle. The boy has fallen in a little way behind them, as if he were travelling the same road alone. 'Speaking of widows, as we were, I hope you will forgive my raising a delicate matter.'

The boy replies with a sharp look, but says nothing.

'You have left behind your mother, have you not? I mean no accusation. You would go to her if you could, but the town is no longer safe for you.'

He stares down at his hands, working the reins into their stained creases.

'It is not safe for you,' Mr Crowe continues. 'You would be putting your own neck in the noose. When you killed the man whose rifle that was – and I do not blame you in the slightest for acting as you did – you left behind the life you had. You left those you loved, both the living and the dead.'

'Don't,' says the boy. 'Don't talk about them.'

Mr Crowe pulls his horse up and turns to him. 'There is pain in this for both of us,' he says. 'I have no wish, believe me, to revisit what occurred. I mean only to offer you what comforts I can.'

'Comforts?' the boy says. 'What comforts?'

'You may not return,' says Mr Crowe. 'And nor may I. Our friend Cromer, however, is under no such injunction. He is a man, moreover, who could do your mother's case much good if he were to apply his arts.'

'What arts? What are you saying?'

Mr Crowe spurs his horse onwards. 'The law, young man, that most tenebrous of all arts. Cromer has taken silk, you know, and defers to no man in his juridical guile. He could have the Magna Carta itself struck down if he put his mind to it.'

Cromer dismisses this with a small gesture. He rides on without looking back, adjusting his misshapen hat and shaking the drizzle from his coat.

'We are still close,' Mr Crowe says. 'Cromer could go back and see to it that your mother is protected, that her home remains inviolate and that she herself is not harassed. Provisions could be made for her comfort also. A sum could be put at her disposal that would give some repose to her thoughts. Let us aid her, my friend. I would take it as a kindness. And it would give us time to settle upon a suitable name.'

Mr Crowe studies him intently as he waits for his reply, but the boy says nothing for a long time. He listens to his own breath, then shakes his head in weariness. 'I have no name,' he says.

'Wait!' Mr Crowe says, bringing his horse up short. 'I have it.'

Eustace took the river road, at last.

It was strange to think that he had not done so until now. He had thought, when he first came back, that it was to see the old places. It was what a man did, surely, when he found he could go no further: he followed his course as far back as he could, sought the vanished things that gleamed still among the reeds. There would be a certain propriety in coming back this way, even if the prospect gave him no comfort. It was no more, surely, than a matter of time.

Yet the day had not come. He had not woken, one dismal morning in the boarding house, with a quiet certainty of purpose. He had not put his walking shoes on and struck out westwards, his intention unvoiced even to himself. He had kept to the quays and the centre of the town, to places he had seldom been even as a boy. The day had not come, and now he could no longer wait for it.

He left Abel at breakfast. There was one more visit he must make, he told him. He would be gone for two hours at the most. Abel was not best pleased. He was anxious to be on the road, and no more inclined than before to be trusting. He insisted at first that they would go together after they had eaten, that he would wait in the car, relenting only when Eustace mentioned his destination.

'Don't get lost,' he said. 'Or I might have to find you a plot of your own.'

He found the ferry house long gone. A railway bridge had been built a little way downstream from the bank where it had stood, and rubble had been sunk for its footings. Around this, the silt had accreted, narrowing the river's course. Eustace could tell the character of the water still from its complexion, from the tensions in its rucked and gathered surface. It was faster and deeper now than it had been in any part of the old crossing.

Further upstream, the reshaping of the bank had allowed a string of cottages to be built, some of them adjoined by places of business: a roughly built workshop with a roof of corrugated iron; a scrapyard where engine blocks were piled alongside the rusting wheelhouse of a boat. The cottages gave way, at a bend in the road, to a more desolate stretch of the bank. A low stone wall enclosed a scrubby and irregular field that was scattered here and there with chunks of old masonry. At its far side stood a low ruin, separated from the river by a margin of reeds and shingle.

He looked around, taking his bearings as well as he could, but it was difficult to be sure. The surrounding country was as flat and featureless as it had always been, with few landmarks worth the name. The river had so much altered its shape that the place was almost strange to him. Only the distances gave him any guide. It had stood about this far from the ferry house, he thought, and at this remove from the church, whose low steeple he could now see.

Eustace stepped over the wall, descending the shallow bank beyond to a rough pasture of sedge and rushes. It was grazed by a single dishevelled pony that lurked at its eastern edge, a greasy rope about its neck. The animal considered him balefully for a moment and lowered its head again, as if it had hoped to go unseen.

He slowed as he drew near to the ruin. It was roofless, and half of one gable had fallen in. About its lintels a faint blackening could still be seen, as if from some long-ago fire. From behind its northern wall rose the crazed splay of a young willow.

He stopped to figure his position, taking sight lines to the church tower and as far downstream as he could see. Circling the structure from outside, he hacked at the briars that had risen about the walls. He stepped back now and then, when he had revealed some part of the choked stonework, to see if it had become recognisable.

Crossing the threshold, he saw that none of the interior walls remained. The field had encroached on the floors, all but reclaiming them. He wandered over the rough grass, searching it for the traces of vanished rooms. He plotted out the area, bisecting it in his mind into two unequal portions. Scanning the larger of these, his gaze settled on a place at its inner edge. Slowly now, he made his way towards it. The wind was harsh, even for January. Blades of dry sedge flicked at his ankles.

The grass straggled thinly over the place where he stopped. He scraped at it with his heel until he had stripped away a thin swatch of turf. Beneath this, he found what he had expected: a plate of blackened stone, deeply encrusted with ash and charcoal. He crouched to touch it, holding his smudged fingertips to his nose as he stood upright.

He crossed to a vacant window in the front wall, looking up towards the road to be sure that he was not observed. Returning to the place he had uncovered, he lowered himself slowly to the ground. He tried to think of the age he had been when he could lie outstretched here, between the range and the kitchen wall. He had all but outgrown it, he remembered, even before Eleanor took his place.

He lay on his side, folding his knees as closely to himself as he could manage. He closed his eyes, listening for the sound beneath the wind, for the slow persuasion of the water.

The boy eyes the boat dubiously. Mr Crowe catches sight of him and claps the Frenchman's shoulder in amusement. 'Look, Lavoisier. Our Eustace is not reassured by the sight of your vessel. He knows an oarlock from a cock ring, mind you, so you should sit up and take notice.'

Lavoisier, who wears the grease-stained tunic of some indeterminate military office, hurls a bolt of tobacco from his mouth and stalks away to attend to the cargo.

Mr Crowe laughs at his retreating back. 'It is only the dinghy, Eustace.' He pauses, as if contemplating his own words. '*Eustace, Eustace* – I do hope it pleases you as it does me. I feel an intense satisfaction, I must confess, at having hit upon it. At any rate, the good ship Sainte-Justine lies at anchor somewhere in that interminable greyness. You did not think, surely, that we proposed to make the crossing in a rowboat?'

The boy stares out to sea. 'I never said I was coming.'

'*La belle époque*, they are calling it. An age of beauty, Eustace. A gilded age. You will have seen pictures of the tower, I imagine, and it is very splendid certainly, but I will show you more than that. I will show you Jane Avril, her legs like black flames of silk in the footlights. I will introduce you to a *vicomte* of my acquaintance who was shot through the cheeks in a duel and now smokes his cigars through the holes. And of course we must visit Debussy, though he labours now against illness and lives in great discomfort. You have never heard music, Eustace, until you have heard him. It is made of starlight and of first kisses. It seems scarcely to belong to our world.'

'I haven't forgotten,' the boy says. 'I can't forget.'

'And nor should you. Have I denied what you charge me with? Have I sought to deflect you from your retribution? I have not, and I will not. Lavoisier, come here. This young man, *mon ami*, will have need of his weapon when we have reached France. It may be necessary for him to shoot me in the Left Bank. Will you permit it, if we entrust the rifle to you during the crossing?'

Lavoisier looks from Mr Crowe to the boy. He searches his hair and drags a palm over his unshaven face. 'I would say *non*,' he says. 'I would say *hors de question*, but if it is you he want to kill—' He sucks at his cigarette and shrugs elaborately.

Mr Crowe claps his hands together. The wind tugs at his dark cloak and plasters his hair over his cheek. 'There, you see? What could be more reasonable, Eustace?'

He turns and looks back up the beach, to the horses huddled at the foot of the cliff, to the rain massing endlessly to the north. He hands the rifle to Lavoisier.

Eustace steps aboard the boat.

It had not been so cold, on the morning in March when he had last visited this place. The verges were darkened now by passing traffic, and he had little hope of finding daisies in flower. He managed, after twenty minutes or so, to come by five frail specimens, their petals greyish and curling inwards. They made a poor garland, all wiry stems and barely large enough to encircle a child's wrist. Still, he wrapped it carefully in a handkerchief and tucked it away in an inner pocket.

When he reached the churchyard, it took him some minutes to find the graves. He was mistaken, it seemed, in his memory of where she lay, though the scheme of the place had been clear enough in his mind: the hulking transept with its blackened stonework and high, mullioned window; the shadow of the yew, blue-dark and obliquely spreading. It was the new memorials, perhaps, that confused him, the ranks of the dead that had deepened in the years of his absence.

The gravestones too were unfamiliar. Though they had been erected on his instructions, Eustace himself had not seen them until now. Eleanor's resting place, when he had last stood by it, had been marked only by a wooden cross. Cromer had seen to it that the adjoining plots were purchased, and that the best materials were used.

He laid an approving hand on the upper edge of Eleanor's monument. Like her father's, it had been cut from handsome granite and bore the simple inscription he had wished for.

The other plot, to the left of Eleanor's, lay empty still.

He lowered himself to one knee by her gravestone. With his forefinger, he traced the chiselled strokes and serifs, the places where her name had weathered. He unwrapped the bracelet of daisies, re-threading it where one stem had broken. He pressed it briefly to his lips, then arranged it at the foot of the stone, using a pebble to secure it against the wind.

Eustace got to his feet, standing only for a minute or two before turning to leave. Abel would be restless by now. He would not be put off any longer.

It was Abel he expected to see when he reached the gate of the churchyard, hearing a car pull up on the road outside, and a discreet thump as one of its doors was closed. He had followed him here from the boarding house, his trust or patience exhausted. He would want to set off directly from here, would tolerate no further diversions.

But a second car door was closed, and another set of footsteps joined the first. He heard a man's voice, gentle and solicitous, as if to a child. Not Abel, then. Some other visitors, though it was early still for the paying of respects, and the morning was not temperate.

It was Cromer's hat, absurdly, that he fixed upon when they appeared. If that was Cromer's sunken and irregular hat, then it must be Cromer who stood at the gateway, who stilled the child gently in front of him, his hands bracketing her shoulders, Cromer who bent to her ear and pointed him out.

Beyond that, Eustace understood nothing. He saw her raise her hand against the low winter sun, saw how thin her wrists had become. He knew her, knew every hesitant flexion of her posture, every softness and hollow of her face. He saw and knew, but he could not – even as he ran to her, as he clutched her and felt himself dissolve – he did not understand, had understood nothing, all this time.

Clara, Clara, Clara.

Twenty-Four

⌒

The house, at twilight, is just as Clara remembers it. She has seen it most often like this, slipping at first light from the kitchen door, or returning at evening when the lawns are crossed by long shadows. It is at these moments that she has always loved it most, standing partly revealed in the half-light, its splendour inked among the incomplete colours. As the car nears the end of the avenue, she glimpses starlings, venturing in diminishing flourishes from the eaves.

They pull up on the gravel before the front door and Abel silences the engine. There is no sign from within that their arrival has been noticed. Only a few of the windows on the lower floors are lighted. Abel turns to Eustace and passes him something, a hard shape wrapped in newspaper.

'For the duration,' he says. 'It don't mean we're engaged or nothing. You have your business here and I have mine.'

Eustace glances back at Clara. 'It is for one purpose only. I will not leave her side.'

Abel raises his spread fingers, disclaiming interest. He nods and climbs from the car. Eustace turns to her again. 'You are ready?' he says. 'The danger has not passed, but it is greatly lessened. You your-self have seen to that.'

Clara watches as he looks over her face. She has told him all she remembers of the night of her abduction, but has shared little so far of the weeks of her captivity. Of what happened to Nazaire she has revealed only a little, scribbling oblique responses to his ques-tions. He has understood only partly. He is struggling still with how much she is unknown to him. It is something that must wait. She leans forward and touches his face. Eustace lays his own hand over hers.

'And you will stay close to me?' he says. 'You have no reason, I know, to trust me any longer with your safety. But it will never— Clara, I will never—'

She raises her other hand to his cheek, effacing the tear with her thumb.

They follow Abel up the steps. One of the great doors stands ajar, lurching sluggishly in the wind. Inside, a drift of leaves skitters across the unlit hall. Some leak or spill has left a brownish delta on the wall of the staircase. Eustace surveys the scene, his face hardening, and closes the door behind them.

Clara caught the sound when they came in: a current of music, remote but persistent. As they cross the hallway, it reaches her again – a jazz record, she thinks, playing in a distant part of the house. The instruments are etiolated, drained of their lushness, leaving only the dark gaiety of the rhythm.

Eustace turns to her, trusting to the acuity of her hearing. At her gesture, he leads them towards the west wing. They walk in silence, moving more cautiously as they approach the source of the music. At the doors of the orangery, he brings them to a halt, inching for-ward until he can see inside.

'It is her,' he whispers. 'She is alone. Abel, we are agreed? You have no account to settle with this one? You will keep watch while I attend to this?'

'Be my guest,' Abel replies. 'I'm here for the main event.'

Eustace faces Clara. 'She can do you no more harm. I will make sure of it. You need not even look at her.'

She takes his wrist, smoothing out his palm as she chooses her words.

I want to see her. I want her to see.

She meets his eyes calmly, not releasing his hand until she is sure he has understood.

He lets out a long breath, and there is weariness in his face as he draws out the object that Abel passed to him in the car. It alters him to see it, blunt and purposeful against the skin she has just touched.

Her scrutiny makes him uneasy. 'It is only to keep you safe.'

She shakes her head, not meeting his eyes. He forgets still. It is not the first time she has seen him hold a gun.

In the orangery, it is not quite dark. Above its vaulted arcade of glass, the dusk has faded to lilac and ash. Arabella reclines on a chaise longue beneath the central dome, her back turned to the door. She holds a wine glass and is smoking a long, white cigarette. The gramophone is on a table at her shoulder. As Eustace approaches her, the stylus crosses a scratchy interval and a new song begins. Trumpets prowl, low and insidious, while a male voice sidles towards melody.

Arabella raises her head without looking around. 'Is that you, darling? I see you so seldom now, I can hardly tell.'

'Get up, Arabella.' Eustace speaks quietly.

'Oh, it's you.' She exhales languidly, the smoke gathering in the still air. 'I thought you'd run away. I'm glad you're back, I must say. Things have gone rather downhill here.'

He stands at her shoulders. With the muzzle of his pistol, he knocks the stylus from the record. There is an abrupt swerve of sound, as if the song has been torn in half.

'Get up, Arabella.'

Carelessly, she crushes out her cigarette. She rises unsteadily, tottering as she seeks out a discarded shoe. 'Were you always quite this rude? Remind me to speak to—'

Clara watches her as she turns, the instant of indecision that follows her surprise.

'Why, Clara,' she says. 'How wonderful to see you. We've been so terribly worried.'

Her expression is amused as she raises the wine glass to her lips. Eustace wrenches it from her and hurls it across the room. It bursts against a veiled goddess, staining the deep folds of white marble. Without warning then, he slaps her face. She staggers a little, keeping her eyes fixed on him, keeping her hand from her face. It is like a convulsion, this abrupt violence, and seems to surprise even him. He steps backwards.

'The performance is over,' he says. 'You may spare us your curtain call. We do not know everything yet, but we know enough. You do not address the child. You do not approach her. If you do, there will be no one who can protect you from me. No one. Do you understand?'

Arabella straightens, bringing her livid face close to his. 'I always told him there was something brutal in you. He would never believe me, but I could see it.'

Eustace turns away. He takes the gramophone record from the turntable, inspecting it briefly before sliding it into its sleeve. 'Where is he?'

'Where is he ever? He is in his precious library, finishing whatever it is that the old man wants. I hardly see him.'

'And Chastern? Do you see no more of him, now that you have served your purpose?'

'You'll find him there too, if he hasn't died in his sleep or fallen down the stairs. He arrived a few days ago, and they have been meeting there in the evenings. Chastern waits for whatever scraps of pages he will show him, like a sickly dog whose master feeds it from the table. It's all rather revolting.'

Eustace regards her coldly. 'Your distaste for the enterprise is late in coming. How soon will it be finished? Do you know?'

'The fuck do we care,' Abel says from the door, 'whether it's finished or not? *This* is finished, right? That's what we come here for, to finish it.'

'Another charmer,' Arabella says. 'It is finished, or I think it is, but he can't bear to leave it alone. He says he's *labouring towards lastness*, whatever that means.'

'We will join them in the library,' Eustace says. 'We will have their forbearance, I trust, if we do not dress for dinner.'

Arabella shrugs. 'Sounds lovely.'

'And you,' Eustace says. 'You will take your seat quietly and remain directly in my sight. You will speak only when I address you. Is that understood?'

She answers with a parodic curtsey.

Eustace makes a courtly gesture with his pistol. 'Shall we?'

The house is in decay. There is no sign now of the battalion of new servants that Clara encountered in the days before she was taken. Even Alice has gone, for reasons Eustace only hinted at. Everywhere, there is evidence of neglect. Grand chambers stand deserted and unlit, emitting the damp breath of rooms that have gone for too long without warmth. As they pass the music room, a cat glares from the top of the piano, where it crouches intently amid a drift of feathers.

In the dim hallways, the surviving bulbs flicker over tables clothed in ruined linen, over waterless vases and the parched tatters of lilies.

Outside the library, Eustace pauses by a fruit bowl. At its centre is a cluster of sunken and unrecognisable husks, their rucked skins ashen with mould. He studies them with fascinated distaste, before covering them with a discarded napkin. Arabella turns with a slow smile.

'Something amuses you?' Eustace says.

'Not anymore,' she replies. 'But this comes close. It upsets you more than anything else that's happened, doesn't it? This decline in housekeeping standards? Poor Eustace. What will you live for now?'

He gestures with his pistol towards the doors. 'There are certain prospects still that I find consoling. After you.'

The library is lit only with candles. Mr Crowe, as they enter, stands at the hearth, prodding at the remains of a fire. Chastern is huddled in a nearby armchair, his knees draped in a blanket. He raises his eyes from a thin sheaf of pages, detaching a pair of half-moon spectacles from his nose.

Mr Crowe turns from the fireplace, still loosely gripping the poker, and stares in silence as Arabella takes the seat that Eustace has indicated. Abel saunters to an armchair opposite Chastern, where he reclines comfortably, his boots resting on a low table. He sets his shotgun on his knees and lights a cigarette, tossing the spent match into the embers.

'My darling child.' Mr Crowe turns to Clara, spreading his arms. 'You are restored to us.'

She moves closer to Eustace, slipping her hand into his.

Mr Crowe turns again to the fire, agitating the dim coals. 'And you, Eustace. It is a very pleasant surprise, of course. And I shall savour the moment all the more fully when you explain why it is that you are menacing my fiancée with a gun.'

'Your fiancée?'

'You are as gladdened, I trust, as I am. We thought of a summer wedding, now that the grounds have been so admirably restored.'

'That is unfortunate,' Eustace says.

Mr Crowe tosses the poker aside. It clatters against a coal scuttle and comes to rest noisily on the hearthstone. 'Unfortunate?' he says. 'Is that quite the proper form of congratulation? I defer to you, normally, in matters of etiquette, but here I feel you may have misspoken.'

'Perhaps it would be best if I excused myself,' Chastern says, leaning forward a little in his chair. 'I do not wish to intrude upon such delicate matters.'

Abel lifts his shotgun. 'You just make yourself comfortable,' he says. 'This won't take long.'

Chastern clucks with irritation as he sits back, looking to Mr Crowe as if expecting him to intervene. Mr Crowe, though, has not taken his eyes from Eustace.

'You are right,' Eustace says. 'It is not quite the right word. It hardly seems adequate, now that I reflect upon it, and yet I cannot think of a better one. I lack your gifts, remember, in matters of language. Here is what I suggest, then. Let her tell you herself, your fiancée. Let her explain her part in what happened the last time we were all gathered here. When she has finished – and I expect, since she has chosen to devote herself to you, that she will be entirely truthful – when she has finished, and when you have had leisure to reflect on what she says, then do please tell me what you feel is the right word.'

Mr Crowe retrieves a squat tumbler of whisky from the mantelpiece. He gulps from it and massages his neck. 'Eustace,' he says. 'Do not think that I am ungrateful for your long service, or that I forget the indulgence you have so often shown. We have lived an irregular sort of life, have we not? Yours has not been an easy station. I have not been blind to that, though I expect I shall go to my grave without learning the full extent of your sacrifice. My greatest failing, I think—'

'She betrayed Clara.'

'Is that so?' says Mr Crowe, his manner almost absent.

'Your showgirl,' Eustace says, keeping his voice steady. 'When she led Clara from the dining room, she was doing their bidding. She betrayed her, the child who was in our care.'

Arabella begins to sing, her voice somnolent and viscous. Clara recognises the words – there is something about a dream, about tumbling from paradise – and the sluggish current of the melody. It is the jazz song that she was playing on the gramophone. There is some meaning in it, perhaps, that is intended only for Mr Crowe.

She laughs to herself, spooling her hair around her fingers. 'Oh, don't look so cross, Eustace. After all, you weren't quite what you seemed either, were you? But now, I suppose, I'm expected to make my tearful confession.'

'Haven't we had quite enough of this spectacle?' Chastern interrupts. 'The lady has had rather too much to drink, I fear. She is in no condition to give a clear account of anything.'

There is a crisp click as Abel draws back the pump of the shotgun. 'I'm not going to tell you again,' he says. 'You sit there, you cuddle your hot-water bottle and you keep your fucking mouth shut.'

He turns to Arabella. 'You were saying.'

She tips her head back and releases a slow furl of smoke. 'He came to the club, after I started seeing you. He told me I was a "striking talent". A *striking talent* – can you imagine? There were people he knew at Covent Garden, roles I might be considered for even if I didn't have *quite* the right background. Of course, I duly imagined it all. Isn't it pathetic? But the best lies begin with a dream come true.'

'Oh, for heaven's sake,' says Chastern, looking away in disdain.

'He said he could speak to the musical director, remind him of certain obligations. In return, all I had to do was give a little performance. That's all it was, a little performance.'

Mr Crowe turns his back to the room, bracing himself with both arms against the mantelpiece.

'I didn't know,' she says, quietly this time. 'I didn't know what he wanted, not all of it. David was supposed to make a big show of being jealous when he found out, and you were supposed to – I don't know – to overreact. To *compromise yourself*, he said, so he'd have some kind of hold over you. I didn't know you'd *kill* him, for Christ's sake.'

She puts out her cigarette, crushing its remnants between her fingertips and scattering them over the ashes.

'And I didn't know they were going to take her, not until that night. I didn't want to go along with it, but the other one, Nazaire, he threatened me. My God, the things he said.'

Mr Crowe drains his whisky and dashes the glass against the back of the fireplace.

'And I loved you by then. I wasn't supposed to, but I did. But you know that, don't you? Why else would I have stayed?'

'Thank you, Arabella,' says Eustace. 'You will perceive your situation, Dr Chastern. This transaction, whatever its nature, will not be completed. Clara, as you can see, is no longer yours to bargain with. Even if there are other means by which you can compel Mr Crowe to give you what you want, we will not allow it.'

'*You?*' Chastern says. '*You* will not allow it? Do you think I am some footman, that I should take direction from the likes of you? The child authored some small deceit of her own, I suppose, to overcome Nazaire's vigilance, but he will not be far behind you. Do not think this contingency went unconsidered.'

Eustace glances at Clara. When she releases his hand, he takes the package from an inner pocket and hands it to Chastern without a word. He unwraps it with brisk irritation, seeing only the white cloth of the handkerchief at first. He flings it to the floor, when the bloodstain is revealed, and stares at it in revulsion.

'You will recognise the monogram, no doubt,' Eustace says.

Chastern closes his eyes and spreads his fingers over the arms of his chair.

Eustace continues in an even tone. 'Clara observed him closely, as you may imagine, in the days before his death. She has offered certain insights into the nature of his malady. I cannot say that I fully grasp her explanation, but it has to do somehow with certain susceptibilities in the nature of living things, with the errors that occasionally arise, and with their multiplication.'

Clara takes his hand again. She forms a quick sequence of characters. Eustace looks doubtfully at her, but she draws her fingertip emphatically across his palm, underscoring what she has written.

'And with the rose,' he says. 'With the rose itself.'

Chastern opens his eyes at this. He seeks Clara out, his lips taut with scorn. 'Is that what she told you?' he says. 'I encouraged these delusions myself, I suppose, but I see now how much I was mistaken. She is a pitiful and afflicted child, that is all. She has spent too long alone, wandering the woods like a pygmy. She is capable only of untutored excesses, of *abominations*.'

Clara tightens her grip on Eustace's hand. He glances at her, strokes her tensed knuckles with his thumb.

'Whatever the case,' he says, 'the implications are not altered. We are here to bring matters to an end.'

Chastern sits up, clasping the handle of his cane. 'How melodramatic you are, Eustace. You have savoured this prospect, no doubt. You have rehearsed this little set piece many times, I expect, in your moments of solitude. And you, Crowe. You would do well to remind the prodigal butler whose house this is. Perhaps you will impress on him also that your obligation to me is not so easily set aside.'

Mr Crowe does not turn from the fire. For a moment, he appears not to have heard. 'I will do as you asked,' he says quietly. 'I will give you what I have written.'

Chastern reclines in satisfaction, settling his velvet collar about his chest. 'You see, Eustace? This is a matter that does not concern you; a matter that lies, if I may say so, somewhat beyond your sphere.'

Abel uncrosses his legs and sits up with a sigh of impatience. He shoulders the shotgun, aims at a point above Chastern's head and fires. The noise, even in the large and richly furnished library, is colossal. Chastern cowers in his chair as flakes of masonry settle around him. Mr Crowe turns at last to face the room, dusting off his smoking jacket with a look of abstracted irritation.

'If I might interject,' Abel says. 'I mean, pardon me and all that, but speaking as someone from this sphere, allow me to clarify our position. No, allow me to clarify *my* position. I don't give a toss what his obligations are. I have an obligation to put some fucking holes in you. I have an obligation to leave you worse off than your hired help left my brother. As soon as Eustace takes that little girl outside, that's exactly what I intend to do.'

'Crowe?' Chastern's voice is shrill. 'Do you have nothing to say? Will you let this person reduce your house to rubble and butcher everyone in it?'

Mr Crowe saunters to the drinks tray. He brushes plaster dust from his sleeve and half-fills another glass with whisky before taking a seat next to Abel.

'My house? My house has been crumbling for years.' He glances at Arabella. 'Lizards crawl now among its stones. And you? I can offer you no shelter, Chastern. I cannot hope even to save myself. He has been coming for a long time, this man or someone like him. I will not stand in his way.'

'You would sacrifice all you have?' Chastern says. 'You will be shown no more clemency, Crowe, not even if I am dead. Another will take my place. There are procedures.'

'Procedures?' Mr Crowe takes a slug of whisky and closes his eyes. 'Do you not see, Chastern? Do you not see what you have set in train? Our time is past. We are eclipsed. And I find that I face the prospect with deep ease. It is my age, I suppose. There are sacrifices, you see, that I have already made, sweetnesses I tasted so long ago that they might as well have been plucked from the tree by Eve herself. I have a memory, you know, a memory so faint that when it comes to me, I hardly dare to breathe. I am a boy, or there is a boy. The boy is running under a wide and perfect sky. He is running, or I am running, towards a river. The water is dark and unrushed. The boy runs – he runs towards the river, and all around him the grass bends beneath the wind. It is almost nothing, you know, and might belong to anyone, but I can see it. I can *see* it, and I hunger for it more than anything. For that grass, for that river.'

He turns to Abel, laying his hand gently on his forearm. 'You are right to seek retribution,' he says. 'It is a pure wish, as blameless as thirst, and I will do nothing to hinder it. I ask only that you grant me a single concession. Let me show him what I have done. Believe me, I beg you, when I tell you that it will deepen his torment. To see what I have made, and to know that he will not live to possess it; that he will not tout it as his own, as he had planned, will not be consoled by glory until his rattling husk is finally tossed into its pit. You could devise nothing, I promise you, that would torture him more perfectly.'

'What do you take me for?' Abel says. 'You know how long I've waited for this? You think I'm going to let him out of my sight now, after all that's happened?'

Mr Crowe leans towards him, draping an arm over his shoulders. 'Look at him, Abel. You see how frail he is. Surely you do not expect him to clamber out of the window and bound away across the lawns? You will lose nothing by this, I assure you. Have I not given my word that I will not oppose you in this? And do not mistake me, my friend. You will have what you wish for because I will give it to you. Do not think that I could not have it otherwise. Your gun, in this house, will not always find its mark. It is old, this place, and its shadows are full of secrets.'

He uncurls his fingers as he lifts his hand from Abel's shoulder. The movement seems careless, and Abel does not see the spider at first. It is as plump as a date and lightly furred, descending his arm with patient deliberation, as if it were a flight of stairs. He leaps from his chair, the shotgun clattering to the floor, beating in terror at his sleeve until he catches sight of the spider again, creeping under the edge of the hearthstone.

He stoops to retrieve the gun, but Mr Crowe hooks it towards himself with his heel, scooping it from the floor and examining its mechanism with apparent curiosity.

Abel crosses the room to another chair. 'Very fucking clever,' he says. 'You're just full of surprises, aren't you?'

'Forgive me,' says Mr Crowe, returning the shotgun with a negligent toss. 'A conjuring trick, merely. It is a weakness I have never quite managed to eradicate.'

Abel turns to Eustace. He scrapes his knuckles self-consciously along his jaw. 'There's one way in and out of here, right? No trapdoors? No secret passageways, any of that?'

'The doors may be locked from the outside. Once that is done, there is no way out. The windows are twelve feet above a terrace.'

'Ten minutes,' Abel says, facing Mr Crowe again. 'And I'll be right outside the door.'

'I am deeply grateful. You have put my mind at ease.'

'How easily consoled you are, after all.' Arabella reclines languorously on the sofa now and stares at the ceiling. 'Are you so untouched by betrayal? You had more heat in you than this when I first met you.'

He gives a low and joyless laugh. 'Betrayal? Is that what you thought it was? Belief, my love, is a species of innocence. I have been rather longer in the world than you, and there is little left, I'm afraid, of whatever innocence I once possessed. And you, Chastern, did you think your puppetry was so very cunning? The woman brought more calamity in her wake than a starving army, and you thought I would suspect nothing? I have engineered more plausible coincidences while at stool.'

'It is a wonder to me,' Eustace says, 'that you did not think to share these misgivings of yours before so much harm was done. It is a wonder too that they have proved to be no impediment to your affections for this creature, that she was installed here long after the child was taken from us.'

Mr Crowe does not look up. 'Have you not been long enough acquainted with me, Eustace, to doubt what is apparent? You of all people should have learned to distrust what you see. It was doomed from the beginning, this little ruse of theirs. The child was not in our care, any more than Sirius is in the care of the Greenwich Observatory. No, it was not for me to intervene. I would only have hindered her progress. It was necessary to give him the satisfaction of his deceit, to appear to accept his little trinket.'

Clara feels a hardening in the muscles of Eustace's hand. 'His little trinket? You are engaged to be married to the woman.'

'She has bound herself to me, and shares my fate now. Do not think it any great gift, Eustace.'

'Such tenderness,' Arabella says. 'Do you see now why I could hardly help myself? May I at least have a drink, since I have to sit still for all this?'

Eustace ignores her. 'She may be bound to you, but I am not. You and your bride, I'm sure, will wish to retain someone better suited to your habits.'

Mr Crowe shakes his head sadly. 'Ah, Eustace,' he says. 'You thought I could dispense with you so easily, after all we have seen? No, that need will not arise.'

'Very well,' says Eustace. 'But I have other obligations. I must think of the child now. I must think of Clara, and her place is here. Her place has always been here.'

Mr Crowe sets his glass down and turns to her. He says nothing for a long moment, and all the gaiety is gone from his face. 'That much is true,' he says at last. 'It is Clara's in a way that it was never mine. But it is all in hand, Eustace. I have spoken to Cromer, and he has seen to the formalities.'

'You have given up the house? The library?'

'They were never mine, Eustace, not truly. I cherished them once, but these things must pass from us, sooner or later. I was a custodian, nothing more, until such time as their rightful owner should take full possession. And she has returned, as I knew she would – as nothing on this Earth could have prevented. She has come into her estate. I am surprised only that it has taken this long, and that she left anyone living. There is some consolation in that, Chastern, surely? In living long enough to glimpse the truth.'

Chastern regards him bitterly. 'Consolation?' he says. 'I would hardly recognise it. I have been too long untouched by pleasure.'

'Have you indeed? Well, there is no shame in it at your age. But come, it is time. Abel, if you are still agreeable, perhaps you and the rest of the company would be good enough to wait outside?'

Abel stands, holding the shotgun across his chest. 'Ten minutes,' he says.

Eustace motions Arabella towards the door, and she rises languidly to precede them. As she passes Mr Crowe's chair, she pauses, laying her hand along his jaw. Clara cannot read her expression. It is not quite regretful, not quite scornful. He detaches himself, kissing and releasing her hand before getting up and crossing towards his desk. As he does so, he begins to sing.

'*Tu che a Dio spiegasti l'ali, o bell'alma innamorata* . . . Come, Chastern. Let us do as Lucia did. Let us unfold our wings before God.'

At first, Clara is not sure of what she is hearing. While Abel paces at the doors, she and Eustace have seated themselves in the passageway. Arabella has arranged herself on the sofa opposite, and has lapsed again into her jaded singing. Clara puts her head on one side, listening intently.

Eustace looks at her, immediately alert. 'Clara?'

She shakes her head. The noise is indistinct, and Arabella's slurred melody distracts her.

Eustace turns to her angrily. 'Hold your peace, can't you?'

When she hears it again, the sound from the library, she stands and approaches the doors. It is Chastern's voice, reedy and beseeching. Seeing her concern, Abel turns and raps sharply on the door.

'Time's almost up,' he says. 'When I come in there, he'd better be reading a bedtime story.'

There is no answer. From within, Chastern's pleading can still be heard, though it has softened now to something barely more than a whimper. There are other noises too, dull and irregular, that Clara cannot identify.

Abel bangs on the door with his fist. 'That's it,' he shouts. 'You've had your fun. Story time's over.'

In his agitation, he fumbles with the lock. Clara steps quietly in front of him, placing her hand on his. He moves aside, his face colouring. She turns the key easily and looks at him with a slight smile. There was always a trick to it.

'Clara.' Eustace touches her shoulder and motions her from the door. 'Please. Anything may happen still.'

She withdraws a little and Abel grasps the door handle. He pauses, turning to Eustace to see that he is ready, and turns it. The doors flex inward by a fraction but will not open. Abel hammers on them.

'*Open these fucking doors, you hear me? We had an understanding!*'

There is no answer. Chastern's voice can still be heard, querulous or weakly keening, but rising steadily above it are sounds that Clara can make no sense of: a series of juddering knocks, a persistent and sibilant scraping.

Eustace comes to Abel's side, and both put their shoulders to the doors. They strain and slam against them, faces contorted with effort, but still they will not yield.

'Stand back,' Abel says, pulling away. Eustace takes Clara by the arm, drawing her back against the wall while Abel brings the shotgun level with the lock. When he has taken aim, he turns his face from the doors. 'Close your eyes,' he says. 'Cover the child's ears.'

Before she can object, Eustace turns and presses her against him, clamping his hands to the sides of her head. She struggles, wanting to see, but it lasts only an instant. The shot is fired and Eustace releases her. An immense chiming, as if from a gigantic tuning fork, fills her hearing. The air is acrid, curtained with smoke and settling dust.

The doors lurch gently open.

'Listen to me, Clara.' Eustace takes her gently by the shoulders.

'Whatever has taken place, we need see no more. We have done what we came to do, or most of it. I will not put you in the way of any harm that may be avoided. Let Abel do as he must.'

She shakes her head. Taking his wrist, she scribbles urgently on his palm.

See the end.

Eustace looks gravely at her. 'Clara, I beg you,' he says. 'Let me keep you safe.'

She writes again, her fingers quick and agitated.

Here. My place is here.

He is about to say more, but the rising tumult distracts him. Abel has pushed the doors fully open and stands in a thickening drift of smoke, much more than the shot could have produced.

'*Fire!*' he shouts. '*He's started a fucking fire in there!*'

Eustace turns to Arabella, raising his pistol again. 'Get up,' he says. 'We are leaving.'

He grips Clara's hand, but she twists free of it, darting through the doors of the library. Abel clutches at her collar as she passes, but she slips by him too. Calmly, she weaves through the smoke, navigating the room as she has done so often in the dark. As she makes her way among the bookcases, she begins to understand the noises. All around her, the shelves are groaning and cracking, spilling books to the floor. It is the books that are burning, the flames rupturing them even as they fall.

She moves steadily, finding a familiar course among the armchairs and tables, stopping only when she reaches the desk. Mr Crowe is seated behind it, she thinks, though she cannot see him clearly. He is at his usual ease, from what she can discern of his shadowed form. He may even be writing still. She hears, amid all the strange and jarring noises, the supple intonation of one of his arias.

Chastern is on his knees before the desk, supporting himself with one swaying arm as he sifts through a pile of manuscript pages, each written in Mr Crowe's dense but fluid longhand. The paper has a faintly sulphurous cast, darkening at the edges to a brownish black. They curl even as he turns them over, rippling with incandescence, becoming ash almost before they fall.

Still, he reads what he can of each one, scanning the lines with such urgency that he lapses into childlike mouthing, shadowing the words with his lips. From time to time, something moves him to look up at Mr Crowe, to implore him, his voice hoarse and feeble, to save something of what remains.

'*Clara!*' Eustace is calling her from somewhere near the door. '*Clara, for the love of God, where are you?*'

Chastern looks around then, and sees her standing over him. His gaunt face is raw and smeared, encrusted in places with soot; his eyes are avid, though at first he is confused, seeming not to recognise her.

He spreads his hand over the pages then – suddenly, as if some realisation has come to him. 'Child,' he says. 'You remember what I told you?'

She looks down at him, crouching over his blackening sheaf. He licks his lip as a scale of ash settles on it.

'It is not only the rose,' he says, his hand flailing over the manuscript. 'It is all of nature. All that I have adored.'

From somewhere behind him, Mr Crowe persists in his aria.

'You see?' His voice is feeble and rattling. 'You see how undeserving he was of his gifts? And you, you wretched imp, where did you crawl from to make your claim?'

He turns fully towards her, scrabbling for his cane and bringing himself half upright, but before he can get to his feet, he is flung by some force against the desk. An instant passes before Clara can account for it, and for the ragged occlusion of his face. She hears the shot only afterwards, as the wound – a sprawling inflorescence of charred flesh – gapes and bleeds. At its centre, she glimpses the slowing machinery of his mouth; the shorn teeth, the twitching heap of the tongue.

Eustace is there, lifting her clean and entire from the floor. She sees Abel, standing rigid and intent, smoke coiling gently from the shotgun.

'Clara, oh Clara.' Eustace clutches her as he heaves her towards the doors. 'Oh, my child. It is all gone. It is over.'

She cannot reach his hands, so she turns in his arms until she can touch his face. She traces the words on his cheek.

All of it. I remember.

From behind them, with an almost vanishing faintness, comes the sound of singing.

Arabella has fled. When they reach the front door, she is already in the car, turning it in a series of erratic lurches. Eustace leaps from the steps without a word and pounds across the gravel towards her. As Abel saunters after him, he breaks and reloads the shotgun. Seeing them, Arabella wrenches at the wheel and reverses violently, shattering an urn and sending the rear wheels slipping onto the banked lawn. Eustace weaves from side to side as he gets nearer, trying to judge the course she will take.

Arabella looks wildly about her, working the motor to a shrill pitch as she struggles to find traction. As Eustace crosses in front of the car, its wheels are skidding in deepening ruts, but before he is clear it lunges from the grass. He tries to spin from its path, but it catches him at the knees. He buckles, and is slammed against the bonnet, held there for a moment before being flung aside as the Jaguar jerks to the left.

In Clara's chest, a coldness spreads. She holds still for a moment, forcing herself not to look away from the car, waiting for Arabella to look back. When she does, it is only for an instant. Her face, behind the glass, is wild and whitened, then the car speeds away. Clara follows its course as it veers past the stable yard, onto the west lane and into the beech woods.

She moves with violent urgency then, reaching Eustace in seconds, still poised and tense as she lowers herself to one knee. She must see him – must take his hand and hear him speak – but it can only be for a moment. She will not stay long, no matter what.

He has brought himself up on his elbows, seeing her approach, and tries to dust himself off. He is pale, his face grave with pain. She can see no blood.

Abel crouches behind him, and Eustace allows himself to be helped to a sitting position. 'It is only my leg,' he says. His voice is weakened, disturbed by a slight rasp. 'It will mend well enough, I daresay, and we shall have a story to tell.'

Clara reaches for his hand, glancing as she does so in the direction of the beech woods, attentive to every sound.

'It is no great calamity,' he says. 'And not entirely undeserved, perhaps. At any rate, we need no longer think of her. Forget her, Clara.'

She smooths out his palm, as she has always done, and holds his eyes. She traces the words quickly but gently. They are small and simple, and it does not take long. He clutches her fingers, reading her intent, but she tugs them free and gets to her feet. She looks at him for a moment longer, pressing her fingertips to her chest.

'Clara,' he says. 'Clara, please.'

But she is gone. She is running.

It is cold in the woods, but not quite dark. Though it is after nightfall, the moon is almost full, and a glaucous light touches the limbs of the beech trees. It is not elation that she feels, or not yet. For now, there is only a strange levity, a weightlessness almost. When she followed Arabella, she acted without thought. Even now, she does not try to account for it. She trusts to the clarity of her instinct, its knife-like simplicity of purpose. She runs.

She follows the sound of the engine, the strained grinding of repeated gear changes. Arabella is driving without lights still, hoping to evade pursuit. She is some way ahead, but has gone no great distance yet. She does not know the lane, and she will not find its twisting course easy to navigate in the dark. Clara glances behind her, to gauge her own distance from the house. Above the treetops, there is a faint bloom of heat.

She stops abruptly, holds herself still and alert. The labouring of the engine is gone, cut off in a dense spasm of noise. It was close, only a little way ahead. She waits, listening through the work of her own breathing. There is the scattered alarm of small creatures, but nothing more. The woods are otherwise silent.

She runs again, skidding down a shallow bank at the edge of the trees and into the laneway. She is faster, on this firmer surface, and she need not weave around roots or jump clear of briars. Without stopping, she tugs her coat off and flings it aside. She will not need it, not for this. She no longer feels the cold.

She sees it at a bend in the lane. The road is blocked by the glazed hulk of a fallen holly tree, and the nose of the Jaguar is embedded in its shadowed underside. A tree so large ought to have been easily visible in the moonlight, but it lies half hidden by the bend and Arabella had been driving at speed.

Clara is cautious, peering through the rear window before approaching the open driver's door. Inside, the rim of the steering wheel has been snapped. The arc of wood that hangs from the fracture is thinly lacquered with blood. She takes the keys from the ignition and stands back from the car, slowing her breathing and forcing herself to be still.

Arabella is on foot, injured at least slightly. Even so, she has a head start, and Clara cannot be sure which way she went. She approaches the fallen tree, skimming the smooth bark with her fingertips. If she went straight ahead, the lane would take her to the edge of the Estate, with little risk of losing her way. But what if she is hurt, badly enough to slow her progress? She would expect those following to catch up, and on the road she will be easy to find.

Clara scans the surrounding woods. If she did seek the cover of the trees, it would have been easier to leave the road on the left. From there it is downhill all the way to the Windbones. She moves quietly to the roadside and drops to one knee. Holding herself tense on her spread fingertips, she scours the verge for signs of disturbance.

She sees nothing at first, but catches the faint scent of wild garlic. It is early still, and it has just come into growth, a scattering of its bright nibs showing among the dead leaves. Clara strokes one tender blade. She has a deep fondness for ramsons. They belong to the time of year she loves most, to March and April, when they throng the borders of every path in the woods. In spring, she brushes against them with every footstep, and the air is ribboned with fragrance. This scent is hardly a thread in the air, but it is not quite nothing. Somewhere, the leaves have been crushed.

She releases the leaf and gets to her feet. Slowly, taking care not to disturb the foliage, she skirts the edge of the drift. She inclines her head so that her face is out of the breeze, so that she breathes the undisturbed air. There – she stops, lowering herself again to her haunches. She cranes forward, hunting in the cold and vacant air. It is somewhere near.

She stops, drawn by something that catches the light: a dark convexity, its gloss too perfect for anything living. Grasping it between finger and thumb, she lifts it free of the litter of leaves. It is a slender and elegant thing, its shorn strap inset with tiny gems. The heel is three inches long, as narrow as a child's bone. It was not made for running through woods.

She reaches the Windbones, as always, sooner than she expected to. The beeches dissipate overhead and she finds herself on the edge of the valley's silent expanse. Above her in the rich darkness, even the Milky Way is visible, a lavish drift of radiance that crosses the entire sky.

As she leaves the trees, Clara slows to a gentle, loping walk. She ran through the lower part of the beech woods at a speed that almost frightened her, but the stillness of this place makes such exertion unthinkable. The urgency she felt is easing too. She is surer now of finding Arabella. If she came this way, emerging as Clara did from the wood, she will find that she has few choices. She can cross the shallow valley towards the mountains, but it is a trek of eight or nine miles that will take her first across the river.

No, she will not go that way. She will be making still for the public road on the western edge of the Estate. To reach it, she will have to keep between the river and the beech woods, skirting the edge of the Windbones and following its slow incline until she rejoins the lane, a journey of a little over a mile. Clara could find the way in her sleep.

She will find her. If she is here, she will find her. Wandering through the rippling grass, she feels a strange ease. Her chest and limbs are filled with the exultant afterheat of running. She is home. She is in the place she loves, and she will never again be separated from it. She will not allow it.

She looks up, her attention caught by a small disturbance of whiteness. The swans are arriving, unfolding themselves from the darkness in pale apparitions of twos and threes. They gather just out of sight, where the edge of the lake is hidden by a steep bank of reeds. Without thinking, Clara seeks out the place.

When she finds her there, the woman, she feels hardly a flicker of satisfaction, as if she had only chanced upon her. She has knelt on the shore to tend to a wound, sluicing her torn forearm with dark palmfuls of lake water, and there seems no reason why she should be elsewhere, why the settling swans should not have drawn her to this place.

They cluster near the woman, and one or two approach her, stalking from the water, their undersides dark and sodden, crooking their necks to investigate the soiled whiteness of her gown. She rises in alarm, catching sight of Clara as she backs away.

'Clara?' she calls out. 'Is it just you? There's no one else coming?'

More swans arrive, their pale wings shuddering from the unseen air. There are two dozen or more, and almost half of them are now on the shore. They trudge around her with squat menace, taking turns to flare their wings or lunge forward, necks out-thrust. She turns helplessly on the spot, jerking away from each new incursion.

'Is Eustace all right? It was an accident, Clara, a terrible accident. I was frightened, that's all, and I panicked. And look, I'm hurt too. Can you get help? Please, darling. It's my arm. I think it's broken.'

Clara stands perfectly still among the reeds at the crest of the bank. There is a chill in the wind as it tugs at her hair. She feels it on her neck, on her bare arms, but gives it no particular thought. There is nothing she wants or needs.

'Clara, please. I know what you think, but I had no choice. It was just a part. You know, like in a play? Or a story – I know how you love stories.'

Retreating from one bird, she stumbles over the back of another. When she rights herself, she is knee-deep in the water. Shocked by the cold, she launches herself towards the shore, but the movement alarms the swans. They crowd more closely around her. Above their arched wings, their necks sway and snap. She loses her balance again, her uninjured arm flailing. She goes under.

Clara turns away. She looks out over the Windbones, where the grasses are combed and silvered by the air, to the shadowed beech woods massing at the edge of the valley. Above them, the smoke spreads and deepens in the clean darkness, suffused by its roiling underglow. In the morning, she and Eustace will survey the damage. They will circle the blackened carcass of the house, keeping their distance from its collapsing ribs.

They will see what can be saved.

For now, the house and its undoing are hidden beyond the trees. She will leave the lake, when this is over, will sleep wherever there is shelter. When she stirs, finding the darkness tainted by heat, she will close her eyes again, thinking nothing of it. She will inhabit her sleep still, and the house will be as she dreamed it. She will wander at dusk among its quiet rooms, where nothing has been touched by fire.

Acknowledgements

To Linda Grant, counsel and confidante, who knows that all art, at last, is fugue.

To John Self, who reads, as he lives, without creasing the spine.

To Jane Casey, Ian Ellard, David Hayden, Rachel Heath and Olivia Laing, who were there when it was dark.

To Helen Macdonald, tender falconer, who instructed me with such patience in the care and feeding of cygnets.

To Richard Beard, who repaid a small favour twice, the second time fatefully.

To Lucy Luck, for whom I would gladly slay a thousand more unicorns.

To Arzu Tahsin, custodian of the opera glasses, who kept safe so much else that was precious.

To Benjamin Dreyer, the gentlest of hierophants, whose word is final.

To Sophie Buchan, John Gallagher, Rebecca Gray, Jennifer Kerslake, Jonathan Gibbs, Jennifer Hewson, Belinda McKeon, Sandra Newman, Kim Nielsen, Liz Nugent, Damien Owens, George Szirtes, Juliet Pickering, Max Porter and Catherine Taylor.

To Patrick and Beryl O'Donnell, for everything.

To Sinéad O'Donnell, eternally, who first saw something swan-like in this tissue of flaws.

blog and newsletter

For literary discussion, author insight,
book news, exclusive content,
recipes and giveaways, visit the
Weidenfeld & Nicolson blog and
sign up for the newsletter at:

www.wnblog.co.uk

For breaking news, reviews and exclusive competitions
Follow us 🐦 @wnbooks
Find us 📘 facebook.com/WNfiction